A MASQUERADE

It was several breathless moments before the black domino slowed their pace. He looked down into Henrietta's upturned smiling face and said in a thoughtful voice, "Your Louis XIV was a stupid fellow indeed to believe you experienced in dalliance. Rather, I would say that you are a young lady enjoying her first ball."

He was right, damn him, but had she been so obvious? Surely not. She wouldn't let him fluster her. "I know why you said that. You think I'm inexperienced just because I don't want you flirting with me. That's it, isn't it? Just a male's conceit." She grinned up at him shamelessly.

"I wonder," he said, "if you would goad me so much if we were to remove your mask."

"Touch my mask and I'll make you very sorry."

"As sorry as you would have made Louis XIV?"

LORD HARRY

ANNOUNCING THE
TOPAZ FREQUENT READERS CLUB
COMMEMORATING TOPAZ'S 1 YEAR ANNIVERSARY!

THE MORE YOU BUY, THE MORE YOU GET

Redeem coupons found here and in the back of all new Topaz titles for FREE Topaz gifts:

Send in:

 2 coupons for a free TOPAZ novel (choose from the list below);

- ☐ **THE KISSING BANDIT**, Margaret Brownley
- ☐ **BY LOVE UNVEILED**, Deborah Martin
- ☐ **TOUCH THE DAWN**, Chelley Kitzmiller
- ☐ **WILD EMBRACE**, Cassie Edwards

 4 coupons for an "I Love the Topaz Man" on-board sign

 6 coupons for a TOPAZ compact mirror

 8 coupons for a Topaz Man T-shirt

Just fill out this certificate and send with original sales receipts to:

TOPAZ FREQUENT READERS CLUB-1ST ANNIVERSARY
Penguin USA • Mass Market Promotion; Dept. H.U.G.
375 Hudson St., NY, NY 10014

Name_____

Address_____

City_____State_____Zip_____

Offer expires 5/31/1995

This certificate must accompany your request. No duplicates accepted. Void where prohibited, taxed or restricted. Allow 4-6 weeks for receipt of merchandise. Offer good only in U.S., its territories, and Canada.

LORD HARRY

by

Catherine Coulter

A TOPAZ BOOK

TOPAZ
Published by the Penguin Group
Penguin Books USA Inc., 375 Hudson Street,
New York, New York 10014, U.S.A.
Penguin Books Ltd, 27 Wrights Lane,
London W8 5TZ, England
Penguin Books Australia Ltd, Ringwood,
Victoria, Australia
Penguin Books Canada Ltd, 10 Alcorn Avenue,
Toronto, Ontario, Canada M4V 3B2
Penguin Books (N.Z.) Ltd, 182–190 Wairau Road,
Auckland 10, New Zealand

Penguin Books Ltd, Registered Offices:
Harmondsworth, Middlesex, England

Published by Topaz, an imprint of Dutton Signet,
a division of Penguin Books USA Inc. Originally published in a somewhat
different version in a Signet edition under the title *Lord Harry's Folly*.

First Topaz Printing, January, 1995
10 9 8 7 6 5 4 3 2 1

Topaz is a trademark of New American Library,
a division of Penguin Books USA Inc.

Printed in the United States of America

To my parents,
Charles and Elizabeth Coulter.
Thank you for being there
for everyone. Here's to the
second time around.

Chapter One

"Lord Harry? Lord Harry, are you ready yet? You've been an age and your friends are getting impatient." Pottson pressed his ear to the closed door to hear the reply, for he couldn't enter unless given permission.

Lord Harry gave his cravat a final twitch, decided enough was enough, and called out, "I'm ready, Pottson, you may come in now."

Although Mr. Scuddimore and Sir Harry Brandon were comfortably seated near the fireplace in the small parlor down the hall, Pottson looked back to make sure before he went into Lord Harry's bed-chamber. He stood in the doorway, critically eyeing Lord Harry's appearance, as was his habit and duty. "By heavens, you've become an accomplished dandy," he said with a humorless grin after inspecting Lord Harry's shining black hessians, fawn breeches, and Weston coat of dark blue superfine. "And just what would that creation be called?" he asked, his eyes on the white starched cravat twined artfully about Lord Harry's neck.

"I call it A Clever Copy of Lord Alvaney, Pottson. I've been practicing for hours at home. It's three folds under and two over and then a few quick turns of the wrist. I don't think I've done too badly. I drew a quick sketch of his lordship's cravat at White's one afternoon. Hopefully, the gentleman in question didn't notice. And I've changed the style sufficiently so that he shouldn't recognize it as his own." Lord Harry followed Pottson's eyes as he looked at the hopelessly rumpled cravats Lord Harry had thrown aside, and grinned. "Come now, I only ruined seven cravats this time. I've heard it said that the Beau rarely achieved perfection before his twelfth try."

"Well, that don't make it any less work cleaning up after you." Pottson swiped up the discarded cravats. "At least you don't go trying to ape those tight-knit pantaloons the gentlemen wear. You still have the good sense for that, I hope." Pottson's grumbling had grown markedly less severe with repetition. Lord Harry gave a hearty laugh, perhaps a trifle high in pitch for a gentleman grown, but certainly passable for a young buck of nineteen or twenty. "I'm not such a fool as that. Of course, Scuddy and Sir Harry are forever twitting me about my abominably fitting breeches. They think me still a rustic in my tastes. It's fortunate for me that their minds aren't of a more tenacious bent."

There was a loud knock on the bedroom door and both Lord Harry and Pottson froze to the spot. "Ho, Harry," Scuddy called out. "We're already late for the first act. Dawdle much longer, you young fop, and Harry and I will come in and drag you out."

"Go about your business, Scuddy. Drink some more of my excellent brandy. I'll be ready in a minute, two at the most."

Pottson groaned aloud and mopped his forehead with a wrinkled cravat, but only after he was certain that he heard retreating footsteps from the bedroom door. "You're making an old man of me, Lord Harry. I've got more gray hairs than I can count now."

"All your hair is gray, Pottson. Stop complaining."

"I'm not complaining, just telling the truth. My heart nearly bounded into my throat. That young Scuddimore, I'll just bet he and Sir Harry have drunk a good bottle of that brandy you stole from your father's cellars. I've had no more than the smallest nip of it."

Lord Harry grinned and patted Pottson on the arm. "Take a good snort after we leave, you deserve it. Come on, stop sweating like a stoat. We've come through unscathed so far. Trust me to carry it off. For God's sake, Pottson, do hide that wretched gown."

After one final look in the mirror to ensure that the blue coat and the fawn breeches didn't show off his hips more than necessary, Lord Harry gave Pottson a mock bow. "Do stop fussing so. It will be all right, you'll see. I'll try not to be too late tonight." After a brief pause, Lord Harry added, "Lord Oberlon is returned just recently to London." His voice grew chill and distant. "It's been eight months that he was away, Pottson. Undoubtedly, the marquess was loath to leave Italy and the plump arms of willing Italian ladies who assisted him to assuage his grief for his dead wife. Certainly since his return to London, he has wasted no time. I, myself, have seen him in the company of a beautiful new mistress. It's even possible that he and his lovely new ladybird will be at Drury Lane tonight. God, I hope so. I want to see him, look him straight in the face."

This bit of information produced a groan from Pottson and more sweat.

Lord Harry smiled his cold smile and patted his valet's arm. "There can be no going back, Pottson. Finally, the plot thickens. Remember what Damien used to say: *Many a battle was lost because the generals were scurrying the other way.* I shall soon have the first close look at our enemy, at least I pray I will."

"I never knew what Master Damien meant when he said that," Pottson said. "I still don't, but that isn't important. Now listen to me, you take care." He wanted to say more, but he knew it wouldn't do any good. Lord Harry was set on a course that was too late to be changed.

Lord Harry waved a negligent hand and sauntered from the room with a swagger of a young gentleman bent on an evening's pleasure.

It wasn't long after Lord Harry had entered the hired hackney with Sir Harry and Mr. Scuddimore that his gay mood dimmed, his thoughts returning to Lord Oberlon. He just wanted to see the man's face. He knew he'd see the guilt in his eyes, he just knew it.

"Never seen you so sunk into silence before, Lord Harry," Mr. Scuddimore said, eyeing his friend in the dim light. "What the devil ails you?"

Lord Harry brought his thoughts back from Lord Oberlon and said, "Not a thing, Scuddy. I was just thinking about the first time I came to London—not above four months ago, you know. Unlike you and Harry here, I'm not yet jaded by all the marvels."

Sir Harry Brandon tapped his cane on Lord Harry's knee. "Knowing you, it's probably female marvels that haven't yet jaded you. But you were quiet and we don't like it. It won't do for you to get the reputation of being a dead bore. It'll make people believe you think too much and that won't ever do. You'd be out of favor in a fortnight." He sat back against the soft swabs and took in his friend's appearance, his blue eyes narrowing with distaste.

"Really, Lord Harry, you must allow us to go with you to Weston's. Pottson's a good valet, but it's naught he can do if you don't give him the proper-fitting clothes to work with. I am shocked that any of Weston's fellows would make a coat that hangs off the shoulders in such a way. As for the seat of your trousers, there's room in there for another small fellow's butt."

Mr. Scuddimore laughed aloud. Sir Harry was offended. "Bedamned to you, Scuddy. I just gave him some excellent advice. Why, Lord Harry here—"

Mr. Scuddimore only laughed more, then hiccupped. Lord Harry thumped him hard between his shoulder blades. When he caught his breath, Scuddy said, "No offense, Harry, it's just that I still can't get used to you being plain Sir Harry and Harry being *Lord* Harry. It's damned amusing."

Sir Harry said in the tone of one instructing a slow, yet good-natured child, "Scuddy, I've told you several times how it must be. I'm a mere baronet and Lord Harry here is the son of a Scottish laird—something outlandish like that. In any case, the both of us can't be Harrys—damned confusing that would be. Since Lord Harry is of higher rank, it's only right that he be the lord and I simply a sir. I know you aren't always strong in your mental workings, Scuddy, but I swear, if you bring this up one more time, I'll take you out to the Hounslow Heath and put a bullet through your toe."

"You won't shoot me in the toe, Harry. I'm a better shot than you."

"Ha, the devil you are. Why I—"

"He's right, Harry," Lord Harry said with a wide grin, displaying even white teeth. "He is the better shot. Now about this Lord Harry and plain Sir Harry business, it is strange, but I think we've solved the problem rather neatly. After all, I didn't want to be called Sir Buttris, after my father. Now, about that other fellow's butt in my trousers, let me tell you that you can line up the possible candidates and I'll pick one."

Sir Harry grunted, then eyed Mr. Scuddimore with as much distaste as he had Lord Harry a few minutes before. "Lord, I hope my reputation doesn't suffer being seen with the likes of both of you. Here is Lord Harry with baggy breeches and coat, and thinking himself so amusing in them, and you, Scuddy, *you* are simply too heavy to be sporting yellow knitted pantaloons. You've got to stop stuffing all those sweetmeats down your gullet."

Lord Harry patted Sir Harry's arm. "We will walk ten paces behind you, Harry, if you wish it. The way the women do in those Muslim countries, to show you our respect."

Mr. Scuddimore said, "I don't like the sound of that at all, Lord Harry. Imagine us behaving like women. The mere thought of being a female shrivels all my favorite manly parts. No, I don't like the sound of it at all."

Lord Harry turned away, grinning into the darkened carriage. "I'll tell you what Scuddy and I will do, Harry. If we happen to see the Honorable Miss Isabella Bentworth at the play tonight, then we will pace back ten steps. You know, give you an opportunity to play the gallant, to gain the young lady's attention."

Sir Harry Brandon shifted uncomfortably against the carriage swabs. Although he was the first to proclaim the lovely Miss Isabella to be a diamond of the first water, he didn't think that as a sophisticated man of the world his deeper feelings concerning the lady should be so obvious. He blanched at the thought of his friends even thinking of him proposing marriage to the young lady. "Oh, very well," Sir Harry said. "The two of you loudmouths win. I won't say another word about your wretchedly fitting clothes if you and Scuddy will keep mum about Miss Bentworth."

"But why should we, Harry? You're not planning to make the young lady an offer?"

"By God, I'm only twenty-four years old, far too young by half to be leg-shackled, even to Miss Bentworth." He said a silent plea of forgiveness to Miss Isabella. If only she were still in the schoolroom, say fourteen or fifteen years old, instead of a marriageable age, ripe to be plucked from the marriage mart. Even his very self-assured brother-in-law, the Earl of March, had not met and married Harry's sister, Kate, until he was twenty-eight, and Kate, very rightly, was but eighteen. That was the right way of it. Curse Isabella for being born too early. It wasn't fair. What was he, too young a man, to do about it? He said, "Listen to me, both of you. You've got to keep quiet about it. You know word like that gets around and before you know it, a fellow is the butt of wagers at all the clubs. The next step is an announcement in the *Gazette*."

Mr. Scuddimore said, "Same thing happened some time back, I remember. There were several gentlemen in the running. Lord Oberlon, you know, the Marquess of Oberlon," he added at the sudden peculiar look in Lord Harry's eyes, "won a vast sum from Sir William Filey. A vast sum. I remember he ended up marrying the lady."

Lord Harry sat suddenly forward in the carriage. "Were there other gentlemen involved in the wager, Scuddy?"

Mr. Scuddimore narrowed his eyes, a sign of profound concentration. "Yes, I think so. There was another gentleman. A military man as I recall. Always in his damned uniform—quite turned all the ladies' heads, the bounder."

"Do you remember his name, Scuddy?" Lord Harry asked.

Mr. Scuddimore cudgeled his brains, then suddenly brightened. "The fellow's name was Rolland—yes, that's it—Captain Damien Rolland. Lord Oberlon never collected the wager from him—Rolland up and left England, later got himself killed at Waterloo, if I remember correctly. In fact, some wagging tongues put it about that Rolland sheared away, put himself out of the running before the lady made up her mind. One day he was pursuing her, then the next—gone off without a word to anyone."

Lord Harry went suddenly pale, but since the interior of the carriage was in dark shadows, Sir Harry and Mr. Scuddimore didn't notice. Lord Harry asked in a voice of casual interest, "Do you recall the lady's name, Scuddy?"

Mr. Scuddimore shook his head and shot a hopeful glance at Sir Harry.

Sir Harry shrugged. "Sorry, Scuddy, it was before my time. Remember I was over in Spain at the time."

Lord Harry said quietly, "Did the lady's name happen to be Springville?"

"Yes, that was it—Springville. Elizabeth Springville. Lovely little filly she was. Dead now, really quite a pity. Life does sometimes serve up the most unexpected and revolting dishes."

"Ho," Sir Harry said. "We're finally here." He leaned his blond head out of the carriage window. "Damnable crush tonight, and being late doesn't help."

Lord Harry said nothing more. Since all of Mr. Scuddimore's attention was focused upon extricating his ample body from the carriage, and Harry didn't want to be bothered by ancient history, it would simply have to wait. It was enough for now that Lord Harry had discovered there had been a wager, and that Lord Oberlon and Damien had been a part of it.

As the three friends made their way into Drury Lane Theater, Lord Harry had but one goal, to find Jason Cavander, the Marquess of Oberlon.

Chapter Two

"You're naughty, your grace," she said in a voice so soft and tempting that it would make any man's toes curl, even his grace's. "You give me this lovely ruby necklace and then hold me prisoner. Would you not like someone other than yourself and my maid to see its beauty?"

Her eyes glittered at the thought of the many envious glances that would come her way. It would serve those twitty young misses and their prune-lipped hypocritical mamas right to see her, Melissande Challier, more richly jeweled than they. Let them put their noses in the air, let them thrust out their bosoms and sail past her, as if she were a bad smell to be ignored. Her escort would be one of the most eligible peers of the realm, and her gown and jewels unparalleled. It was a delicious thought.

Jason Cavander touched his fingers lightly to the ruby necklace, an expensive bauble he'd bought in Italy on a whim. Having no one else upon whom to bestow it, he'd willingly given it to Melissande. It was a welcoming present, he'd told her. Welcoming him home from Italy and welcoming her to his protection. Since the exquisite necklace was the only item of apparel she was wearing, his fingers soon strayed to her soft shoulders and white breasts.

Actually, he admitted to himself, he was quite sated, Melissande having most superbly seen to his pleasure. But he was tired, tired of the seemingly endless stream of agents, advocates, solicitors, and tenants who had occupied his waking hours since his return from abroad. He would have preferred to spend the evening quietly with Melissande, perhaps allowing himself to emerge from her charmingly furnished apartment on the morrow, not a tired, but an exhausted man. But he saw the gleam of excitement in her eyes, really quite a dazzling sight, and knew without her telling him that she wished above things to tempt and bewitch the gentlemen and ladies at Vauxhall Gardens this evening.

He lazily propped himself up on one elbow, gazed appreciatively once more at her very nicely arranged body, then smiled. She was exquisitely beautiful and she didn't yet bore him. He didn't mind in the least giving her what she wished. He wondered though, in the dark hours of the morning when sleep didn't come easily, what it was that he wished. And, he'd wondered, even if he ever did figure out what he wanted, who would be there to give it to him? He had no one, not a blessed soul. He'd been home from Italy for only a short time, a trip he'd not wanted to take, not really, but he'd had to leave England because of the speculation, the interminable sympathy shoveled at him by friends and enemies alike upon the death of his wife in childbed. Ah, she'd been so young, so beautiful to die so tragically, so needlessly. He'd not been able to bear it, all the mournful expressions, the endless silences around him because of his sorrow, a sorrow so deep that he simply wouldn't speak of it or refer in any way to his dead wife. And there'd been Sir William Filey, of course, that damnable bastard, who'd delighted in questioning Elizabeth's death, raising rumors that had no substance to them. Not that anyone had believed Filey or the rumors, but he'd had to leave else he'd have likely killed Filey. He shook his head, picked up his breeches, and left Melissande in the hands of her maid, Ginny.

He had to see to himself, a small mirror in the adjoining dressing room his only assurance that his appearance wouldn't shame the exquisite rubies around his mistress's white neck.

Ginny was carefully tugging a long curl of rich auburn gently into place on Melissande's shoulder when Lord Oberlon returned to the bedroom. Melissande rose and smiled at him with the confidence of a lady who knows herself to be the elixir of pleasure and beauty. She touched her fingers to the ruby necklace that lay nestled in the hollow of her throat. "You approve, your grace?"

She had pleased him. The darkness deep within him was at bay. She did look as succulent as a prime partridge. "You'll make all the other ladies present want to go hide themselves in the shrubbery."

Ginny paused a moment from straightening her mistress's brushes when she heard Melissande say with great relish to her lover as they left the room, "How I hope that Lady Planchey will be in attendance this evening. Why the effrontery of her ladyship to believe that you could be interested in her spotty-faced daughter." Although Melissande was very much aware that wives and mistresses were poles apart in a gentleman's mind, she knew that even the loveliest of young misses would receive no

more than a disinterested glance from Lord Oberlon
while she was leaning gracefully on his arm.

He smiled down at her, knowing exactly what she
was thinking. He appreciated her predictability, was
amused by her fascination with herself. She soothed
the bleakness, made him forget how bloody serious
life could be.

Miss Henrietta Rolland nearly cracked her jaw on
a prodigious yawn the next morning. She only
opened her eyes when Millie made a loud snorting
noise for the third time, this third time, not more
than three inches from her ear.

"That's it, Miss Hetty. Open your eyes. Your
father will no doubt miss you if you don't join him
for luncheon."

"Yes, you're right about that, Millie." She
stretched and groaned. "Goodness, but I'm tired."

"You can't expect much else if you stay out until
the chimney sweeps begin their work."

While Hetty bathed from the porcelain basin atop
the marble commode, Millie, with practiced efficiency, told her mistress of the previous evening's
events. "You should know that your father was
engaged with Sir Richard Latham, Mr. Alwyn Set-
tlemore, and Sir Lucius Bentham. These gentlemen
arrived at about eight o'clock. They drank sherry in
the drawing room until half-past eight, discussing
politics all the while, then left for Sir Mortimer
Melberry's house. Of course, your father didn't
think to say good night to you, so we had no worry
there. Grimpston informed me that Sir Archibald
returned just after midnight with two of the gentlemen, drank more sherry, and held more political

discussions until just after two in the morning. Sir Archibald rose at his usual time of nine o'clock and repaired to the study after breakfast. And," Millie finished, glancing at the clock on the mantelpiece, "If you don't soon finish pulling up your stockings, miss, you'll ruin his blessed schedule and then we just might be in a rare mess."

"A rare mess that could prove fatal. We must never interfere with his schedule. Indeed, I imagine he's already planning how he will talk God around to his way of thinking once he arrives at the Pearly Gates. It boggles the mind, Millie, it truly does."

Millie quickly brushed out her mistress's short blond curls, threaded a white ribbon through the hollows and fastened it at the nape of her neck. "There," she said, stepping back to survey her handiwork. "No one could accuse you of not looking the perfect young lady of fashion except that your gown is two inches too short, but Sir Archibald wouldn't notice such a thing, thank the lord. Now, go, Miss Hetty, I just heard the clock chime twelve."

Hetty ran down the carpeted stairs into the small entrance hall. "Good morning, Grimpston," she said to the Rolland butler, who'd dandled her on his thin knee and burped her as well.

"Good morning, Miss Hetty. Off with you now, Sir Archibald is already at the table."

Hetty sped past him down a small corridor that led to the dining room. She turned and waved a friendly hand before disappearing through the open door. She stopped short, took a deep breath, and smiled. Her father, Sir Archibald Rolland, esteemed member of the House of Lords, Tory by birth, economic persuasion, and passionate conviction, sat at the head of the long table, his head buried behind the *Gazette*.

Mrs. Miller, the Rolland housekeeper, stood at his elbow, a look of patient resignation on her face, waiting to discover his preference of soups. It was a sacred rule among the servants that Sir Archibald was never to be interrupted in his ritual reading of the newspaper. She looked heavenward and Hetty could almost hear her silent sighs.

"Good day, Father," she sang out, carefree as any nightingale, and walked to her father's side.

"Father," she repeated, as his silver head didn't emerge from his newspaper.

"Damned idiots," he said to himself. "I ask you, why can't they understand the simplest economics? Their constant, radical inveigling against the Corn Laws makes me wonder if they share an entire brain amongst the lot of them." He jerked his head up. "Eh? Oh, Hetty? My dearest child, I trust you slept well?"

"Excellently, Father," she said fondly and dropped a kiss on his smooth forehead. "And you, my dear?"

"Like a top, my dear, like a top. I wonder where that odd saying came from? Why a top, I ask you? Well, I suppose it's far less important than the Corn Laws. If it were not for these infernal, cursed Whigs, I'd sleep even better than a top. How I'd like to send the lot of them to perdition." He chuckled at the thought and Hetty smiled, somewhat surprised that her father could joke about the Whigs, the bane of his political existence.

"Sir Archibald, may I now serve the soup? Would you prefer the turtle or the potato?" Mrs. Miller's very matronly face was nicely matched to her patient voice.

"I say, Mrs. Miller," Sir Archibald said, giving a start. "You really ought not creep up on one like that. Ah, turtle soup, did you say? Yes, the turtle soup will be fine, Mrs. Miller. Cook has a fine hand with the turtle. Not at all the thing with the potato soup, though, thick fleshy things, potatoes are. Come, dish it up. We mustn't dawdle all afternoon. Man wasn't meant to live by bread alone. Ah, my dearest Hetty, you do look lovely, my child, but your gown is rather short, isn't it? Is that a new fashion? Or have you grown again? Aren't you rather old to be still growing?"

She just smiled at him, biting her tongue so she wouldn't blurt out that she was thirteen years old and still growing. She wondered if he had any notion as to how old she was. But he had noticed her gown was too short. That was something she didn't like. That was scary. She would have to be very careful around him.

She shook her head and thought her father's condemnation of the potato soup had naught to do with Cook's inability, but rather with the circumstance that potatoes had the disadvantage of being a vegetable. And that, she decided, grinning to herself, reminded him of the Corn Laws. Not wishing to sound like a reprehensible Whig, no matter how farfetched her vegetable comparison, Hetty hastily concurred with the turtle soup.

As Mrs. Miller suffered from arthritis in her knee joints, Hetty, as was her habit, dismissed the housekeeper. After standing ten minutes by Sir Archibald's chair, unnoticed, Mrs. Miller wanted nothing more than to take the weight off her aching legs. She dipped a stiff curtsy and left father and daughter to their luncheon.

As Hetty spooned a mouthful of turtle soup to her lips, she thought about her activities for the afternoon. Sir Harry Brandon had insisted that they ride to Cowslip Hollow to see a local mill. She had no particular liking for prizefights. Yet, not to show a tad of enthusiasm for one of the most popular of the gentleman's sports would surely not hold her in good stead with her companions. At least, later, they would ride in Hyde Park. In all likelihood, Lord Oberlon would be among the glittering *ton* that made their daily appearance during those fashionable hours of four to six in the afternoon. She smiled, her turtle soup for the moment forgotten. How very grateful she was that Mr. Scuddimore did not possess the most awesome of intellects. He'd offered her the use of a hack without the slightest hesitation, and more importantly, without questioning her feeble story that her father needed her own bay mare for stud purposes.

"Studding, eh? Laudable solution. England has need of more bay horses. Mares love it, my papa told me."

Hetty looked up to see her father smiling at her in that vague way of his. He surprised her by saying, "I trust poor Drusilla's sick sister hasn't hampered your activities, my dear child. Your first trip to London and all that—I would not wish you to be bored."

She could but stare at him. He'd noticed her gown was too short yet he'd not realized that poor Drusilla Worthington had left London a good four months ago? She reached out and clasped her father's hand. "Dear sir, I assure you that I am never bored. I have made many friends and am never at a loss for something interesting to do. In fact, after luncheon, I am promised to meet friends and go to, ah, Richmond Park to walk through the maze. Have you ever been there, Father? Do you know the secret of the maze?"

He looked at her as if she'd asked him for a key to Bedlam. She wondered if he even knew what Richmond Park was. "Never mind, sir. I shall find my own way." She saw Sir Archibald couldn't manage to hide his relief. She knew he was delighted that she'd settled so quickly into London life. He wanted her to attend all the routs, balls, but the thought of chaperoning his daughter to such affairs would never even occur to him.

Looking at her father now, she realized he loved her, that he knew she was a good daughter, not at all bothersome, never demanding this or that from him. She never overspent the generous allowance he made available for her and ran his house with silent, uncomplaining efficiency. He made Hetty blink in an effort to understand his mood when he said sadly, "How very much like your lovely mother you are, my dear child. Never importuned me for a thing, did that wonderful woman." He heaved a heavy sigh and turned his attention back to a wafer-thin slice of ham.

"Why thank you, Father." Goodness, where had that come from? She was about as much like her deceased mother as Mr. Scuddimore was like her father. Poor Mother. Even as a small child, Hetty could remember Lady Beatrice complaining bitterly of her husband's neglect, of his blind preoccupation with all that *political rubbish*. When she contracted a chill and died swiftly of an inflammation of the lung, it required a stirring eulogy by the curate to make Sir Archibald aware that an important member of his family had passed to the hereafter. He grieved for her perfunctorily, focusing his beautiful, vague eyes on Hetty and patting her on the head in recognition of their mutual sorrow for the better part of two weeks. But then, suddenly, there was an election. Perceval became Prime Minister, and as a result, the Whigs began to wield such political power that Sir Archibald sought to throw himself immediately into the fray. He patted Hetty on the head for a final time and set off to London to launch a counteroffensive. Hetty went back to her prim governess with the natural dread of a lively child condemned to sewing samplers in a cheerless schoolroom. And then Damien had arrived to rescue her. Wounded in a skirmish on the Peninsula, he was packed to the country to recuperate. How quickly he had realized that the country offered very little in the way of amusement. He had turned to her, recognized her deep loneliness, and instantly taken her under his wing. Miss Mills, Hetty's governess, was charmed to her very soul by Damien's brotherly treatment of her, and so raised no great fuss. Thus it was that Hetty had found herself riding to the hunt, shooting at bottles with Damien's dueling pistol, and quickly becoming the most skilled ten-year-old piquet player in England.

Hetty felt a lump rise in her throat. Although she did not in the least resent her father's vague dismissal of her mother's demise, she couldn't help but think Sir Archibald oddly selfish when he had shown no more emotion at his son's death. She wondered with a tinge of bitterness if her father would even remember Damien if it were not for the large portrait of him that hung in the drawing room over the mantelpiece. Lady Beatrice, unfortunately, had never achieved a like immortality through the artist's brush.

Hetty was brought up short by her father's impassioned voice. "Of course, as *true* Englishmen, we would never consider the application of such vile methods as those employed by those more radical members of parliament. Yes, gentlemen, I speak of the incitement to riot, the unconscionable exploitation of the workers by the more irresponsible members of our company. Nay, I would not wish to indict the whole of the opposition—"

"Bravo, Father," Hetty said when he reached a long pause. "A speech for the House of Lords? You speak this afternoon?"

"Eh?" Sir Archibald jumped at his daughter's interruption, the words of his next sentence waiting impatiently on his tongue. "Oh, excuse me, my dear, I did not realize that you were still about. You haven't yet finished your soup? Didn't we also have some ham? Oh dear, I dislike potato soup, and that's what she brought, isn't it? Do you think perhaps Mrs. Miller could bring us something else?"

"Certainly, Father. Is there anything else I may do for you, sir?"

"Do for me? Other than have Mrs. Miller fetch me some ham soup? No, my dear. Such a good, considerate girl you are, Henrietta. Now, my dear, I'm off to make a speech this afternoon. If you are dining in, my child, don't have Cook hold dinner. Sir Mortimer and I will be discussing whether or not we should journey to Manchester, to determine if large scale insurrection is in any way a possibility. I will, of course, inform you if I am to leave London."

"I would expect nothing less from you, Father." Hetty rose and kissed her father's brow. As she closed the dining room door behind her, she heard her father's beautiful resonant voice rise to an impassioned crescendo.

Chapter Three

Later that same day at Rose Briar Manor in Herefordshire, Lady Louisa Rolland pursed her lips and steepled her fingertips, tapping them lightly. "Jack, do listen. This is all very odd. I've a letter from Drusilla Worthington, that mousy little dab of a woman who is supposed to be chaperoning Hetty in London. She is full of apologies that she had to leave the dear child suddenly to attend to her sick sister in Kent."

"Sounds proper for her to inform you." Sir John didn't look up from cleaning his favorite hunting rifle.

"What is odd, Jack," Lady Louisa said, frowning at his bent head, "is that she left nearly four months ago. In fact, but four weeks after Hetty arrived in London. Neither Hetty nor Sir Archibald have mentioned it in their letters."

Sir John looked up, a look of patent disbelief on his square, handsome face. "Surely you're mistaken, old girl. Quite impossible, in fact."

"I assure you it's what she writes," Lady Louisa said.

"But I've never known my father to write a letter to anyone. Something strange there, Lou."

Fighting back an urge to cosh her husband, which

seemed quite the natural thing to do, Lady Louisa managed to control herself. "Attend me, Jack, and cease your jesting. You know I didn't mean that. I merely used Sir Archibald's name in a manner of speaking. You know very well that Hetty is the only one who ever writes. And she," Louisa continued, "hasn't mentioned it at all."

"Now, Lou, you're not thinking about playing a dragon mother-in-law, are you? Lord knows if you want to, don't. Send your own mother instead, she'd scare the sin out of the prince himself. She could give a dragon lessons. As for Hetty, I can't say I blame her for not telling us. The Worthington woman was probably a damned nuisance, probably drove poor Hetty quite mad. Good thing she's gone to that sick sister." He paused a moment, looking worriedly at his rifle. "I hope the sister doesn't die. That would mean the Worthington woman would be back in poor Hetty's hair again."

"Damned nuisance or not, my love, Hetty is but eighteen years of age. Even though she's in mourning for Damien and won't be attending Almack's or any of the large *ton* parties, it concerns me that she's not attended by anyone. It simply isn't done."

Finally, his wife got all his attention. Sir John put his rifle down for a moment and looked at her. "I don't frown upon it. Do you mean that poor Hetty might have to forego the pleasure of having some elegant, worthless idiot asking for her hand in marriage? Really now, Lou, Hetty's got a sound head on her shoulders. And I'll wager she hasn't even stirred much from the house these last four months, much less offended any of your great ladies." He added on a sigh as he hefted his rifle over his left shoulder, "Maybe it would be better for her to kick up her heels and offend one of those stiff-butted old gossips. At least we'd know that she's not still prostrated by Damien's death."

"My point exactly. The poor child should have someone with her. You know that Sir Archibald might as well be on the moon, for all the attention and comfort he offers her."

"You said yourself, Lou, that Hetty hasn't mentioned a word about the Worthington woman leaving. Shows you, doesn't it, that Hetty is perfectly content not to have anyone with her." He grinned and put down the now sparkling clean rifle again. "Got you there, old girl," he said, grinned at her like a sinner and pulled her to her feet. "No need to worry about Hetty. We'll be going to London next month anyway, you know. You can content yourself that your sister-in-law is feeling just the thing, before we continue on to " Sir John's voice trailed mysteriously off.

"Oh, Jack, do you really mean it? You have arranged it? We're really going to Paris? You're not trying to get away with something, are you?"

"Give me a kiss and I'll tell you the truth."

Louisa gave him more than a kiss, she bit his earlobe, then hugged him until he groaned. He dropped a kiss on the chestnut curl that lay provocatively over her left ear, a delicious little ear that he loved to kiss. "Of course I mean it. Will you be satisfied to spend a few days with Hetty then?"

"Certainly. Hetty's a lovely girl. I just hope she's adjusting. I just want her to be happy."

Sir John said quietly, his dark eyes hooded, "I doubt she'll be happy for a very long time. Damien is dead now. When we saw Hetty at the funeral, the poor girl was so grief stricken that she barely spoke a word. Even without a chaperone. I don't think you have to worry that she'll get herself talked about. Lord, I just wish she would. I wish she'd go out and kick up her heels and make everyone stare at her. But she won't. Damnation, I miss Damien, too. What a loss, what a damnable waste."

"He died a hero for England, Jack. We must remember that. We must believe that he made a difference, that his death meant something."

"To hell with England. Oh damn, now I've pulled us both down. Tell you what, Lou, let's go see if Little John has driven Nurse to distraction."

Less than a week before Miss Drusilla Worthington left Sir Archibald's town house on Grosvenor Square to attend her sick sister, she had sat quietly in the drawing room across from her charge, Miss Henrietta Rolland.

She gazed up several minutes later to see that the young lady's eyes were focused upon the brightly dancing flames in the fireplace. Yet, Hetty didn't seem aware of the fire, much less the rest of her surroundings. Lady Louisa had told her that Henrietta was much affected by her brother Damien's death at Waterloo. Miss Worthington had been with Henrietta for three weeks, but all her efforts to suggest appropriate amusements didn't penetrate the shell of grief that enveloped her young charge.

Miss Worthington's eyes clouded as she gazed at Hetty. All that unremitting black the girl persisted in wearing. What a pretty picture she would be if she but attended to Miss Worthington's repeated, gentle suggestions. True, perhaps she was a trifle tall for society's current whims, but regal in that straight, proud way she carried herself. Miss Worthington thought of Sir Archibald, a decided glint in her normally unassuming gray eyes. Probably off at some political gathering, all his mental energies focused upon his one passion. It seemed that there was scarcely a moment in the day when he was aware of the presence of his daughter, much less of Miss Worthington's tireless efforts to provide a normal atmosphere in his home.

If the truth were told, Miss Worthington felt like a floundering fish in a fisherman's net. It wasn't that Henrietta was unkind to her or made her feel unwelcome in any way. But the only visitors to be seen were Sir Archibald's political cronies, severely dressed gentlemen whose curt nods made Miss Worthington feel woefully inadequate and twittery as a caged chicken. To make matters worse, if Henrietta wasn't sitting quietly in front of the fireplace, simply staring off at nothing in particular as she was now, she would take long walks by herself, an activity of which Miss Worthington disapproved. When she had very tactfully pointed out that a young lady walking about by herself was not at all the thing, Henrietta had merely cocked her head to one side and appeared to look straight through Miss Worthington. "You needn't worry that I'm ogled by all the young gentlemen, Miss Worthington," she'd said. "All these heavy black veils keep them at their distance."

She saw that Henrietta's hands were knotting and unknotting a handkerchief in her lap. She sighed and put down her needle. "Hetty, dear child, do look outside. The fog is lifting and I believe that the sun will be out soon. Would you like to accompany me to the Pantheon Bazaar? You haven't visited there, you know."

Hetty raised dark blue eyes, which looked suspiciously red about the rims, and slowly shook her head. "No, thank you, Miss Worthington. If you would like to go, I shall be happy to ring for John the coachman."

Miss Worthington felt the familiar naggings of defeat. "No, Hetty, I am quite content to finish my mending." They sat in silence until the afternoon sun began its descent into the distance. As Miss Worthington rose to light a branch of candles, a knock sounded on the drawing-room door.

Grimpston, the Rolland butler, and in Miss Worthington's opinion, a man of great efficiency and tact, appeared in the doorway. "Miss Henrietta," he said and waited. As his mistress did not turn, he cleared his throat to gain her attention.

Finally she looked up. "Yes, Grimpston?"

"There is a person here asking to see Sir Archibald, Miss Hetty."

"Sir Archibald isn't here at the moment, as you very well know, Grimpston."

"I know, Miss, but there's a man here, a Mr. Pottson. He tells me that he was Master Damien's batman."

"His batman?"

Miss Worthington watched her in surprise as Hetty nearly leapt from her chair. "Oh, do have this Mr. Pottson attend me in the back parlor. I shall be there directly."

He returned to the entrance hall and said to the diminutive gray-haired man who stood still clutching a crumpled wool hat between his hands, "Miss Henrietta Rolland will see you. If you will follow me."

Pottson was certain that he'd made a mistake in coming when he was ushered into the presence of a tall young lady who stood watching him come toward her, an unreadable expression in her eyes. Drat the butler anyway, he thought. What he had to say was for Master Damien's father's ears—not for a gentle young lady all draped in black. He found himself gazing at her curiously, for unlike his late master, Miss Henrietta was very fair, with short curling blond hair framing her face. Yet, the eyes were the same—a deep blue and wide, set beneath distinctively arched brows. There was a dreaming quality about such eyes, Pottson thought.

"Miss Rolland," he said, stepping forward, his wool hat still between his hands.

"Yes, I am Henrietta Rolland. Grimpston said you were Damien's batman." She moved gracefully forward and clasped the startled Pottson's hands in hers. The hat fell unnoticed to the floor.

"Yes, ma'am. I had intended to see Sir Archibald, but the butler insisted that I was to see you instead."

How very like dear Grimpston, Hetty thought, and how very perceptive of him. She drew a deep breath and smiled warmly. "Yes, I'm the one for you to see. Do sit down, Pottson, I believe we have much to discuss." Hetty didn't spare a moment's thought about the pain the batman's words must inevitably bring her, laying raw her grief. She knew only that she had to know what had happened to Damien during those long months after he'd suddenly left London.

Pottson eased his small person to the edge of a

chair. Saying what he had come to say would have been bad enough with Sir Archibald. But Master Damien's younger sister. Damnation, scratching old wounds, that was all he was doing. It was that thought that had kept him away these summer months since Master Damien's death.

"I only came because of the letter!"

"What is this about a letter? What letter are you talking about, Pottson?"

"You see, ma'am, me and Master Damien were together for nine months, traveling from Spain to Italy, carrying dispatches to and from the generals and such as that. Master Damien was always a right proper gentleman, ma'am, yet never too starchy in the collar, if you know what I mean. I quite liked him. He was greatly respected by the men, made them laugh, he did, and he was trusted by the generals. General Brooks always asked for Master Damien, always."

Hetty swallowed the lump in her throat. Now wasn't the time. What letter was he talking about? She was content to wait.

"Always ready for a good joke was Master Damien, never seeming to worry much about what the next day would bring. Several of those dispatches he carried, well, I can tell you, ma'am, they weren't about the weather. I thought a lot of him, I did."

"Yes, Pottson?"

"Well, ma'am, sometimes it seemed to me that all wasn't right with Master Damien. Just when I'd expect him to be charting the route for some important document he had to deliver, I'd find him instead sitting alone in his room, not even a candle lit, brooding-like, you know. I didn't mean to be forward or anything, ma'am, but I'd ask him if there was anything bothering him. He'd just smile at me, a kind of sad smile. And he'd say it wasn't anything to bother me with, naught of anything really, he'd say, and I knew it was just to protect me, to make me go away and leave him to his thoughts.

"Just before Waterloo, back in the early days of June, he got his orders to attend the Prince of Orange in Brussels, a safe spot, I told him, seeing as how we all knew it was coming to a bloody battle and all. Next thing I knew, he was assigned under a General Drakeson, a very different kettle of fish, I remember him telling me, a man on the prince's staff, a gentleman with spiky side whiskers and a back so stiff he couldn't bend, I was sure of it. I was with Master Damien when he got orders to lead a frontal cavalry charge, right in the thick of the fighting. He wouldn't let me come with him, ma'am, just patted me on the shoulder, that sad smile on his face. I'll never forget what he said. 'Well, Pottson, I must believe that my charmed existence is about to come to an end. It looks, old fellow, as if I'm to be the sacrificial goat.' That's all he said, ma'am. I never saw him again, ma'am."

Pottson saw that the young lady's face was as white as her gown was black. Her hands were trembling in her lap, but she didn't cry, didn't sob, didn't do anything. She just said calmly, "What about the letter?"

"Well, I got to wondering about what Master Damien said before he left, ma'am. When I was preparing his personal things to be sent back to your family, I found a letter folded up and tucked inside

the lining of his valise. I read it, ma'am. I'm sorry,
but I couldn't help myself."

"Let me see the letter, Pottson." Hetty unfolded
the single sheet of paper and slowly began to read.
She looked up, past Pottson's right shoulder, then
lowered her head and read the letter yet another
time.

Dearest Love:
    I cannot believe that you have been torn from my
arms. Oh, Damien, if only we'd had time to be
together, if only I had some hope that you could return
to me. You must see now that I have no choice. I do
not know what Lord Oberlon will do now, but you
must understand that my own fate is no longer in my
hands.
    May God damn him to hell for what he has done. I
will love you forever, my darling. Adieu—
                    Your Dearest Elizabeth

Hetty straightened and carefully folded the letter.
She looked up, directly into Pottson's face. "You did
quite right to bring the letter to me. Yes, you've
done excellently."

Even though Miss Worthington considered it a
trifle odd for her charge to spend nearly an hour in
the company of a servant, she gave it only cursory
thought, for not twelve hours later she found herself
in a sudden whirl of activity. The quiet young lady
who had sat so very many long hours staring into
the fireplace, who had taken long walks, had disappeared as if she'd never drawn breath. It was Henrietta who suggested over breakfast that they visit the
Pantheon Bazaar. At last, Miss Worthington
thought, her patient efforts had reaped their

rewards. She had succeeded in redirecting Henrietta's thoughts. Being a Christian woman, she also admitted to herself that the timely visit by the late Captain Damien Rolland's batman must have, in some small way, assisted Henrietta to recover her spirits. She most willingly assisted her charge to exchange some of the black gowns for soft gray ones and pack them, black veils and all, in an old attic trunk that had belonged to Hetty's grandmother.

When she received her sister's plea a few days later to attend her in Kent, she gazed up at an innocently smiling Henrietta. Miss Worthington was torn, not knowing precisely where her duty lay. Although Henrietta very prettily begged her to remain, she did hasten to say that she, of all people, well understood one's feelings toward one's own dear family.

Miss Drusilla Worthington departed London two days later with the happy conviction that she had performed her duty by Henrietta. She never realized that Henrietta was fairly itching for her to be gone.

Three days after Miss Worthington's departure, Lord Harry Monteith made his first appearance in London.

Chapter Four

"Thompson Street will suit us just fine, Pottson. It's just a short distance from St. James, so we needn't worry about the expense of hackneys. How much did you say the furnished rooms would cost by the quarter?"

Pottson grunted a price that he secretly hoped would put an end once and for all to Miss Hetty's mad scheme. He was doomed to disappointment, for Miss Hetty beamed at him. He supposed that he really shouldn't be surprised at anything Miss Hetty proposed now, though he had thought himself entered into bedlam, when, but three days before, she had summoned him back to Grosvenor Square and poured her idea into his ear.

She said now, clapping him on his thin shoulders, "Of course, we must now see to my clothes, and, to be sure, set aside enough money to secure my debut into the fashionable world. Thank heavens that Damien saw to my education in piquet and faro. I vow that with any luck at all at the gaming tables, we will live in a most sumptuous manner."

"Ah, Miss, it's a crazy scheme. You just ain't a man and no soul in his right or left mind would ever believe you to be one." He tried to add punch to his words by critically eyeing her from breasts to hips.

She merely laughed. "Stop worrying. I have ideas on *that* score. I have made out a list of my measurements and colors of breeches, waistcoats, and coats that I would like. The gentlemen's current whim toward those tight-knitted pantaloons are, unfortunately, out of the question. I have no desire to tempt fate."

"Say we can dish you up to play the young gentleman. You still must approach the Marquess of Oberlon. From what I hear, he's a powerful gentleman and an acclaimed sportsman. You tell me that you will have your revenge on him for your brother—but how, Miss Hetty? How?"

Hetty's eyes clouded. "Didn't I tell you, Pottson? Besides teaching me gaming, Damien also saw to it that I was a crack shot. As to fencing, I admit to needing lessons. I have been making discreet inquiries myself, you know, and will begin fencing lessons with a Signore Bertioli very shortly. However, it is my plan to face down the marquess with pistols."

Pottson felt his grizzled hair grizzle even more. He tugged on it. He wanted to curse, but he couldn't, not in front of a lady who would soon be a man. But he couldn't keep quiet, he had to make one last try. "Oh gawd, this is pure nonsense, Miss Hetty. You can't go aping gentlemen's ways. It's against God and Nature. It's against everything I can even contrive to think of. It's probably even against the law."

"Come on, Pottson, it's far too late for you to be carrying on with these nonsensical arguments. My mind is quite made up. Either you help me, or I shall simply find someone else." She spoke with more confidence than she felt. When Pottson nodded finally, she wanted to shout with relief.

"I'd like you to tell me one thing, Miss Hetty. Master Damien, like I told you, was always a proper gentleman, treating ladies just as he ought. Why would he teach his own sister such unladylike activities?"

She laughed. "He was bored, Pottson. Perhaps, too, he felt a trifle sorry for me, for Mother had just died and Sir Archibald had returned to London to carry on his never-ending battle against the Whigs. He was recovering from a wound, as I recall. He said I was an apt pupil."

"Now there's another thing, Miss Hetty. I can't be dressing you. And more than that, you can't be sneaking back here to Sir Archibald's house looking like a gentleman."

"Already you lack confidence in me. When next you come to visit me, I will introduce you to my maid, Millie. You can both preach doom to me, if you like. But I warn you, I have quite secured her cooperation, so it will do you no good to plot against me."

"All right, all right. I'll bite my nails and keep my mouth shut. Ah, yes, I'll need some guineas for the rooms, Miss Hetty, not to mention a credit for the tailor."

"Thank you for reminding me, Pottson. I shall see to it now. It's fortunate that my mother left me my own money. We shall use my quarterly allowance until circumstances or my ill-luck at the gaming tables force me to dip into the principal. One other thing, Pottson, don't forget that my new name is Harry Monteith."

"Where'd you get such a name, Miss Hetty?"

"From an old atlas of world explorers. I really don't remember what the man discovered," she added, the lie clean. She knew very well that hundreds of years ago, a Baron Monteith had set himself against the de Medicis, vowing revenge for the poisoning death of his sire. It had seemed like the biblical David and Goliath struggle, and Hetty's casting herself in the role of the avenging Monteith had quite stirred her imagination. The only note that jarred her fantasy was the fact that she could not discover whatever became of the baron.

Someday she'd tell Pottson the truth.

"Come, my lord, your wrist is flaccid. An iron wrist, my lord, you must have an iron wrist." Signore Bertioli stepped back from Lord Monteith and leaned lightly on the handle of his foil. Not one bead of perspiration was evident on his forehead, and his bushy black brows drew closely together at the heaving, sweating young gentleman. How very intense and eager the young lord was, so unlike the vast majority of his other pupils—young dandies who sought to exhibit good form and style, the practice required to become truly proficient in the art an abhorrent thought to most of them. He softened his tone, but it had to be said. "It is strength you lack, my lord."

Hetty wondered if she would survive her first lesson, for her heart was pounding so wildly that she feared it must burst. She managed to gasp out between heaving breaths, "Yes, Signore, I fear what you say is true. But there must be something I can do." At least, her main fear—that Signore Bertioli would realize that he was instructing a female—had not come to pass.

Signore Bertioli drew back, surprised at the seriousness in the lad's voice. "Actually," he said, "strength need not be everything. You have the grace and agility. Perhaps with much work, my lord, I can teach you some of the more, er, unusual techniques. It would hold you in good stead, if," he paused pointedly, "you are willing to apply yourself."

Damn, Hetty thought, rubbing her arms, he was right about her endurance and her flaccid wrist. She focused upon his last words. "You mentioned unusual techniques, Signore?" Hope reared itself and she gazed at the olive-skinned master with such intensity that he turned suddenly away from her. "Signore, I'll do anything, anything you say."

"Sit down, my lord," he said, sweeping a face guard from a chair.

Hetty nodded gratefully and sank down, wiping her white full sleeve across her sweating brow.

"You are new to London, my lord?"

"Yes, Signore, I arrived just this past week. You wonder at my lack of skill. I come from the far north of England, where, unfortunately, there were naught but cows and girls to fence with. My apologies for being such an inept pupil, Signore."

There was much earnestness in the young gentleman's unabashed candor. And yet, he thought, even if Lord Monteith never became a credit to the noble art of fencing, it made no great difference, at least in England. With dueling outlawed for some years now, fencing had become a showy sport for Englishmen, just as playing the harp was for the young English ladies. An accomplishment, nothing more. He fanned his hands and said with a chuckle, "Cows and girls, you say, my lord? It's a pity to be sure. You have courage, my lord. But no duels for you as yet."

To his surprise, Lord Monteith suddenly squared his shoulders and sat board straight, his mouth drawing into a thin line. "You say I have courage, Signore. I will tell you that I am willing to do anything. You spoke of unusual techniques. You must teach me. I will learn. I must."

The young gentleman didn't take his words as a frivolous joke, Signore Bertioli thought. He paused and cocked his thin, intense face to one side. "You press yourself, young sir, far beyond the limits of most of the young gentlemen who come to me. It is certainly not to prepare yourself for war. You English, after all, have finally dispatched that pig Corsican to his island hell. And even if it were for war, young sir, the art of the foil becomes outmoded, just as the bow and arrow. Were I not in England, my lord, I would think that you prepare to execute a *vendetta*."

"*Vendetta*, Signore?"

"A *vendetta* is a sworn act of revenge. In my country a *vendetta* can carry from father to son for many generations. Many times the cause for revenge is lost over the years. Yet the desire for revenge upon one's enemies remains, as if it were born into the soul itself."

"I like your word *vendetta*. Yes, it is perfect."

"If you carry such an idea for revenge, my lord, I would suggest the pistol. You have a keen eye, and to kill a man with the little ball requires no more strength than your cows or girls have."

"You must know, Signore, that in England, in a duel of honor, the one who wishes the revenge cannot select the weapon. I am an excellent shot, Signore, but it is not enough. You must teach me so that my *vendetta* isn't simply an empty wish."

Signore Bertioli gazed down into the young set face. But a boy the lord was, a mere boy, with smooth cheeks and many years of life before him. He felt sudden fear for Lord Monteith. If he was truly in earnest about a duel of honor, Signore Bertioli seriously doubted his ability to endure in the face of a more powerfully built and skilled opponent. He said quietly, "Yes, I will teach you. We will contrive. If you are rested, my lord, there is much more for you to learn today."

"Thank you, Signore," Hetty said simply, and rose with new energy to her feet. "Yes, I am rested."

"*En garde*, then, young sir." Signore Bertioli slashed his foil through the silent air, its gleaming steel soon connecting with Lord Harry's blade.

At each clash, the impact sent quivers of pain up Hetty's arm. She gritted her teeth, silently repeating her catechism of hate against the Marquess of Oberlon, to keep her mind from the pain. *I shall send you to hell, your grace, just as you sent Damien to his death. As your blood flows from your body, I shall tell you who I am and why you are dying. I'll stand over you and laugh when you draw your last breath.*

Chapter Five

"I say, Lord Harry, you're not looking at all the thing tonight. Some bleater insult the cut of your trousers?" Scuddy leaned his yellow and green striped elbows on the card table to look more closely into his friend's exhausted face.

Hetty's arm was so sore that Pottson had had to take great care when assisting her into her coat. "No, it was Signore Bertioli. He's a stern taskmaster, Scuddy, as I've often told you. He very nearly unmanned me today with the pace he set. I've taken lessons with him for nearly as long a time as I've known the both of you, yet I still stagger out of his apartment like a drunken loon."

"Any hope for you, Lord Harry?" Sir Harry asked with a wide grin. "Surely there's hope. You're endowed with superior physical stamina, just look at the size of your muscles, pathetic little mounds of nothing, but hey, you're a smart fellow, for what that's worth."

"You mean," Hetty said, "that God couldn't make me both strong and smart so he gave me the smart only?"

"That's it, only I said it in a more clever way. Now, as I was saying, I'm just really guessing about your muscles since you insist on wearing your bloody clothes so damned loose. Tell us, are your muscles superior? Or just your brain?"

"In my case, it's both. Why, superior is just the word Signore Bertioli used for me. He said I could have butchered you months ago."

"Well, in all fairness," Sir Harry said on a sigh, "my own sister did nail me when we fenced. Of course that was before I bought a commission and went to Spain. Now I'm up to snuff, my boy, so don't try to insult me. I just hope you aren't too tired for what I have planned for tonight. Time to test your northern mettle."

"What northern mettle? You want me to trounce you in piquet again, Harry? I've already fleeced you of five guineas. You're an abominable player."

"Lord Harry's got you there, Harry," Scuddy said. "Ever since I've known you, you've always told me what an accomplished player *you* were. Lord Harry's beaten you regularly. Now what is this about northern mettle?"

"Much you would know about any sort of mettle," Sir Harry said. You're naught but a lazy hedonist. Just look at that belly of yours, oozing from beneath your waistcoat. It turns my stomach, and at your age, too, Scuddy."

Scuddy said after he'd poured another long drink of wine down his gullet, "Where did you learn that word hedonist? Ha, you must have got it from your sister or her husband. Lord knows you aren't all that much into words longer than a grunt."

Hetty sat back in her chair, amused by their squabbling. She twirled a delicate crystal goblet of wine between her fingers, only halfheartedly listening to their bickering. The four months she had been Lord Harry Monteith seemed an eternity to her, the demands of being a young gentleman exhausting, sometimes dangerous, but always exhilarating. How very lucky she had been that Sir Harry Brandon and Mr. Scuddimore had so quickly and unreservedly taken her under their collective wings. Her thoughts went back to that first evening, four months ago, when she had emerged from Thompson Street as Lord Harry Monteith. Her deep fear had been that the first gentleman she would meet would look at her, stare in the direction of her womanly parts, then look horrified. She had pomaded down her normally fluffy blond curls and tied the queue securely with a black ribbon. Her cravat had caused her to gulp with fresh anxiety, for to any experienced masculine eye, it was indeed an abomination. She'd forced herself to leave the apartment, all her thoughts firmly focused on swaggering like a young gentleman, her hips resisting every urge to sway. She had tried to nonchalantly swing her black malacca cane in her hand, as if she hadn't a care in the world, and had made her way to Drury Lane, whistling and humming even as her heart pounded against her ribs.

She would never forget her first evening at the theater, the title of the melodramatic play, *The Milkmaid's Dilemma,* and the freak accident that had brought her together with Harry and Scuddy. A very rowdy play it was, following the adventures of a seductive milkmaid who, in the most maddening manner, refused to be bedded by her ardent young man. The hero had finally been about to succeed in his amorous endeavors when the milkmaid's cow—a very real bovine specimen—became suddenly irked with the proceedings, mooed loudly, kicked over the milk can, and after gazing balefully at the uproarious audience, took violent exception. But a moment later, the cow lumbered off the stage, down into the pit, with frantic stagehands, a harried director, and the tousled heroine chasing behind her. The laughter suddenly turned to panic and Hetty found herself being pommeled and pushed roughly this way and that by the now stampeding audience.

"Out of me way, m'lad," a very fat man yelled behind her, buffeting her on the shoulder. She would have gone sprawling to the ground had not a strong hand grabbed her arm and pulled her upright and back from the aisle.

"I say, old fellow," a laughing voice said. "You really must keep out of the way of the rabble, you know. Hope that damned cow kicks in a few of their heads."

Hetty looked up into twinkling blue eyes, set in a quite handsome young face. "Thank you, sir. It's my first visit to the theater. Does this sort of thing happen very often?" Oh God, had she squeaked? Or had her voice been low enough?

The young gentleman grinned. "We were lucky tonight. They usually don't have livestock that's truly alive onstage. Once the audience threw rotten apples at the players. You should have seen the look on poor Macbeth's face. Ho! They've finally got the poor beast in tow." A sudden look of surprise crossed the young gentleman's face. "First time to Drury Lane, you say?"

Hetty nodded. "Yes, I've just arrived in London— from the North. It is all rather new to me."

"Don't mean to tell me you're a rustic? Well, I'll

be damned. Hey, Scuddy, pay attention, old boy, we've got an oddity here and I saved him from being trampled."

Hetty looked past her rescuer at a heavyset, cherubic-faced young man who had an openness about him that made her lips curl into an instant smile. Not a drop of guile in him. Probably not many brains either.

"What's your name? It's only fair that you tell me since I saved your hide."

"Monteith. Lord Harry Monteith."

The cherubic-faced young man blinked. "Damned coincidence. His name is Harry, too—Sir Harry Brandon. Me, well, you can call me Scuddy." He gave Hetty a plump hand that had probably never rubbed down a sweating horse in its life.

Hetty had worried about her soft white hands, but had discarded gloves. She would worry no longer.

Sir Harry poked Scuddy in the ribs. "His name's actually Mr. Thayerton Scuddimore, but we don't like to hang the poor fellow with that mouthful, so Scuddy it is. He doesn't deserve such a noble name either."

"It's a pleasure, Scuddy." So far, so good, she thought to herself. Both Harry and Scuddy appeared bluff and good-natured. She couldn't help but wonder just how they would have introduced themselves had they known she was a female.

Sir Harry turned to gaze at the now empty stage. "Well, it looks as though our milkmaid ain't going to tumble in the hay after all, at least tonight. Scuddy and I were going to White's for a late supper. Why don't you come along with us."

Hetty said slowly, "You see, because I'm so new

to London and have no friends here, I'm not a member of White's. I'm not a member of anything."

"Scuddy and I are," Sir Harry said. "You may come along as our guest. No harm done there."

"I say, Lord Harry." She heard Scuddy's voice, impatient now, "I've asked you the same question three times."

Hetty blinked away her memories and brought her attention back to the present. "I was just thinking about the cow at Drury Lane."

Scuddy laughed and thumped the table with the palm of his hand. "Damned funny sight. First time we met you, eh, Lord Harry? Damn it seems longer than what—four months ago?"

"Well, it was four months ago," Sir Harry said, his voice testy, an unusual event. "Stop prosing about the distant past else it will be close to dawn before I can tell you what I've got planned for the evening."

Hetty recognized the rakish gleam in Harry's sweet blue eyes, that, were it any other gentleman's eye, would have been decidedly lecherous. Her palms were beginning to sweat as she forced herself to ask, "Tell us, Harry, what is this plan of yours?"

"A visit to Lady Buxtell's house on Millsom Street. It's been a damned long time since I've been there. About time to make another call."

Palms sweatier still, Hetty knew she had to ask. "Lady Buxtell? A friend of yours, Harry?"

Scuddy gave a chuckle and tapped Hetty on her very sore arm. She managed to keep the gasp behind her teeth, knowing such a display wouldn't be manly. "Good grief no, Lord Harry. She ain't his friend—much less a lady—it's her girls Harry's interested in, not that bloody old besom."

It had been with something of a shock to her when she discovered gentlemen's conversations frequently settled in a most direct way upon the assets or lack thereof of various young ladies of their acquaintance. It was to their credit, Hetty supposed, that young ladies of quality were excluded from such frank and detailed comparisons, at least most of the time. But the bodily charms of females of a different class were bandied about in quite another manner. Up until now, Hetty believed that she had performed well, aping their rakish remarks and behaving in as lusty a way as her friends.

She wondered what the devil she was going to do now. She shrugged her shoulders and tried to look bored. "Really, Harry, a brothel? I, myself, prefer to partake of goods that aren't displayed to so many customers."

"Mighty high in the instep you are, Lord Harry. I tell you, it's a very select house, not at all in the common way. You'll not catch the pox there." Sir Harry turned eagerly to Mr. Scuddimore. "Come, Scuddy, you ain't said a word about the matter. I know for a fact you haven't had a girl since you tossed one of your father's serving maids. You said she gave you the grandest lessons imaginable. Time to try out your new knowledge."

Scuddy sputtered into his glass of port. "No need to shout it to the world, Harry. If you will know, I'm not too plump in the pocket, it being midway through the quarter. M'father wouldn't take it too kindly if I showed up on his doorstep with my hand out. Again."

"Damnation, Scuddy, this one visit ain't going to send you up the River Tick. And as for you, Lord

Harry, I begin to wonder if you've ever even been to a house of pleasure. Just what is it you chaps do in the North Country?"

"Chaps in the North Country do much the same as you do, I suspect." How the devil was she going to get out of this? "Actually, we tend to marry before we become old men. Solves a lot of problems, you know."

It was Scuddy who turned upon her, his eyes filled with disbelief. "Damned silly notion. M'father is forever telling me that marriage has nothing to do with pleasure. Don't tell me you're that old fashioned?"

"Scuddy's quite right, Lord Harry. A man's got to have his pleasure. It has nothing to do with marriage, either before or after. Well, what do you say, chaps? I'm off to Lady Buxtell's. Do you have red blood in your veins or are you all talk and excuses?"

Scuddy painstakingly calculated the remainder of his allowance until the first of the next quarter, brightened and said, "I'm with you, Harry." He downed the rest of his port and turned an owlish stare at Hetty.

In that moment, Hetty knew she couldn't refuse, for to do so might plant suspicious seeds in her friends' minds that Lord Harry Monteith really wasn't the lusty young man they believed him to be. She had to be manly and that meant not complaining about her sore arm muscles and going to a brothel. She tossed down her wine as Scuddy had done, thumped her glass on the table and rose with a swagger. "Well, my lads, the night grows late. Lead on, Harry. I, for one, am ready to sample Lady

Buxtell's wares." She turned and allowed a hovering footman to assist her into her cloak.

Sir Harry frowned. He should be the one leading Lord Harry, not the other way around. It had been his idea, after all. He clapped Scuddy on the shoulder, recovering his good humor at the thought of a lovely young woman pleasuring him and said to Lord Harry, "We're right behind you."

Hetty cudgeled her brain as street after street melted away beneath her boots, bringing her nearer and nearer to Millsom Street. Somewhere, she thought, there must be some humor in this ridiculous situation.

She was momentarily surprised at the somber picture Lady Buxtell's establishment presented to the passerby. It was a huge, three-story brick structure that dominated a street corner, its façade of Georgian columns unpretentious to the point of austerity. No more than a modicum of candlelight shined through its front windows, and for an instant, Hetty thought that Harry had made a wonderfully welcome mistake. Perhaps it was closed for the night. Both wishes were soon dashed when Harry stepped smartly up the stone steps and loudly sounded the heavy brass knocker. Only deep silence followed the echoing knock, and again, Hetty allowed herself the hope that Lady Buxtell was not receiving gentlemen this evening.

She heard a slight grating sound and realized someone was looking at them. More minutes passed before the heavy oak door was eased smoothly open, and a tall, gaunt-looking man, all dressed in severe black, stood silently before them. As the man's eyes rested briefly upon her, Hetty felt her heart thump madly. She had the uncanny sensation that somehow he knew her to be an imposter. But then the man stepped back, offered a negligent bow, and motioned for them to enter. How strange, she thought, that I am relieved to be allowed to enter a brothel. Another man, also clothed all in black, took their canes and cloaks. Hetty would have sworn that the rheumy old eyes leered as he silently pointed them down a long, narrow hall toward the back of the house.

"Very discreet," Hetty said to Harry, trying to keep condemnation from her voice. She wondered if the Marquess of Oberlon would be in attendance tonight. Stupid thought, she realized but an instant later. His grace kept his mistresses privately. She doubted if the marquess had given up such pleasures even during his brief marriage to Elizabeth Springville.

She quickly forgot the marquess as Sir Harry confidently directed them into a spacious drawing room. He gave her a sly look. "Well, what do you think, Lord Harry? More elegant than you expected, eh?"

On first glance, Hetty was inclined to agree. The long, rectangular room was richly appointed with heavy crimson velvet hangings in marked contrast to delicately wrought clusters of chairs and sofas fashioned in the gold and white style of the late Louis. At least half a dozen black-clad footmen moved unobtrusively about the room, quantities of drink held on large silver trays. A closer look showed her that the occupants of the room were a far cry from the habitués of Almack's. There were many more ladies than gentlemen present, and though they were garbed in keeping with the elegance of the room, there was more white bosom showing than Hetty ever considered possible without showing a navel as well. She noticed with growing dread that although conversation appeared lively and high giggling laughter was a commonplace amongst the *ladies*, the gentlemen still managed to caress and stroke any unclothed flesh that was near to them. She felt frightened and embarrassed to the tips of her toes at the spectacle before her. "What did you say, Harry? Oh, it's elegant. You're right. Why a more tasteful brothel I've never encountered."

"Gawd, ain't *she* ever a beauty," Mr. Scuddimore whispered in awe, his widened eyes fastened upon an ethereal-looking girl whose shining hair lay long and thick and black as polished ebony down her slender back. Her brown eyes were curiously slanted at the corners, giving her an exotic appearance.

"Ah, I can see that you are taken with Lilly, young sir. She has come to us just recently from a faraway land called China. Most charming, is she not?"

Mr. Scuddimore jumped and reddened, unaware that his remark had been overheard. He turned, just as had Sir Harry and Lord Harry, to gaze into the light green eyes of a tall, willowy built woman, who, unlike the rest of the females in the vast room, was dressed in a blue velvet gown that revealed not one patch of bosom. The smile on her reddened lips was one of tolerant amusement. Hetty realized that she was the *madam*, the woman who procured and sold the bodies of these other women. Without thought to her precarious position, she looked the woman up and down, and said with all the haughty *sang froid* of a peer of the realm, "How interesting that you must needs search to the ends of the world to procure *ladies* for your establishment. Is procurement that difficult? Perhaps it is very costly?"

Chapter Six

Sir Harry shot a look of confused surprise at Lord Harry and Hetty forced herself to swallow her anger. She shrugged her shoulders and turned away from Madam Buxtell to look about the room.

"I'm Sir Harry Brandon, Lady Buxtell. Perhaps you remember me. I was here not above a month ago."

Lady Angelique Buxtell, Martine DuBois by birth, cloaked her anger and forced a polite mask of recognition and welcome to her painted face. Actually, she had no memory of him at all, but he appeared eager to please, and somewhat embarrassed by his friend's churlishness. Thus, she nodded her dark brown curls, only slightly brightened by the dye jar, and stretched her hand to Sir Harry. "Of course, Sir Harry, I remember you well. I see that you have brought two friends. Perhaps some champagne, cards, or pleasant conversation with one of my lovely girls?"

Mr. Scuddimore, having gathered his scattered wits back together, replied with unabashed directness to Lady Buxtell's suggestion. "Didn't come here for cards, ma'am. Already lost too much blunt to Lord Harry here."

Ah, so the rude young man is a lord, Lady Buxtell

thought, instantly revising her opinion and forgiving the insolence. Lords were, after all, the making of her success. It wouldn't do at all to offend one of them. "In that case, gentlemen," she said, focusing a bright smile on Hetty, "champagne and conversation it shall be."

"Didn't really come for conversation either," Scuddy said. "I ain't much in the line of talking at the best of times."

"I can see that." Lady Buxtell ushered them to a generously laden sideboard at the far end of the room and poured each of them a glass of sparkling champagne. "To your evening's pleasure, my lords," she said with practiced gaiety, motioning toward the girl, Lilly, as she spoke.

Sir Harry leaned over to Hetty and whispered, "See, I told you Lady Buxtell's was far above the common touch. There's Lord Alvaney next to the fireplace and over there is Sir John Walterton."

Hetty interrupted. "Yes, and the gentleman already far into his cups is Lord Darcy Pendleton. Bedamned. Sir William Filey. How I pity the poor girl who must see to his wants."

Hetty despised Sir William Filey, for he was debauched, cunning, and ruthless. That a good part of her hatred of him was heavily mixed with fear, she freely admitted. At White's, several months before, he had made a mocking remark about the inordinate smoothness of her cheeks. That very evening, she had made an obvious show of departing with Sir Harry and Scuddy, leaving no doubt that she was off to enjoy a man's pleasures. She had contrived whenever possible to avoid Sir William's company, fearful that he would see through her disguise. When Scuddy had told her and Harry about the wager, her condemnation of him had been complete.

"Lord Harry, for God's sake, stop staring like an idiot at Sir William. The last thing you want to do is offend him. He's dangerous."

"You're right, Harry. It's just that he offends me." Her thoughts returned to her own predicament. She realized that she wasn't behaving as a normal gentleman would. After all, the only reason a man would come to Lady Buxtell's establishment was to gratify his appetites and that meant, pure and simple, having sex with one of the girls present. She watched as the diminutive Lilly bore off a suddenly tongue-tied Scuddy. She found her eyes again wandering to where Sir William Filey sat, one of his hands resting possessively over the full breast of a raven-haired girl. In that instant, as if he was aware of being observed, Sir William swiveled about, his dark eyes meeting Hetty's over the rim of his glass. He gazed at her in a way that made Hetty feel as though she were standing naked on display, and then, lazily, lifted his glass in her direction in a mock salute. Knowing that she'd paled, Hetty quickly nodded and turned back to Sir Harry. It was with a mixture of dismay and relief that she saw Sir Harry's attention was no longer even partially on her. "I'll leave you now, old boy," he said over his shoulder as he took off in the direction of a long-legged blonde, whose features were remarkably like his own.

Hetty felt as if she were frozen in her boots. She knew that she had to do something, at least act interested in one of the girls. She watched as Sir John Walterton led a giggling, flushed girl from the room and toward a wide circling staircase that began its ascent just outside the door of the drawing room.

What the devil was she going to do?

She forced herself to attend to those females in the room who appeared as yet unattached by any of the gentlemen. It was only the second time her eyes swept over the occupants that she chanced to notice a slightly built redheaded girl who stood partially hidden by a red velvet hanging. Even across the room, Hetty sensed the fear in the girl. New, was she? Hetty made her way slowly toward the girl, halting only to procure two glasses of champagne from a footman's tray. As she neared, she was aware that the girl had seen her approach, and had started guiltily. Dear God, Hetty thought angrily, she appeared to be younger than Hetty herself was. She looked to be no more than sixteen, if that.

She heard herself say calmly, "Hello, my name is Lord Harry Monteith. Would you care to join me for a glass of champagne?"

"Oh yes, certainly," the girl said quickly, too quickly, Hetty thought as she handed her the glass. She watched the girl's eyes dart past her. She turned her head slightly and saw that Lady Buxtell's sharp eyes had narrowed to slits as they rested on the girl. Hetty took a step sideways, hopefully blocking Lady Buxtell's view.

"What's your name?"

"Mavreen, my lord."

"You seem very young to be here, Mavreen."

"Oh no, my lord, I'm not young at all, unless you want me to be. What do you want, my lord?"

For a moment, Hetty was so shocked she couldn't

think of a thing to say. She saw that Mavreen's hand was trembling slightly, the champagne sloshing close to the rim of the glass.

Hetty suddenly felt a ray of hope as she gazed down upon the girl's pale face. Mavreen was as yet quite inexperienced at her trade, of that Hetty was certain. At least, she prayed for this certainty, since it was quite likely that her future as a gentleman rested on her assumption.

Mavreen started nervously at the touch of his lordship's hand on her bare arm. "Please forgive me, my lord, would you care to be seated?"

As Hetty seated herself beside Mavreen, she had the sudden fleeting picture of herself in the girl's situation, her livelihood dependent upon pleasing gentlemen. As Hetty didn't have the luxury to dwell upon this particular injustice, she turned abruptly to Mavreen and said in a no-nonsense voice, "You need not lie to me, Mavreen. You can't be more than sixteen, I know. Come, tell me the truth."

Mavreen jumped. Normally, gentlemen weren't the least interested in her age, or, for that matter, any thought she might have in her head. She tried to assess his lordship's intentions, but her lack of experience didn't provide her any clues. She said hesitantly, "I am telling you the truth, my lord. But I am just turned sixteen but three months ago." She saw the young lord's jaw tighten and hastened to reassure him as best she was able. "Even though I'm young, my lord, you mustn't believe that I am not adept at whatever you would wish of me." Mavreen saw a look of sadness pass over the young gentleman's face, and was at once alarmed and confused.

"How long have you been in this establishment, Mavreen?"

"Two weeks, my lord, but all you have to do is tell me what you wish. I'm very good, my lord, truly."

She imagined it was so. She heard Sir Harry laughing and looked up. Like Scuddy, he was now headed toward the staircase. She couldn't quite grasp it. Her friends were going to take off their clothes and be intimate with females they didn't even know and then they were going to give them money. It was more than she could begin to understand, and here she was in the middle of it.

"Have I displeased you, my lord?" Hetty looked back at Mavreen, and saw that she was staring at Lady Buxtell who was speaking with a newly arrived gentleman.

"No, you don't displease me, Mavreen." She patted the girl's hand. "Tell me how you came to be here."

"My Uncle Bob was killed, fighting with Wellington at Waterloo," Mavreen blurted out. "Oh goodness, forgive me, I shouldn't have said that. Oh dear, Lady Buxtell will surely be displeased with me."

"Mavreen, I trust that Lord Monteith is receiving all that he wishes." Hetty jerked about to see Lady Buxtell hovering at her side.

Hetty replied smoothly, a touch of arrogance in her voice, "I was just telling Mavreen that the room is close. I dislike all this noise. And the smell of cheap perfume. If you will excuse us, Mavreen is going to take me for a stroll." She rose, her back turned insolently to Lady Buxtell, and assisted Mavreen to her feet.

Lady Buxtell would like to smack Lord Monteith, but she couldn't afford to have it get around that she ever insulted a nobleman. She watched as the couple slowly made their way across the room and disappeared from her view up the staircase. She wasn't at all a stupid woman and found herself wondering at the young lord's ill-concealed distaste for her famous establishment. She glanced up at the clock and saw, with some irritation, that it was nearly one o'clock in the morning. Many of the fancy gentlemen were still dawdling about, evidently content to fondle her girls and pour her expensive champagne down their gullets.

"You're unhappy about something, my dear Angelique?"

Lady Buxtell swiftly planted a complacent smile on her lips and said to Sir William Filey, "Nothing in particular, my lord. It appears though that the gentlemen are more fond of drink tonight than the pleasures my lovely girls offer." Sir William gave her pause. Although he was always polite to her in that slightly mocking manner of his, she knew there was a deep streak of cruelty in him. Even though it was never directed at her, she was afraid of him.

He laughed softly and she found herself shivering at the sound. "Don't worry, Angelique, I shall myself lead the gentlemen upstairs where they belong." He proffered her a mocking bow, turned, and said over his shoulder, "My thanks for the young French girl, Marie. A tidy morsel, my dear, exactly to my tastes. So young and so very untouched. Not now, of course, ah, but I enjoyed her whilst I taught her her trade. I congratulate you, Angelique, upon your means of procurement."

Lady Buxtell offered a silent prayer that the foolish, whining Marie had learned her lessons well. Not, of course, that she begrudged the time she had spent with the girl, cursing and threatening her each time she seemed to rebel against the description of what Sir William would require of her. If nothing else, Sir William was most generous when he was pleased. She looked after Sir William as he made his way back to Marie. Despite the habitual sneer that marred the line of his full mouth, he was a handsome man, not above forty. He showed to advantage in his tight-knitted pantaloons and his coats had no need of buckram padding. She had heard that by the time he had reached thirty-five, he had already buried two wives. She thought about these two faceless ladies and decided it was probably fortunate for them that they had passed to the hereafter. A night spent in Sir William's bed was not an experience that any of her girls relished. Just imagine how those prudish, simpering innocent young ladies had reacted to his demands. Well, it was none of her affair. She did wonder, though, about the rumor that had recently come to her ears. It seemed that Sir William was casting about for another wife—a very rich one—in all probability. Lady Buxtell shrugged and took a glass of champagne from a passing footman.

Hetty, in the meanwhile, followed closely after Mavreen, with what she prayed was a convincing display of male eagerness. They passed down a long, thickly carpeted corridor, Mavreen finally drawing to a halt in front of a closed door. Hetty pushed the knob and preceded Mavreen into a small room

furnished almost entirely in dark blue velvet. Exotic
pictures showed in blatant detail various positions.
Goodness, some of those positions looked remarkably difficult and all of them were embarrassing. As
for the pictures of the men, they looked ridiculous,
all hair and muscle and their sex sticking out. She
looked toward the four-poster bed in the center of
the room and felt her heart jump into her throat.
At that moment, Mavreen leaned heavily against
Hetty and threw her arms about her shoulders.
Hetty quickly thrust her away, an instinctive reaction, for she couldn't trust her tightly laced chemise
to completely flatten her breasts. A look of dismay
and consternation settled upon Mavreen's face.
Hetty thought quickly, knowing that at the very
least, she mustn't give Mavreen any reason to think
that she didn't appreciate her woman's charms. She
took the girl's hands in her own and lifted them to
her lips, slowly kissing each slender white finger.
"You are exquisite, Mavreen." She forced herself to
look at the girl's gently sloping shoulders, and then
down to the fullness of her breasts. Her waist was
small, an asset, Hetty supposed.

"Oh, thank you, my lord," Mavreen said, her voice
breathless and filled with relief. She dared not think
what would have happened to her if she failed to
please Lord Monteith. "Would you like me to dis-
robe now?"

Hetty pretended to ponder Mavreen's question.
Lord, the last thing she wanted was to have a naked
girl standing in front of her. She tried to determine
exactly what a man would say and do. As the answer
was an obvious one, she was forced to charter new
ground. She replied casually, "No, I think not now,

Mavreen. Actually, I would know more about you, and why you are afraid of Lady Buxtell."

Oh God, Mavreen thought wildly, he wasn't a customer. He must be one of her spies. "Oh, my lord, she is really a very kind mistress. She most kindly took me in when I would have starved in the streets."

"I doubt that. You're terrified of her. You may trust me, you know."

"I don't know what you mean, my lord." She saw a gleam of anger narrow Lord Monteith's dark blue eyes. "I'm being stupid. Let me undress you, my lord. Shall I take you in my mouth? Shall I fondle you with my hands?"

"No," Hetty said. "You may tell me if you're a trollop."

"Oh God, I'm not, I swear it. I was a virgin, my lord. It is true that she pulled me from the street, but it wasn't my fault that I was there. After word came that my Uncle Bob was dead, the creditors came to our milliner shop and all but threw me out. I had no money and no family I could go to. She told me that I was very lucky, that I would be deflowered by a handsome lord. It was Sir William Filey." She gazed helplessly up at Lord Monteith. "It was awful. He hurt me horribly. He was worse than the others. Some of them were even nice to me, petting me like I was a dog or something if I managed to please them."

Through a haze of unshed tears, Mavreen realized that she had disgraced herself. Lady Buxtell would be informed that she was unworthy of her protection. She would starve in the streets, alone, friendless. She jerked her hand free of Lord Monteith's and covered her face. She sank to her knees and began to sob. "I don't want to starve in the street, I don't. I'm too young to starve."

Hetty stared down at the crumpled girl at her feet. Sudden anger exploded through her. That this girl—no more than a child—should be forced to be a whore just to survive. It wasn't right.

Hetty became suddenly brisk. "Come, Mavreen, no more tears. We have work to do." She pulled a handkerchief from her waistcoat pocket. "Dry your tears. I believe that you and I have much to talk about."

"You're not going to tell Lady Buxtell that I wasn't what you wanted?"

"Oh no," Hetty said. "As a matter of fact, I'm going to save you."

Chapter Seven

Gray streaks of dawn lit the black sky when Pottson at last delivered Miss Hetty through the servants' entrance into Millie's hands. He'd argued with her only briefly, for her soul-deep anger had stilled his tongue.

He sighed and shook his head as he turned from Sir Archibald's town house in Grosvenor Square to make his way back to Thompson Street. This latest exploit of Miss Hetty's was making his gray hair frizzle even more than the last time she'd teased him about it. Imagine Miss Hetty—a young, gently reared lady—in a brothel. He lowered his head into the howling February wind, so tired from his long night of waiting for Miss Hetty that his legs trembled with fatigue. He wondered what Millie was going to say when she heard about Miss Hetty's surprise.

"You've not got long to sleep, Miss Hetty," Millie was saying in her matter-of-fact voice, still ignorant of what had happened during the night. "Sir Archibald and his holy schedule, you know. I'll awaken you just before luncheon."

By the time Millie had quietly closed the bedchamber door, Hetty was already asleep.

To Millie's surprise and relief, near to eleven

o'clock that morning, Sir Archibald informed the housekeeper, who then informed Millie, that he would be lunching with Sir Mortimer Melberry. Such an unheard of change in Sir Archibald's schedule left the servants stunned. "But you can set every clock in the house by Sir Archibald," Grimpston said, throwing his hands into the air.

"It's not what I'm used to," Mrs. Miller, the housekeeper, told Millie over a cup of hot tea in the kitchen.

Millie said, "I, for one, would never think of talking against the master, but it's a sad thing that Sir Archibald doesn't even think to send a message to Miss Hetty. I tell you, Florence, if the master cared as much for his own flesh and blood as he did for those dratted Tories, then perhaps Miss Hetty would not—but that's neither here nor there."

To Millie's relief, Mrs. Miller didn't seem to notice her sudden lapse. Indeed, to Millie's eyes, it seemed that Mrs. Miller was suffering more pain in her joints. She looked at the kitchen clock and smiled. Miss Hetty would get much-needed sleep, the poor lamb.

Hetty awoke in a panic. She knew instantly that it was long past noon. Her eyes frantically sought out the ormolu clock on the mantelpiece. Half-past two in the afternoon. Where the devil was Millie? She dashed out of her warm bed and pulled vigorously on the bell cord.

Millie entered her room a few minutes later, a faint smile puckering out her thin cheeks. "No need to fret, Miss Hetty. Sir Archibald did not lunch at home today."

"That's impossible. Don't lie to me, Millie. You

felt sorry for me and didn't wake me up. Oh dear, what did he say? Is he upset with me?"

"Your father informed Mrs. Miller that he was lunching with Sir Mortimer Melberry. In fact, Grimpston overheard Sir Archibald muttering about some elections and how he must keep a very close eye on the Whigs. I don't believe that he will be back for dinner."

Hetty dropped the shift she'd just grabbed up. "Good heavens, Millie, these elections must be something to send Father out of the house before noon. I daresay I shall discover what is afoot tomorrow—over luncheon. Surely he would never be gone two days in a row. This entire household would come to a halt were he to do that."

"No doubt. Now, Missie, back into bed with you. No playing the young gentleman tonight. I've told Cook to send a tray later to your room."

After Millie quietly closed herself from the bedchamber, Hetty snuggled down into the warm covers, not to sleep again, but to think. It seemed fantastic to her, now that she was once again the protected young lady of quality, that she could ever have become entangled in such an incredible situation. She raised thankful eyes upward that she had managed to come through with her identity as Lord Harry Monteith without question. She wondered now how many other young girls were in Mavreen's situation—forced to sell their bodies so that they would not starve? As much as she hated the inevitable answer to her silent question, she realized that her hands were quite full enough trying to untangle just Mavreen's future. She had made firm promises to the girl, promises that she was honor-bound to fulfill.

Hetty sat up in her bed and fluffed a pillow behind her head. She had promised to settle Mavreen in some sort of position. As her knowledge of these matters was limited, the only ideas that came to mind centered around governesses and ladies' maids. She pursed her lips, deep in thought. Suddenly, she remembered Louisa, her sister-in-law. Indeed, it was inspiration. Dear Louisa was always complaining how Little John wore her to a frazzle and then it was Big John's turn. Were not Louisa's letters full of how she wished for a younger person to chase after him when his mother fell exhausted onto a sofa? Well, she now had the perfect solution. She felt rather smug for coming to such a neat resolution so quickly. She couldn't help but remember though that she hadn't felt one single whit of smugness the night before, when she'd had to face down that dragon, Lady Buxtell, at four o'clock in the morning. Oh God, she thought even now, remembering how she'd watched Lady Buxtell standing in the empty drawing room, undoubtedly relishing her success in dispatching all the gentlemen either upstairs with her girls or politely removing them from her establishment. Hetty had approached her with a brisk stride, a frown on her face.

"My Lord Monteith," Lady Buxtell had said, managing to dredge up a brittle smile, not forgetting or forgiving his sneering rudeness upon his arrival. "You leave us very early. You were with Mavreen, were you not? So untouched she is, so innocent yet skilled, so—"

Hetty interrupted with all the contempt she could muster, "Yes, I had the misfortune to be with that whining, fearful little fool. I was told, my dear Lady Buxtell, that a gentleman would not leave your house unsatisfied. I shall regret telling my friends that your establishment is sorely lacking in service, ma'am."

Lady Buxtell's thin face grew alarmingly red and Hetty knew a moment of fear. To her surprise, Lady Buxtell's wrath fell instantly upon Mavreen's head. "That damned ungrateful little tart. And here I picked her out of the gutter, I did. Gave her the best of everything, held nothing back, I did. I should have known when Sir William did not approve of her that the little wretch would cause me nothing but trouble. I'll kick her arse back in the streets, where she and that skinny arse of hers belong."

"It's what she deserves," Hetty said. "I'm glad that you agree with me."

Lady Buxtell realized with some irritation that she had allowed her carefully polished speech to slip. She turned her eyes to Lord Monteith, and said in a tone that licked his lordship's boots, "Dear Lord Monteith, of course, there is no charge at all for the evening, let me assure you. Perhaps you have a fondness for redheads? I shall install another such a one for your pleasure, but this time, I shall find a girl who knows her place. I would hope, my lord, that with my assurances to make amends, you won't feel it necessary to inform your friends of this incident."

"Another redhead for my pleasure, you say?"

"Oh yes, my lord."

Hetty flipped an indifferent hand. "Very well, ma'am. I shall say nothing if you promise that this one blighted specimen is out of your house this very day. I want none of my friends to make love to a sniveling, limp excuse for a female. I require more creativity in my pleasures, just as, I understand, does Sir William." Hetty realized instantly that she had scored a master stroke with this added glaring lie. Lady Buxtell's eyes gleamed and she smiled slyly. "Ah, so, my lord, now I quite understand you. It will be just as you say, my lord."

Hetty bowed slightly and made as if to take her leave, then stopped and said sharply, "Well? Do you plan to wait until noon? Perhaps you won't toss out the little slut until three o'clock? I want to see the wench thrown out now, madam. Not of course that I disbelieve that you will do what you agreed to, but—"

"This very instant, my lord." Lady Buxtell walked briskly from the room, gritting her teeth at the officious young man.

Moments later, a well coached, sobbing Mavreen was roughly dragged down the stairs, her arm painfully held in Lady Buxtell's very strong grip. "Here's the little trollop, my lord. As for you, you ungrateful little wretch—" She viciously boxed Mavreen's ear. "Now, you little fool, get out of my house. The street is too good for the likes of you. And don't you try to come sniveling back, my girl!"

Hetty watched with her jaw clamped tightly closed for fear that she would tear into the old termagant, as Mavreen was roughly hurled through the front door into the cold night.

Hetty said evenly as Lady Buxtell turned triumphantly back to her, "You have done just as I wished, ma'am. I shall bear you no grudge. I bid you good night."

Hetty pushed back the bedcovers with a sudden spurt of energy. She felt at once elated and quite pleased with herself. She padded over to her writing desk, lit a branch of candles, and sat down to quill and paper. She might as well inform John and Louisa of their good fortune in obtaining the services of a young person perfectly suited to Little John's temperament.

Words flowed from her quill and before she had done with her letter, she had covered two pages of flowing, heart-touching prose about Mavreen. Of course, she made no mention of Mavreen's brief professional stay at Lady Buxtell's.

Hetty rose and stretched. Both Mavreen and her letter of introduction would be dispatched from London on the morrow by dear Pottson. She only hoped that he wouldn't let anything slip; Mavreen must always believe that her rescuer was Lord Harry Monteith. Miss Henrietta Rolland was only a dear friend who was sending Mavreen on her way to a different life.

Pottson, in the meanwhile, had finally settled the excited Mavreen into Lord Harry's bed, and bid her a more friendly good night than he would have considered possible only that morning. When he had first laid eyes on her, Mavreen had looked her profession—a painted little harlot. But after their shopping this afternoon, when she had shyly but proudly paraded before him dressed in a modest dove gray muslin gown, her fiery red hair smoothed down into a bun at the nape of her neck, all the paint wiped clean from her young face, he was of the firm conviction that Miss Hetty had behaved just as she ought. Poor little mite, he thought, Mavreen deserved much better from life than being a gentleman's whore. Before he had tucked her in a fatherly manner into bed, she asked wistfully, "Mr. Pottson, will I see Lord Monteith again?"

"No, Miss, he is staying with friends, not wishing to compromise you in any way by staying here."

If Mavreen thought that was a bit absurd, she didn't say so. She said instead, "Do you know what will happen to me, Mr. Pottson?"

"Don't worry your head about it, Miss. Lord Harry will inform me as to your future plans on the morrow."

He received his summons to call upon Miss Hetty in Grosvenor Square very early the next morning. As he sat opposite her in the small back parlor listening to her unfold her plan for Mavreen's future, he felt his respect for her grow to impressive heights. He readily applauded her solution, thinking to himself that kin of Master Damien would undoubtedly behave toward Mavreen with a great deal of kindness. Thus, it was with a light heart and a wide smile on his leathery face that he assisted Mavreen onto the mail coach that same morning.

"Now, be careful, Miss, not to lose your letter of introduction to Sir John and Lady Louisa." He lifted her gloved hand and pressed five guineas into her palm. "It's a gift from Lord Monteith. He said, Miss, that self-respect doesn't have anything to do with money, but it helps in many other ways."

She returned his smile, but felt a large lump rise in her throat. "Please thank his lordship, Mr. Pottson, and tell him that I shall never forget all he has done for me."

Mavreen's gratitude to Lord Harry made Pottson uneasy. He hastened to say, "Don't forget that you know only Miss Henrietta Rolland. It is she who is your benefactress. It won't do at all for you to ever mention Lord Monteith. You won't go forgetting, will you, Miss?"

Mavreen sighed and shook her head. "No, Mr. Pottson, I shan't forget."

When Pottson returned to Grosvenor Square before noon to give Hetty an accounting of what had happened, he found her looking much like the cat who had swallowed the cream.

"It's done, Pottson?" she asked, looking up.

"Yes, the poor little mite was so grateful, Miss Hetty. Said she'd never forget you."

"Never forget Lord Harry, you mean."

"There a nab of the truth in that. I'll ask you not to be going to any brothels again, if you please."

"As a young gentleman with no mistress in keeping, it is what one does. Ah, don't fret further about it, Pottson, for we did manage to scrape through unscathed and did a good deed in the bargain. I have devised a plan that will, I trust, keep me away from such establishments in the future."

He was afraid to ask but he did. "What plan?"

"When I see Sir Harry and Mr. Scuddimore later today. After I endure a recital of their exploits at Lady Buxtell's, they will undoubtedly want to know how I fared. I shall tell them that I found Mavreen to be just what I require, and have set her up as my mistress. It will do marvelous things for my reputation."

Pottson groaned.

"I shan't tell them where I've installed her. That,

I am convinced, will only add to my consequence as a confirmed young man of the world."

Pottson groaned louder.

"You know, Pottson, Sir William Filey was at Lady Buxtell's. He is really a vile man. Just the story Mavreen told me about him made my blood run cold. I can't believe that Sir William ever intended to marry Elizabeth Springville. I suppose if Lord Oberlon did marry her, his intentions, at least toward the lady, were honorable. Of course, we need have no doubts whatsoever as to Damien's intentions." She rose, becoming suddenly brisk. "Well, I must get back to business. I will lunch shortly with Sir Archibald, then Sir Harry and Mr. Scuddimore and I will be doing something doubtless naughty this afternoon. Then, tonight, there's a rout at Blair House. As to Lord Oberlon being in attendance—I will make no more predictions. The wretched man continues to unwittingly evade me."

Chapter Eight

Jason Charles Cavander, Marquess of Oberlon, sat comfortably in the reading room of White's, his long breeched legs stretched out toward the fire. He had been reading a rather involved article in the *Gazette* that recounted in grisly detail a recent murder on Hounslow Heath. But now, he was just staring into the flames, and rising every once in a while to kick the embers again into life with the toe of his boot. His thoughts were black, but then again, for well over a year his world had been black, filled with hatred and malice and pain. And here he was now, sitting in White's, quite at his leisure, any number of servants about to do his biding, and there was nothing he really wanted to do. He was becoming a melancholy bore, he thought, and that would surely never do, at least not for him. He had to get a grip on his life again, take a good hard look at the man he'd become since that fateful night some sixteen months before. He looked deeply into the flames and sighed. He was beginning to enjoy his melancholy and that would never do. When he heard a *hummph* beside him, he looked up to see Lord Melberry, namely his Uncle Mortimer, at his elbow. His surprise held him silent for a moment, for his staid uncle, the very cornerstone of the Tory party, hadn't to his knowledge, stepped through the portals of White's in many a long year.

The marquess dropped the paper on the smooth mahogany table at his side and grinned engagingly at Lord Melberry. As humorless as he found the old man, he nonetheless held him in some affection. Melberry had never said a single word of sympathy at Elizabeth's funeral or afterward. He'd been there, standing by him, like a rock. Jason suspected that his uncle hadn't really been aware of what had happened, all his powerful intellect completely focused on politics, but that hadn't mattered then, nor did it now. He'd been silent and he'd been there.

Jason pumped his hand in welcome, but forbore to clap him on his gaunt shoulders. Jason's mood lifted. He studied his fingernails, then said in that bored lazy drawl he knew his uncle couldn't abide, "Don't tell me, Uncle, that the Tories have taken to meeting in this frivolous place? Have votes become that hard for you to collect?"

His uncle wasn't to be drawn, which was disappointing, but one still had to try. Jason smiled at his uncle even as Lord Melberry said, "At least you *do* read the newspaper, my boy. I don't suppose the article has aught to do with politics." Lord Melberry removed his bony hand from his nephew's strong clasp, grunted in vague disapproval at his surroundings, and flipping up his black coattails, sat down in one of White's plush leather armchairs, across from his nephew.

"Nary a bit," the marquess replied cheerfully. "What with Bonaparte no longer pulling our English tails, the only news worth reading is the gossip about the Regent." He gazed with some amusement at his uncle, wondering as he had many times before, whatever possessed his delightful, flighty aunt, Lady Corinna Melberry, to wed herself to this dour, single-mindedly political gentleman.

Lord Melberry looked about the reading room. Although it was a sober enough place, he knew that most of White's members were drawn just beyond the great double doors to the glittering gaming salon.

"You're looking well, Nephew," he said finally, slewing his eyes back to the marquess. "It's a relief. You looked like bloody hell before you left for Italy."

"Thank you, Uncle. I'm pleased you noticed, though surprised that you did. As you can see, though, I'm back to my old habits. Why are you here? Ah, I see. To track down the fox, one must go ahunting to his lair."

"And you don't look any the worse for all those months in Italy," Lord Melberry continued, refusing to be baited. Nor was he quite ready to spring the purpose of his mission on his unsuspecting nephew. "I suppose all that interminable sun and heat must occasionally lift a man's spirits."

"As you see, Uncle," the marquess said. "I trust my aunt is well?"

"Have you ever known your aunt to be otherwise?" Lord Melberry said in a sour voice. "Damnation, here I, a serious man, a man committed to England and her future, I must be plagued with gout. Whereas your aunt, who never concerns herself with anything but worthless amusements, bearing children and the like, is ever the very picture of enduring health."

"Perhaps all the gods who decide such things for we pathetic mortals aren't Tories, Uncle."

"You jest, boy, and it doesn't suit you. It suits your aunt, but not you."

"Ah, well, Uncle, I can but be myself. Now what is it I can do for you?"

The marquess thought of his engagement with the Earl of March and Lord Alvaney—to arrange a boxing match near to London without the magistrates getting wind of it—and wondered if he even cared to go. It seemed a waste of time. His uncle was still silent and Jason raised an eyebrow at him. His uncle was dithering? Surely not. Jason said, "I know that you must be much occupied, sir, what with the Whigs and Tories stabbing political knives in each other's backs. Come, Uncle, why would you search out such a fribble as myself? Not, of course, that I'm not excessively flattered."

"The Cavanders were always a flighty bunch," Lord Melberry said without much heat. It had been several years now since he had ceased his most pressing efforts to bring his nephew into the Tory fold. As all his arguments had met unerringly with a smile of amused indifference, he had eventually admitted defeat. "If you must know, my boy, I am here to execute a favor for your aunt."

"Oh, God, please tell me she hasn't brought out another tongue-tied young miss for my perusal."

"Hardly, Jason, since your own wife hasn't yet been dead a year." He wished instantly that he hadn't been so blunt, for he saw a strange bitter gleam in his nephew's dark eyes.

"Forgive my lack of tact, Jason, but these things happen and a man must get on with life."

That was true, Jason thought, staring at his uncle.

"Now attend me, Nephew. Your aunt asked me to encourage you in the strongest fashion possible to get you to come to one of her soirees."

"What? My poor aunt finds that she suddenly has thirteen sitting down to dinner?"

"It must be so. She was wringing her hands until she recalled that you'd come home. I trust you are not otherwise engaged for tonight, Jason?"

The marquess had planned to escort Melissande to Covent Garden this evening. But then again, he quite liked his good-natured aunt and wanted to see her. A mistress was one thing, but a beloved aunt was another. "I should be delighted, sir. What time does my aunt require my presence?"

"I haven't the foggiest idea. Come when you're hungry. Now, lad, if you'll excuse me, I have much to do this afternoon." The tone of his voice left no doubt in Jason's mind that his uncle considered this commission on behalf of his beloved to be a shocking waste of his valuable time.

He rose and cordially shook his uncle's thin hand. A smile touched his lips as he watched his uncle grunt a stiff greeting to a gentleman who had the misfortune to offer a polite "how d'ye do."

"He may be your uncle, your grace," Mr. Denby said a few moments later, "but I swear that politics does naught to a man but make him act like his trousers are too tight in the crotch."

Jason Cavander laughed. "Be relieved, Denby, that he isn't *your* relative, though he isn't so bad."

Jason strode downstairs, deciding how many guineas he would wager with Alvaney over the new prize-fighter he was backing.

*   *   *

While the marquess was attempting to set a wager with Lord Alvaney, Hetty, having heard the clock strike noon, rushed toward the breakfast room to greet Sir Archibald.

She kissed Sir Archibald lightly on his cheek and rested her hand on his shoulder until he reluctantly turned away from the *Gazette* and looked up at her.

How very handsome he is, she thought, admiring his still smooth forehead topped by thick silver hair, handsome and distinguished. His sparkling blue eyes must inspire trust and confidence. The fact that his eyes normally became markedly vague when he gazed upon her didn't overly disturb her, for, she thought philosophically, she was of no concern to his electorate.

To Hetty's surprise, Sir Archibald's gaze did not, this time, become vague, nor did he seem preoccupied. He said exuberantly, thrusting aside his paper, "Hetty, my dear, we have got those damned Whigs by their radical collars this time. In two borough elections, *two*, mind you, our Tories ousted the incumbents by a great margin! What do you think of that?"

"It's marvelous news, Father," Hetty said, preparing herself for a complete account of the brilliant strategies executed by the Tories. To her further surprise, Sir Archibald showed no disposition to favor her with the details of the triumph. Instead, he said, "Come, child, do sit down, and let us have our lunch. There is much I have yet to do this afternoon. And," he added in a conspiratorial manner that set her antenna aquiver, "I have a surprise for you."

He'd never before in his life had a surprise for her.

Finally, convinced that he'd had a fit of some sort, she said, "Father, you have a surprise for me?"

"Surprise? Certainly, my dear child. Lady Melberry has invited you to attend a musical soiree this evening. Nothing fancy, of course, just some squawking Italian soprano to give you a headache. But I fancied it would be just the thing for you. I accepted her invitation on your behalf."

Hetty went pale. She'd realized that sooner or later Miss Henrietta Rolland must make her entry into London society. She had optimistically hoped it would be much later, perhaps even after she had dealt with Lord Oberlon. If both Miss Henrietta Rolland and Lord Harry Monteith appeared at social gatherings, it wouldn't be long before someone noticed the marked resemblance between them. "This evening, Father?"

Sir Archibald regarded his daughter over the top of his spoon. "I know, Henrietta, that you are still in mourning for your brother. But I didn't think you would mind a small informal gathering. I told Lady Melberry that you were a quiet girl, with no racketty notions at all." As his daughter didn't say a single word, he continued in a stern voice, "You stay too much at home, Henrietta. You must not be concerned that you won't conduct yourself as befits your station. I will, myself, conduct you to Melberry House. I cannot stay, of course, but no matter. Lady Melberry assured me that she would personally make sure that you are seen safely home." Thus having dispatched any argument that in his view would be of concern, he returned, quite satisfied, to his lunch.

She didn't suppose there was any hope for it. She

said, "It's kind of Lady Melberry, Father. I shall be delighted to attend her gathering, but just this once."

She doubted Sir Archibald was listening to her, and she was right.

After dispatching a message to Pottson through Millie to inform Sir Harry and Mr. Scuddimore that she wouldn't be joining them at Blair House for the evening, Hetty curled up in front of the fireplace in her bedchamber. She cupped her chin in her hand and tried to think of a way out of this current mess. Regardless of the fact that Lord Melberry was one of Sir Archibald's cronies, this soiree was to be a social gathering, not a political one, and as such, the guests would undoubtedly include some of those gentlemen and ladies who Lord Harry Monteith had met over the past four months.

She was nearly at the groaning stage when she looked up to see Millie directing Doby, the footman, who was carrying two buckets of hot water for her bath. She sat in the copper tub for some time, thinking and thinking. "I don't know what to do," she said to Millie who was arranging towels. "I have nothing to wear, for all my old gowns haven't grown as I have." She stepped out of the tub and Millie handed her a towel.

Millie said matter-of-factly, "You tell me that Lord Harry is cool and calm in all circumstances. I fail to see why Miss Hetty cannot be the same." She paused a moment and gazed down at the fluffy cluster of blond curls atop her mistress's head. "You know, Miss Hetty, Lord Harry wears a disguise, even pomades down his hair. What would you say if all the high and mighty ladies and gentlemen did not proclaim Miss Henrietta Rolland to be a diamond of the first water?"

Just before eight o'clock that evening, Hetty grinned a final time at her image in the mirror, wanting very much to laugh aloud. She looked a fright. A large, lacy alexandrine cap of pale green covered her blond curls, leaving only the vaguest suggestion that the head beneath the cap was indeed endowed with hair. A pair of spectacles, borrowed from Cook, sat precariously on the bridge of her nose, the narrow prisms dimming the brilliant blue of her eyes. If the cap and spectacles weren't enough to convince even the most tolerant that Miss Rolland had neither taste nor style, her ill-fitting gown of pea green—just one sickening shade darker than the cap—would certainly put the polish on the boots.

Hetty turned from the mirror and pulled the spectacles from her nose. "Since my eyesight is nearly as perfect as my health, I had best not don Cook's glasses until after I leave Sir Archibald. I vow, Millie, that I shall be declared an ape leader before the night is over. Isn't that marvelous?"

Although Sir Archibald would never connect such a vulgar term as ape leader with his daughter, he did think it odd of Henrietta to wear such an overpowering cap. Was she not a bit young for such a thing? Hetty replied with composure that such a cap was all the crack this season. Sir Archibald was a trifle daunted by her absolute assurance. He said, "Well, no matter, Henrietta, you will outshine all the other young ladies. Oh, yes, child, Lord Melberry informed me this afternoon that your ears would not be offended by that squawking soprano I told you about—it's to be a small card party. Just the thing to help you learn your way about."

If she could have boxed her father's ears, she would have. Oh dear, another new set of problems. She would have infinitely preferred the squawking soprano, for it would have meant that all attention would be diverted away from her. As John coachman assisted her into the carriage, she muttered a quiet wish that Lady Melberry's soiree be a very small one, with no persons of particular consequence in attendance. Or, at least, all politicians, for they would never demean themselves by chatting away social nonsense. She sighed, knowing this wouldn't be the case at all.

Hetty alighted from the carriage at the Melberry townhouse with the air of a young lady readying for an evening's pleasure. She waited a moment on the front steps until her father's carriage had bowled away down the cobblestone street. Then she carefully pulled the spectacles from her reticule and balanced them at a most awkward angle on her nose.

She took a deep breath, affected a very noticeable squint, and soundly thwacked the knocker.

The Melberry butler, Higgins, a man of discriminating taste and the keenest of eyes, answered the summons. Although his nose quivered in distaste at the homely looking female on the front doorsteps, his tone was smoothly impassive.

"I say, yes, ma'am?"

An excellent beginning, Hetty thought, noticing the quivering nostrils. If I've offended the butler's sensibilities, perhaps I shall pull through this evening without a second glance from anyone. "I'm

Miss Henrietta Rolland," she said, glorying in the high nasal twang. It sounded pleasingly obnoxious to her own ears.

Higgins blanched visibly at the pea green gown. It came to him suddenly that she must be the daughter of Sir Archibald, a most distinguished man and ardent political crony of Sir Mortimer's. He was profoundly shocked. Such an ill-appearing offspring could scarce do credit to Sir Archibald's political career. No wonder his lordship scarcely ever entertained at Grosvenor Square.

Chapter Nine

Lady Corinna Melberry gazed about her overflowing drawing room, and smiled with the contentment of a successful hostess. Sir Mortimer had obligingly removed himself and the majority of the more somberly clad, serious gentlemen of his political persuasion. The few who remained were clustered austerely apart from the gaily chattering ladies and gentlemen of the *ton*. In a few moments, when she was certain that most of her guests had arrived, she would signal to the orchestra to strike up a waltz. That fast German music would rout the politicians.

She was still smiling when she looked up to see Higgins standing with a pained expression on his face next to a tall, abominably gowned young lady. That wretched green cap and those awful spectacles. Good heavens, she thought with a start, whoever could that be? Perhaps she was at the wrong address. She planted a smile on her lips and moved gracefully forward.

"Miss Henrietta Rolland, my lady."

Goodness, Lady Corinna thought, it was Sir Archibald's daughter. After another glance at Henrietta, Lady Corinna felt the arousal of her motherly instincts. She remembered that Sir Archibald's wife had died many years before, and she saw his poor daughter as a neglected, orphaned waif.

"Ah, my dear Henrietta, how very kind of you to come this evening. Do not tarry, child, I would introduce you to all my friends. You are new to London?" Before Hetty could form two words together, Lady Corinna had clasped her gloved hand tightly in hers and drawn her toward a knot of ladies and gentlemen.

Taken aback by her unwanted warm reception, Hetty finally managed to say, "No, ma'am, I've been in London many months. I'm in mourning for my brother."

"Oh yes, how very dreadful for you." Lady Corinna had forgotten about Sir Archibald's handsome son who'd lost his life at Waterloo. Had this poor child been immured all these months with only the occasional company of her father to bolster her spirits? That in itself was an appalling thought, for Lady Corinna assumed that Sir Archibald, like Sir Mortimer, secreted a limitless array of parental shortcomings. With grace born of long dealings in society, she drew Hetty forward to meet a fat dowager, who was in fact, her very closest friend. "Eve, do allow me to present Miss Henrietta Rolland. She is Sir Archibald's daughter, you know. We must make her welcome in her come-out, if you quite understand my meaning."

Lady Eve Langley, a quite good-natured woman who had not an unkind thought in her head, turned and smiled at Hetty. "So pleased, Miss Rolland." She saw nothing amiss with Hetty's appearance, only wondered at the cap, for only dowagers and proclaimed spinsters donned this proof of their status in society. "You must allow me to present you to my daughters, Maude and Caroline."

Hetty hadn't expected such kindness and was at a loss to explain it. She wondered if, contrary to her common sense, she had sorely misjudged London society.

Hetty was hard pressed to preserve a straight face as she approached one of the young ladies in question. She had seen her at Drury Lane, simpering and smiling enticingly at all the young gentlemen. Lord Harry Montcith had appeared to be much to her taste when he had chanced to gaze up at her box.

Miss Maude Langley, a rather narrow-faced, scrawny-bosomed young lady in her second season, willingly looked away from her younger sister, who was the center of attention of several gentlemen, at the sight of a young lady who was homely enough to make Miss Maude appear a celestial angel by comparison. She smiled down from her thin, long nose. She was delighted. "How famous. A new arrival in London. But surely, Miss Rolland, this cannot be your *first* season?" She eyed the green cap with glee. The spectacles were icing on the cake.

Hetty restrained a smile and said shyly, "Yes, indeed, it is, Miss Langley. You see, I have spent many years in the country." If Miss Langley wished to think her a maiden beyond her years, it was fine with Hetty. Lady Corinna saw that her dear friend, Lady Eve, didn't have the wherewithal to see that her daughter—a most irritating girl—was being rude to Miss Rolland. She nodded dismissal at Miss Maude and drew Hetty away to meet Miss Caroline Langley. Hetty had also seen Miss Caroline at Drury

Lane, and was forced to admit upon closer inspection that this sister confirmed Lord Harry Monteith's initial impressions. Miss Caroline was a beauty, her dark, flashing brown eyes set beneath perfectly arched dark brows. Her black hair, all the rage this season, was a cascade of thick curls, bound only by a blue velvet ribbon over her left ear. She was petite, trim of figure, her full bosom covered modestly—by order from her mama, no doubt—by the most exquisite Brussels lace. Miss Caroline wore a petulant expression. Hetty wanted to tell her it diminished her beauty. Her lovely eyes darted restlessly about the room. What was she looking for or who?

In truth, Miss Caroline was not only peeved, she was bored. She realized that it was highly unlikely that the man she had wanted so badly to see would present himself. The heady experience of being sought out by every young gentleman had paled over the past several weeks, and she refused to consider the thought of bestowing her beauty on any of those worshiping young puppies, as society expected her to do at the end of the season. Of course, she didn't wish to end up like poor Maude, still sitting at the rear of the shelf at the end of her second season. But to wed any of the gentlemen so far presented to her made her want to spit, something that would make her dear mama faint. No, she wanted to attach an older man, a man with experience, a man who wouldn't languish at her feet composing ridiculous lines of poetry that praised her slender swan's neck. She had seen such a man, and the thought that he might be in attendance this evening had brought a delicious flush over her cheeks.

She looked up to see Lady Melberry leading over one of the sorriest excuses for a female that Caroline had ever seen. She shuddered in distaste, then planted a firm smile. After all, one shouldn't ever appear a sour apple, like poor Maude.

"My dear Caroline, I would like you to meet Miss Henrietta Rolland, the daughter of a very dear friend of Lord Melberry's."

Caroline inclined her graceful neck in Miss Rolland's direction. "Charmed," she said, managing not to shudder at the sight, though it took great inner strength not to do so.

"Oh, how very lovely you are, Miss Langley." Hetty thought she owed this enthusiastic compliment to Lord Harry, who, she decided, would have been far more outrageous in his flattery.

Miss Caroline looked again at Miss Rolland, surprise widening her eyes. She wasn't used to receiving such frank praise from another lady. Indeed, she wasn't used to receiving any praise at all from another lady. She revised her opinion, forgot her affected drawl and smiled pertly. "You are a flatterer, I fear, Miss Rolland."

"Oh, have I offended you? Truly, Miss Langley, you are one of the loveliest ladies I have yet seen in London."

"She only arrived yesterday," Miss Maude said.

"Oh no, Miss Langley, I've been here quite some time now. Your dear sister jests."

It occurred to Miss Caroline that such frankness and candor, such generosity of spirit, should be encouraged. After all, she had nothing better to do at the moment, and conversing with such a homely girl as Miss Rolland might very well make her appear noble and virtuous to the dowagers who had jealously proclaimed her to be conceited.

She ignored her sister and said, "Do come sit with me, Miss Rolland. I think I would like to know you better." Hetty nodded and trailed after Miss Caroline to a small sofa by the fireplace. If she continued to fill Miss Langley's ears with compliments, it would at least keep her from further notice by Lady Melberry's other guests.

"Now, Miss Rolland, you must tell me all about yourself," Miss Caroline said, patting Hetty's hand as she sat down beside her.

Hetty knew very well that Miss Caroline could give two farthings about her and so prepared to give a very limited account of herself. She had scarce time to open her mouth, when she realized that Miss Caroline's attention had riveted itself to the drawing room door. She saw her lips part ever so slightly and her vivid eyes sparkle with excitement. Hetty followed her gaze and stiffened.

"His grace, the Marquess of Oberlon." Higgins's voice was deeply resonant, bringing everyone's attention to the gentleman who stood with negligent ease beside him.

Hetty, who had never before seen the marquess at such close range, was aware that her own eyes had widened in surprise. At a distance, she had believed him swarthy and tight-lipped, had imagined his dark eyes cold and hard. Had he displayed horns and a pitchfork tail, she wouldn't have been overly taken aback. But now, with only the narrow room separating them, she saw that his deeply tanned face was quite pleasant to look at and that his dark eyes were warm and alight with amusement. When

he laughed at one of Lady Melberry's remarks, Hetty
found his smile so disarming that for an instant she
forgot who he was. He was a monster, he had to
be, to show the world such a pleasant face and jest
so easily, and yet be so evil beneath.

Miss Caroline grabbed Hetty's hand and whispered, "Is Lord Oberlon not the most dashing,
handsome man you have ever seen, Miss Rolland?
Ah, I feared he wouldn't come tonight, for he isn't
known to come to such insipid affairs as this. He
has just returned from Italy, you know, so I dared
to hope. He is Lady Melberry's nephew, you know."

"No, I didn't know that," Hetty said. She resolutely turned her back upon Lord Oberlon and nodded stiff-lipped, for Miss Caroline to continue.

"Lord Oberlon's father, like Lord Melberry, was
very influential in the ministry before his death several years ago," Miss Caroline said behind her
gloved hand. "Of course, my mama and Lady Melberry are the dearest of friends. Poor man, such
tragedy he's borne. He needs pleasure; he needs
beauty." She rose, her movements intensely feminine, the look in her eyes predatory. "Ah, you must
excuse me, Miss Rolland, but I really must pay more
attention to our kind hostess."

Really, Miss Caroline, Hetty thought, you think
to gain his attention? Perhaps he'll give it to you,
but there will be a price. She watched Miss Langley
move quickly to where Lady Melberry and Lord
Oberlon stood in amiable conversation. She herself
sat back to watch Lord Oberlon with forced objec-
tivity, but she could not. The familiar hatred welled
up inside her. Here he was carefree and quite at his
ease, laughing, damn him, while Damien lay dead,

forgotten by all save his family. Poor man, indeed. How ironic it was that she should finally be in the same room with him, not as Lord Harry but as Henrietta Rolland. The fates must be against her.

She continued to study him. She was forced to admit, grudgingly, that he was a superb guest who would delight any hostess, for he mingled easily with ladies and gentlemen alike. It occurred to her that his good manners might lead him to even seek her out, and she rose swiftly and slipped into a half-hidden position behind a curtain.

Later in the evening, when Hetty had relaxed her vigilance, she chanced to see him approaching her. Not only were the Fates against her, they were trying to kill her. She quickly turned her shoulder and attempted painstaking conversation with the deaf old dowager next to her. She thought she saw a puzzled frown sweep over his brow at her blatant rudeness. But then, he turned easily, and was soon caught up in Caroline Langley's gay chatter. Had he wondered who she was? Had his aunt Melberry told him to seek her out? She wondered what he thought.

What the marquess was thinking was that the Rolland girl his aunt had directed him to meet was wearing one of the most unfortunate gowns and caps he'd ever seen. He didn't know if she was as unfortunate of face as she was of clothing, but it seemed likely. She'd turned away from him. She was either very rude or very myopic. He smiled at something Caroline Langley said, though he hadn't heard anything.

Hetty turned reluctantly at the sour, whining voice of Miss Maude Langley. "I fear my sister must learn decorum. Isn't it shocking, Miss Rolland? She has been hanging on Lord Oberlon's arm all evening. Of course, you must know about him."

Hetty, who had drawn a fatalistic sigh at Miss Maude's jealous attack on her sister, now raised her eyes to the young lady's face, all attention. "No, Miss Langley, I fear I don't know about Lord Oberlon, save that he is Lady Melberry's nephew and the Marquess of Oberlon. He appears to be charming to all of Lady Melberry's guests."

Miss Maude arched a thick brow, darted her eyes once again in Lord Oberlon's direction. "Oh la, Miss Rolland, you are new to London. Our mama wouldn't approve my saying so, but you must know he is a rake. But then, from all that I have heard, I suppose a gentleman who is a rake is perforce charming."

"But why is he a rake, Miss Langley?"

Miss Langley lowered her voice even more and cupped her gloved hand over her mouth. "Listen to this, Miss Rolland. His poor wife died but eight or nine months ago, in childbirth. He left England immediately, scarce after her funeral, and traveled to Italy. His exploits with the Italian ladies were all the talk of London. Indeed, I have seen him with a new mistress; he flaunts her all about London in the most high-handed way. Haven't you seen them, Miss Rolland?"

"Only from a distance, Miss Langley." Elizabeth had died in childbirth? Surely Miss Langley must be mistaken, for had Elizabeth not married Lord Oberlon only seven months before her death? Hetty said, "Who was Lord Oberlon's wife, Miss Langley? How sad that the poor lady died so quickly after their marriage."

"Elizabeth Springville was her name. She and I were both in our first season last year. She was loose, Miss Rolland, and a flirt. I suppose that she was pretty enough, but I can't excuse her easiness with the gentlemen, no lady could. Lord Oberlon was only one of several gentlemen dangling after her. When he suddenly married her by special license, and then removed her immediately from London to one of his estates in the West Country, there was much speculation. I will tell you, Miss Rolland, that I don't need to speculate. My mama is Lady Melberry's best friend, and *she* is, of course, Lord Oberlon's aunt—well, I know for a fact, that Elizabeth was in the family way. She was pregnant with Lord Oberlon's child."

Hetty said, "Then it would appear to me, dear Miss Langley, that Lord Oberlon behaved in a most honorable way. Surely a rake wouldn't have married the lady."

Miss Maude looked pityingly at Hetty. Hetty wanted to smack her. "You didn't let me finish, Miss Rolland. It was rumored that after he took his bride to the West Country, he left her and returned to his old ways. Shocking, is it not? I only pray that my own sister won't fall into the same dire predicament that led poor Elizabeth to her death."

Much later that night, Hetty said to Millie as she pulled her nightgown over her head, "She is a spiteful, jealous cat, Millie, and I'm not at all certain that I can believe all that she told me." Hetty fumbled with the buttons on her nightgown, forcing them into their proper holes. "But you know, the fact of the matter is that Lady Langley is Lady

Melberry's best friend and what with Lord Oberlon being her nephew, well, it does make some sense that Miss Maude could find out that Elizabeth had been pregnant. Oh my God. Millie, you do not think, do you, that perhaps the child was Damien's?"

"Well, it may be the truth, Miss Hetty. You remember that we couldn't understand why Elizabeth would have *no choice,* as she put it in her letter to your brother. It would appear that she wished to avoid a scandal by marrying herself off as quickly as possible. You told me yourself that her father, Old Colonel Springville, was a stiff, proper curmudgeon. Probably curl up his toes were his daughter to disgrace him in such a way. Probably shoot her if he could get away with it."

"Poor Elizabeth. I can see it all now, Millie. She loved Damien, and though I can't condone her behavior, or my brother's, for that matter, they must have planned to marry."

Millie was silent a moment, staring thoughtfully over the top of Hetty's head. "Do you think it's possible that Lord Oberlon married Elizabeth without knowing she was pregnant?"

Hetty nodded, her eyes sad. "Yes, she must have kept silent to protect herself. When Lord Oberlon realized she was pregnant with Damien's child, he practically deserted her, just as Miss Langley said. It's ironic, is it not, Millie? He sent Damien to his death, thus winning the lady, only to discover that *she* had used *him.* How Damien must have suffered, knowing that she carried his child and he could do nothing about it."

"Miss Hetty, hold a moment, there is something

here that simply doesn't let the key fit the lock."
Millie frowned and rubbed her fingertips against her
thin ribs.

"You're thinking that Lord Oberlon's actions
weren't those of a libertine, a man who used women
and didn't care what happened to them once he
was through?"

"Yes, it sounds like to me that his grace loved the
girl. My ma told me that when men are smitten
they will do any number of outrageous things to get
what they want."

Hetty said, her voice as harsh as the winter wind,
"I don't care about Lord Oberlon's motives, Millie.
The fact remains that it was he who is responsible
for Damien's death. No one else, just Lord Oberlon.
And by God, he deserves all that I have planned
for him."

Several hours later, Millie quietly entered Hetty's
bedchamber to ensure that she had indeed locked
away the fine pearl necklace her mistress had worn
this evening, the only item she'd worn that was
worth saving. She stood silently at her mistress's
bedside, the slender candle flame darting shafts of
orange light, and gazed down upon Hetty's face.
Millie felt a sudden wrenching of fear. Deep in
sleep, with her tousled blond curls softly framing
her small face, Miss Hetty looked like an innocent,
vulnerable young girl, which of course she was. Ah,
but she had the heart of a lion. Millie turned, the
candle trembling in her hand. What chance could
Miss Hetty have against such a powerful, ruthless
man as Lord Oberlon?

Chapter Ten

Lord Harry and Sir Harry Brandon stood outside the Earl of March's elegant three-story town house on the northern corner of Grosvenor Square. A strong February wind whipped their greatcoats about their ankles and tugged at the top hats set rakishly over their pomaded hair.

"I tell you, Lord Harry, if my brother-in-law backs you, you'll be a member of White's by this very evening. You can't go on missing out on all the good sport. Just be yourself and Julien will like you well enough. I already dashed him a note, telling him all about your pedigree."

"If you're certain, Harry. I have no wish to bother him."

"Julien doesn't bite, but he does make me very nervous sometimes. It's just the way he is. He looks down his nose at you and you turn red, but he isn't bad. He and my sister, Kate, have just returned from St. Clair. Since he hasn't seen me for a good while, I expect he'll be pleased enough to see me. Time away from me does make him more tolerant I've found. Come along, my boy."

Sir Harry grasped Lord Harry's arm and pulled him up the front steps. Hetty wasn't certain why she felt so uneasy about making the acquaintance of the powerful earl of March. But the die was cast. She really couldn't afford to draw back now. It was imperative that she become a member of White's, a regular habitué of that famous club, the club where Jason Cavander, Lord Oberlon, spent a good deal of his time.

But an instant after Harry rapped the large brass knocker, the door was opened by one of the most distinguished-looking men Hetty had ever seen.

"Good morning, George," Sir Harry said, grinning at the butler. "It's me. It's been a long time, you know. His lordship should be delighted to see me. What do you think, George?"

"Certainly your sister will be delighted, sir." George stepped quickly aside for them to enter. "As for his lordship, I just heard him laughing. He should welcome you pleasantly enough. Ah, you've brought a friend. Do come in, both of you."

"My sister well, George?"

"Quite fit, Sir Harry, quite fit." George shifted his kind gaze to Lord Harry and lifted an elegant gray brow inquiringly.

Sir Harry said with a wide grin, "This gentleman is another Harry, George—Lord Harry Monteith. He's from up north where there's nothing but cows and moors and byres. No society whatever, poor chap, but that's changing now. I've taken him in hand."

"An interesting thought. Ah, a pleasure my lord." George bowed and unobtrusively snapped his fingers. A footman appeared in practically the same instant, and assisted the gentlemen out of their greatcoats.

"Kate never was a lazy sort. Is she up and about?"

George looked a trifle discomfited, Hetty thought, before he answered smoothly enough, "Yes, of course, Sir Harry. Her ladyship and lordship are in the library."

"Excellent. You said you heard his lordship laugh? That's good. Now, come on, Lord Harry, we don't want to dawdle about all day. My brother-in-law doesn't like it when I dawdle. He says it makes his bile rise."

An embarrassed frown passed over George's face. He called, "Don't you want me to announce you, Sir Harry?"

"Don't trouble yourself, George. I know my way well enough."

The footman, Mackles, was grinning behind his white-gloved hand. George rounded on him. "Enough of your wicked loose-lipped grins, my lad. Off with you, his lordship wants this coat taken to Weston's this very morning."

"Damned elegant house, ain't it?" Sir Harry asked, as they made their way down a long corridor. Hetty had no time to reply, for as they neared the library, they drew up in unison at the sound of angry voices.

"Damn you, Kate, I should thrash you to an inch of your life, then lock you in a convent. You little idiot, why didn't you deign to tell me that—"

"Don't be stupid, Julien," came an angry lady's voice clearly through the closed door. "I'm some sort of fragile little miss who will fall apart just because of a little sport. You're being altogether ridiculous—acting just like a man—and I won't have it."

"Damn you, I am a man."

Sir Harry grinned at Lord Harry. "That's my sister, you know. Quite a way with words, she has. She always has just the proper insults to drive Julien quite mad. She's always making him furious, so furious in fact that he's always kissing her and touching her. Odd that, and they're married. Come on, let's pull them apart."

Hetty felt her unease grow and grabbed at Sir Harry's sleeve. "Surely, Harry, this isn't the time to broach the subject of my membership to his lordship. He sounds ready to kill."

But Harry had already turned the knob to the library door and swung it open. Hetty stood rooted in the open doorway, blinking rapidly at the scene before her eyes.

A gentleman and lady stood facing each other across the expanse of a large oak desk. Of all things, the lady was dressed in tight-knitted men's breeches and a white silk shirt. In her hand was a foil. She was young, very beautiful, her dark auburn hair flowing down her back, bound only by a narrow black ribbon. The young lady suddenly turned. "Harry." She dropped her foil on the desktop and rushed forward. She threw her arms about Harry's neck and hugged him hard. "Oh, my dear, it's so good to see you again. She drew back, and Hetty saw her vivid green eyes were sparkling with pleasure. "How very smart you look, my dear, that waistcoat—all those lovely yellow stripes, goodness. Oh—" She drew to a halt and looked past her brother into Lord Harry's embarrassed face.

"Now, Kate, don't ruin my waistcoat, old girl. It is quite the thing, this waistcoat of mine. Every gentleman wants one. The tailors can't make them fast enough, but I'm the first, don't forget that. Ah, this is Lord Harry, a special friend of mine. My sister, Kate."

There was no sign of discomfort on the countess's face as she sent a dazzling smile to Lord Harry. "How very nice of you to visit, my lord. Julien, come away from the desk and say hello to your brother-in-law. Come, my dear, you haven't seen him for a good seven weeks. Surely you've forgotten how he drank the best of your claret then got violently ill on the Aubusson carpet in the library, haven't you? It isn't just Harry, you know."

Hetty saw that the earl of March didn't take any offense at all. He straightened, smiled lazily at Harry and strode forward. "It's good to see you again, Harry. Now, who is your friend here?"

"Lord Harry Monteith, Julien. You know, I wrote you about him yesterday. Dashed good fellow, and needs your backing for White's."

"I'm honored, my lord," Hetty said formally, her voice as deep as she could make it, and bowed. She had the inescapable feeling that his lordship's gray eyes saw straight through her coat, waistcoat, and shirt to her chemise. He was an extraordinarily handsome man, and as a woman, Hetty appreciated his smile in a way that Lord Harry couldn't begin to.

"So you're another Harry, eh?" the earl said with a smile, and pumped Hetty's hand. He turned to Sir Harry. "As always, Harry, your timing is impeccable. Your sister and I were just having a rather heated discussion. It will be difficult, but if Kate agrees, we will turn the battleground back into a library."

The countess lightly poked her husband's arm,

and said, "My dearest Harry, I'm becoming quite accomplished with the foil. And now, just because I'm breeding, Julien must play the possessive overbearing husband. Don't you think it dreadful of him?"

"Breeding! That's wonderful news, Julien, Kate. Oh my God, you're breeding, Kate? You're actually breeding and you're still hopping about in boy's clothes and fencing? I don't believe it. Good Lord, you should be locked in a closet, for your own good."

"No help for you from that quarter, Kate," the earl said, his eyes resting upon his wife's face. There was such tenderness in his gaze that Hetty felt suddenly like a chair in the middle of a crowded ballroom. "Your termagant of a sister just informed me a few minutes ago, else I would never have allowed her to batter me with her foil."

"Batter? It was more than just battering, Julien. I had my foil at your throat at the time. But look at you now, all puffed up in your husbandly conceit. Just like a man, acting like a crowing bandy rooster, so proud of your prowess. And you, Harry, agreeing with him. I ask you, Lord Monteith, is it just for a woman to sit docilely about, doing nothing at all that is any fun, just because she is pregnant, while men issue all the orders and strut about?"

"It isn't at all fair," Hetty said promptly, forgetting that she was a gentleman. "I've heard that exercise is very beneficial for a lady who is in the family way." Oh dear, the earl was looking at her now, and he was surprised.

Kate rounded on her husband with a crow of delight. "You see, Julien, not all gentlemen are so confoundedly staid and pompous. I insist that you back Lord Monteith instantly for White's. How I wish that I could be a member of White's. What sport it would be. I would wager that I would best you in fencing within six months."

Hetty looked away from Harry's sister to see that the earl's eyes were still on her face. Drat the man. The earl said easily, "A most unusual stance you take, sir. A member of White's you shall be. Perhaps your unconventional views may sway some of us more pompous, staid gentlemen to more moderate stands."

"I thank you, my lord," Hetty said.

"How kind of you, Julien." The countess threw her arms about the earl's neck and hugged him fiercely. Laughing, he clasped her about her still slender waist and lifted her above him. Her long hair swirled over her shoulders and onto his face.

"Let me down, you great brute. We mustn't shock poor Lord Monteith. He isn't used to your ways, my lord."

"Your ways as well, madam," the earl said. "Lord Monteith will learn soon enough that I must fight for every shred of male dignity. Come, Kate, should we not offer our guests some tea. Perhaps some claret for your brother? Ah, but first, let's remove this carpet."

But not a moment later, George entered the library carrying a beautiful silver tray that held tea and morning cakes. The earl laughed. "George helps us maintain decorum. Do sit down, Lord Monteith and take some refreshment. I assure you that we aren't always so rough and tumble. Well, perhaps most of the time we are, but if there's warning, then—"

"You will hold your tongue, Julien," the countess said, and took a bit of lemon seed cake.

"Dashed good cakes," Sir Harry said, his own mouth full with his second bite.

The earl said to Hetty, "Harry here informs me that you hail from the North Country. I suppose you must find London ways a bit unusual."

She agreed readily, thankful the earl hadn't asked her to be more forthcoming about her specific origins. "It is different in many ways here, but I like London very much. Everyone has been most kind to me. Particularly Harry here. He's a great friend."

Sir Harry beamed. "Lord Harry ain't so much the rustic anymore either. Except for his clothes, that is."

Kate said, "Don't be unkind, my dear. I find nothing at all wrong with Lord Monteith's clothing. It is just that you have an overfondness for yellow-striped waistcoats and very tight breeches. Not that they don't look well on you, for they do, the tight breeches, that is."

"Certainly they look well on me. Now, Lord Harry—his breeches are far too loose. His coats, too."

"A grave shortcoming," the earl said with a smile. "Harry tells me that you fence with Signore Bertioli."

Hetty nodded, unconsciously rubbing her arm. "I have a fondness for the sport, as does, it appear, her ladyship."

The earl said, "I have, myself, fenced with Bertioli upon occasion and found his techniques most unusual. He knows tricks that few Englishmen have ever seen. Perhaps you would care to cross foils with me, Lord Monteith."

Hetty thought the possibility quite unlikely, if she had any say in the matter, but she smiled and nodded. "I would say that her ladyship must have first claims, my lord. If her quickness of wit is any measure of her skill, you hold in her a very worthy opponent."

"She's a damned brute," Sir Harry said. "She nearly thrust her foil through my gullet once. Lord, Kate, but that seems ages ago. Goodness, Father was still alive and—"

"True, Harry, and of no interest whatsoever to Lord Monteith. Tell me, sir, do you also shoot wafers at Manton's?"

"Now no one can beat Lord Harry at that," Sir Harry said before Hetty could even open her mouth. "Never challenge him to a duel, Julien, for I vow he could trim your sails, at least with pistols. He never misses."

"You exaggerate, Harry."

"Narry a bit. You must come with us to Manton's, Julien. You can see for yourself that Lord Harry is quite the expert."

"I just might do that," the earl said easily, looking closely at Hetty.

When at last Hetty rose and took the countess's hand in hers, she said simply, "Harry is an excellent friend, my lady. He has the sunniest of tempers."

Sir Harry turned to his brother-in-law. "Now don't forget, Julien, to take care of Lord Harry's membership this afternoon. We've a wonderful celebration planned for this evening."

"That's a frightening thought," the earl said. "Both of you rest assured I shall do what I've promised. Take care, Monteith. No doubt I shall see you at White's."

"Thank you, my lord, for your kindness," Hetty said, bowing formally to the earl.

Late that same evening as the earl and countess of March lay close together in their bed, Kate nuzzled her cheek against her husband's neck and whispered, "Now, my lord, will you allow me to continue with our fencing lessons? You must admit that it is no more strenuous than our lovemaking."

The earl shifted so he could look into his wife's vivid green eyes. "You think so, do you? You have your way with me, allowing me only to lie here whilst you enjoy my man's body, then you claim this to be strenuous. If you would know the truth, this is much more like riding than fencing."

"What a vulgar thing to say. Ah, very well, I suppose that perhaps I shouldn't fence with all that much vigor for a while yet. At least until the babe is born."

"I appreciate your compromise. Now, tell me what you think of Harry's new friend."

The countess pondered a moment then said slowly, "I think he is somewhat different from Harry's usual friends. He seems sober and quite mature for his years. You know, Julien—and do not tease me—but at first I thought him to be a rather effeminate young man, for he is quite a pretty fellow. But after listening to his calm good sense, watching him handle Harry quite expertly, I must own that I like him."

"Regardless of the fact that Lord Monteith is a pretty fellow, he has already gained something of a reputation for being a young rakehell."

"No, Julien, you cannot mean it. Lord Monteith? Why he is modest and kind and soft spoken and—"

"Harry was quick to inform me that Monteith has already installed a mistress here in town. The story goes that he found her in Lady Buxtell's establishment, plucked her out and set her up the first night he was with her."

"Having a mistress doesn't necessarily make him a rakehell. He isn't yet married. After all, my love, you had a string of mistresses in keeping before we met."

"Well, no matter," the earl said quickly, not wanting to fall into that quagmire. "In any case, I have seen to the young man's membership at White's. I don't doubt that he and Harry have already registered Lord Monteith's name in Henry's famous book. I find young Monteith most interesting. Now that he is a member of White's, I can more easily follow what I believe will be an interesting career. Now, my dear, enough of both Harrys."

Chapter Eleven

Both Harrys and Mr. Scuddimore were seated at that moment in the small dining room at White's, toasting one another from a seemingly endless supply of champagne bottles.

"Keep the best coming," Sir Harry said to a harried waiter, turning a wide grin on Lord Harry. "Damned fine banquet, Lord Harry. Ah, yes, another toast."

Hetty thought of the price of this orgy of food and drink, and blanched. She knew she must keep a close watch on her purse strings, just on the off chance that Sir Archibald might inadvertently speak to his man of business. There wasn't all that high a chance of this happening, but still . . . A game of piquet or faro would be just the thing to cover the cost of her celebration.

Sir Harry, seven glasses of champagne swirling about in his belly, said happily, "Now that Lord Harry is officially one of us I think it's only fair he tell us where he's hidden his little ladybird."

"I will say only that she is quite well and, naturally, supremely happy." Hetty silently toasted the absent Mavreen, praying that what she said was indeed true.

"Don't suppose you will be coming with us again

to Lady Buxtell's," Scuddy said over the rim of his champagne glass.

"Perhaps, if my little ladybird ceases to please me. Who knows? A gentleman's taste changes swiftly and unexpectedly. Yes, we'll see."

Sir Harry carefully stored away Lord Harry's words, changing them about just a bit so that they would be in his style, hopeful that at some time he could say them with the same negligent indifference to other gentlemen in his acquaintance.

Hetty rose, straightened her powder blue waistcoat and gave a salute to her friends. "Since you two are drinking up my assets, I can see that my only recourse lies with the luck of the cards downstairs. Now that I am an esteemed member, I can hold the faro bank. To your health, gentlemen." She tossed down the remainder of champagne in her glass, and left Sir Harry and Mr. Scuddimore to their own devices. It was, in truth, her second glass.

When Hetty entered the elegant gaming salon, she felt a tinge of smugness mingle with her excitement at finally being an accepted member of this exalted male stronghold. She looked up at the heavy chandeliers, their twinkling prisms catching the glowing light from the candles and shimmering down upon the gentlemen's heads, and gave them a conspiratorial wink. The array of black and gold clad footmen, the trademark of White's, still impressed her with their silent efficiency. They hovered unobtrusively about the gaming tables, holding exquisite crystal decanters on silver trays, ready for the snap of a gentleman's fingers.

She sauntered to the faro table and stood quietly at the elbow of Lord Alvaney, a very likable gentleman whose cravat styles she copied regularly. His amusing pronouncements upon the misfortune of existing in the same era as Beau Brummell made Hetty feel that he cared not a whit about the vagaries of his fellow men. She felt no fear of a snub at standing near to him.

She had thought Lord Alvaney engrossed in the play, and was surprised when his soft voice reached her, without his even looking up. "Ah, Monteith, allow me to felicitate you. New blood and youth you bring us. I daresay that you will stir up the arid old bones rattling around at White's. You play at faro, my boy?"

"Yes, I much enjoy the game."

"Sit, lad, sit. Ah, did I tell you how much I admired the distinctive style of your cravat this evening?"

She knew he was mocking her, but it was in gentle fun, and she merely grinned and sat down on a delicate French chair next to his lordship. "Now that I am a member, sir, I can hold the bank."

Lord Alvaney smiled kindly at this ingenuous remark, and made his play. He didn't guess aright, having forgotten the suits already placed to one side of the dealer, and grimaced slightly.

"What a ridiculous way to lose twenty guineas." He rubbed his hand against his rather pointed chin. "Would you care to take on Sir Robert, Monteith? Robert, attend, old fellow, I am giving you a new lamb for the fleecing."

Robert Montague, a tall, gaunt gentleman, renowned for his exquisite tact and near worship of propriety, raised his dark brown eyes to the newcomer. "Monteith? You hail from the North Country, I understand."

Hetty knew that the gently phrased question

cloaked the most vital of concerns to Sir Robert, namely whether Lord Harry's pedigree and prospects were sufficient for him to be considered as a future son-in-law.

Not wanting to be considered anything remotely close to a possible son-in-law, she merely smiled, and nodded.

Hetty eased herself into the seat vacated by Lord Alvaney and sat forward to cut the deck. She lost the cut, not much liking it because Damien had always told her that being the dealer gave her not only the advantage but luck.

Sir Robert neatly inserted the shuffled deck into the faro box, an elegant, hand-lacquered affair, so exquisite a piece that it effectively masked its purpose of preventing the dealer from any false-carding. Sir Robert shoved the bank forward and withdrew the jack of diamonds from the box. The two of hearts followed, and Hetty set her memory into motion. It was vital to remember the suit and value of each card played, and Damien had taught her any number of quaint devices to remember the order of play. She repeated to herself that Jack loved the two of diamonds but the evil queen of spades must interfere. And on and on, weaving a nonsensical rhyme and story with each turn of the cards.

Sir Robert noted the intense concentration on Lord Monteith's young face. After some five more minutes of play, he decided to offer a rather unusual wager, to test the young man's mettle. He rather liked the thought of having a son-in-law who wasn't a complete wastrel. "Twenty guineas, my lord, if you can call aright the last three cards in the box."

The king lost his heart when the eight of spades

clubbed the trey. Hetty looked up, eyes sparkling. "Yes, indeed, Sir Robert, I accept your wager. I declare the seven of hearts, the ace of spades, and the four of clubs, but I cannot guess at the order."

The ace of spades slipped from the faro box. Next came the seven of hearts and finally, to Hetty's incalculable delight, emerged the four of clubs.

Sir Robert, for the first time, was pleased that he'd lost. "Well done, my lad, well done," he said, sitting back in his chair. "You have your wits about you. Remarkable, I think, for one so young."

"Monteith shows his prowess in other areas, I see," came a drawling, mocking voice from behind Hetty's shoulder. She turned quickly in her chair and looked up at Sir William Filey.

"Ah, what's this, Sir William? In what other areas does young Monteith show prowess?" Sir Robert didn't particularly care for Sir William Filey. He was vulgar, ruthless, and not at all likable. However, Sir Robert's strict code of civility forbade him to ignore the gentleman.

Sir William's eyes were narrowed on Lord Harry's face. His hands fisted and opened at his sides, but when he spoke, it was with that same mocking drawl that made her skin crawl. "Quite a reputation Monteith is acquiring with the ladies. I, of course, use the term loosely, as the harlots in Lady Buxtell's house can scarce lay claim to it."

Hetty wanted to hit him, but she forced herself to perfect stillness. She saw Sir Robert's dark eyes widen in surprise. Then she saw the disappointment. Damn Sir William.

Hetty said quietly, her eyes hard, "Perhaps, Sir William, the pot shouldn't be calling the kettle black, particularly when the pot is renowned for boiling over on so many stoves."

Sir William bared his teeth in a snarl, and she knew she'd gone too far. Not Sir William, dammit. But then she heard a laugh behind her and turned quickly. She swiveled in her chair to see Lord Oberlon standing negligently beside Sir Robert, an elegant Sevres snuffbox in his hand.

Oh, my God. She froze, not believing that he was here, that he'd overheard Sir William, that he was actually not three feet away from her. But not like this, she thought. She didn't want to meet him like this.

Sir William ignored the marquess. He leaned down over Hetty's chair. His voice was a soft hiss. "You've a careless tongue in your head, Monteith. I suggest you keep it behind your teeth, else you may find yourself quite mute one of these days."

Hetty felt Lord Oberlon's dark eyes upon her. I'm baiting the wrong man, she thought, but couldn't help herself. Sir William was loathsome. Above all things, she would never let the marquess believe that she was a coward. She relaxed into her chair and lifted a booted leg over the brocade arm. "I fear you mistake my harmless metaphor, Sir William. When I spoke of the pot and the kettle, I was in error. Rather, sir, I should have said *pot de chambre*. It is much more fitting for you at least, don't you agree?"

"You damned arrogant puppy." Sir William's large hand lifted to strike. "By God, I'll make you pay for your ill manners."

Lord Oberlon's seeming indolence disappeared in that instant. Hetty sensed, actually sensed that his powerful body was tensing for action. "Hold, Filey.

You provoked the lad, as I think Sir Robert will agree. I suggest you respond with wit rather than with threats or fists."

Sir William turned angrily. "Your grace interferes with no invitation. Monteith needs to be taught manners."

Sir Robert rose suddenly, his gaunt frame a looming shadow commanding attention. "I must concur with his grace, Sir William. Monteith is new to London ways, just today made a member here."

Lord Oberlon said, "If it is a duel of honor you seek, Filey, turn your anger upon another man, not a mere boy. You know that I will most willingly oblige you. You have but to name your second and the time. Name your weapon."

Sir William drew back, a glimmer of fear in his eyes.

"Ah, I see that you aren't about to face me. By God, it's your manners I find execrable, not the lad's." Jason looked toward the boy as he spoke. His face was pale, there was banked rage in his eyes, yet he held himself in excellent control. He was motionless, showing nothing of what he was feeling or of what he intended to do. The marquess was impressed.

Hetty felt as though someone had jerked the chair from under her. Damn Lord Oberlon for coming to her aid. She didn't mind Sir Robert speaking up, but not this, not Jason Cavander being her knight, damn his eyes. Finally she'd managed to come face-to-face with him and what had it gained her? A damnable protector. This was her first opportunity. She couldn't just let it slip by her. She uncoiled from her chair and rose to stand between Lord Oberlon and Sir William. Though her eyes were on a level with Sir William's, she was forced to tilt back her chin to look into Lord Oberlon's face.

In a calm low voice, she said, "I didn't know your grace was a defender of all gentlemen who haven't yet reached your exalted years. I'm not a callow youth who is in need of your protection, your grace. I shall fight my own fights, and find one bully much the same as another, no matter the guise. I do not wish or need your interference."

There was a sharp intake of breath behind her, but whether it came from Sir William or Sir Robert, Hetty neither knew nor cared. She thought fleetingly of Signore Bertioli and his feigned optimism at her progress with the foil. Was she at last to be put to the test?

Not a flicker of emotion registered on Lord Oberlon's face. He was very tanned, she thought, thinking of his time in Italy. She thought she saw a gleam of surprise in his dark eyes, but he looked down so quickly, she doubted what she saw. She found her hands balling into fists at her sides. Why didn't he strike her?

With studied, almost indifferent movements, he flipped open the Sevres snuffbox, and with an elegant flick of his wrist, inhaled a pinch, then breathed deeply. He brushed a fleck of snuff from his sleeve, and to Hetty's surprise, looked her full in the face and smiled gently.

He wanted to take the boy's white neck between his long fingers and gently squeeze until he apologized for his unmeasured words. But he knew he couldn't, at least not here at White's. He wondered what was in the boy's mind, why he was attacking him. For what purpose? It made no sense. He kept his own voice low, almost meditative. "It would appear, Filey, that Monteith has no use for either of us." He paused yet again, his gaze roaming over Monteith's face. "Your tongue is sharp, my boy, your words barbed. May I suggest that in the future, you temper your fits of arrogance and swagger, particularly in my presence."

Sir William said, "You'd best heed his grace's advice. You may be certain, callow youth or no, that you will pay for your insults." Sir William sensed that young Monteith had so thoroughly offended Lord Oberlon that his own closing shot wouldn't draw his grace's wrath upon his own head. He glanced a final time with loathing upon the lad's flushed face, turned abruptly and strode away.

Sir Robert, his mouth prim and disapproving, bowed with the slightest dip of his thin shoulders and retired to another table. Hetty found herself alone, facing her enemy. At last. She sensed his strength, his sheer physical power, and another power that was deep within him, that was part of him, that was, indeed, what made him what he was—ruthless, utterly without morals, yet he'd defended Lord Harry Monteith, a perfect stranger to him. It made no sense and she refused to think about it, to grant him any credit. She thrust up her chin. A bullet or a foil would bring him to the ground. Let him be strong, let him be powerful, it mattered not. She was going to kill him. He deserved it.

He spoke again, the gentleness of his tone stark with naked warning. "You're young, Monteith. Although I applaud your dislike of Sir William and indeed, find myself amused at your wit in felling him, you must take care. I don't think you stupid, my lad, so attend me carefully. Know well your victim before you lash out with your cutting words."

"*Victim*, your grace? How oddly that word sets upon *your* shoulders. I see you in the light of the predator, without conscience, without remorse. You may be certain that I will indeed know the predator before I lash out. I do heed your advice, your grace, with only the minor adjustment to your character." She saw the smooth line of his jaw harden, the twitching of a small muscle beside his mouth. He will strike me now, she thought, bracing herself. An arrogant man as he is will never tolerate such insults.

Lord Oberlon slowly replaced his snuffbox in his waistcoat pocket. He gazed down at the boy standing stiff as a young sapling before him, not with anger, but with tolerance. Good lord, had he ever been so young? So arrogant? So utterly certain that he was invulnerable? Yet there couldn't be more than seven or eight years between them. He supposed that he must have once been as great a fool. Most young gentlemen were. Of course, there'd been no excuse for the greatest foolishness of his life, none at all. He said finally, his voice amused, "I find you tolerably entertaining, Monteith. But really, lad, you call me a predator? I can't imagine how you come to that conclusion. It would appear to me that you have decided to number your years by willy-nilly insulting every gentleman who is unlucky enough to come into the sphere of your spiteful tongue. I doubt you are twenty-one yet. If you wish to see another year, you'd best mind your tongue and your manners."

Hetty struggled to find words to push him to anger. She didn't understand him. Why didn't he take her by the throat and shake her? She managed more coldness, more disdain. "Nay, your grace," she said, chin as high as it would go, "in your case, I don't insult a gentleman, but rather a nobleman. Even with my few years, I know there is a difference, is there not?"

It was beyond what he would take. Jason grasped the boy's wrist hard, twisting the bones, realizing as he did so that the bones were delicate, that he could break the wrist with just a twist of his hand. But he didn't twist the boy's wrist. He saw pain in the boy's eyes, but he made no sound, merely looked down at Lord Oberlon's hand, his look cold and dispassionate. Jason didn't want to be impressed, but again, he was.

It was all Hetty could do to keep herself from crying out. His fingers were long and squared at the tips, overlapping about her wrist. I've succeeded, she thought, her elation overcoming the pain in her wrist. He jerked suddenly on her wrist, pulling her within inches of his face. He said softly, "I deplore bad manners and scenes, Monteith. You push me. On purpose. I ask myself why. Why, lad, do you do this?"

Damien's name formed on her lips, but she bit it back. He deserved no explanation, not until she'd put a bullet through his black heart. As his lifeblood flowed from his body, then and only then would he know the reason for his death.

"Hey ho, Lord Harry, what are you about? Are you brewing some mischief with his grace? Don't tell me, Lord Oberlon, that Monteith has false-carded you at faro? It's impossible, he's far too good a gamester. He never loses."

Hetty bit her lower lip in frustration. Lord Oberlon dropped her wrist. He didn't even bother looking at her again. She wasn't important enough for more of his precious time. God, she wanted to curse at him, tell him he was a murderer, without honor, responsible for her brother's death, and how she would kill him. There would be another time, she promised him silently, watching him turn into a bored gentleman as smoothly as a chameleon.

"No, Brandon, Monteith does not, to the best of my limited knowledge, resort to such subtle tactics as cheating at faro. However, what he is I have yet to determine."

Jason turned to look at the newcomer, Mr. Scuddimore. "I trust, Scuddimore, that your parents are well? Your father has recovered from his hunting accident? They survive without your presence?"

Scuddy bowed deeply, cognizant of his grace's signal honor of speaking to him. "So kind of your grace to inquire. No problem there, your grace, my father goes along quite well now. They haven't said that they miss me overly."

The marquess merely nodded, saying now to Harry, "Brandon, give my regards to your charming sister and Julien. I shall call upon them presently. As for you, Lord Harry, doubtless we will chat again. Mind what I've told you, lad. Think before your mouth leads to your demise." He flipped his hand in an indifferent salute and strolled away.

"What was that all about?" Sir Harry asked, looking after the marquess.

"Nothing at all. Now, tell me how much more champagne have you consumed for *my* celebration? I won only twenty guineas at faro. Ah, but let's drink it down. Lead on, MacDuff."

"MacDuff?" Scuddy said. "Don't know him. Does the fellow like champagne? It wouldn't do to bring him along if he don't."

Chapter Twelve

Jason Cavander stirred a cube of sugar into his rich Spanish coffee and savored the pungent dark aroma before swallowing. Although it was after nine o'clock in the morning, it promised to be another dreary winter day, and the marquess wished he could have stayed abed. A howling wind was battering noisily against the long French windows in the small breakfast room, and heavy pellets of rain blurred the triangular park just opposite his town house in Berkeley Square.

A damned depressing day it would be, he thought, pouring himself a second cup of coffee. Poor Spiverson. He could picture his stooped gaunt man of business, walking hunched forward against the rain and wind, presenting himself to Lord Oberlon in a dripping shiny black suit, his sparse gray hair plastered about his small square face. He paid an extraordinarily generous fee to his man of business, yet Spiverson would sooner risk an inflammation of the lung than part with a few shillings to take a hackney.

The marquess cupped his hands about the coffee cup, rose from the table and strolled to the fireplace. He controlled the urge to inform his butler to send Spiverson away when he arrived. Although such caprice from a wealthy master wouldn't be blinked at, the marquess had no desire to emulate his late father, who, with a snap of his fingers, blithely canceled appointments, leaving his house in chaos whilst he went off to drink with one of his cronies or inspect a new hunter. The marquess had returned order to the house, and he had no intention of allowing himself to slip into indolence at the sacrifice of his responsibilities. This once, though, he was sorely tempted, for his head ached from too much revelry the previous evening. The rest of his body was none too pleased either, for following a not-altogether-steady walk from White's to Melissande's apartment on Pemberley Street at two o'clock in the morning, he'd roused his sleeping mistress and turned her bed into a shambles before pulling on his clothes and staggering out into the dismal cold dawn back to Berkeley Square.

He knew in more objective moments that such orgies of excess could be viewed as an opiate, a not altogether satisfactory manner of burying unpleasant memories, but, perhaps, still better than nothing at all. It really was a pity that one couldn't learn wisdom, maturity, and temperance without causing exquisite pain in the process. It was a pity that one couldn't make the pain and the blackness simply disappear.

He turned at the tread of his butler's catlike footsteps outside the breakfast room door. He could even hear Mrs. Gerville's wheezing breathing before she got within ten feet of a closed room he was in. It was at times like this, attuned to every sound in the house in which he had reached manhood, that he was most aware of his aloneness. None of his friends or family knew what his short marriage had meant to him, and he, of a certainty, hadn't talked about it. If they believed his abrupt departure to Italy after his wife's death had shown he was distraught, that was fine with him. He knew that was what most of them had believed.

His butler's cat's feet drew to a halt and a muffled tap sounded against the door. The marquess looked at his watch. Damn, Spiverson was early. "Come in, Rabbell." He set his empty coffee cup onto the table.

"Your grace," Rabbell said, looking for the world like a Cornish piskey with his spiky red hair and his pointed nose.

The marquess sighed. "I know, Rabbell. Please tell Spiverson I'll join him shortly in the estate room. Oh see to it he gets himself dried off. We don't want him croaking from an inflammation of the lung."

"It isn't Spiverson, your grace," Rabbell said, and gave his master a big impudent grin. "Oh no, it's the earl of March and here he is right on my boot heels."

"St. Clair," Jason said, rising. "Good lord, man, whatever sends you out on this dreary morning?"

"You might well ask, Jason," the earl said, shaking his friend's hand. "Actually, I expected you to still be in bed, it's where any sane man belongs this morning. Bloody nasty weather."

"My man of business that has me up and about at this ungodly hour. Come, Julien, join me in a cup of coffee."

"It's your Spanish blend, I trust. Ah, yes it is." He took a cup of coffee and drank deeply. "I don't suppose you'd be willing to give me the recipe for this blend for a Christmas present?"

"If I did, you wouldn't have reason to visit me anymore."

The earl just smiled and sat himself down. "How did you find Italy, Jason?"

He wanted to say that it was naught but a place, that he could have traveled to Russia and it wouldn't have made a difference, that he'd simply wanted to exile himself. But he said instead, "Too warm for my tastes, if you would know the truth. One cannot fault the beauty of Florence, and yet, you know, I could not escape the feeling that I was somehow treading on an overripe fruit."

"A peach perhaps," the earl said. "Italy reminds me of peaches." The earl knew that Jason's extended trip was the result of his wife's death. He and Kate had been in Paris when Jason's wife had died in childbirth. It was odd, but Jason had never invited either of them to meet his wife during the months before her death. Since Jason was a friend, he wasn't about to ask. But he wanted to. He was frankly tired of worrying about his friend.

"Your forbearance is alarming. Come, Julien, I won't call you out if you speak your mind, which I can see you're dying to do."

"What would you have me say, Jason? That I've heard stories of dissolute behavior? That you took every woman who looked your way, and given that you're not a troll, many did? I want to know the truth, damn you."

The marquess was very still. He then smiled, a slow bitter smile that made the earl frown deeply at him. He said after a moment, his gaze fastened on the orange glowing embers in the fireplace, "I have an excellent notion of the drivel spouted from the gossips' mouths. The truth, then, Julien. I did go to the devil himself. I am very lucky that I didn't get the pox. It was an interesting experience, particularly hearing sex words I didn't understand. I laughed many times, and yet—" He paused, his spoken thought left unfinished.

The earl said slowly, "And yet, Jason, it was no balm for the soul."

The earl was exactly right, only for the wrong reasons. Jason just shook his head. "Enough of this. More truth, my head aches from too much brandy and I have the most unpleasant notion that Spiverson will keep my nose in his damnable account books until the afternoon. Now you will tell me what you're doing in Berkeley Square. Surely your mission wasn't just to see if I still lived or not."

"No, I have other ways of knowing whether your breathing is steady," the earl said. "Actually, I was on my way to Tattersall's. I want to purchase a sporting phaeton for Kate, and unfortunately I must rise with the birds, if I want to keep her in the dark. It's a surprise for her." The earl sat forward in his chair. "Congratulate me, Jason. Kate is pregnant."

"My God, that is good news indeed." He shook the earl's hand, clapped him on his back, and grinned at him like a fool. "Ah, now I understand your problem. Kate balks at being a lady of leisure."

The earl laughed. "She even went so far as to inform me of the fact in the middle of our fencing lesson. I remember wanting to strangle her and knowing that I couldn't, when she was saved by her brother Harry and that new friend of his came to

visit. Which reminds me, Jason, what do you think
of my new protégé? I saw to making him a member
of White's yesterday."

"What protégé?"

"Monteith is his name. Harry Monteith. An interesting lad, soft spoken, yet older than his years. I
think he's certainly a good influence on Harry."

Jason stared at him. "You don't mean to tell me
that you are responsible for that young whelp running free in the club? No, that isn't possible. The
lad I'm thinking of is slight of build, has fair coloring, and a damnably sharp tongue."

"Yes, that sounds like Monteith. What's going on
here? Have you already met the lad?"

"Met him? By God, Julien, I was sorely tempted
to beat the fellow to a pulp. The arrogant puppy
called me not a gentleman but a nobleman. He did
it on purpose, too, for what reason I have no idea.
I asked him but he wouldn't say a word."

"You say you didn't kill the lad?"

"Not this time, but I'll tell you, Julien, if he
doesn't keep his tongue in his head, he isn't long
for this world. You believe him soft spoken and
mature for his years? I think he's singularly stupid.
God, and the bravado and arrogance. If Filey gets
him alone, it will be all over for him. If I hadn't
stopped Filey, the boy would be dead at this
moment by Filey's hand."

"Since he's offended you, my friend, I wonder
how I could have seen him in such a different way.
But the fact is that I did. Is it possible that you
didn't push him in some way to retaliate in such a
manner? Come, tell me what happened."

"I didn't push him at all. Monteith was playing

faro with Sir Robert when I chanced to overhear that ass, Filey, blatantly draw the boy. Monteith rounded on him—" The marquess paused, memory forcing him to grin. "Damned fine job he did on Filey, I tell you. Said something to Filey about the pot calling the kettle black. Then, with all the poise in the world, he told Filey that he was mistaken in his metaphor—a *pot de chambre* was what he had intended to say. As you can well imagine, Filey turned quite purple, then nasty. The villain was on the point of calling Monteith out, when, fool that I am, I stepped forward into the fray and drew Filey off. Instead of gratitude, Monteith turned on me. He made unflattering comparisons between me and Filey—called me a bully, a predator, and the like."

"He's young. Could it be that your interference wounded his pride?"

"No, it wasn't that," the marquess said slowly. He leaned forward and rested his elbows on his knees. "If I could think of some likely reason, I would believe that the lad hates me. His insults were deliberate and vicious. He was pushing me to violence, Julien, of that I am certain. It was as if Filey were in the way. It was me he wanted. It was me he wanted to fight, not Filey, not anyone else, just me. Why? I haven't the foggiest notion, as I told you."

"Do you think there's a seduced sister somewhere in the background? Monteith has no Italian relations hanging about Florence, does he?"

The marquess laughed. "I did wonder about that, so stop your laughing at me." He shook his head. "No, I can't believe that. There was purpose and design to his attack. Oh, what the hell. No doubt I'll discover enough if there's a seduced sister somewhere or if the lad just disliked the cut of my coats. Now, Julien, when is the future earl of March to make his appearance into this world?"

"Late summer or early fall, Kate obligingly informs me. Now, I must go. I'll leave you now to the mercy of your man of business. You know, Jason, you're always welcome at Grosvenor Square?"

"Oh yes. Who wouldn't welcome such a *noble*man as myself to his home?"

The earl of March just grinned at him and rose to take his leave. "You will take care, won't you, Jason?"

"As always," the marquess said.

"Oh my goodness, Miss Hetty, do wake up now. You'll not believe who just landed on our doorstep. Oh lordie, what a shock it is."

Hetty jerked the covers over her head. "Oh, Millie, no, not yet. It can't be time for luncheon, not yet, please. Just another thirty minutes, even twenty."

"Come, Miss. It's Sir John and Lady Louisa. Sir John was surprised that you weren't up and about."

"But I have a hangover. You wouldn't believe the number of bottles of champagne—well, that's neither here nor there. Jack and Louisa, here? But no one told me they were coming. You're right, what a shock."

"They're here nonetheless. In the drawing room, Miss, with Sir Archibald. You might well guess that he's fairly itching to be gone. You must hurry, else they will be left quite alone with poor Grimpston wringing his hands."

Hetty groaned and swung her bare feet to the

floor, wiggling her toes about for the warmth of her slippers. "Is Little John with them?"

"No, just their servants and mountains of luggage. Blink your eyes, Miss Hetty. It will make the puffiness go down. Here now, here's your shift. Ah, you have a royal headache, do you? A hangover, you said? You?"

Hetty just groaned.

"My baby has a hangover. The good Lord preserve us, a hangover, just like a bloody man. No, don't hold your head in your hands. You've got to be still. Your hair is a mess of tangles."

Hetty moaned. "Bring me some coffee first, Millie. If you don't want me to die, bring me coffee."

Chapter Thirteen

After two cups of coffee and holding her face in ice-cold water for three minutes, Hetty decided she would live. Not twenty minutes after that decision, she was walking down the main staircase, wondering what in heaven's name Jack and Louisa were doing in London, and with no warning.

Grimpston was waiting for her at the foot of the stairs. "Sir Archibald just retired to his study. Mrs. Miller will bring tea and morning cakes to the drawing room within the next five minutes. Sir Jack and Lady Louisa are comfortable but getting restive."

"Thank you," she said, and nearly ran to the drawing room. "Jack, Louisa. How wonderful to see you." But why, she wanted to demand, didn't you at least write me a letter?

She took two quick steps into the room and found herself swooped up in a tight embrace. "Ah, Jack, you wretched giant, you're breaking my ribs." She was laughing, her arms tight about her brother's neck.

"Don't crush her just yet, Jack. I want to hug her first."

"My little Hetty's made of stern stuff, Lou," Sir John said, but drew back, releasing Hetty. He studied her pale face and felt the months roll back to the past summer. Damn, she was still mourning Damien. He suppressed his own pain at the thought of his brother, and said, lightly cuffing her shoulder, "Not on the go too much, are you, kitten?"

Hetty saw the concern in her brother's blue eyes. She couldn't see herself telling him she'd drunk too much champagne with her cronies the night before and was suffering for it this morning. "Oh no, don't worry about me. But you know, London is a busy town and there's so much to do. Everyone here is always struggling to get enough sleep. Now, let me go, for it has been an age since I've seen Louisa."

Hetty gathered the smaller Louisa into her arms and kissed her cheek. "You're looking wonderful. So marriage with my brother here suits you?"

"I nearly have him trained, Hetty. He scarcely ever tries to climb on the furniture or whines at the front door."

There was a loud snort from Sir Jack.

Louisa just grinned, then took both Hetty's hands into hers and smiled. "You grow more lovely by the day, my dear Hetty. And that paleness Jack so heartily condemns is all the style. At least it used to be. Come, my dear, let's sit down. You must tell me all the latest gossip."

"First, Louisa, tell me what you are doing here in London? And where is Little John?"

Sir John sat back in a chair that creaked under his weight. "It just so happens, little sister, that London is merely the first stop for Lou and me. Yes, we've got places to go and things to do. Paris is our final destination."

"Paris? Louisa, I began to think you are no mortal woman. However did you manage to pull Jack from his cows and crops? Goodness, you certainly have trained him well."

"All right, both of you females. Lou knows I'm a man who keeps to his word. I promised my sweet malleable little wife a holiday before she got too fat to travel."

"Fat? Louisa's not fat. You're wretched, Jack, to tease her like that."

"Er, Miss Hetty."

"Yes, Grimpston. Ah, here's the tea and morning cakes. How lovely everything looks. Do thank Mrs. Miller."

She handed her brother the plate of cakes, saying, "Now, Jack, what do you mean you're taking her to Paris before she gets too fat?"

Sir Jack had a mouthful of seed cake. It was quickly gone. "Goodness, little sister, what an innocent you are. Are you eighteen? Time you learned a bit more about life."

"Jack, don't tease your sister. What my darling husband refers to, my dear—oh well, I'm breeding. It's only fair, he told me, that we have a second wedding trip before we have a second child."

"Oh, how marvelous. I'm so happy for you. Goodness, I believe your babe will be born about at the same time as Kate St. Clair's." She bit her tongue. Damnation, how could she imagine that Miss Henrietta Rolland could have ever met the earl and countess of March. "But that's not important. Where are you staying in Paris? How long will you be there?"

"Did you hear that, Lou? Our Hetty's made some powerful friends. So you've been rubbing shoulders with the countess of March, have you?"

Drat your tenacious mind, Jack, Hetty thought, wanting to hit him and then herself. "Not exactly," she said. "I just know of her, that's it. I just hear things and that was one of the things I just happened to hear."

"Don't you know, Hetty, that Jack has known Julien St. Clair, the earl of March, for quite a few years. Neither of us has met his countess as of yet. I understand she's a charming girl."

Hetty pictured Kate St. Clair in her tight black breeches with a foil in her hand, mercilessly goading her husband. "Yes, that is what I've heard, too."

"Enough gossip, ladies. Tell us, Hetty, what have you been up to for these past months?"

Hetty silently breathed a prayer of thanks to Lady Melberry. She launched into a description of the soirée she had attended, embroidering upon the event sufficiently to lead Louisa and Jack to believe that she had been gaily flitting from one party to another. As she prattled on, she chanced to see her brother gaze meaningfully at his wife. She said, "Did you believe I was sitting about still mourning Damien?"

Sir John said, "Don't deny us the right to be concerned about you, Hetty. We had thought you weren't going out at all since that Worthington woman left you months ago."

"Don't worry about me, either of you. I do go to routs and parties and there are always kindly dowagers about to chaperone me. Now," she said abruptly, her chin going up. "Enough about me. Do tell me about what you think of Mavreen. Does she get along well with Little John and Nanny?"

Neither Sir John nor Lady Louisa were ready to

delve more deeply. Louisa said, "Mavreen is a dear girl. Jack thinks so, too. Little John adores her. She's the only one in his confidence now. Here he is only five years old and he's in love. And not with his mother. He has even shown her his rock collection. She is one reason why we have no second thoughts about leaving him for a while. Hardly a sad look he could muster when we took our leave of him."

"Thank you for taking her into your home. I prayed she would work out well for you."

Sir John stretched out his long, muscular legs toward the fireplace, and said with a frown darkening his brow, "There must be many such waifs as she, I fear. Many such men as her uncle Bob were hailed as heroes, yet the government did naught for their widows and children. At least we have all done the right thing in this one instance. Don't worry about her, Hetty. She's safe and content with us. We will see to her future."

Lady Louisa said, "She's such a bright, pretty girl. Jack's right. And when the time comes, we will see to it that she makes a suitable marriage. In the meanwhile, she will have the security of wages and a good home."

She wanted to cry, she was so relieved, but she managed to swallow down the sob. She tried to smile, and was saved by her perceptive brother. He said, laughing, "Our father never changes. Lord, Hetty, how do you ever manage the care of him?"

"Ah, a fine question. Do you know that the servants tell me that Sir Archibald's schedule is a flawless clock. Once, but last week, he had luncheon with one of his Tory cronies, and left the servants bewildered for the remainder of the afternoon. My only interference has been to give Cook the hint never, never to serve any dish to him that contains even the remotest suggestion of corn." At the puzzled frown on Louisa's face, she added with a grin, "You must know that the wretched Whigs are brewing all sorts of mischief with the Corn Laws. I don't think that I could endure another impassioned lecture on their collective deceit, which, I assure you, would be the outcome."

Sir John said, sitting forward in his chair, "I would never, of course, even dream of talking politics with Father. Yet, being a farmer myself, I begin to see that there are flaws with our new Corn Laws. Not importing corn until our own English corn reaches eighty shillings a quarter—well, it seems to me that our poorer people are going to have a hard time of it. Already the price of bread is out of reach for the poor wretches in the larger cities. Damien, I know, was beginning to grow quite concerned about the worsening conditions, particularly in Manchester. I can remember him saying that in not too many years there would be trouble there and demand for sweeping reforms. Damnation, I wonder if Father will ever admit to the fact that there are other points of view."

"You speak blasphemy, Jack." Hetty swept her eyes heavenward for forgiveness. "Father was born a conservative Tory and he will die a conservative. Actually, he's beyond a mere conservative. I don't think there's really a party for him, but he strives to bring all his cronies into his way of thinking."

Louisa rose suddenly and shook out her stylish traveling skirt of twilled gray muslin. Sir John, seated, was nearly the height of his wife standing.

She leaned over and kissed him lightly on the lips, then remarked in a teasing voice to Hetty, "You see, my dear, how you deal with one of his size? You must show affection to your oversized brother when he's seated. It quite saves one from being crushed or getting an ache in one's neck. Now, Jack, you have done your duty. Both Hetty and I excuse you. You're probably itching to visit your clubs, to hear all the manly gossip." She turned to Hetty, eyes twinkling. "Men's gossip, I think, is very much like our gossip, only it would take torture for Jack to admit it. Now, Jack, I will see that Planchard unpacks for you and lays out your evening clothes."

"Dismissed by a little slip of a girl who hardly reaches my chest. I ask you, Hetty," Sir John continued, rising from his chair, "should I box her ears for such an impertinence or kiss her for being so adorable?"

"Kiss her, Jack," Hetty said. "Although it appears you've already done a lot more than just kissing."

"My sister, the virgin," Sir John said, and grinned.

"Off with you, Jack. I don't wish to see that insufferably grinning face of yours until dinner." It was Louisa who kissed her husband.

"She leads me about by the nose, Hetty." Sir John gave his sister a gentle pat on the cheek and strolled from the drawing room, humming a tune whose words were best left unspoken and unsung.

Hetty led her sister-in-law up to the blue guest room to chat about styles, Little John's immense talent in singing, and the new baby that nestled inside its mother's womb. It was finally Lady Louisa who changed the topic of conversation from her own concerns to Hetty's. She gazed pointedly at the hem of Hetty's gown, that was, unfortunately, several inches too short, and said, "You've grown taller since last I saw you, Hetty. I hope that your party gowns are sufficiently long to cover your ankles. Come, love, show me your wardrobe, for if you have need of something, I would like very much to go shopping this afternoon."

As Hetty could think of no polite way to keep Louisa from seeing her pitifully few dresses, she agreed, hoping that at the worst, her sister-in-law would only think her guilty of bad taste.

Louisa made a rapid inspection. She was appalled by the outmoded gowns and wondered just exactly what Hetty wore to all the parties she attended. Because she knew Hetty's pride to be as great as Sir John's, she held her tongue, and silently determined to get Hetty to a dressmaker's that very afternoon under the guise of selecting several new gowns for herself. Unjustly, she blamed Sir Archibald for not providing Hetty sufficient funds to gown herself properly. Didn't the wretched man realize that a young lady preparing to embark on her first full season was in need of gowns that did not positively shout that she was fresh from the country? Of course he could never realize any such thing.

Hetty agreed to Louisa's proposed shopping expedition in good humor, knowing full well that her sister-in-law was shocked by her meager wardrobe. Well, she could hardly tell Louisa that Lord Harry was excessively expensive to dress. There was no reason to spend any grouts on Henrietta who was, after all, a mouse and needed only a pair of spectacles and a pea green gown and matching cap.

Hetty knew a moment of fear when they entered

her father's carriage, bound for Madame Brigitte's. She could only hope that Lady Melberry and the other ladies she had met at the soiree wouldn't be out and about. Upon their arrival at the select little shop on Bond Street, Hetty's eyes darted to every corner of the fashionable outer display salon in search of anyone who might recognize her. *My luck is holding so far*, she thought to herself. She then turned her attention to a very décolleté cerulean blue satin gown that would, Madame Brigitte assured her, transform her into a regal princess. "Yes, indeed," Madame assured her. "It's just the thing for a young lady of your regal height."

"Do let me make it a present to you, my dear," Lady Louisa said. "After all, I didn't get you a birthday present." She had, but she lied well to her sister-in-law, just hoping that Hetty had forgotten.

Hetty *had* forgotten. If only Lord Harry would complete his *vendetta* with the Marquess of Oberlon so that Henrietta Rolland could emerge into society as she really was. Only then could she wear the lovely gown.

When the ladies returned to Sir Archibald's town house, they found Sir John in the drawing room, dressed in severe black evening clothes, his cravat meticulously arranged by his perfectionist valet, Planchard. To Lady Louisa's fond eye, he presented a very handsome picture. Hetty appeared to agree with Lady Louisa, exclaiming, "Good heavens, Jack. What a handsome devil you are."

He grinned engagingly down at her from his noble height. "Damned if you aren't right, little one. I suppose that I haven't a groat to my name with both of you gone for such a long time."

"Two groats left," Louisa said.

"I'll even add a groat if you're going to insult us," Hetty said. "You only purchased me a belated birthday present." Hetty pulled up short and looked at him, cocking her head to the side, for there was a certain smugness in his smile. "All right, Jack. What have you done? Come clean, else you won't leave this drawing room alive."

He flicked an invisible speck of something from his coat sleeve. "I, ah, well, my dear sister, I'm glad you've arrived home in time to make yourself beautiful. Er, even more beautiful, I should say."

"Beautiful? Why? What's this all about? Come clean, what the devil have you done, Jack?"

"If you must know, my dear, we will be having a guest for dinner this evening. Don't worry, for I have already spoken to Mrs. Miller and she's right now in a dither of cooking. I believe, Lou, that you will be quite pleased."

"Who the devil is coming to dinner?" Hetty said, poking him in his massive chest with her finger. "Tell me now, and wipe that idiot grin off your face, or I'll give you to Louisa for some more training and taming."

"Very well, I've invited Jason to dinner."

Hetty frowned, for she knew no gentleman named Jason. To her surprise, Louisa flung herself into her husband's arms. "Oh how wonderful, Jack. It's been an age since we've seen him. Is he quite recovered from his tragedy?"

"I don't know, Lou. You'll have to judge for yourself." Sir John was aware of the irrepressible gleam of matchmaking in his wife's eyes. He probably had the same gleam himself.

"Jason who?" Hetty said, tapping her foot.

Sir John looked mildly surprised, then shook his head. "I guess you wouldn't have met him yet, Hetty. He only just returned to London. When he and I were close, you were still in the schoolroom. He's Jason Cavander, the Marquess of Oberlon."

"Lord Oberlon," she repeated, her brain numbed, her voice flat as her chest was when she was fifteen. "Lord Oberlon," she said again. "You know the marquess? Jack, how come you to know him?"

Louisa said, "Ah, you didn't know that Jason Cavander and Jack were thick as thieves some years ago? They were both in the same college at Oxford."

Hetty shook her head, couldn't seem to take it in. But it was true. She said finally, "Did Lord Oberlon also know Damien back then?"

"Of course," Sir John said. "Not as well as I did, of course, for they were separated by some five years. He promised me to keep an eye on Damien whenever he was in London, after Lou and I married and left for Herefordshire. He's the best of fellows, poor chap."

By God, she thought. How could Jack be so taken in? He believed that vile man to be his friend? Was he bloody blind? Had he no sense at all? Words tumbled out of her mouth, unchecked. "How dare you invite Lord Oberlon here? I'm mistress of this house, and you had no right to invite anyone without my leave, damn you."

Louisa gasped.

"Well, what's done is done. Since you, Jack, have invited that despicable man to this house, he can't now be uninvited. But I tell you, Jack, I will have none of him. Do you hear me?" She drew to an abrupt halt, realizing how much she'd just blundered. Sir John and Lady Louisa, mouths agape, stared at her.

Sir John was the first to recover his tongue. "What the devil are you talking about, Hetty? How can you possibly become such a shrew over a man you've never met? Damnation, girl, this passes all bounds. What do you mean he's despicable? That's utter bloody nonsense."

Her brother's words had a calming effect on her. She drew a deep, shaking breath and said, "Please forgive my ranting, Jack, Louisa. You will, I pray, give Lord Oberlon my apologies." She backed toward the drawing-room door. "Unfortunately, I'm already engaged for the evening, and indeed, must go now and dress. I shan't be home until very late, so please don't wait up for me. I shall see both of you in the morning."

"But, Hetty, we are just arrived. Surely you can send word, you can—"

"I'm sorry, Louisa, truly I am, but I can't. It's an engagement of long standing. There's no choice at all. I must attend." She saw the flushed anger on her brother's face, and before he could demand an explanation of her, she grabbed up her skirt and fled the drawing room.

"This is a fine kettle of fish," Millie said after Hetty told her what had happened. "Well, there's no hope for it. You must leave, Miss Hetty. I can't imagine that the marquess is a stupid man. He is certain to recognize you, or at least wonder about you. And, knowing you, you couldn't keep a civil tongue in your head where he is concerned. Lord,

I can just see Miss Henrietta Rolland challenging him to a duel."

"Of course you're right," Hetty said, only to whirl about when there came an urgent knock on the door.

"Hetty, Hetty, my dear." It was Louisa. "Can't I speak to you for just a moment?"

Hetty steeled herself. "I'm sorry, Louisa, but I must hurry. I mustn't be late. Please, Louisa," she added, a plea in her voice, "just leave me be. I'll see you in the morning."

Hetty heard her sister-in-law sigh deeply. She could easily picture the troubled, confused look on her face. She didn't move or again speak, and, at last, she heard Louisa's retreating footsteps down the corridor.

"Damn," Hetty said. She saw the marquess as she'd seen him the previous night, Lord Harry's insults cold and clear, not making a particular impact on him, damn him. Would he know her if he saw her as Henrietta Rolland? She knew, deep down, she knew that he would.

Millie said quite calmly, "If you don't leave soon, you just might meet Lord Oberlon on the doorstep. That would be another fine kettle of fish."

Ten minutes later, Hetty was clutching her cloak about her shoulders and peering outside her bedroom door. It appeared that Jack and Louisa were either in their room, or downstairs awaiting the marquess. She slipped quietly to the servants' stairs and made her way quickly down to the side entrance, Millie following closely behind her. "You stay here," Millie said, "I'll fetch a hackney." Millie disappeared around the corner and Hetty huddled back against the servants' entrance until she heard the sound of carriage wheels drawing to a halt in front of the house.

"Psst! Come, Miss Hetty."

Hetty slipped from her hiding place and hurried around the corner to a waiting hackney. "You take care, Miss Hetty. I'll be waiting for you. It doesn't matter what time it is. I'll be here, just inside the servants' entrance."

Chapter Fourteen

Upon the arrival of the Marquess of Oberlon, Grimpston bowed lower than was his wont, indeed, lower than his stiff back normally allowed him to. He recognized the signal honor paid to Sir Archibald by the visit of such an exalted personage, and made haste to lead his grace to the drawing room.

"His grace, the Marquess of Oberlon," he announced in a deep, rich voice. Both Sir John and Lady Louisa gave a guilty start, for he had been the subject of their conversation.

Louisa recovered herself quickly, jumping to her feet. "Jason, oh goodness. How very marvelous to see you again."

"You are as beautiful as ever, Louisa," he said in her ear as he swept her up in his arms. "When will you leave this oversized oaf and come away with me?"

Sir John looked benignly upon this scene, then stepped forward and clasped Jason Cavander's hand in a strong grasp.

"Beautiful she may be, Jason, but you'd soon be back at my door begging me to take her back. It would look damned awkward, you know, prancing all over Europe with a pregnant lady in tow."

"Good God," the marquess said, holding Louisa

back in the circle of his arms. He gave her a dazzling smile that revealed his strong white teeth. With his face deeply tanned from the harsh Italian sun, he looked so devastatingly handsome that Louisa thought Hetty must assuredly have lost her wits to have taken him into such strong dislike.

He added, "It would appear that I'm to be surrounded by pregnant ladies. Kate St. Clair is also breeding. Julien told me of it just this morning."

"Yes, Hetty told us." Louisa gave her husband a wild look and bit her tongue.

"Hetty?" he said, looking down at her, then over her head at Sir John.

"My little sister," Sir John said shortly. "Ah, a glass of sherry, Jason?"

"Don't mind if I do," the marquess said easily, giving no sign that he'd noticed anything amiss. "Come, Louisa, let's sit down. It's only right that little John waits on you now. Tell me, how did all this come about?"

Louisa gave a trill of laughter, poked him in the arm, and conversation turned to the five-year-old heir, Little John. The marquess spoke about how fast the time went now. As he sipped at his sherry, he said, "I begin to think my presence this evening has put you out. Does no one live in this house when you aren't here?"

As if to a cue on the theater stage, the drawing-room door opened and Sir Archibald entered, the habitual look of distraction on his face disappearing at the sight of the marquess.

"My boy, welcome to my home. How are your dear mother and sister?"

"Both are quite well, sir." The marquess shook

Sir Archibald's hand. "You recall, of course, that my sister, Alicia, married Henry Warton last summer."

Sir Archibald had no such memory of either the sister or the marriage, but he nodded in gentle agreement. He asked, "Warton? Is that Sir Waldo Warton's son? Excellent, just excellent. Good Tory family, the Wartons."

The marquess wondered with a sinking in his stomach if Sir Archibald would beleaguer the company with Tory tales. He reckoned without Louisa.

Artfully, over the first course at dinner, she maneuvered the conversation to the sights they should visit in Paris and the people that they would be meeting. The Bourbon Louis was discussed at length, but only in terms of the festivities offered by the French court at this time of year. By the main course of flaky fish in a rich wine sauce, the marquess found himself describing the wonders of Italy. In deference to the polite company, he dwelled upon the spectacular ruins, the endless number of paintings of the Virgin Mary and Child, and the warmth of the weather.

Sir John was pleased with his father. His sire asked such sensible questions, with no political overtones, at least to Sir John's sensitive ears, that by the time Grimpston served apple tartlets topped with rich whipped cream, he was quite in charity with his father.

"I say," Sir Archibald said suddenly, "I thought something was not quite right. Where is dear Hetty?"

Louisa's eyes flew to her husband's face. Seeing no immediate help from that quarter, she said with as much nonchalance as she could muster, "Hetty was otherwise engaged this evening, Sir. She regretted that she couldn't be here, but she wasn't able to cancel."

"But where did she go? I swear she said nothing about an evening out to me." Sir John could only stare at his father. He would have sworn that Sir Archibald didn't even know the color of Hetty's hair.

"Ah, to Covent Garden," Louisa said, and nearly choked on a bite of the apple tartlet.

At last she could rise and she did so. However, she was stopped by her father-in-law. He rose and smiled in a general sort of way at everyone at the table. "I hope you young people will excuse me. There are pressing matters of economics that the Prime Minister has asked me to look into. I mustn't shirk my duty no matter how delightful the company I am forced to leave."

As the door closed behind Sir Archibald, Sir John said, grinning at his wife, "At least Jason understands Father's preoccupations, Lou. Isn't your uncle, Lord Melberry, also a rabid Tory?"

"Yes, and it quite drives me to sleep. I hope you'll agree, Jack, that we don't need to have our port this evening? I find myself far more animated in Louisa's company than in yours, old fellow."

"He's a damned rake, Lou," Sir John said. "I should probably keep you hidden in the wilds of Herefordshire while the fellow's running loose in London."

Louisa gave her husband a wicked smile. "You're one to talk, Jack. The stories Jason's told me about you. My ears turned red and if you'd been married to me at the time I would have boxed your ears."

"Well, enough of that," Jack said and sped into

the drawing room, leaving his wife and his friend laughing at his retreating back.

Louisa played a Mozart sonata for them. They drank tea and ate Cook's delicious lemon cakes. The marquess sat back in his chair and said suddenly, "You were always an abominable liar, Louisa. Covent Garden? Had you been in town but several more days, you would have heard that the play there is vulgar in the extreme and not fit for a young lady. I gather that Hetty is a young lady?"

"Oh," Louisa said.

Sir John tugged at his cravat. "Damnation, I don't believe this, Jason. If you would know the truth, Lou and I really have no idea where Hetty is this evening."

A dark brow arched up a good inch. "May I inquire as to the age of your sister, Jack?"

"Dammit, she's eighteen."

The black brow remained arched.

"Oh, very well. It seems my sister, for some reason unknown to either Louisa or me, holds you in strong dislike. We don't understand this at all because we don't think she even knows you."

"How very unsettling. It seems my popularity is shrinking by the day." He thought briefly of young Harry Monteith. At least that young cub sought him out rather than fleeing from him like Henrietta Rolland. He looked meditative for a moment, saying nothing more.

Louisa said suddenly, "Perhaps I understand. Hetty told us she attended a soiree at your aunt Melberry's last week. Jason, were you there?"

"Yes, but what has that to say to anything, Louisa?"

"You must have offended her in some way, inadvertently, of course. Can you remember meeting her?"

The marquess stroked his chin with long fingers. "What does you sister look like?"

"She's quite a pretty little thing. Bright, laughing, full of fun. Not one of those damned simpering misses."

"Oh, Jack, you're still seeing Hetty when she was five years old. Jason, she's the beauty in the family. She's not little at all, rather tall and slender. If you can imagine Jack the giant here as a female, blond hair and all, you'll have Hetty."

"Her nose is shorter than mine," Sir John said. "And she comes only to my chin."

"A female giant then," Louisa said.

The marquess remembered his aunt Melberry asking him to speak to a Miss Rolland and pointing toward a very nondescript female seated with a deaf old dowager. Yes, he remembered now stepping toward the young lady, but she had turned her face pointedly away from him. At the time, he had thought her quite rude. He pictured a hideous alexandrine cap of the most putrid shade of green imaginable. Oh yes, and a gown of pea green, equally as revolting as the cap. He remembered wondering if her face were as unfortunate as her wardrobe. No, certainly that female couldn't have been Jack's beautiful sister. But why hadn't he met her? If she were like Jack, then she certainly wouldn't be a wallflower.

"She's a beauty, you say, Louisa?" he asked slowly.

"Yes, she's lovely. Did you meet her at your aunt's?"

"No, I did not. Ah, then it's a mystery we have on our hands. The young lady has taken me into dislike, yet I know I've never met her. Such a beauty as you describe, well, rest assured that I would have remembered her." It was all very odd.

"Enough of my little chit of a sister," Sir John said. "I want to talk about that dandy cravat you're wearing."

While the occupants of Sir Archibald's town house were discussing in high good humor the vagaries of fashion, Hetty was wiping the remains of cold chicken from her lips and fingers.

"It's a problem, Pottson. I can only hope that Louisa doesn't want to take me to Almack's or some other exalted place before she and my brother leave for Paris."

Pottson removed the tray to the sideboard, remarking in a gloomy voice, "Bound to meet Lord Oberlon, particularly at Almack's. It was a narrow escape you had tonight, Miss Hetty, too narrow for the warmth of my blood. Yes, another gray hair. I'll find it in the morning."

There was a sudden knock on the outer door. Hetty jumped to her feet. "Good God, who the devil can that be? Hurry, Pottson, you must answer. Oh yes, I've told you a dozen times, you already have gray hair, all of it is gray. Maybe you'll find a black hair." Hetty picked up her skirts and ran down the narrow hallway that divided the small drawing room from Lord Harry's bedchamber.

She heard Scuddy's voice. "Ho, Pottson. Is Lord Harry about?"

Hetty reached a quick decision and called out in

Lord Harry's deeper voice, "Hello, Scuddy. Do come in, old boy. I'm dressing and shall be with you shortly. Fetch Mr. Scuddimore a glass of sherry, Pottson."

As she stood in front of her mirror arranging her cravat into The Pavilion, an elegant yet uncomplicated series of folds inspired by the Regent's residence in Brighton, various schemes on how she would spend the evening with Scuddy flitted through her mind. Suddenly, an idea burgeoned in her head, an idea so daring and outrageous that she refused to examine its less desirable consequences. Was Lord Oberlon not otherwise occupied for the evening? Indeed he was, she thought, rubbing her hands together. She'd observed cynically over the past months that gentlemen were far more possessive toward their mistresses than toward their wives. What better way to push the marquess to fury than to poach upon his preserves? She glanced up at the clock above the mantelpiece. Only shortly after nine o'clock. Ample time, indeed more than enough time, she thought, knowing that Sir John and Lady Louisa loved to entertain. She resolutely banished a seed of guilt at using her brother to further her own ends. After all, wasn't Lord Oberlon playing a far more perfidious game than was she, posing as the friend of a man whose brother he'd killed?

As she shrugged into her coat, she thought of Melissande. Indeed, an unforgettable name and an equally unforgettable woman. Hetty had seen Melissande only upon two brief occasions, neither of which had provided her with many clues as to the lady's character. If Melissande happened to be faithful to her protector, then Hetty—or rather Lord

Harry—would just suffer a wasted evening. But one never knew. She looked at herself in the mirror. She looked at Lord Harry and she winked at him.

Although Mr. Scuddimore frowned at the mention of visiting someone in Pemberley Street, he could think of no reason not to accompany Lord Harry, and thus climbed into a hackney alongside his friend.

"I say, old boy, who the devil does live in Pemberley Street? If it's your mistress, I really don't think I should be tagging along. Why, whatever would I say to her?" His protest was a halfhearted one, for he realized that Sir Harry would willingly give a guinea to be in his place. Were they really going to visit Lord Harry's mistress? Scuddy couldn't wait. He mentally tried to make room in his brain to store up all the memories this night would bring.

"Don't worry, Scuddy. It's not my mistress we're visiting. But she is a woman and she is lovely. I just want to better our acquaintance, that's all. You'll enjoy yourself, you'll see."

Well, that wasn't too bad, Scuddy thought. What woman?

The hackney creaked and swayed upon turning into Pemberley Street. Hetty perused the small, elegant town houses that lined the brick pavement, and dug the head of her malacca cane into the roof of the hackney when she spotted the small Queen Anne residence. The jarvey obligingly drew to a halt and Hetty jumped to the pavement, smiling. "Come along, Scuddy," she said over her shoulder, after tossing the cabby a goodly number of shillings. "I promise you an interesting evening." Had Mr. Scuddimore realized that this charming house was owned and maintained by the Marquess of Oberlon, Hetty with all her persuasions, wouldn't have been able to extricate him from the relative safety of the hackney.

Since Melissande wasn't expecting Lord Oberlon this evening, particularly given his excesses in her bed the night before, she was attired in a negligee, a frothy confection of green silk and gauze that revealed more than covered her delicious self. A slender red vellum book lay in her lap, and as her eyes traveled down the page, she sighed in boredom. Really, she was thinking, the heroine is such a stupid, whimpering little miss. She hasn't a gut in her limp body. Must she fall into a swoon at the end of every scene? Lord, what would the young maiden have done if Lord Oberlon visited her as he had Melissande the previous night? Melissande grunted. The stupid chit would have probably screamed her head off and removed herself to a convent. But still, she thought, torn somewhere between envy and cynicism, the dashing hero appeared to cherish the heroine all the more for her frailty and feminine weakness. He appeared to adore her lack of guts. In a moment of pique, she flicked her finger against the thin volume and sent it spinning to the carpet. She wasn't at all certain that she had any desire to be so cherished, but still it might be nice to be offered the choice.

She rose from the settee and stretched lazily. Her house was beautifully furnished, and she had, after all, most of what she desired. When Jenny, her maid, tapped on the small drawing-room door, her lips were pursed in deep concentration, her uppermost thought being how she could bring the marquess around to the idea that she would look most charming driving her own phaeton and pair in the park.

"There are two gentlemen here to see you, Madam," Jenny said, so surprised she'd forgotten to curtsy. "His grace isn't with them. Whatever shall we do, Madam? This has never happened before."

"How very nicely peculiar," Melissande said. She looked at her image in the mirror above the mantelpiece. Boredom slipped from her shoulders and she felt a tingle of excitement. Someone to visit her besides Lord Oberlon. It couldn't be bill collectors. Lord Oberlon was generous. Men, she thought. No—gentlemen—a very different stripe of man. She felt like singing. "Don't just stand there like a gutless heroine, Jenny, do show the gentlemen in. Oh, Jenny, your bosom is sticking out. Bow your shoulders a bit. Yes, that's good."

Chapter Fifteen

"Lord Harry Monteith and Mr. Thayerton Scuddimore, Madam," Jenny said, trying to sound important as a butler in a grand house.

Melissande's first thought upon the entrance of the gentlemen was that the infantry had just invaded her house. Why, they were but boys. She frowned ever so slightly before advancing toward her unexpected and uninvited guests.

Hetty was very aware of Melissande's initial response, but wasn't at all surprised or disturbed by it. Of course she and Scuddy presented a far less prepossessing image than the older, more experienced Marquess of Oberlon and any of his rakehell friends. Well, I can but try, she thought. She halted in her tracks and stood poised in rapt wonder, causing Mr. Scuddimore to bump into her.

"You're much more beautiful than I could have imagined." She breathed deeply, and hopefully, reverently. Then, as if gathering her scattered wits, she coughed in mild embarrassment. "Oh dear, do forgive our intrusion, ma'am, but both Mr. Scuddimore and I have worshiped you for many weeks now, always from afar. To be allowed to see you, to be in your divine presence but a moment—it is all a man could desire, it is beyond what most men ever gain, it is the very elixir of pleasure." She thought she'd puke if she didn't stop, so she did.

Melissande wondered fleetingly if she had just stepped into the pages of her discarded novel. Though she had thought the hero rather asinine in his high-flown phrases to that silly fragile heroine, she wondered if she hadn't been too abrupt in forming her opinion. She gave the young gentleman a dazzling smile and said, voice as sweet and encouraging as a virgin's with her beau, "Fie on you, sir, such flattery, but it's quite nice, I won't scold you for it. Now, who are you?"

"Lord Monteith, ma'am, Lord Harry Monteith. And this is my friend, Mr. Scuddimore." Hetty stepped forward, as if propelled by a powerful unknown force, and reverently clasped Melissande's white hand. She turned it over and planted a mothlight kiss on her palm. "It's beauty such as yours, ma'am, that launched the ships to Troy."

Melissande arched a perfect brow, and Hetty rushed on, "No, it is too paltry to compare you to Helen. I should be flayed for my smallness of imagination. Ah, yes, you are Aphrodite emerged from the ancient myths to cleanse the jaded palates of Englishmen." I will surely puke, she thought, and smiled.

Although such names as Helen and Aphrodite meant very little to Melissande, she was, nonetheless, able to deduce from Lord Monteith's passionate tone that he was paying her high tribute indeed. None of the gentlemen she had ever known had compared her to an ancient myth. She smiled an enticing woman's smile, and with an effort, turned her attention briefly to the plump gentleman—were those indeed cabbage roses on his waistcoat?—at Lord Monteith's elbow. "Mr. Scuddimore," she said only, one glance at his flushed countenance assuring her that dazzling compliments to her incomparable beauty would not be coming from his quarter.

"Yes, ma'am, but you may call me Scuddy. Everyone does, you see, even my parents."

Melissande smiled and motioned for them to be seated. She ordered the staring Jenny to bring sherry for the gentlemen. She wanted gin, but knew it wouldn't be wise of her to drink such a thing, not in front of gentlemen, not in front of this lovely young lad who had honey flowing from his tongue.

Melissande turned willingly back to Lord Harry, and was taken aback to see him gazing with a frown on his fair forehead about the small drawing room.

"My lord?" she asked. She felt a twinge of disappointment that he hadn't continued in his praise of her person.

Hetty turned readily back to Melissande. She'd seen the novel lying upon the carpet and had made out its title—a dripping, maudlin story. She smiled and said, "Oh, my dear ma'am, do forgive my wandering wits. It's just that your parlor—lovely though it may be—doesn't adequately reflect the loveliness of the person in its midst. It's a palace you require, beautiful lady, with silken draperies and mirrors to cast your image to every corner. I would have a lutist to play for you whenever your heart desired it. I would have a minstrel sing to you of your loveliness and your goodness. I would feed you the finest of delicacies. Perhaps escargots from the finest French gardens, well cleaned and cooked, of course. One wouldn't want to take a chance with your precious health."

Had she gone too far? To her relief, Melissande sighed and seated herself in a graceful, languishing pose, and patted the chair beside her. Hetty cast a quick glance at Mr. Scuddimore, saw that his eyes were glazed in bewilderment, and said under her breath, "Come, Scuddy, sit down."

"Nice house you have, ma'am," Scuddy said. "I agree with Lord Harry. The draperies and furnishings are very nice. Er, maybe they're not nice enough for you, but I'd take them, in a flash."

"Thank you, Mr. Scuddimore. Ah, here is your sherry. Do allow me to pour for you, my lord."

Hetty accepted the crystal goblet, her eyes never leaving Melissande's face. "A toast to your eternal beauty, Aphrodite. But I am wrong. You're a goddess in your own right. Aphrodite, bah. No, you're now the goddess Melissande, goddess of beauty and grace." She allowed the goblet to tremble ever so slightly in her hand, then raised it to her lips and sipped. She lowered the glass and gazed soulfully into the deep rich sherry. Her voice was intense with adoration. "But look at the depths of the color, ma'am, it glistens and glimmers with the lights of your hair. I beg you will forgive and understand my poor mutterings, dear Melissande, but these moments in your exquisite presence turn my very thoughts into water."

Melissande made haste to reassure her slave.

"Oh no, my lord, your words are quite gratifying. Improvement would be nice, but you do well. It isn't often that a gentleman such as yourself is so forthright and honest in his speech to me."

It was fortunate that Hetty wasn't sipping her sherry, for she would most assuredly have choked.

So, my dear marquess, she thought gleefully, you don't cozen your mistress with charming flattery. She is starving for it. A mistake, your grace. Now a woman will show you the way to your mistress's heart.

"Beauty must always inspire truth, Melissande. Your face is the eternal food for gods, the gentleness of your person is the inspiration of the poets. Ah, dare I go on? No, I think not."

Melissande was on the verge of placing herself in the slippers of the frail, weak heroine. For a brief moment, she even felt as though she could swoon in the most helpless fashion if this worshipful youth continued. If she swooned, she wondered if he would be strong enough to hold her. She controlled these fancies, and said, "Do tell me, Lord Monteith, you said you have viewed me from afar. Where, sir, was that? You see," she added on a small sigh, "I'm not often out in company nowadays."

"That is infamous. Dear ma'am, I cannot believe such a thing."

Melissande lowered her vivid green eyes demurely and fingered the silken folds of her peignoir. "His grace, the Marquess of Oberlon, doesn't care for the entertainment one enjoys at the theater or say, Vauxhall Gardens. At least not often. I must practically beg him."

Scuddy leapt up, looking like a fox suddenly cornered by the hounds. "The Marquess of Oberlon? Oh my God. Oh goodness. Oh, Lord Harry, say it isn't so. We'll be dead by morning." Several drops of sherry splashed on Mr. Scuddimore's red cabbage roses. He sputtered to regain his breath.

Hetty said easily, "Didn't I tell you that our gracious hostess is a close acquaintance of Lord Oberlon, Scuddy? Well, no matter. Do sit down, Scuddy, and control yourself." She chose to ignore the horror on Mr. Scuddimore's face and turned quickly back to Melissande. "How very odd, to be sure. Why, Mr. Scuddimore and I often see his grace at White's and, of course, riding in the park. But that, indeed, isn't my concern, is it? Do forgive me, Melissande. You asked where we had drunk in your ethereal beauty, it was two weeks ago, at Drury Lane." Pleased with herself for sowing seeds of discontent, Hetty willingly turned the topic. From the corner of her eye, she saw that Mr. Scuddimore wore a hunted look. He looked ready to write his will. She would tell him later that since he didn't have all that many worldly goods to leave, he didn't have to bother with a will.

Hetty was gratified to her toes when Melissande said suddenly, a warm glow in her eyes, "I believe I do remember remarking on you, my lord. Weren't you seated in the pit, looking up at his grace's box? Didn't you smile at me? Ah, yes, I remember your smile, so very adoring."

"Oh yes, adoring is just what I feel whenever I look at you, Melissande. I'm honored you remember me, for there were so many gentlemen vying to catch your eye, all of them adoring." Hetty looked up at the ormolu clock on the mantel. Goodness, they had to leave. There was no way of knowing if Lord Oberlon would come tonight after he'd left Jack and Louisa. She quickly rose, Scuddy, scared to his toes, followed suit. Hetty managed to look chagrined and guilty and charming, a look that Millie had evaluated for her many times. "It was wrong of me to seek you out, Melissande, very wrong of me, yet I couldn't help myself. Cupid's arrow has pierced my breast. I know his grace—such a proud, disdainful man—wouldn't be gratified if he discovered that one of your many adoring admirers had visited you unattended —" Hetty let her voice trail off in meaningful silence, praying silently.

Melissande was much touched, more by Lord Monteith's declared admiration of her person than by his concern over the marquess. She gazed at him under her lashes. He was much too young for her, admittedly, yet he was so much like the hero from her novel. She was far too experienced to believe that she would ever live under his protection, but she could see no harm in a light flirtation. She thought speculatively about Lord Oberlon. Perhaps just such a flirtation with a gentleman some years his junior would make him realize her value. Maybe, she thought, he would purchase her the phaeton and pair to keep her delicious person all to himself.

"Don't concern yourself about Lord Oberlon. You've committed no impertinence, my lord, by visiting me." She rose and laid her hand lightly on Lord Harry's sleeve. "What is your direction, my lord, so that I may send word to you when the opportunity presents itself? I do love to ride in the park," she added on a small sigh, a gutless sigh that that damned heroine would make. She even managed to wilt just a bit, but not enough to lose the impact of her cleavage.

Once Lord Harry's direction was written down in a thin white book, Hetty clasped Melissande's hand once again and brought it to her lips. "*Au revoir,* my goddess," she said. Melissande's flesh was warm and soft. Hetty felt distinctly odd, kissing another woman's hand.

No sooner had the front door closed behind them than Mr. Scuddimore nearly tripped over his tongue with outrage. "Damn you, Lord Harry. Have you taken leave of your senses? That *lady* is under the protection of the Marquess of Oberlon. His grace, the Marquess of Oberlon. Jason Cavander. Good God, he would slit your throat without a second thought if he found out. Are you lost to all reason? By God, after your argument with the marquess at White's—" Mr. Scuddimore drew to a sudden halt, his brain having finally leaped to an obvious conclusion. "You're doing this on purpose," he said slowly. "You planned it. All that damned flattery to that empty-headed woman, all that praising of her eyebrows, all that silly mythology, all of it was a lie. You want to provoke the marquess. You want to enrage him, you want—What do you want him to do, Lord Harry?"

Hetty poked him in the arm. She laughed. "Scuddy, you've misread the entire situation. I find Melissande lovely. I told you and Sir Harry that I don't like to be bored. Melissande pleases my eye. So what if the Marquess of Oberlon is currently her protector? Things change. Who knows?"

"You're being blind, Lord Harry. Unlike you, I wish to reach my thirtieth birthday. Powerful man, the marquess, powerful and ruthless. Not one to cross, that's for sure. Ask anyone, he's one of the best swordsmen in England. Come, Lord Harry, what is this all about?"

But Hetty only smiled and shook her head. "I just find his mistress lovely and to my liking," was all she would say.

"No good will come of this, you'll see."

"Don't fail me now, Scuddy. Now, I need a mare to escort the fair Melissande to the park. You will oblige me?"

Mr. Scuddimore drew up, mouth agape. He nodded his head from habit.

"Excellent. My thanks, Scuddy, and stop your worrying. All will be fine. Now, the mare has to be a bit showy—perhaps white so Melissande can quite think of herself as a fairy princess. Yes, she would like that. Now, let me see, I think an emerald green velvet riding habit, with a dashing plumed hat, of course, would be just the thing to set off her beauty. Well, don't stand there, Scuddy, it grows late, and I, for one, have much to do tomorrow. Don't forget, a showy mare."

Chapter Sixteen

Sir John didn't waste any time. He yelled at his sister across the breakfast table, "Just where the devil were you, Miss? Damnation, it's bad enough that Lord Oberlon knew you refused to be in the same house with him, but to boot, you stay out until all hours then sneak in the servants' entrance. Damn it, Hetty, I won't have it."

She tried not to smile, but she could just picture herself telling her giant of a brother that she'd been visiting with Jason Cavander's mistress, tell him that she'd insulted his grace in his own club, but that hadn't done any good, so what was poor Lord Harry to do?

"I won't have you grinning at me, damn you." He pounded a fist onto the table, making the eggs jump. "Where were you? What were you doing?"

Louisa gently laid her hand over her husband's. "It was awkward, my love. Unfortunately I made the situation worse. When Jason Cavander asked me where you were, I told him you were at Covent Garden."

"Good God, Louisa—Covent Garden. That's too much. Goodness, no lady of any breeding would attend Covent Garden this week."

"I wonder if you have any breeding," Sir John

said. "Stop dodging the issue. Where were you last night?"

Well, a lie it must be, Hetty thought as she gazed at her brother's implacable face. "If you must throw such a tantrum about it, Jack, I'll be glad to tell you. I wasn't at Covent Garden but rather at Vauxhall Gardens. Lou got half of it right. Now, no more. I'm not a child and I shall do exactly as I like. Leave me be. Let's talk about Paris."

"By God, I feel pity for the poor mortal man who has the taming of you."

Hetty unwisely said, "You wretched men. Why must you always think that if a woman shows any spirit at all she has to be tamed? Tamed? Like some sort of bloody animal. I had hoped that being married to Louisa would have given you more sense."

"Hetty, Jack has sense, truly he does."

"Not from what I see. You, Sir John, may be a domestic tyrant in Herefordshire, but here you have no authority at all. In short, dear Jack, I shall do exactly as I please, and with no interference from you. Now, finish your breakfast."

Sir John's fork clattered to his plate, this time sending his scrambled eggs plopping to the tablecloth. Before Hetty could draw another breath, he jerked her from her chair, clasped her about the waist, and lifted her above his head. He shook her until her teeth rattled.

"Jack dearest," Louisa said, tugging on his sleeve, "you must remember that you're just a wee bit larger than Hetty."

But Hetty wasn't the least bit afraid of Sir John's attack. As he swung her above his head, she remembered times long ago when her giant of a brother would gleefully toss her about. "Oh, Jack," she said between gasps of laughter, "you're such a bully. I do love you so."

He shook her once more, then lowered her to her feet. Slowly, he drew her against his chest.

Hetty snuggled her face against his shoulder and said, her voice breaking, "How I wish Damien were here. God, I miss him so much. Every day and I still miss him. I can't bear it sometimes." She burst into tears.

Sir John's eyes met his wife's above Hetty's head. She nodded silently and slipped quietly from the breakfast room.

He gently stroked his sister's soft fair curls, momentarily bereft of speech. It was several moments before he said softly, "I know, Hetty, I know. Damien was a part of me too. I miss laughing with him, hell, yelling at him. He was the finest of brothers."

Hetty raised her tear-streaked face. "I'm sorry, Jack, for being so selfish. Of course you feel his death as strongly as I do." She pulled herself suddenly from his arms and whirled about, pounding her fist upon the table. "It's so damned unfair."

She managed to gain control. "Forgive me again. I've upset you quite enough. Please, Jack, don't worry about me. I go along quite well, really."

Sir John sighed and patted her on the shoulder. "I suppose you do, Hetty. It's just that Sir Archibald takes no notice of you and I do worry. So does Louisa. You're so damned young."

"Father is Father, Jack, and will never change. I am quite used to his ways, and, indeed, wish him to be no other way. He doesn't interfere with my activities, you know."

"Does that mean you still refuse to tell me why you didn't wish to see Jason Cavander?"

For one long instant, Hetty wanted to pour out the truth to her brother, to tell him that Jason Cavander was no friend. She thought of the letter, safely locked in her dresser drawer, Elizabeth's heartrending farewell to Damien. She shook her head, her tongue still. No, revenge was hers—and Lord Harry's. She realized that were she to tell him, and were he to believe her, the outcome could be disastrous. Jack was all the family she cared about, Sir Archibald being of little influence in her life. Were he to die in a duel, she would be alone. As would Louisa, little John, and the small unborn infant in Louisa's womb. Yet, she couldn't bring herself to lie outright to her brother.

"Please, Jack, don't demand that I give you an answer. Suffice it to say that I loathe the Marquess of Oberlon. My reasons must remain my own."

Sir John, his little sister's defender, said, "He didn't insult you, did he, Hetty?"

"No, he's in no way offended Henrietta Rolland."

"Good. It's unimaginable, but still, I wish you'd talk to me, Hetty."

"No, Jack, leave it be."

He did then, saying as he took his leave of her, "Louisa wants to visit Richmond, a picnic, you know, and a visit to the maze. And tonight there is a masked ball at Ranleagh House. Lou told me she wants to recapture some of her wild youth before turning stout and matronly. You're not promised to something tonight, are you? You will join us, won't you, Hetty?"

A masked ball. She could act herself, without fear of discovery. "A masked ball, as in really masked?"

"Yes, you can cover yourself from toe to ear, if you like."

"Ah, I should love that. I do wonder what Louisa's going to wear."

He watched her skip from the breakfast room, an eighteen-year-old girl. It had frightened him, that controlled anger, that too-old look on her face when she'd spoken of Jason Cavander. He remembered he'd also asked Jason the previous evening if he planned to attend. His grace's reply had been quick, a wicked smile on his face. "I had planned to, Jack. Melissande would much enjoy herself. I don't suppose your sister will be there? The one who dislikes me? The one I've never met?" Sir John had nodded, hopeful that Hetty would agree.

And now she had. Hopefully, he would discover this evening just why his little sister held one of his best friends in such dislike. He thought if Jason were to come close to Hetty, she might discover he wasn't a bad sort after all. Since it was a masked ball, she could easily escape him if she really disliked him. As he strolled to Sir Archibald's library to bid his sire a good morning, he grinned, wondering just how the devil his very experienced friend was going to react coming face to face with his sister.

While Sir John and Lady Louisa explored the maze at Richmond, Lord Harry trained his eyes on the circular targets set at twenty paces from the marking line at Manton's and stroked the trigger. A shout went up from Sir Harry.

"Bravo, Lord Harry, yet another bull's-eye. At twenty paces, too."

Mr. Franks, the gruff, excellent attendant at Manton's, added his praise. "An excellent marksman, ye be, my lord. Now, Sir Harry, ye see the way his lordship caresses the trigger, his eyes never leaving the target? Ye mustn't be in a hurry, Sir Harry, no sir, never be in a hurry. Not with a lady, nor with a gun."

Sir Harry grunted. "Well, I for one have had enough practice for one day. What say you, Lord Harry, I am off to Gentleman Jackson's. You've never joined me, you know. Let us see if you're as fine in the ring with your fists as you are at caressing triggers."

Hetty handed the pistol to Mr. Franks before replying, "Harry, I've told you countless times that you could dash me down in but a moment in the ring. No, I thank you, but I've no taste or ability to embroil myself with fists. Besides, I have my fencing lesson in but an hour with Signore Bertioli."

Appeased by Lord Harry's frank admission of his superior skill at boxing, Sir Harry said, "Does the Italian think you've improved?"

"I think he's from Sardinia, not Italy. Yes, he's forever giving me encouragement, but I confess I believe his sense of diplomacy is stronger than his honesty." Hetty didn't add that Signore Bertioli had ceased several weeks ago to concern himself about her lack of endurance. All their time together was spent in practicing his master's techniques—delicate feints, subtle flicks of the wrist that could catch an opponent off guard.

"It isn't a matter of life or death," Sir Harry said. A queer gleam shone an instant in Lord Harry's blue eyes, then disappeared.

Sir Harry said, eyeing his friend with suspicion, "Look here, now, Lord Harry, you aren't thinking of a duel, are you? It isn't done. It isn't smart. My brother-in-law would have my innards for breakfast if I got involved in a duel." Then he thought of the Marquess of Oberlon and the outlandish story he had heard just this morning from Mr. Scuddimore of their visit to Melissande's house the previous evening. He blanched.

"Of course not, Harry." She turned quickly from his inquiring gaze and allowed an assistant to help her into her greatcoat. With the knowledge that Jack and Louisa were leaving on the morrow, she said over her shoulder, "Why do you and Scuddy not come to my lodgings tomorrow evening? I promise you a substantial dinner, an excellent claret, and a sound thrashing at cards."

"Sorry, but I've other plans for tomorrow night."

"Does the fair Isabella Bentworth play a part in them?"

"No, she doesn't, but it's none of your business anyway. I almost forgot. My sister, Kate St. Clair, wants both of us to come to dinner tonight."

"I'd like to, Harry, but I can't. I promised I'd go to the masked ball at Ranleagh House."

"Which one of you charming ladies is my Louisa?"

"My dear John, it's obvious," Sir Archibald said seriously, "Little Hetty is half a head taller than Louisa."

"Right you are, Father. The short, plump one it is."

"Louisa, hit him, he's abominable." Hetty was laughing, her eyes twinkling from behind the slits in her red mask.

"He'll be sorry, Hetty. I intend to dance him into the ground this evening. You know these oversized men, no endurance. He'll be begging for mercy. I think I just might try dancing on his big feet."

"And I'll be there to see it," Hetty said. Then she thought: Endurance. Louisa knows nothing at all about endurance. Her arm still aching from the hour she had spent with Signore Bertioli.

"Father, we're off. Have a pleasant evening."

"Grimpston told me he's off to Lord Melberry's house," Hetty said to her brother as she seated herself in their coach.

"Those damned and dratted Whigs again, no doubt," Jack said. "Move over, Hetty, I've got long legs. Lou, you're grinning and I don't trust it. What are you thinking about? No, don't answer. You're going to tell Hetty how I found our way out of the maze."

"Actually, I was thinking about your begging me to let you rest after your sixth dance."

Hetty sat back, thinking of the evening ahead of her. Although Jack, in that big brother way of his, had demanded that Hetty stay close to him, parroting nonsense about there being too much license granted at a masked ball, she had no intention of doing so. The red mask gave her anonymity. Staying by Sir John, whose size and deep voice would be recognizable to even a slight acquaintance, she would be instantly known. She had every intention of thoroughly enjoying herself, and that meant keeping the dowdy Miss Henrietta Rolland as well as Lord Harry well in the shadows.

Her excitement mounted as the carriage pulled off the main road onto a long, circular graveled drive in front of Ranleagh House. It was a mammoth three-story building that sprawled atop a slight hill. Scores of lighted candles sparkled from every window, making it appear more a huge diamond, aglow against the backdrop of the black night. A seemingly endless line of carriages lined the drive, and it was with some difficulty that John coachman maneuvered around them to deposit Sir John, Louisa, and Hetty at the front stone steps.

They were met inside the front doors by a deeply bowing butler and three footmen, who deftly removed their cloaks. The laughter coming from the great ballroom down the corridor mixed with the strains of a fast German waltz made Hetty laugh aloud with anticipation. "Come, Jack, Louisa, don't wait all night," she said over her shoulder as she picked up her skirts and moved swiftly after the butler.

She paused for a moment at the entrance of the grand ballroom, taking in the imaginative decorations. Yards upon yards of red and white satin had been gathered at the ceiling and dipped down like countless sultan's tents over the heads of the guests. Huge urns filled with every imaginable flower graced each corner, their sweet scent filling the room. There must not be a bloom left in the Ranleagh greenhouse, she thought, turning her attention to the magnificently arrayed guests. She laughed aloud her excitement as a gallant Robin Hood clad in forest green bowed low in front of her and offered his arm. Without a moment's hesitation, she turned from Sir John and Lady Louisa, smiling at her brother over her shoulder, and whirled away with her partner into the throng of guests.

Sir John raised his hand to stop her. "Don't you dare, Jack," his wife said. "Let her enjoy herself. No harm can come to her here, and, you must admit, it has been too long a time since Hetty has showed such pleasure." She clasped her husband's hand. "As for you, my lord, it's time to prove your mettle. I've been thinking what I'll give you for a reward if you manage to dance every dance I wish you to."

No sooner had Hetty's Robin Hood left her than she found herself locked in the arms of an English knight. After several more waltzes and a score of country dances, Hetty's feet felt as though she had danced with every gentleman in the room. Ah, but here was a Greek God. When she asked him if he was Zeus, he said in a very low voice that he was Bacchus and he fancied he could already taste the sweet wine on her lips, perhaps taste it other places as well, if she were willing.

Hetty pictured wine in her shoe. She laughed and laughed, pushing him away, and he went after easier game. At the end of another lively country dance, Hetty was shocked to hear her partner, a rather paunchy gentleman dressed as Louis XIV, say between heaving breaths that it was near to midnight.

"Midnight? But the ball just began. Surely you must be mistaken."

"The time has flown by in your exquisite company, my Scarlet Queen," he said. Hetty didn't like his tone. It sounded husky and too low, just as Bacchus's had sounded. She looked pointedly at his face and thought his eyes overly bright behind the white satin mask. So he'd had a bit too much of the champagne punch. The poor fellow wasn't the least bit dangerous. She smiled. "I must leave your majesty now, for there are so many of your subjects awaiting the pleasure of your company." She thought her parting line nicely diplomatic, and was thus utterly chagrined when the gentleman didn't release her hand. "A king has but to command, my Scarlet Queen, and his wishes are fulfilled. You're heated, my dear. May I suggest a stroll on the balcony? I have a fancy to see those white shoulders of yours, mayhap even uncover your breasts. You've not birthed a child yet, have you?"

Hetty gave him a disgusted look. How many gentlemen had she seen like this at White's? But now she was a female and thus prey to him. She forgot charm and fell back on common sense. "A masquerade this may be, sir, but you are still a gentleman. I expect you to behave as one. Now, excuse me. I'm returning to my brother."

The gentleman had other ideas. He laid his palm gently against her cheek. "No, my little innocent, I don't want you to go just yet. I've watched you flirt outrageously with many gentlemen this evening. Now it's my turn. As to your having a brother— I don't believe that for a minute. Tell me, who's your protector?"

Just because she was a female she had to put up with this nonsense. If she'd had her pistol, she'd shoot him. She just looked at him with disgust, saying low, "You're a bore, sir. I've enjoyed the evening until now. I've had fun. I haven't flirted. If you are too stupid to know the difference then I suggest you return to your nanny so she can teach you. Perhaps she can also instruct you in good manners."

He clutched her all the tighter.

"I really suggest you let me go or I promise you I will hurt you badly."

"Hurt me? *You* hurt *me*? Ha, that's funny, my girl. Come now, no need to play coy with me. I'll see you continue to enjoy yourself. Why, please me and I just might consider setting you up."

Chapter Seventeen

"I believe the lady is tired of your company, Your Majesty. Why don't you take yourself off and take a little nap behind that palm tree over there. The music is loud enough so that no one will hear your snores."

Hetty whirled about to see a tall man in a black domino and mask standing close behind her.

Louis XIV turned glittering eyes to the intruder. "I don't know who you are, probably one of those gamblers who sneak into such functions as this. It doesn't matter. You can't have her until I am done with her."

"What if I told you I was the lady's protector?"

If Hetty had had her pistol, she would have shot this man between his eyes.

"Pah, she doesn't have a protector, at least not yet. I just might offer, if she pleases me enough. Go away now. She's mine."

"I do wonder what lies beneath that white peruke," the black domino continued in the same cold officious voice. "No doubt it covers an empty and foolish head. Leave go of the lady now, else I shall personally tip you over the balcony into the lovely fish pond just below."

Louis XIV's hand loosened slightly on Hetty's

wrist, and in his moment of uncertainty, she wrenched her hand away and moved back toward the black domino. Her anger with the man was now turning to amusement. She just shook her head at him. "Sir, this scene is becoming boring, indeed it is past boring. Please, just go now. Doubtless you will find a lady who has imbibed enough punch to find you quite acceptable. However, I do not."

"Then I'll give you all the punch you will need," Louis XIV said eagerly.

"It would take two casks before you would be acceptable to me," she said, and rolled her eyes when he looked thoughtful. "Three casks, at least," she added. She knew the man in the domino was grinning like a sinner. Louis XIV said to her rather than to the man, "Three casks? You aren't worth it. You're probably very young. I won't be your protector. I don't want you. This damned wastrel can have you."

"Why, thank you, Your Majesty."

Hetty watched her erstwhile partner turn drunkenly and disappear into the crowd.

She turned and smiled up into the face of her rescuer. "You have wit and a sense of fun. The poor man is just too drunk to mind his manners. But now he is gone."

"You don't act at all like a damsel in distress."

"Well no, why should I? He was just a man like any other man. I'm glad I didn't have to hurt him."

"Could you tell me exactly how you would have hurt him? I have never before met a young lady so confident in herself. It is refreshing. Actually, I'm pleased you weren't a real damsel in distress. It might have become tedious."

"Ah, I'm pleased I didn't bore you."

"Oh, not at all. As a matter of fact, I think you begin to fascinate me. Tell me, what would you have done to our poor drunken Louis?"

There was something vaguely familiar in the black domino's voice, in his tone, and teasing deep laughter that stirred just out of reach in her memory. Suddenly, she wasn't quite certain that her rescuer was any less dangerous than the Louis XIV. She sensed that he was pushing her to be outrageous. Behind the anonymity of her mask and domino, she willingly obliged him. Why not? She would never see him again, indeed, she would never see him at all. She was quite safe to do and say anything she wanted to. "Why, sir, I dare say I would have kicked him below his yellow waistcoat. If he'd been too drunk to feel that, then I wouldn't have been in any trouble at all, would I? Now, sir, that you have amused yourself at my expense, I believe I shall go search out some amusement for myself."

She saw his dark eyes flash suddenly, but his deep voice still held laughter as he said, "What an unusual young lady you are. Do you wish to leave my company because I interfered with your fun, or is it because you fear that my intentions may be as low as those of our departed Louis XIV?"

"Your intentions can scrape the floor for all I care, sir. I really don't care. And I'm not afraid of you."

"That's excellent. A wilting lady would be too much to bear. I dearly love to waltz. Surely you would not refuse to dance with the poor mortal who mistakenly thought to be chivalrous?"

"You're unscrupulous. You're also using wit rather than brawn. I shall reward you. Lead on."

Hetty placed her hand in the crook of the black

domino's arm and allowed him to lead her onto the dance floor.

He slipped his hand lightly down about her waist and drew her into the circle of his arms. She responded readily to his lead and soon found herself being whirled in large, sweeping circles about the room. He quickened their pace suddenly, and she laughed aloud in excitement, tightening her hold on the black domino's shoulder.

He lowered his head slightly and whispered in her ear, "Ah, a sign of affection? Or is it that you fear I shall drop you?"

"Please don't flirt with me," she said, leaning back to look up at his face, still maddeningly hidden by the black mask. "This is such fun. Don't bother me with all that nonsense. Now, sir, please mind your steps, you very nearly stepped on my toes."

He threw back his head and laughed aloud. His teeth were strong and white, his throat tanned. She very much liked that laugh of his. Who the devil was he?

She gave him a guileless smile. "There, you see? Making love is a bore, particularly when you're dancing and having such fun."

"So you don't think lovemaking is fun?"

"I haven't the foggiest notion," she said and he tightened his hand ever so slightly about her waist.

Hetty chose to ignore it. He was a man. Men, in her short but pungent experience, were strange creatures. Sex seemed to be the primary thing on their minds. And the secondary thing, too. When the music came to a halt, she was disappointed. "Oh dear," she said. "The dance is over already? You're quite good, but I'm sure all the ladies tell you that."

She saw him raise his hand in some sort of signal to the musicians. In but an instant, another waltz was struck up.

She laughed. "Well done, sir, well done." Without any thought as to the complexities of propriety, she laid her hand on his shoulder.

It was several breathless moments before the black domino slowed their pace. He looked down into the upturned smiling face and said in a thoughtful voice, "Your Louis XIV was a stupid fellow indeed to believe you experienced in dalliance. Rather, I would say that you are a young lady enjoying her first ball."

He was right, damn him, but had she been so obvious? Surely not. She wouldn't let him fluster her. "I know why you said that. You think I'm inexperienced just because I don't want you flirting with me. That's it, isn't it? Just a male's conceit." She grinned up at him shamelessly.

"I wonder," he said, "if you would goad me so much if we were to remove your mask?"

"Touch my mask and I'll make you very sorry."

"As sorry as you would have made Louis XIV?"

"You don't deserve that. Something milder." She stepped on his toes.

He winced, but said nothing more. He whirled her about in a wide circle. When he came to a halt, he landed adroitly upon her foot.

"Ouch!" She jumped, crying out more in surprise than in pain.

"Men are sometimes clumsy. I do apologize. Perhaps if your feet weren't quite so big, I wouldn't have succumbed to the temptation."

She wanted to hit him and she wanted, oddly, to

laugh, just to have him join in with her. His laugh
was lovely.

"Shall I return you to your brother?"

All her fun dissolved in that instant. "You know
my brother?"

"Certainly I do, Miss Rolland."

At that moment, Hetty wanted to murder Jack.
What was he doing anyway—telling all his friends
that his sister was in the scarlet domino and mask,
and in need of partners? She backed away from him,
turned abruptly, and slipped into a throng of guests
before he could stop her.

She heard the black domino calling her name.
She ignored him, wanting now to find Jack and hit
him over the head with a potted palm. Damn him.
Her enjoyment of her first ball was fading rapidly.
The black domino knew who she was. Others might
know also. Her voice couldn't be that different from
the dowdy Miss Henrietta Rolland's voice or, for
that matter, Lord Harry's.

A high, trilling laugh drew her up short at the
perimeter of a boisterously gay group of gentlemen.
In their midst stood Melissande, her lustrous red hair
piled high upon her head and a daring expanse of
white bosom revealed by the extreme low cut of her
green velvet gown. She looked utterly delicious. Hetty
felt her heart start to thump fast and hard. If Melissande was here, then Lord Oberlon was here, too. She
scanned the knot of gentlemen but didn't see him.

She wanted nothing but to leave. Where were
Jack and Louisa? She walked toward the edge of
the crowded ballroom, hoping to position herself
where she would see them. She slipped behind a
huge potted fern to avoid an amorous-looking fel-

low, too deep in his cups, she thought, not to make a scene were she to refuse to dance with him. Wretched men. Lord Harry wouldn't have to put up with such nonsense. She nearly laughed at that.

She suddenly saw Jack, leaning negligently against a curtained wall, in laughing conversation with another man. She stepped forward, then froze in her tracks. It was the black domino.

She ducked quickly behind the potted fern again. She simply couldn't approach Jack while that man was there. For that matter, she couldn't very well hide behind this ridiculous plant for the rest of the evening. What she needed was a very good excuse to remove herself from the ballroom. Her young lady's repertoire wasn't very impressive. She leaned down and gave a vicious tug on her domino, but the velvet was too strong for her fingers. She raised it to her mouth and bit into the hem with her white teeth. She felt it obligingly rip, and without thought to the beauty of the garment, pulled it away in a jagged circular tear. There, she thought with satisfaction, that should keep me from the dance floor for the remainder of the evening. She soon found Louisa conversing with Lady Ranleagh herself, and slipped quietly beside her.

"Louisa, I've ruined my domino and must go see to repairs."

"My dear child," Lady Ranleagh said, leaning over to inspect the gaping tear. "It looks like your partner was a clumsy oaf. Such a pity."

Hetty fervently agreed. Then, as she'd hoped, Lady Ranleagh directed her to a large dressing room at the top of the stairs, where, she was informed, Lady Ranleagh's maid, Celeste, would mend her costume. Louisa prepared to accompany her, but Hetty, having no wish for Louisa to see her dally away the rest of the evening, said, "Oh no, Louisa, I'll be fine. A stupid accident and it was my fault, not a gentleman's. Go dance with Jack. He looked too relaxed and rested."

She'd nearly made good her escape when she heard Jack's deep, booming voice behind her. "Hetty, wait a moment. Where are you off to, little sister?"

She turned reluctantly, fearing to see the black domino with her brother, but Jack was alone. "I just tore my domino. I'll see you later, Jack. I have a few words I have to say to you, you interfering sod."

"It's probably just as well you take yourself out of commission for a while." He grinned, took off his mask and rubbed his cheek. "You've got so many young bucks trailing after you, the ladies are beginning to plan your murder."

She wanted to tell him to go take a good look at Melissande, but she managed to keep quiet.

"Go dance with Louisa," she said, turned and set her foot upon the wide staircase. "Oh, Jack," she said, turning, "who is that gentleman you were talking to in the black domino and black mask? The tall man with a very nice laugh?"

Jack gave a bark of laughter and gazed at her, a deep twinkle in his blue eyes. "I believe you must have enjoyed the fellow's company, Hetty. Didn't you waltz with him twice?"

"When he wasn't laughing, which was nice, he was rude and arrogant, and quite amusing. Still, I didn't like him."

"Well, Hetty, I did put a word in the fellow's

ear—you know, to stay clear of you—but he is always one to tempt the fates."

"You told him who I was. That wasn't fair of you, Jack, damn you. Now, who is he?"

Sir John lifted a fair eyebrow and said in a voice so bland she wanted to scream, "He's none other than your arch enemy, Hetty, the Marquess of Oberlon." He turned about and waved to her impishly over his shoulder. His booming laughter rang in her ears.

Hetty clutched at the banister, staring after her laughing brother. No wonder the man's voice had sounded so familiar to her. She forced herself to draw a deep breath. Obviously, his grace hadn't recognized her. If he had, everything would have been lost. Thank the heavens for something. She would kill Jack, however.

"Had you continued to dance with me, Miss Rolland, I'm sure your domino wouldn't now be in tatters."

Hetty whirled about and very nearly tripped on her skirt at the sound of that shiftless drawl. The marquess stood but a few feet lower than her on the stairs. He was looking up at her, grinning widely.

"You." There was nothing she could say. He might recognize her voice. She hated it, but she had no choice. She gathered up her skirts and fled up the stairs.

"An arrogant and rude man, I grant you, Miss Rolland," he called after her. "But you quite like my laugh and find me amusing? You are a discerning young lady." Rich, deep humor sounded in his voice. Without looking at him, she knew he was grinning like a gambler in a roomful of vicars.

Chapter Eighteen

Lord Harry rose to kick a log in the fireplace with the toe of his boot, sending crackling embers up toward the flue.

A knock sounded on the door. Lord Harry didn't care who was there and didn't bother looking up.

Pottson said, "Look at this, Miss Hetty. Why, it's a message from a lady. The lass who delivered it wouldn't tell me the lady's name."

Henrietta Rolland's folly was promptly forgotten as Lord Harry raised the soft pink envelope and sniffed the heavy musk scent.

"Ah, this isn't from a lady, Pottson," she said, grinning shamelessly at him. She ripped the envelope open and pulled out a single sheet of pink paper, covered with a flowery script. Her eyes widened and she gave a shout of glee.

"What is it, Miss Hetty?"

"Now, I don't want you to screech, Pottson. Here's the way of it. I paid a visit to Lord Oberlon's mistress—as Lord Harry, of course. Her name is Melissande, and she is no lady, I assure you. It appears she's free this afternoon for a ride in the park with me."

"You what? Gawd, you visited Lord Oberlon's mistress? Miss Harry—no, I mean, Miss Hetty—you can't mean you'll be riding with his mistress? If the marquess discovers it, he'll be after your blood. He'll want not just to thrash you, he'll want to kill you."

"I know," she said quietly. "Now, if you will excuse me, I'm off to purchase a green velvet riding habit for my lady and secure a docile mare from Mr. Scuddimore. I just hope the mare is showy enough."

It was a properly unassuming, yet charming young gentleman who strolled into Madame Cartier's fashionable boutique and purchased a riding habit and matching bonnet at an outrageous price, for it had originally been destined for a Miss Caroline Busby. Mr. Scuddimore proved a bit more difficult, but after much wheedling and coaxing, Hetty secured a bay mare named Coquette—a most appropriate name, Hetty thought. At promptly five o'clock in the afternoon, Hetty secured Coquette at the railing outside Melissande's town house.

Melissande was a vision to behold when she glided into the small drawing room where Lord Harry had sat waiting for her for a good half hour.

"You wonderful naughty boy," she said, dancing into the parlor. "However did you know my exact measurements? I vow I would have chosen no other riding habit myself."

Hetty doubted that Madame Cartier would have let Melissande anywhere near Miss Caroline Busby's riding habit. She was forced to admit that the green velvet riding habit, high cut, fitting snugly below her succulent breasts, couldn't look better on another female. Row upon row of frothy white lace sprung from the green to touch her chin. An arched black plume swept in a high circle, framing the thick auburn ringlets about her face.

Melissande knew she looked glorious. She knew that this lovely young gentleman shouldn't have given her such a gift, but after all, a girl had to enjoy herself. Lord Monteith was a charming boy, no more, and if she wished to spend a small part of her time with him—well, where was the harm in that? If the marquess were to find out—she drew up a moment with this rather daunting thought, then shrugged her white shoulders. Perhaps he would take her less for granted. Perhaps he would take her to more balls like the lovely masked ball the previous evening.

Now, as she pirouetted in front of the raptly admiring young Lord Harry, she applauded her decision. The marquess never extolled her beauty in such glowing terms. Nor, she thought, forgetting momentarily the ruby necklace he had bestowed upon her after his return from Italy, had he ever bought her such an exquisite riding habit.

"Men will envy me today in the park, Melissande. They will want to slit my throat. They won't understand why such a goddess as you lower yourself to be seen with me. Ah, you should ride Pegasus, not the mare I brought for you."

Melissande could sit a horse beautifully, but that was about all she could do. Making a horse go or stop was beyond her. Hetty was profoundly thankful that the gentle Coquette was docile almost to the point of being unconscious. She led Melissande carefully through the London traffic and into the park. Few pedestrians were present, for the winter wind was sharp, and the air so chilly Hetty could see her breath.

But it didn't matter. It was that time of day to be

seen and to visit. Phaetons, horses, and carriages were in abundance. Hetty felt her heart jump into her throat as a gentleman astride a huge black stallion cantered toward them. It wasn't the marquess. She had wondered just what she would do were they to meet Lord Oberlon in the park, had ruminated over possible scenes, then finally banished it from her mind. She wanted very much to confront him. She was prepared, she knew, with a limitless array of insults. But not here, not just yet.

They cantered past a closed carriage, and Hetty was delighted to see Lady Melberry's face pressed against the closed window, her eyes fastened in surprise on the magnificent Melissande. Hetty raised her hand in polite salute, suppressing the smile on her lips. Even if Lady Melberry weren't a gossip, Hetty thought, even the most sainted of persons would have difficulty keeping such a juicy tidbit to themselves. Of course, how could Lady Melberry possibly know who she was?

"You aren't too cold, Melissande?"

Melissande had received so many passionate and ardent looks from gentlemen, she wouldn't have cared if her teeth were chattering. Just as long as there was no gooseflesh on her face, she wouldn't complain. She shook her head, allowing the arching plume to brush against her rosy cheeks, and smiled caressingly at Lord Harry.

By the time they had cantered nearly the full perimeter of the park, their presence had been duly noted by at least a dozen very interested ladies and gentlemen. Hetty slowed her horse as a phaeton with a gentleman riding alongside pulled onto the green. She glanced sideways at the driver and drew abruptly to a halt, handily catching Coquette's bridle in her fingers. She looked into the smiling face of Kate St. Clair, the countess of March. She felt nothing but pleasure at the encounter until she realized that the gentleman on the black stallion was the earl, and he wasn't happy.

Well, there was nothing she could do about it. "My lady," Lord Harry said, bowing in the saddle, "I see that you have taken to more mild forms of exercise. Do you enjoy yourself sufficiently?"

Kate gave a trill of laughter, delighted to see Lord Harry. She looked at her husband, expecting to see his easy smile. She was surprised and confused at the sudden set look on his face, that tightening of his jaw, a very stubborn jaw, that happened only during their more ferocious arguments.

"How delightful to see you again, Lord Harry. Such a pity you couldn't come with Harry to dine with us the other evening. Harry sang your praises until my lord here was ready to throw turtle soup in his face. Hitting the target from twenty feet at Manton's is no small feat. Ah, how I should like to go there."

"I should like to take you there, my lady," Hetty said. She was well aware that the earl's eyes were stark and narrowed on her face. He was furious. Excellent, just excellent. Let him gnash his teeth, for he couldn't call her out, only the marquess could.

Hetty smiled as she looked squarely into the earl's set face. "My lord," she said. "It is an exquisite phaeton. I, myself, admired it at Tattersall's. The countess drives it well. I imagine that she could also shoot well at Manton's."

"Indeed." The earl said nothing more. He was now looking at Melissande, who was growing decidedly restive at not being the center of the conversation.

The countess misunderstood her husband's behavior. "Oh, do forgive me, Lord Harry, but who is this lovely lady with you?"

"This is Melissande Challier. Melissande, this is the earl and countess of March."

The countess gave Melissande a friendly smile and nodded. Melissande gave a toss of her plumed hat, never looked at the countess, but stared at the earl, saying, "Surely I'm honored."

Hetty guided her horse away from the phaeton. "We will leave you now. It's cold and I've no wish to see icicles growing off your nose, my lady. Do enjoy yourself. Perhaps someday, we can arrange for you to come with me to Manton's."

The countess stared after Lord Harry as he gently and with great care assisted Melissande's mare into a slow canter.

She turned to her frowning husband. "Lord Monteith is a charming lad. Now, Julien, don't be cross with me. I admit to my rudeness, though it was unintentioned. I was just so pleased to see Lord Harry again. Miss Challier is beautiful, but oddly, I wouldn't have imagined her to be quite in Lord Harry's style. But it's amusing how opposites attract."

The earl tried to smile, he truly did, but he couldn't quite make it. He said, "Kate, I'm not at all angry at you. And, as usual, you are quite correct, the lady isn't at all in Lord Monteith's style."

"Just whose style is appropriate to the lady?"

She knows something is wrong, the earl thought.

He said, "Very well. Melissande Challier isn't a lady. You've just been your most charming to Jason Cavander's mistress."

"Goodness. But Julien, if she's Jason's mistress, whatever is she doing with Lord Monteith? Surely it isn't at all the thing to do."

"No, it isn't at all the thing to do. It's insane, actually." The earl followed the retreating figures of Lord Harry and Jason Cavander's mistress. He was remembering his conversation with Jason but a few days before. What a fool he'd been to so blithely discount his friend's story about Lord Monteith's flagrant provocation. God, when Jason found out, as most certainly he would, about Lord Monteith openly flaunting Melissande with all society to see, the young man might very well find himself thrashed to an inch of his life. Why the devil was the young man doing this? Did he wish to be beaten soundly, or perhaps have a foil run through his gullet? He decided that it would be better that he himself tell Jason Cavander. Jason had the devil's own temper when aroused.

"Julien, what is it? What are you thinking?"

She knew him far too well for him to lie to her. Thus, he spent the next hour relating to her all that he knew about this strange situation.

When he finished, his countess was silent for a very long time. "Come," he said, "what are you now thinking?"

"I think," she said in a very quiet voice, "that Lord Monteith is far too intelligent to embark upon such a course as you describe without an excellent motive. He's an unusual boy, Julien. There is something very different about him. I would hate to see him cut down so young by Jason Cavander. Yet, you feel that he is purposefully pushing Jason until there is no choice but retaliation. Is there nothing you can do, Julien?"

The earl said frankly, "Probably not much. But I will speak to Jason on the morrow. Perhaps between us we can determine just what is driving the lad to such fatal extremes."

Chapter Nineteen

Pottson was busily engaged in adding a dash more garlic to a steaming mutton dish upon Hetty's return from her ride in the park with Melissande. She breathed in deeply, demanded a spoon, and dug in. "Oh goodness, Pottson, it's wonderful. It's much too good for Sir Harry and Mr. Scuddimore. We can save it for just the two of us. Haven't we several apples we can give Harry and Scuddy?"

"Go on with you, Miss Hetty," Pottson said, waving his own spoon at her.

Hetty was changing into Lord Harry's clothes, when there came a knock on the bedchamber door. It was Pottson wiping his hands on his apron, looking like a man hunted. Behind him stood Millie.

"Oh, Pottson. You startled me out of my skin. What's happened?" Hetty quickly pulled a robe about her shoulders. "Don't tell me Sir John and Lady Louisa have returned to London? Oh no, that can't be."

"No, it's not Sir John, thank the good Lord. The cat would have jumped out of the bag if they'd stayed any longer in London. No, it's your father, Miss Hetty. He's up and done it again. Lady Melberry has invited you to another party and Sir Archibald accepted on your behalf. He wanted to see you,

Miss Hetty, but I told him you were resting. You must know that I had to tell him that you would be delighted to go, so as to keep him from suspecting you weren't at home."

"You did just the right thing, Millie. Drat Sir Archibald anyway. I doubt he even remembered that I asked him to consult me before he accepted any more invitations. Oh well, it's done. Now, we must hurry. Quickly, Millie, fetch a pen and writing paper from Pottson. There is just enough time for him to pay a visit to Sir Harry and Mr. Scuddimore and cancel our evening together. Pottson, you'd better not eat all that stew by yourself."

A scant two hours later, Miss Henrietta Rolland, the dowdy specimen who had made her debut but a week before, climbed into Sir Archibald's carriage, pressing the green alexandrine cap against the top of her head to keep it from being whipped away by the harsh evening wind. As before, she didn't balance the spectacles on her nose until she pounded the knocker at the Melberry town house. The Melberry butler again looked at her as if he prayed devoutly she'd disappear. She gave him a big swarmy smile and a bigger squint.

She quickly scanned the assorted ladies and gentlemen clustered in small groups in the drawing room. Her sense of wariness eased. She didn't see Lord Oberlon. Miss Henrietta Rolland wished to avoid his grace to the same extent that Lord Harry Monteith wished to be thrown into his presence. She said all that was polite to Lady Melberry and quickly made good her escape to a far corner of the drawing room, there to observe, and hopefully, not to be observed by any of the other guests. Her gaze soon fell upon a lovely, dark-haired girl who was seated demurely beside her mama, looking for all the world as if she would yawn loudly from boredom at any moment. Hetty grinned. The vision of loveliness was none other than Miss Isabella Bentworth, the delight of Sir Harry Brandon's heart. Lord Harry had met the young lady only briefly, and had exchanged only superficial civilities. Perhaps Miss Henrietta Rolland could make Miss Isabella's acquaintance. She had a lively curiosity about the young lady who had captured Sir Harry's devotion, though not as yet, a proposal of marriage.

As Hetty drew closer to Miss Bentworth, she began to believe Sir Harry mad. Isabella was indeed a beautiful girl, her deep brown eyes soft and warm. She looked kind as well as beautiful. Hetty wondered if Sir Harry deserved her. Her hair, glossy black with no hint of red, was swept high atop her head, with myriad small curls framing her ivory face. Hetty decided Sir Harry didn't deserve Isabella.

Hetty was at the point of gaining Miss Bentworth's wandering attention when she was drawn up suddenly by the grating voice of Miss Maude Langley.

"My dear Miss Rolland," Maude said in that sticky sweet way of hers that set Hetty's teeth on edge. "How very delightful to see you again. Do forgive me for not calling upon you, but I was invited to so many balls and routs that I scarce had time to purchase new gowns."

Fat chance of that, Hetty thought, and took a deep breath, her only ambition to rid herself of the unwelcome Miss Maude. "I most readily forgive you, Miss Langley," she said, raising her voice, thus forcing her vowels to be irritatingly nasal. "Where is your beautiful sister? Surely, the gentlemen will be howling soon if she doesn't come."

Miss Maude became less friendly. "Oh, Caroline is probably off in some corner flirting outrageously. Mama quite despairs that Caroline's unladylike behavior will drive away the more serious of eligible gentlemen."

"That's difficult to believe, Miss Langley. Gentlemen adore lively, beautiful girls. She will probably have half a score of marriage proposals before the season has even begun."

Miss Maude decided that Henrietta Rolland was as impertinent as she was homely. She looked down her long thin nose, taking in every aspect of the pea green gown that hung shapelessly on Miss Rolland's shoulders, and gave a tittering, tight little laugh.

"You, certainly, Miss Rolland, need not concern yourself about being so bothered by the other sex."

Hetty choked back a laugh, squinted at Miss Maude and said in that ghastly nasal twang, "Perhaps you can bear me company during the season, Miss Langley. We can criticize all the beautiful girls as we sit along the ballroom walls watching them dance."

"Impertinent little twit," Miss Maude said under her breath, but not under enough.

"Such an insufferable girl, isn't she? However did you get rid of her so neatly?" Hetty turned about to see Miss Isabella Bentworth at her elbow.

"It's not all that hard if you know how to insult her properly. Do forgive me, but I'm Henrietta Rolland. I wanted to make your acquaintance. You are quite the most beautiful girl in the room, you know.

I'm sure Miss Maude could find ever so many awful things wrong with your person, your clothes, and your character."

Miss Isabella Bentworth smiled, then grinned widely. "I haven't met you before. Are you new in town?"

"Somewhat. I've seen you, Miss Bentworth, with a very handsome young gentleman. He's tall and fair complexioned. Very dashing and princely I thought him." That was going too far, she thought, with the princely part, but to her relief, Miss Isabella's cheeks turned suddenly warm and she looked quickly down at the toes of her blue satin slippers. "I believe you're speaking of Sir Harry Brandon."

Hetty wasn't deaf to the depression in Miss Bentworth's voice. She knew she shouldn't make a judgment of character on such short notice, yet she couldn't help being drawn to Miss Bentworth. She said carefully, "I've heard of Sir Harry. He's considered a very eligible bachelor, isn't he?"

"I suppose so," came a dull answer.

So Miss Bentworth did return Harry's affection, Hetty thought, giving Sir Harry a mental kick for holding back from the young lady. Princely, ha. "You hold him in some regard, I gather."

Miss Isabella eyed the sympathetic Miss Rolland, and said in a rush of confidence, "Oh, yes, Miss Rolland, but you see it doesn't matter. My mama wishes to see me wed by the end of the season, for I have three sisters who must come out, and Harry blanches at the thought of marriage. He is all of twenty-four, yet he believes himself too young. That's because his brother-in-law, the earl of March, was twenty-eight when he wed and that's the age Harry agrees on, none other. He tells me I should only be fourteen-years-old right now instead of eighteen. He says it's all my fault. He is sometimes more stubborn than my mama, which is a terrifying thought when one considers a lifetime with such a mate."

It did indeed. And that sounded just like Harry's logic, Hetty thought. She felt no sympathy whatsoever for the three unknown sisters and wondered fleetingly if her own mother, were she alive, would have pushed her to wed at the end of her first season as Isabella's mama was doing. Goodness, and the season hadn't even begun yet. She asked, "Does your mama have anyone in particular in mind, other than Sir Harry Brandon?"

"Yes, Sir William Filey. He's very rich and a toad. He flatters Mama until I want to yell that she should marry him. They're nearer the same age. He's always polished, always says just the right thing, yet there's something about him. I'm not at all certain that he is what he seems."

"He's old enough to be your father, just like you said. You're right, have your mama wed him. It's nonsense to think you should marry him. Surely, your mama couldn't believe that such a match would prosper, surely she couldn't believe you'd be happy with such a husband." She wondered if Sir William had an affinity for young misses, at least very rich young misses.

Miss Bentworth said, "It's true, he is too old for me. But if Sir Harry doesn't wish to wed me, I fear that I shall have no other choice in the matter. My mama is strong-willed, you know. My papa quakes in his boots whenever she speaks. And there are my sisters, of course. All three of them. She's even pushing me to marry before the Season begins, so she may save money, which is silly, since my father's made of money."

"Nonsense, Miss Bentworth, everyone has choices. You just must have some resolve."

Miss Bentworth thought privately that the homely Miss Rolland could well afford to state her mind and have all the resolve in the world, for she couldn't imagine any gentleman threatening to do away with himself if she didn't wed him. How could Miss Rolland possibly understand?

Hetty misunderstood Miss Bentworth's silence, and began to believe her spiritless. She knew she shouldn't be meddling, but someone had to do something about these two. "As I said, Miss Bentworth, it just takes a bit of resolve, and a sound strategy. Listen and tell me what you think."

Miss Bentworth obligingly bent her dark head close to the pea green cap. Hetty became so engrossed in weaving her plot and in gaining Miss Bentworth's agreement, that she was unaware of Lord Oberlon's arrival. Thus, when the sound of his deep rich voice came to her ears, not ten feet away from her, she jumped, the remainder of her words dead on her tongue.

Miss Bentworth was too involved in Miss Rolland's daring plan to notice anything amiss. When Hetty grabbed her arm and pulled her into a corner, she believed merely that Miss Rolland had no wish to be overheard. It was some five minutes later when the orchestra struck up a lively country dance and two gentlemen were purposefully approaching her to secure the dance, that Miss Bentworth finally agreed. "You're certain Lord Monteith will agree, Miss Rolland?" she asked yet again.

"Yes, I am. He'll call on you tomorrow, Miss Bentworth. Remember, you mustn't breathe a word of this to anyone."

Hetty slipped even further into the corner, Miss Bentworth and her trial with Sir Harry for the moment forgotten, her eyes upon Lord Oberlon. He was laughing easily with Miss Caroline Langley. She glanced at a clock, saw that it was just after ten o'clock and realized with a sinking in the pit of her stomach that it would be quite rude for her to depart so early in the evening. She thought about a sudden, painful headache. Yes, that just might do it. So busy was she in planning her migraine that a light touch on her sleeve made her whirl about in consternation and stumble into a table.

"Did I frighten you, Miss Rolland?" Jason Cavander, quite eager to tease the spirited, outspoken young lady whose company the previous evening at the Ranleaghs' masquerade ball he'd found stimulating, actually more than stimulating. He realized he couldn't wait to see her again. But then she whipped about and his horrified eyes took in the hideous green cap, the squinting eyes behind wire spectacles, and the most ill-fitting gown he had ever seen in his life.

"You're Miss Henrietta Rolland?" he asked slowly, praying that this daunting vision gaping stupidly at him was some errant relative of Lady Melberry.

Hetty, after her initial shock, was well aware of the effect of her appearance upon him. Without thought, she snapped with all the natural arrogance in her character, "Certainly I'm Henrietta Rolland, sir. Unfortunately or fortunately, depending upon one's perceptions, I find I'm not acquainted with you. Nor do you look the sort of gentleman who would interest me in the least. Do feel free to take your leave."

She instantly regretted her rudeness, for the marquess was staring at her, his dark eyes puzzled and one black brow lifted in confusion.

"I believe," he said even more slowly, "yes, I'm quite certain we danced together at the Ranleaghs' masquerade ball last evening, Miss Rolland. My aunt, Lady Melberry, pointed you out to me but a few moments ago."

"Did we really dance, sir? Odd, but I don't remember you at all."

"Perhaps I've made a mistake," he said, but he knew full well he hadn't. Somehow, the wretched specimen before him simply didn't appear to be what he thought she must be—her parts just didn't fit themselves logically together. That is, he thought, striving to make sense of the situation, everything fit, but her voice and words. The coldness, the quickness of wit, the arrogance . . . decidedly something was quite wrong.

Hetty saw the myriad emotions on his face and knew she must stop taunting and insulting him. He'd found the masked Miss Henrietta Rolland to be entertaining the previous evening. She must become all that Miss Rolland was not. She placed a firm clamp on her tongue, squinted, and simpered.

"Oh la, sir. You've found me out." She wished she had a fan so she could tap him playfully on his sleeve. "Pray don't think Jack too naughty for telling you that I had taken you into a strong dislike." She managed an obnoxious titter at the incredulous look on his face, silently begged her brother's pardon, and simpered on, disgusting herself at her own performance, "Indeed, sir, or rather *your grace*, you are so very popular with the ladies, I believed my little joke the only way to dance with you. Surely such a spanking handsome fellow as yourself didn't mind a little deception?"

Hetty wanted to laugh aloud at the look on Lord Oberlon's face. Was she that bad? Something repellent and maybe even smelly? Then suddenly, his look again became puzzlement. He was certainly angry. He was ready to throttle Jack for making him appear the fool. He wanted more than anything to remove himself from as far away as he could from Jack's wretchedly vulgar sister. But there was a nagging doubt in the back of his mind. Those damned parts again—something still didn't fit properly. Though his dislike was clear on his face, he managed to say calmly, "How very curious, Miss Rolland, that you seem so terribly in need of spectacles now. Yet, I recall last evening that you could read the spots off playing cards in the other room. Indeed, one would think that you had the vision of an eagle."

Hetty produced a grating, high-pitched giggle. It made her own flesh crawl. "Ah, fie on you, *your grace*. It's impossible to wear spectacles and a mask at the same time. Such a smart gentleman you are, I vow my heart is still fluttering. Jack did give me such a scold for our little ruse, but I told him you were ever such a wonderful dancer and so gallant and ever so naughty—"

She got no further, for the marquess no longer

cared about the parts fitting properly together. The look he gave her was so very cold and contemptuous that had he not spoken, she might not have been able to control her tongue.

"Congratulate your brother on his joke, ma'am. If you will excuse me, I wish to enjoy some fresh evening air."

Hetty couldn't prevent the deep chuckle that burst from her throat. To her consternation, the marquess stopped in his tracks, stood quietly for a moment, then continued on his way without looking back.

Well, you arrogant devil, she thought as the marquess was charmingly waylaid by Miss Caroline Langley, Miss Henrietta Rolland need no longer be concerned about your unwanted attentions. She'd handled him well. She wondered idly just how long it would be before Lord Oberlon discovered Lord Harry's underhanded poaching with his mistress. To doubly ensure his wrath, she decided to take Melissande to the park again. Hetty just prayed that Melissande wouldn't yet try to seduce Lord Harry into her bed. That, Hetty thought with a crooked grin, would prove most interesting.

Chapter Twenty

For Lord Harry Monteith to pay the promised morning call to Miss Isabella Bentworth required a great deal of hurried activity and exquisite timing. Under no circumstances could Sir Archibald's luncheon be postponed even a second past the noon hour, and Hetty's presence at his table was nearly as requisite as the hour itself. Not quite, but nearly.

When Lord Harry sat with Miss Isabella in the company of her mama, a tall, beak-nosed lady, who tried her best to determine the exact degree of affluence among Lord Monteith's relations, it lacked just five minutes until ten o'clock in the morning. Hetty smoothly parried Lady Bentworth's none too subtle questions. She saw that Isabella was in an agony of embarrassment and prayed devoutly for Sir Harry's sake that Isabella wouldn't in the future fall into her mama's more grating mannerisms. She also prayed that Isabella's mama would live as far away from them as the land allowed.

All in all the visit achieved its purpose. Hetty had excellent hopes that Sir Harry would be jealous and furious at Lord Harry for his poaching, an excellent combination. What, she wondered, would Sir Harry do? The numbskull. The *princely* numbskull.

It lacked but a minute to noon when Hetty

slipped into her seat at the dining table, her gown slightly askew and one slipper loose on her foot.

There wasn't the familiar newspaper in Sir Archibald's hands. He greeted her with the enthusiasm of a parent who hasn't seen his offspring in at least a decade. "My dear Henrietta, how very charming you are looking, my child. Ah, yes, just the picture of your charming mama."

While Hetty gazed at him in some surprise, he turned to Mrs. Miller. "Serve the soup now, if you please. Then leave us, for Henrietta and I have much to discuss."

Hetty's eyes flew to Mrs. Miller's face, to seek enlightenment. The housekeeper gave an infinitesimal shrug and went about ladling the soup, beef soup, thank the lord. Hetty felt a nervous knot begin to grow in her stomach. Up until now, Sir Archibald had always stood as an unmovable rock amid the uncertainties that surrounded her. Had he somehow discovered that his daughter wasn't always what she appeared to him? She forced herself to sip at her soup, and waited.

Upon Mrs. Miller's departure from the dining room, Sir Archibald said with great good humor, "Well, my dear child, I must tell you that I visited a moment with Lady Melberry last evening, after you had left her party."

Oh, God, Hetty thought, paling, she'd told him about the pea green gown and the spectacles.

"She told me, Henrietta, that you were quite the popular girl. No, not dancing and all that folderol, but rather intimate conversations, one after the other."

She felt a touch of amusement, for obviously the

good Lady Melberry had found herself in a situation that required diplomacy of the highest order. "I think Lady Melberry perhaps gives over to a bit of exaggeration, Father," she said finally.

"Now, my dear child, I applaud your natural modesty, but facts are facts."

Whatever was he talking about? Sir Archibald leaned over and took her hand into his. "Do you like the Marquess of Oberlon, my dear? Lady Melberry thought that you quite encouraged his grace in his attentions."

Hetty dropped her spoon, sending the beef soup over the edge of the bowl onto the tablecloth. "The Marquess of Oberlon," she repeated. She shook her head. No, it was ridiculous. "Listen, Father, I promise I didn't encourage his grace. Really, I barely spoke to his grace. I barely even saw his grace. He spent most of his time very far across the room from me, Father. Besides, it doesn't matter. I don't even like him."

To her horror, Sir Archibald merely smiled at her indulgently. "A coy little miss you are, Henrietta, just like your dear mother. Why, I remember that she swore up and down to her parents that she didn't care for me at all. Protested in that ridiculous manner until the day we were married."

I have sorely wronged you, Mother, Hetty thought, remembering Lady Beatrice as a rather cold, constantly complaining parent. You were far more perceptive than I had ever imagined.

"Yes," Sir Archibald said, "it wouldn't be such a bad alliance. Cavander is, after all, a Tory, even though he doesn't often appear in the House of Lords. Well, perhaps he's never appeared in the

House of Lords. He's young. There's time to train him properly. There is John, too. He and Cavander have been friends since they were up at Oxford together. No, my dear child, if you wish the marquis for a husband, I won't forbid it." He pursed his lips a moment, caressing his chin in thought. "Ah, I've got it, my dear. You're such a shy little thing. I'll call upon the marquess, perhaps invite him to dinner. Give him my approval. Yes, that will do the trick."

She was close to fainting and shrieking at the same time. She drew a deep breath. Calm, calm. "No, no, Father, please. Listen to me. His grace has no interest in me whatsoever. I promise. He dislikes me. He can't stand me. He thinks I'm ugly and a sorry excuse for a female, truly, you mustn't. Why, the only reason he spoke to me at all was because he and Jack are friends. He was just being polite, nothing more. Please, Father, I don't want to know Lord Oberlon better. I don't ever want to see him again."

Hetty had always been rather proud of her stubborn streak, as Damien had called it, eyeing her several times like he wanted to smack her. But now she found herself silently cursing it, for her stubbornness came directly from Sir Archibald. She knew well enough that once his mind had grasped a certain course of action, there was no budging him. Indeed, it would take less effort to change the flow of the river Thames. She looked up, realizing that he hadn't even paid her any attention. So much for her calm good sense approach.

Sir Archibald fixed Hetty with a patriarchal, benign smile. "You are such a good child, Henrietta.

Trust me, my dear, to do what is best for you. Now, let us finish our luncheon, for I must meet with Lord Bedford, whom we have elected to whip Sir Edwin Barrington into shape for the upcoming election."

"Which election, Father?" Anything, Hetty thought, to divert her father's thoughts.

"The borough at Little Simpson. Up to this time, the wretched farmers have refused to listen to reason. But Sir Edwin is a popular man, though he hasn't yet grasped the need to use whatever means necessary to achieve what is right. Political necessity is a concept that eludes him."

"But if he isn't the sort of political material you want, then why do you back him?"

Sir Archibald grinned indulgently at this errant bit of nonsense from his naive daughter. "Don't worry your head about it, child. Sir Edwin will do well enough. I will teach him all he needs to know."

Hetty thought fleetingly of Damien's desire to enter the political arena. She wondered if he would have had an honored Tory member whip him into shape. Or would Sir Archibald have been his mentor? No, she couldn't imagine it. According to Jack, Damien hadn't even leaned toward Torydom, far from it.

Sir Archibald spoke no further of the marquess of Oberlon at lunch. Hetty sent a plea heavenward that once her sire got involved in his political activities in the afternoon, he would forget all about his matchmaking.

She excused herself shortly from the dining room, giving her father a hurried hug, and slipped out of the house to make her way to Lord Harry's lodgings.

She forced herself to be lighter of heart, for, even if Sir Archibald happened to approach Lord Oberlon, she was fairly certain that the damned marquess had found Henrietta Rolland such a repellent creature that he would never accept such an invitation to dine.

As she slipped into breeches, frilled shirt, and hessians, she quickly reviewed her schedule for the remainder of the day. First she would be meeting Sir Harry at Manton's. Now that would be a most interesting experience. Lord Harry would start the worm of jealousy gnawing in Sir Harry's breast. With any luck at all, that should make Sir Harry realize that Isabella was ripe for the plucking in more than one orchard.

Oh yes, Hetty thought as she bade Pottson a good afternoon, he must take a note to Melissande, inquiring if the fair lady would deign to ride again in the park with Lord Monteith.

At the thought of how she would be spending her evening, she grimaced in distaste. Impossible to extricate herself from going with Harry and Scuddy to that wretched cockfight.

Still, it was with a light step that Hetty strolled to meet Sir Harry at Manton's, her face down against the winter wind.

As for the marquess, he neither felt light of step nor light of heart. Indeed, he was frozen with cold deadly anger as he listened to his friend, the earl of March.

"So, Julien, I'm now fast bidding to become a laughingstock of London, am I not?" His voice sounded so very calm that no one save his closest friends would have realized that his grace was ready to kill with his bare hands.

"Most likely," the earl said.

"Now you will believe me that the young whelp wishes death by my hands?"

The earl paused an instant, seemingly intent upon removing a fleck of dust from his coat sleeve. "It's all very strange," the earl said at last. "I do agree that young Monteith wants something. Whether it's death at your hands—well, I must believe that a bit extreme."

The marquess didn't say anything. The earl sat forward in his chair. "You know, Jason, Kate immediately agreed with our conclusions that there is something driving the boy to behave in such an outrageous manner. You are certain that you have never before heard his name, that you can think of no insult ever made to him? Come, think, Jason."

"Damn it, no, Julien. We've asked ourselves these questions, even before this latest exploit. I tell you, I know nothing about Monteith save that I intend to beat him to a bloody pulp, then kick his hide into a ditch."

"Tell me, Jason, do you care so much about Melissande? I recall only the other day your telling me that you were rapidly becoming bored with her."

"I'm not a fool, Julien," the marquess said quietly. "It hardly matters what I think of her now. She is, after all, still under my protection." He rose and strolled to the fireplace, his dark eyes resting a moment on the glowing coals. He turned to face the earl, digging his hands into his breeches pockets. "It's now a question of honor, Julien. Surely you see that I can't ignore this insult."

The earl sighed and nodded slowly. "No, of course you can't ignore it, and yet—"

"And yet, you don't want to see me kill the boy," the marquess finished, gazing searchingly at the earl.

"Don't think I'm becoming lost to all sense of honor, Jason. Yet again, I must concur with Kate's opinion. There is something deuced unusual about Monteith, as if he were a complex puzzle whose pieces simply didn't fit together. I ask only that you do not act rashly. Surely, if the lad continues in his outrageous behavior, you will have no choice but to call him out."

"Strange you say Monteith is like a puzzle whose pieces do not fit together."

"I thought it apt, Jason. Why?"

"It's of no importance." The marquess shrugged. "Damnation but this is an impossible situation. Were it a snake like Filey, I wouldn't feel the slightest hesitation, indeed I'd welcome such a chance. But hellfire, Julien, as you say, Monteith is just a boy. The difference in our ages—eight years at least—and in our experience . . . why, I would look little less than a murderer were I to call him out."

"That's true," the earl said. "I think though, that if you remain, shall we say, impervious to the boy's taunts, it is he who will call you out. Think on it, Jason. Now, I must be off. George informed me on my way out that Kate was preparing to direct the carpenters in the refurbishing of the nursery wing. If I know her, she will be climbing about the rafters with them." The earl rose and clasped his friend's hand.

"I'll take your advice until I can do naught else, Julien. Give my love to Kate."

The earl turned at the door of the drawing room and gave the marquess a lazy grin. "Are you certain, Jason, that one of your succulent beauties in Italy wasn't distantly related to any Monteith? Say a virgin who wanted to get you out of your breeches and you couldn't bring yourself to say no?"

"Damn you, St. Clair."

After the earl of March had taken his leave, Jason Cavander, in a fit of excess energy, departed to Gentleman Jackson's boxing salon, where his hapless opponent in the ring took on the features of a fair, blue-eyed youth with a mouth that was filled with more insults than a bordello was filled with randy men.

Chapter Twenty-one

"You what?" Sir Harry Brandon dropped his pistol into its case and turned in stunned surprise to Lord Harry.

"You really should be more careful with your guns, Harry. Thank God it wasn't loaded. You might have shot your toe off or worse yet, my toe."

"Damnation, Lord Harry, it's bad enough that you must tweak Lord Oberlon's nose by adding his mistress to your string of females, but you will leave Isabella alone."

"But, Harry, I find Miss Isabella Bentworth very charming. Surely you remember that both Mavreen and Melissande are redheads. Isabella has the most beautiful black hair—smooth and shiny like a bolt of black silk or do I mean a raven's wing?"

Sir Harry ground his teeth. "I won't have it, damn you. Isabella is pure and innocent. She won't let you flirt with her, she's not that kind of girl."

"Ah, so that's it. Don't mistake my intentions, Harry. I don't intend to trifle with the lady. She isn't a brief amusement. After sitting with her an hour this morning, flirtation was the furthest thing from my mind. She's a glorious creature, so soft and gentle, so sweetly deferential to my wishes."

"But that's impossible, utterly ridiculous—" Sir

Harry's voice trailed off. He stared at Lord Harry in baffled silence. He leaned over and very carefully fastened the clasp on his gun case. As he straightened he said heavily, "Then you're thinking of marriage, Lord Harry?"

"Perhaps."

"But you're younger than I!"

Hetty replied with a laugh, "Neither of us is in the infantry, old fellow. If you wish to admire the fair Isabella from afar until you have reached the exalted age of twenty-eight, in keeping with what you believe to be your brother-in-law's edict, then you'd best give her up right now. Don't you know that fortune-hunting mama of hers is fair to forcing Isabella to wed Filey by the end of the Season? Mayhap even before the end of the Season, to save money. Really, Harry, as a gentleman, I can't allow that lecherous old satyr to warm her bed. It turns my stomach."

"Yes, of course I knew that. But it's nonsense. Her harridan of a mother can't force Isabella to wed Filey. These are modern times, not the thirteenth century." Sir Harry didn't like this, any of it. Of course he knew about Filey's attentions toward Isabella, and it irked him. But still, surely she wouldn't marry the old fool.

Hetty gave him a look of utter disgust. "Are you pleased to wear blinders, Harry? Are you content to throw Isabella to Filey? Listen to me, young ladies don't have the choices you seem to think they do."

"You really believe that Isabella will be sold to that old lecher, Filey?"

"Don't forget, Harry, that Filey is titled and as rich as Golden Ball. It would take a gentleman of similar qualifications and much persuasion to convince Isabella's mama differently. The old eagle was appraising me openly this morning. Her questions were impertinent in the extreme. I think I found favor in her mercenary eyes, but not as yet as much favor as you have." Hetty paused a moment, then added lightly, "But I daresay that I shall bring her around. After all, old boy, it isn't as though I were cutting *you* out. You've left the field wide open."

Sir Harry suddenly turned on her. "I don't want you to see Isabella. You're a damned rakehell, Lord Harry, and I'll not let you break the poor girl's heart."

"Ah, but it won't be I who will break her heart."

"Damn you for a meddler." Sir Harry flung from the shooting range into the large outer parlor at Manton's.

Hetty grinned at his stiff back and followed him slowly, not at all displeased. If only she could enlist the help of the earl of March. A few well-chosen words from that powerful peer would hang the icicle on the eave. She sighed, knowing such a conversation with Harry's brother-in-law was out of the question. Still, she'd done quite well enough, she told herself. She left Manton's whistling.

Her complacency grew when, upon returning to Lord Harry's lodgings, she found awaiting another flowery note from Melissande, begging Lord Monteith's charming company for another ride in the park. Sir Harry's problems slipped from her mind as, not long thereafter, she cantered through the London traffic to Melissande's apartment, leading the docile Coquette. She found herself shivering with a kind of frightening anticipation. Surely Lord

Oberlon must have found out about her meeting with Melissande the day before. She knew that no gentleman would accept such an insult. It can't be much longer now, she told herself. No, not much longer now.

Melissande stood arrayed in the green velvet riding habit Lord Monteith had presented to her the day before, peeking through the curtains onto the street. She realized that she had, in all honesty, accepted yet another invitation to ride with the young Lord Monteith because she was indulging in a fit of pique. Not that she minded all the languishing phrases that seemed to flow in an endless stream from the young gentleman's mouth. Yet, Lord Oberlon seemed not even to be aware of her minor transgressions, for after that altogether delightful evening spent at the Ranleaghs' masquerade, he hadn't come to call, hadn't even sent her a note, hadn't even sent a servant with a note to her.

Lord Monteith suddenly came into view astride his bay mare, leading her mare, Coquette. She pulled quickly back from the window and schooled her features into a welcoming smile. Perhaps his grace would come visiting while she was out with Lord Monteith. She shrugged an elegant shoulder. Well, if he did come, Jenny could simply inform him that Melissande was otherwise occupied. Should she have Jenny tell the marquess with whom she was otherwise occupied? Such a disclosure bothered her. She didn't want Lord Oberlon to blow out Lord Harry's brains. He was too pleasant a young gentleman to be dead.

"Ah, my dear sir," she greeted Lord Monteith. "How kind of you to escort me again today."

As Hetty was becoming more adept at her constantly shifting roles, she managed to greet Melissande with a soulful sigh and a profound look of admiration. "You have but to command me, my fair Melissande." She tenderly brought Melissande's white hand to her lips and kissed the soft skin. It tasted of jasmine. Very nice. "It is, of course, my good fortune to find you unoccupied. What a shame though to find you so much alone. And on such an excellent day. Not a single rain cloud in the sky. Ah, did I say something that upsets you, Melissande?"

Hetty wanted to laugh, but she didn't. She'd just scored a major point. If nothing else, Melissande would be in a god-awful snit the next time she saw Lord Oberlon. Come to think of it, Melissande did deserve a bit more attention, didn't she? Surely she was expensive. She realized then that a mistress was dependent upon her protector for all her needs. That of course wouldn't advance Lord Harry's goal. She wouldn't dare ever mention another gentleman's name in her master's presence. Ah, Hetty thought, there were many others who would relish filling Lord Oberlon's ears with tales of his mistress and another gentleman.

Melissande said, "Yes, it's just as you say, my lord. But now that you are here, I won't think of the marquess. Perhaps he isn't even in London, for I've not heard from him."

Hetty suddenly gulped down a sinking thought. Had Lord Oberlon perhaps dismissed the beautiful Melissande? Lord, if that were so, Lord Harry's antics were not only needlessly expensive but also pointless. But as Hetty had no evidence that such a break had occurred between the marquess and his mistress, she was careful to maintain the depressingly romantic chatter that Melissande appeared so much to admire. She pressed Melissande to ride two turns about the park, ensuring again that the usual habitués had an excellent view of Lord Monteith in the company of Lord Oberlon's mistress.

When Hetty returned to Lord Harry's lodgings to change for dinner and the inevitable cockfight, she wanted nothing more than to sink chin deep in a hot bath. She could still sniff faint whiffs of Melissande's heavy perfume.

Shortly after eight o'clock she took a hackney to Mr. Scuddimore's lodgings on Queen Street, hopeful that the wretched cockfight wouldn't last very long. There were several aspects about being a gentleman that made her stomach turn over.

A closed carriage, the eagle and raven crest barely visible on its paneled doors, drew to a jolting halt on Thompson Street. A cloaked gentleman flung open the doors and alighted before the driver scarce had time to quiet the steaming horses.

"Walk the horses about, Silken. I shan't be above thirty minutes within," the gentleman said over his shoulder.

"Aye, your grace."

The Marquess of Oberlon took the front steps two at a time. He felt such fury that he wanted to choke on it. He pounded his fist upon the closed oak door.

Pottson, who was enjoying a warm mug of ale, contemplating a quiet, uneventful evening by himself, jumped in his chair at the sudden loud knocking, spilling some of the lovely ale to the carpet. His eyes flew to the clock over the mantelpiece. It was scarcely after nine o'clock. It couldn't be Miss Hetty, that was for certain. He set down his ale and hurried to the door.

"Who is there?" He pressed his ear to the door.

"Open the door, damn you. Be quick about it man, else I shall kick it in."

Pottson fumbled with the latch, suddenly sweating with premonition. He pulled vigorously on the knob. He could practically hear another curse forming on the visitor's tongue. No sooner had he unfastened the latch than the door burst open and a large, black-cloaked man strode past him into the room.

Lord Oberlon took in every empty corner of the small, cozy drawing room in an instant. He whirled about to the small, plump man who stood, mouth agape, in the open doorway.

"I presume you are Monteith's man. Fetch the wretched young puppy this instant. I would have speech with him."

Pottson knew without being told that he was face to face with the Marquess of Oberlon. Miss Hetty had succeeded.

He licked his tongue over his suddenly dry mouth and stammered, "I—I am sorry, your grace, but Lord Harry isn't here."

"Your grace, huh? So, my good man, you know who I am. I should have expected as much."

"Yes, your grace. You must believe me, Lord Harry won't be back for hours. I don't know where he is, but he's with his friends so it will be very late before he returns."

"Somehow I disbelieve you." Lord Oberlon turned

abruptly from the trembling Pottson down the small corridor to Lord Harry's bedchamber.

It struck Pottson forcibly in the few moments he stood alone in the drawing room that making all sorts of plans and plots in no way came close to the dreadful reality he now faced. Obviously, his grace had discovered that his mistress had flaunted herself with Lord Harry and was now in the blackest of rages. Gawd, Pottson thought, his legs beginning to tremble beneath him, the marquess was fit to kill.

He searched about frantically in his mind for some way of protecting Miss Hetty. Of all evenings when she might return early, it was this evening. "That disgusting cockfight," she'd said grimly. "I pray only that I won't heave all over those pitiful birds."

Pottson looked up helplessly as the marquess strode back into the room. "What in God's name is this?" he shouted. He waved Miss Hetty's gown in front of Pottson's horrified eyes.

It's all over now, Pottson thought, not without a feeling of relief. How stupid of him not to have hung up her gown. What an ironic way for all of Miss Hetty's plans to come to an end. She would skin him alive. "It's a dress, your grace," he said, and waited. There was nothing else he could do. Just wait.

"Do you think me blind as well as stupid? Of course it's a dress. It's a lady's gown. It's obvious that your master is a dissolute young rakehell. Damn, his gall knows no bounds. Because I'm a gentleman, I didn't search through the closet. If I had, I would have found a trembling naked young maiden awaiting Monteith's return."

Pottson thought the world had suddenly taken a faulty turn. He shook his head stupidly.

"You protect him, do you, my good fool? You may now tell me where I can find the perfidious young puppy, else I shall break your skinny neck." The marquess flung down the gown and walked purposefully toward Pottson.

"I don't know where Lord Harry is this evening." Pottson drew himself up to his full diminutive height. "He's with his friends, that's all I know."

Jason Cavander looked fully for the first time into the ashen-hued face of the terrified valet. Damn, the little man had pluck. He didn't deserve to be beaten for his master's sins. He reined in his black rage and forced himself to survey the situation rationally. It wouldn't solve a thing were he to throttle the hapless valet. That the man was loyal to his master, well, he had to admire that, even if his master was a rotten little sod.

Perhaps it was just as well that he hadn't found Monteith at home, for he admitted to himself, the consequences of his anger might have produced very unpleasant results. He felt like killing the young man, slowly, with great relish.

"Very well," the marquess said finally. "You will tell your master that the Marquess of Oberlon is desirous of seeing him. If Monteith is not a coward, I shall expect him at White's tomorrow evening. There, you may tell him, he will apologize to me, in full company." The marquis paused a moment, then added with deadly preciseness, "If he doesn't choose to make full apology, or if his bravado extends only to the bedroom, you may expect me to call again. Is that clear?"

"I'll tell him, your grace." Pottson had an almost irresistible urge to tell the marquess the truth. He couldn't bring himself to serve her such a turn. He stood in miserable silence as the marquess swept past him and slammed the door behind him.

Pottson walked slowly over to Miss Hetty's discarded gown and automatically picked it up, smoothing out the wrinkles. The marquess had held the answer to Lord Monteith in his hands, yet hadn't realized the truth. She had fashioned herself too fine a reputation as a wild, dissolute young gentleman.

Pottson walked slowly into Lord Harry's bedchamber and hung up her gown in the closet. He looked about the room. Had the marquess not been so angry, he would have noticed the ribbons and hairbrushes scattered about on the dressing table.

Pottson walked back into the drawing room, his shoulders hunched forward. The marquess's words burned into his mind. There would be no going back now.

Chapter Twenty-two

Signore Bertioli faced the sweating, red-faced Lord Monteith. He placed his foil carefully into its velvet case and handed the young gentleman a white lawn handkerchief to mop his brow.

"You fight with the calm desperation of a man who knows the test of his courage to be near," Signore Bertioli said softly. "The *vendetta*, it draws to a close, my lord?"

Hetty's lungs were going to burst, she knew it. She tried to answer him but couldn't. Signore Bertioli gently removed the foil from her unresisting hand and waited patiently.

"Yes, Signore, as you say, the *vendetta* draws itself to a close." She read concern in the Italian's dark eyes. "Ah, don't fear for the outcome, Signore. All will be resolved with pistols, not foils. I am an excellent shot."

Signore Bertioli frowned. "Then why have you pushed yourself to learn the tricks of the masters, my young lord?"

"They say, Signore, if a man goes into battle with but one weapon and a prayer on his lips, he is a fool. In all truth, I would have much preferred foils, yet despite your excellent instruction, I must face the fact that I have not the endurance nor yet the skill to dispatch my opponent."

Signore Bertioli wanted very much to know the name of Lord Monteith's enemy, yet he knew the young man would never tell him. "Your opponent, my lord, he is much skilled with the foil?"

"Yes, so I have heard. And he has at least eight more years experience than I have."

"Then he also has at least eight more years experience with a pistol as well."

"True, but as I told you, I'm quite excellent with a pistol. If you have a biblical turn of mind, you could liken me to the small David. The tiny ball from my pistol will bring down my Goliath. The pistol levels all our differences. Now, Signore, I must leave you. It will be a most interesting evening and I have no wish to be late."

Hetty shrugged into her greatcoat and drew on black leather gloves. She said as she turned, "Signore, thank you. I've been a disappointment to you. I'm sorry for that. If I don't see you again, well, you will know that the young lion had no more than a great roar. Goodbye, Signore."

Hetty gazed with glittering eyes about the vast gaming salon at White's, noting that fewer gentlemen than usual lounged about the gaming tables. She registered surprise until she remembered the races at Newmarket. Many of the *ton* were drawn away to wager their guineas in the company of the Regent.

She turned to a footman who stood at her elbow balancing a silver tray that held an array of liquor. "Have you yet seen Sir Harry Brandon?"

"Yes, my lord. He's at the faro table."

"Has the marquess of Oberlon yet arrived?"

"I haven't seen his grace, my lord."

Hetty nodded and walked to the far corner of the room where the faro tables were set up. Her footsteps were sure, her back straight. She wouldn't allow herself any doubts about what she would do.

She saw Sir Harry lounging in one of the Louis XV chairs, observing the game's progress. She wondered why he wasn't playing.

Sir Harry was depressed. He'd already drunk too much brandy, and his bowels were fiery warm. If only he could wipe away Isabella's pale, pensive face from his mind. He hadn't meant to argue with her over receiving Lord Harry, yet when she herself had spoken so enthusiastically about Lord Monteith, he hadn't been able to keep his mouth shut. She'd said to him in a tight little voice, "I would rather marry him than Sir William Filey," and he'd yelled at her, "Ah, then do it, Madam. Both are rakehells. Yes, take the younger, why not? He'll show no more fidelity, you'll see."

He gulped down another swig of brandy, and gazed morosely into the glass.

"I'm glad you are come tonight, Harry."

Sir Harry looked up into the face of Lord Harry and grunted. "You said it was urgent that I come to White's this evening. What is it—you wish to announce your marriage to Isabella?"

Harry looked like hell, she thought. "No, this has nothing to do with Isabella, though there is much I could tell you on that score, would you but listen."

Sir Harry gave Lord Harry a nasty look then drank more brandy.

"Don't become foxed, Harry. I have need of you this evening. I need you clearheaded. I need you with me."

Sir Harry looked up quickly. "What the devil are you talking about? What are you brewing? You sound damned serious and I don't like it." Lord Harry turned suddenly, his attention riveted toward the doorway.

He followed Lord Harry's gaze and quickly placed his brandy glass on the table. In the doorway stood the Marquess of Oberlon and Harry's brother-in-law, the Earl of March. He felt Lord Harry stiffen beside him.

"Come, Harry, you must not fail me. I can count on you, can't I?"

"Of course." Harry rose quickly to stand next to Lord Harry. "Dammit, tell me what's going on. By God, what have you done?" Even across the room, he sensed the tension from the earl and the marquess. He saw the tight closed look on Lord Harry's face. He walked beside his friend toward the earl and marquess. As they drew closer, he saw his brother-in-law's cool gray eyes alight upon him, first in surprise, then in anger. He would have liked to stop dead in his tracks, yet his feet moved forward.

"So you have come."

The marquess spoke directly to Lord Harry, his words so very simple, yet Harry felt the icy spray of unspoken words fill the air.

"Yes, I am come. I have many failings, your grace, but I submit that cowardice and arrogant cruelty aren't among them. Perhaps your grace would care to elaborate upon these most interesting flaws of character."

Sir Harry was too stunned by his friend's insult to do more than gaze at him openmouthed.

Strangely enough, at least in Sir Harry's eyes, the Marquess of Oberlon didn't so much as flick an eyelid at Lord Harry's outrageous remarks. Indeed, his dark eyes seemed to gleam all the brighter.

Actually, Jason Cavander felt a strange sense of anticipation. He'd known that young Monteith wouldn't apologize to him. He didn't know why he was so certain, but he was. He'd hoped at the very least to push the young gentleman into explaining his obvious hatred for him. So, he would just have to push a bit more. He raised a black brow that made him look haughtier than the Prince Regent, and drawled with an obnoxious sneer, "You have but to provide me with suitable circumstances and I would be most willing to explain cowardice and cruelty to you, Monteith. Without a frame of reference, though, I fear I am unable to the task. If you wish to pursue flaws of character, perhaps you can readily enlighten me upon the seduction of other men's women. It begins to seem that you're another Sir William Filey in the making. Shall I counsel you to beware of the pox or are you already well schooled on the pitfalls of falling in bed with so many women?"

He'd turned her own arguments against her. He was a master at this, she'd known that he must be. He was a nobleman, a Corinthian, a man who was ruthless, a man who would do whatever was necessary to gain his own ends. Knowing all that, she hadn't been prepared. She could but try. She raised her chin, trying to achieve that disdain, that cold ridicule that flowed so easily from him, that contempt that told her without words that she was less than a fly on the table, that she was nothing.

She said, "How very interesting that you mention Sir William, your grace. I had thought him the most vile of creatures when I first came to London, yet,

I found readily enough that I was quite mistaken. Vile though he may be, he wears his villainy openly and doesn't slither about like a snake, hiding his dishonor under his belly."

"Your insults wander about in too many different directions, Monteith. They have no substance, and no ring of truth to them. Are you too shy to speak your mind? Perhaps you are afraid to say what you mean? If so, you may simply apologize to me and I shall gladly be rid of your irritating presence. I am finding you frankly annoying. I do not like to be annoyed."

He spoke calmly and indifferently, as if she were naught but a troublesome boy. Frustration and anger mounted in her, words poured from her mouth. "I would as soon apologize to that monster, Bonaparte. You spoke of my seducing other men's women—I don't think the fair Melissande quite thought of herself as belonging to a *man*. Indeed, she was so eager for my embraces, that, if I didn't know of her intimacy with your grace, I would have thought she'd been marooned alone for many a long month."

"God, Lord Harry—"

"Shut up, Harry," she said low and mean over her shoulder, her eyes never leaving Lord Oberlon's face.

Finally, she'd succeeded. She saw rage in his eyes, saw the tightening of his lips, saw the pallor of his high cheekbones. Yes, she'd made him pale with rage. Soon now, at last. She stood proudly, stiff and erect, waiting for him to strike her. With his palm? With a glove? She didn't care. She waited.

She felt as though someone suddenly whipped her feet from beneath her when the earl of March threw back his head and laughed loudly.

Jason Cavander unclenched his fisted hand. He

blinked rapidly several times and turned to the earl. "Damn you, St. Clair, what the hell are you laughing at?"

The earl, amusement still lingering in his deep voice, said more to Lord Harry rather than to the marquess, "You pick the wrong barb, my boy. Cavander here has been so plagued by women that he must needs flee from them. As for his mistresses, it has been said that their sighs of pleasure can be heard from two rooms away. Now, Monteith, may I suggest that you either tell Lord Oberlon why you find him so abhorrent or simply apologize for your many unprovoked insults and be done with this nonsense. Like his grace, I, too, grow annoyed with your inconsequential chatter."

"Yes, do, lad," the marquess said, his temper restored. He stared a moment at the young man. "Come, Monteith, I hesitate to kick a bothersome puppy. What is it about me that sticks in your craw?"

"Lord, Harry, please, leave go," Sir Harry pleaded in her ear.

Hetty felt helpless. More, she felt impotent. It wasn't until she tasted her own blood that she realized she'd bitten her lower lip. She could think of no more insults, no more sarcastic taunts. She had vowed so long ago not to tell the marquess the reason for her hatred until he lay bleeding away his miserable life at her feet. She could see all the months of her careful charade as a gentleman crumbling into failure in front of him. It was her lack of years that made her look ridiculous. For an instant, she pictured herself as the marquess must see her— an arrogant, foolish young boy. They could afford to be amused, these proud gentlemen. She was naught to them but a bothersome puppy, just as Lord Oberlon had drawled to her. Had Lord Oberlon thought Damien just as insignificant? So unimportant, in fact, as to send him out of the country with no self-recrimination? Only dimly did she hear Lord Oberlon give a crack of rude laughter, and say to the earl, "Come, Julien, the farce is ended. I need no apology from a young whelp who is scarce breeched, and who now appears to have lost his tongue. Bravado in the young should be discouraged, don't you agree? There's nothing behind it, nothing at all. It's very trying."

She felt a surge of hatred so strong that she shook with it. A footman passed by, bearing a tray of glasses filled with chilled champagne. She grasped the slender stem of a glass and held it in front of her, as if readying for a toast. She heard her own voice spilling out words with surprising calmness.

"That I have afforded you such entertainment, your grace, leaves me most gratified. You find my insults nonsensical. Perhaps it's true, for I haven't your years of studied brutality. Where my words have failed, perhaps this will not." She dashed the champagne into Lord Oberlon's face.

She heard a moan from Sir Harry. She heard the whispers from shocked gentlemen who were even now drawing closer. But her attention didn't waver from the marquess.

She watched him pull a white pocket handkerchief with a deft, graceful movement, and slowly mop the champagne from his face. In a voice so quiet that she had to lean forward to hear, Lord Oberlon said, "You give me now no choice, Monteith. Do you wish to fight in the middle of White's, or can your mad rush to dispatch yourself to hell wait until the morrow?"

"A night to anticipate your demise will give me great pleasure."

"Very well," he said, his voice flat. "Julien, will you act for me?"

"Yes, if it must be, Jason."

Sir Harry felt his brother-in-law's gray eyes. Even as Lord Harry turned, he knew that he had no choice but to second his friend. His *yes* was a croak.

The earl of March stepped forward and laid his hand on his brother-in-law's sleeve. He said formally, "It is my duty as a second to seek reconciliation."

At the silent set faces of Lord Monteith and Lord Oberlon, he continued slowly, "As you will. Tomorrow morning at seven o'clock at the north end of Hounslow Heath. Harry, come with me now, we must make arrangements."

"Such a fool you are, Monteith," Lord Oberlon said in a pensive, almost sad voice. "Will you tell me anything before you die?" He turned finally and strode from the gaming salon.

Hetty was left standing alone, the empty champagne glass still held tightly in her hand. Whispering gentlemen began to disperse back to the gaming tables. She thought she saw a footman speaking behind a white-gloved hand to one of his peers. Slowly and with great deliberation, she strode to the footman and placed the champagne glass down upon his tray. She wondered fleetingly if her own face was as pale as the footman's. She drew a deep breath and walked from the gaming salon, not looking back.

Chapter Twenty-three

Strangely, Pottson said not a word when Hetty, an hour later, tried with as much calm as she could muster to relate to him what had happened.

"We both knew this night had to come, Pottson, for there was, after all, no other reason for Lord Harry's existence. On the morrow, Damien will be avenged."

Pottson raised weary troubled eyes to Miss Hetty's young, innocent face. "Aye," he said quietly, "Master Damien will be avenged, or you, Miss Hetty, will follow him to the grave and it will all have been for naught."

She felt a sudden chill touch her heart and shivered despite the warmth of the small parlor. "Pray don't seal my fate so quickly. A man's chest is a much larger target than the wafers at Manton's." She paused a moment and looked about her. Odd how this small apartment seemed more her home than Sir Archibald's town house.

"When we return tomorrow morning, Pottson, we must decide what is to be done with Lord Harry Monteith. And, more importantly, my friend, we must discuss your future. If you have a liking for Herefordshire, my brother, Sir John, would, I am certain, be most willing to engage Damien's batman."

Pottson merely grunted an unintelligible reply, and Hetty, mindful of being refreshed on the morrow, rose and walked slowly into Lord Harry's bedchamber to change into a gown.

As was his habit, Pottson accompanied Miss Hetty back to her father's town house. As they drew up to the servants' entrance, where Millie stood waiting, Hetty said, "I'll see you at six o'clock, Pottson. When it is over, we shall enjoy a hearty breakfast and bid Lord Harry a fond adieu."

Pottson just looked at her for a long moment. Then he lowered his eyes, nodded, and disappeared into the night.

"What's wrong with him?" Millie asked once they were in Hetty's bedroom. "Ate too much of his own cooking?"

"Yes, lamb stew," Hetty said. She had no intention of telling Millie anything.

If Hetty hugged Millie a bit longer than was her wont, Millie didn't say anything. She left her young mistress, her own thoughts on the fair that was coming to Bidlington the following week where her sister lived.

Hetty didn't climb into her bed. She carried her candle to her writing desk and prepared herself to perform a task for which she had no liking, but a task that had to be done. She smoothed out a piece of plain white paper, dipped the quill into the ink pot and began to write. "My dearest father," she wrote, pausing to chew on the quill handle before continuing. "When you read this letter, you will know that you will never see me again. I pray that you will find forgiveness in your heart for the inevitable scandal that my death will cause. I have tried to act in accordance with principles that carry the highest honor, and although my failure must leave you in the forefront to deal with the unpleasant aftermath, I beg that you will try to understand my motives."

Motives? Her motive was there, for all to see. She'd simply wanted to avenge Damien. Would she die in the attempt? She hated the fear that surged through her. She didn't want to die.

The single candle had gutted in its socket before Hetty laid down her pen and rubbed her cramped fingers. Her explanation had covered five long pages, and although she feared much repetition, she had no wish to reread her work. Wearily, she stood and stretched. She saw with a shock that it was past midnight.

Hurriedly, she drew forth more paper, took quill in hand, and wrote much in the same style to John and Louisa as she had to her father.

She thought as she sealed both letters into their envelopes that if she were not to leave the dueling field alive, John would have to seek redress from the marquess. John's friend, the man who was responsible for both his brother's and sister's deaths.

She flung away from the writing table and paced back and forth across the width of her room until the chill drove her to her bed. She sank beneath the heavy covers and stared into the darkness, her eyes refusing to close. How strange it is, she thought, that death has happened so very close to me, yet I cannot really imagine it coming to me.

When word of Damien's death had reached her,

she had felt as though a part of her had died with him. Yet, she still breathed, still felt the sun upon her face, still heartily enjoyed her father's political vagaries. Even though the past months had moved with unremitting purpose to this point, the possibility of her own death had always seemed only a vague specter, the meaning of death lying only with Damien and in the final revenge she sought from his murderer.

She thought again of Sir John, his open, bluff good nature, his sincere friendship with the Marquess of Oberlon. Perhaps she should have told him of the marquess, of Damien, of Elizabeth Springville. Oh no, it was *her* revenge, a debt she owed to Damien. She realized with sudden insight that her single-minded goal had hurled her back into life. How very different she was now from the Hetty who had moved through her days and nights after Damien's death like a vague shadow, allowing nothing to touch her.

If she emerged the victor on the morrow, she would again lose part of herself—the proud, outspoken Lord Harry, the brash counterpart of Henrietta Rolland. Which Henrietta Rolland? Parts of her seemed to be strewn all about London, each with a different function, each unwhole, each wanting. How strange it was, too, that Jason Cavander had known each of her parts. The Henrietta Rolland who had attended the masked ball didn't care for this thought. The marquess she'd known at the masked ball was all that was charming and fascinating, not at all the man who'd had Damien killed, the man who'd simply taken what he'd wanted, not caring, not looking back.

The clock chimed one o'clock in the morning. She had but five hours until Millie would awaken her. She finally fell asleep wondering if Millie suspected that something other than an early ride in the park with Mr. Scuddimore was the purpose for arising at such an ungodly hour.

When the Marquess of Oberlon unceremoniously slammed out of White's, his many-caped greatcoat flung carelessly over his shoulders, he was in the grip of such rage that he covered the entire length of Bond Street before he was aware of the frigid night wind cutting unhampered through his elegant evening clothes. He drew to a halt and fastened his greatcoat securely about him, and jerked on the fur gloves that had hung out of his pocket.

It was perhaps the feel of the sticky dried champagne on his face and the still damp touch of his cravat against his neck that finally brought forth the reasonable man. Having a glass of champagne dashed into one's face was certainly not a pleasant experience, yet it had proved to be as effective an insult in 1816, a year when dueling was considered most unfashionable, actually illegal, as a slap with a glove or a few well-chosen words had been to his father's contemporaries in the bygone days when dueling was an honored activity that cut many a gentleman's life short. The marquess remembered his bewigged grandfather, a full-lipped, lecherous old gentleman who, had he not broken his neck cramming his horse over a fence, would very likely have been felled by a ball from a pistol the very next day by a one-time crony whom he'd negligently insulted. As it was, the one-time crony had sniffed copiously at his grandfather's funeral and the marquess's father had sarcastically muttered to his small son that he didn't know if the man's sniffing was from grief or from being cheated out of putting a bullet through his grandfather's heart.

Lord Oberlon paused a moment, realizing that his wayward thoughts had carried his feet into Millsom Street, altogether in the opposite direction from Berkeley Square. He turned and began to retrace his steps. How very ridiculous it was, he thought anew, to be forced to fight a duel with a young gentleman whose very existence had been unknown to him but a month before. There was but one man whom Jason Cavander had ever wanted to call out. Even so, his father's sincere disgust at the waste resulting from duels had stilled his fury, if not his contempt for Sir William Filey. He found himself wondering, even now, what he would have done if he had been able to prove beyond doubt Filey's loathsome conduct in the affair. Damn Filey anyway, and damn Elizabeth. Filey had cared too much for his own skin to ever openly taunt the marquess. As for Elizabeth, he knew that toward the end she had hated him as much as she had Filey. He shut his mind against further unpleasant memories. Elizabeth was dead and long buried, her hatred and bitter unhappiness locked away with her forever.

The marquess walked up the steps to his town house and raised his hand to the knocker, only to have Rabbell open the door. "Ah, your grace. The earl of March awaits you in the study, your grace."

"So my faithful second comes to give me encouragement." Lord Oberlon felt no hesitance in speaking aloud of the duel, for Rabbell's unnatural mannerisms told him clearly enough that every servant was undoubtedly aware in the most minute detail of the evening's fiasco. Sometime, he thought, as his butler helped to divest him of his greatcoat and gloves, I must force him to tell me how the servants' infallible grapevine can be so damnably efficient.

He walked thoughtfully to his study. "Well, Julien," he said, upon opening the door, "I'd call this a fine night's work. Have you come to sympathize or tell me what a damned fool I am?"

The earl was lounging next to the large Italian marble fireplace, looking as lost in his thoughts as Jason had earlier. "Come, St. Clair, I should be the one thoughtfully depressed, not you. Yours is a simple task. You have only to take the boy away after I am done with him."

The earl pushed his shoulders from the mantelpiece and walked to the marquess. "You've been long coming back, Jason. Actually, when you came in, I was plotting the possibility of trussing Monteith up in a sack and having my captain sail away with him to the West Indies. Perhaps acting as a bookkeeper on my plantation in Jamaica will give him a healthier respect for the life he leads here in London."

"I daresay the young gentleman would rule the islands within a month—either through persuasion or by dispatching all the current leaders in duels." Neither man laughed. The marquess said, "It's hellishly cold, Julien, would you care for a sherry?"

The earl nodded and there was companionable silence until both gentlemen, glasses in hand, seated themselves near to the crackling fire. After a moment, the earl said reluctantly, "As much as I dislike it, Jason, I must of course inquire as to your preference of weapons, as Monteith was the challenger."

"Need you really ask, Julien? A pistol is far too deadly a weapon, and you must know that despite all the young puppy has said and done, I have no wish to kill him. He can't be all that experienced with the foil, and I hope to contrive a quick and clean prick through his arm. That ought to cool his murderous instincts, at least for a month."

"That's what I hoped you would say, Jason. I might tell you, too, that Harry informed me that Monteith is a crack shot. I would have feared the outcome had you chosen pistols."

"You believe I could be brought to the ground by a lad who can't even grow whiskers? No, don't answer that. Now, how is poor Harry taking all this? Judging from his openmouthed expression, I gather he didn't know what Monteith intended this evening."

"Harry is torn in two directions. Of course, his honor forbids him to refuse to second his friend. I left him with Kate. Yes, I'm a coward, but she deals well with him. Good Lord, what could I say?"

The earl rose and placed his empty glass on the sideboard. "I must be off now, Jason. It's past midnight and you must be clear and steady on the morrow. I shall be here—with my carriage—before seven o'clock."

"Your carriage, Julien? You terrify me. I'd hoped to ride from the park all in one piece."

The earl merely smiled slightly, but remained silent. Actually, it had been Kate who'd insisted on the carriage. The earl said as he walked beside the marquess from the study, "What do you intend to do about Melissande now, Jason?"

Lord Oberlon shrugged, saying, "Her house has three more months on its lease. She may stay until then. With her beauty and figure, I have no doubt that she will attach another well-breeched gentleman long before that time." He added, a hint of amused incredulity in his voice, "Did you know that Monteith gave her a riding habit? Did you know he provided a mare for her called Coquette? Do you know he likened her to Helen of Troy and to Aphrodite, a goddess I'm certain Melissande has never heard of before? His ingenuity is frightening. His determination to fell me is, well, it's more than frightening. I only wish I knew why."

"A riding habit." The earl laughed, he couldn't stop it. Things were so very grim, yet look what Monteith had done to achieve his goal. It boggled the mind. The earl turned to his friend and clasped his hand. Mindful of Rabbell standing near, he said quietly, "You have acted quite rightly in this wretched business. Until tomorrow, Jason."

Chapter Twenty-four

It was a blistering cold overcast morning. Naked oak and elm trees stood sentinel over the hard frozen ground at the north end of Hounslow Heath. There was no foliage this time of year. There were no onlookers, not on the heath, even the highwaymen who chanced to ply their trade here had long gone back to their lairs.

The dull thudding of horses' hooves and the crunching of carriage wheels were the only sounds to break the monotony of the gently rustling branches, and the chirping of the more hearty sparrows.

Sir Harry Brandon stole a sideways glance at Lord Harry. He shifted uneasily in the saddle at the sight of his friend's set face. His usually shining eyes were narrowed in deep concentration and his lips were drawn in a bloodless thin line. Lord Harry had said not a word to him, save to beg a mount from his meager stable for Pottson. Wordlessly, Harry had obliged, but the precious time this detour had cost put the hour much too close to seven o'clock for his peace of mind. But Lord Harry seemed oblivious of the hour, leaving Harry to wonder if he was aware of the nicety of the gentleman's code that forbade a duel if either of the opponents arrived after the appointed time.

Sir Harry was forced to conclude that Lord Harry knew exactly what he was about, for it lacked two minutes to the hour when their small cavalcade broke into the clearing. Not twenty feet away stood the earl of March's town carriage.

As they dismounted and tethered their mounts, Hetty turned to Sir Harry and said, "I know you thought I'd be late, but you must know, Harry, one must always make an entrance after all the guests have arrived."

Sir Harry could find no witty rejoinder for this admirable display of *sang froid,* and said only, "Quite."

As Harry fidgeted with his horse's bridle, Hetty said gently, "Should you not meet with the earl of March, Harry? The weapons, you know."

"Aye," Harry said, falling back on his mother's Scottish speech. When he was beyond earshot, Hetty turned to Pottson, who stood in grim silence, his hands wringing into the folds of his coat.

"Don't fail me, Pottson. Whatever happens must occur without any interference from you. Give me your promise."

Pottson stood in frozen silence. Hetty grabbed his arm and shook him. "Damn you, Pottson, your promise."

"But Master Damien would never wish for this, Miss Hetty. Gawd, he would never—"

"Stop it now. It's far too late for maudlin scenes. Do you swear to keep a still tongue in your mouth?"

"Yes, Miss Hetty," he said finally, looking squarely into her fierce blue eyes, "I swear. But I hate it."

"Hate is a good thing in this damnable situation. Now, I want you to remain here." She turned on her heel, her boots crunching loudly into the frozen earth, and without a backward glance, strode toward the small circle formed by the three gentlemen.

She knew that concentration was born of calmness, and had, for the past two hours, mentally raised the dueling pistol in her hand, turned her body sideways so as to present the smallest possible target, aimed carefully and tenderly stroked the trigger. Over and over she had played through each minute movement until her mind finally settled with single thought to its one purpose. There was now no room for fear or self-doubt to slip in uninvited.

Her stride was a confident swagger, her hands still inside their warm gloves, steady and dry.

She glanced only briefly at the earl of March, her eyes narrowing on the marquess.

"Ah, I bid you good morning, your grace, my lord March. I don't wish my mare to become restive. Shall we begin?"

Admirable, the marquess thought reluctantly, the boy shows courage beyond his years. But his voice belied his thoughts as he said with a mocking drawl, "By all means, Monteith. I wouldn't wish you to be late for your visit to the surgeon."

"Ah, but you, your grace, it won't be a surgeon to attend to you. It will give me great satisfaction to see your blood seeping into the ground."

The earl said abruptly, "Do you wish to inspect your foil, Lord Monteith?" He opened the long narrow case and carefully lifted out a glittering silver rapier.

Hetty looked stupidly down at the foil. Damnation, what a ludicrous mistake Harry had made. He, of all people, knew that she preferred the pistol. She turned to him, her jaw working with frustration and anger. Her voice was as hard as the frozen earth. "What have you done, Harry? You know I choose the pistol."

Sir Harry's eyes widened in disbelief. "But, Lord Harry, it doesn't matter. Of course you prefer pistols, but there wasn't anything I could say in the matter."

Lord Oberlon watched the two young men, as confused as Sir Harry. How could Monteith ever have assumed that the choice of weapons would be his? He'd been the one to issue the challenge.

The earl of March said smoothly, "As the challenger, Monteith, you have no choice in the selection of weapons. Lord Oberlon has decided upon foils."

Sir Harry added desperately, "Don't you remember, Lord Harry? It was you who dashed the champagne in his grace's face."

The marquess said as he flicked at the sleeve of his greatcoat, "It would appear that Lord Monteith fences well only with words. I will accept your explanation, lad, as well as your apology, if you choose now to sincerely give it."

Hetty's secure mental fortress had shattered into myriad unrelated thoughts, uppermost among them the ridiculous phrase she had spoken to Signore Bertioli the afternoon before—"a young lion with only a roar . . . we shall soon know if I am only a young lion with a roar."

She looked blindly at the three faces staring at her, and saw only contempt, for she was not looking at them but back into herself. She remembered her blithely spoken words, again to Signore Bertioli, that a man who goes into battle with but one weapon and a prayer is a fool.

"You have but to explain and apologize," his words sounded in her mind. He invited her to crawl away with a sincere apology, in shame and dishonor.

She saw Damien, lying lifeless on the bloody battlefield of Waterloo, crying out for vengeance. Her mind fastened upon his image, and in that instant, her thoughts wove themselves together again.

She said, her voice colder than the early morning air, "Foils, your grace? It makes no difference to me how you wish to die."

She picked up a gleaming rapier from the black velvet-lined case and tested its weight in her hand. It was light, steady, and exquisitely forged.

The marquess frowned at Monteith's baiting words, not in renewed anger, but in perplexity. He wasn't blind. The stunned shock on the lad's face, then the empty coursing of fear that had left his eyes glazed, made the marquess suddenly wonder if he weren't playing the part of the villain in some sort of cheap melodrama at Drury Lane, a villain who seemed, strangely, to have the upper hand over the hero.

"Jason."

He shook his head, focusing on the task at hand. He took his foil from the earl's outstretched hand.

"Take care, my friend," the earl said.

The marquess nodded, wondering if Julien meant him to take care of himself or to take care of young Monteith. He found, foolishly enough, that he had to hand the foil back while he stripped off his great-coat and gloves.

"Damn but it's cold, don't you think so, Lord Harry?" Harry wished it were a day from now, even an hour, anything to have this over and done with and he and Lord Harry safe and well and on their way back to London. He didn't think he'd ever been so scared in his life. He watched as Lord Harry unbuttoned his waistcoat.

"Yes, it's cold. Who cares?"

"Lord Harry, I don't think—"

"Yes?"

"God, it's done, isn't it? There's no turning back now. I'll keep your greatcoat warm."

Stripped to a loose, frilled white shirt, breeches and hessians, Harry watched Lord Harry slash his foil through the air several times, testing its flexibility, then watched him move forward to where the marquess stood, dressed in black breeches, black hessians, and white shirt, his side presented.

Hetty flexed her knees, leaning slightly forward, and placed her left hand lightly upon her hip. She slashed the foil again in a wide arc and stood ready for the earl's command.

"*En garde!*" The earl's words rang out harshly in the silent wood.

The marquess began to move gracefully toward her, his blade carefully poised, his eyes intent upon her face. His foil suddenly flashed out wide to her right side, testing for the quickness of her reaction.

Hetty caught his blade handily, parrying his thrust with no particular difficulty, and skipped lightly to bring her weight down on her left foot. The marquess drew back, his foil making small circles, readying like a viper, Hetty thought, to strike again. She sensed his easy control, his practiced mastery, the silver blade appearing to her like an extension of his arm and his will. Thus it was with Signore Bertioli. Give me your skill, Signore, she prayed silently, then with a quick sidestep, lunged forward. The edge of her foil rang against tempered steel and slid nearly halfway up the marquess's blade, until with a powerful flick of his wrist, he parried the strike. The force of his parry sent stabs of pain up her arm.

The marquess was mildly surprised at the quickness of the lunge, but felt the loosening of the lad's foil when he'd disengaged with brutal strength. The lad had quickness, but not the strength and endurance to last for any length of time against him. He needed only to engage the boy in a continuous flurry, giving him no time to rest, and, above all, rigidly control the encounter so that Monteith couldn't slip through his guard. He drew a wide path of control in front of him, discouraging further sudden attacks, but engaging with pounding force. He saw the uncertainty and frustration growing on the boy's face, and held to his strategy.

Hetty knew exactly what he wanted to do. She tried to save her strength, drew back and began to stalk him, lightly on her toes, dancing in a circular direction opposite from his, just as Signore Bertioli had taught her. He drew toward her to force a flurry, and in that exact instant, she lunged forward, her right arm extended to its full length.

He evaded her attack handily, giving ground to her. She followed, her blade dancing in the silent air in the brief seconds between clashes. Then she felt the power of him, unchecked for an instant, driving her back. She saw his powerful thigh muscles bulging in his knit breeches, and felt her own legs begin to tremble. That she wasn't a man would bring her down. That she simply didn't have his strength would mean her death. It wasn't fair. She wouldn't accept it. She would beat him because she was in the right. There had to be justice somewhere. That justice had to be within her.

She was sweating and quickly dashed her hand across her eyes. Her breath was coming heavily now, and she knew she had to retreat at least a moment from him.

She took three light jumping steps backward, disengaging her blade from his, gulping in the precious air. But he was on her in an instant, his lunge curiously shallow, yet clashing against her blade with such force that her fingers nearly crumpled on their grip. She met his eyes in that moment, saw that they were calm and coolly calculating, and felt a quiver of anger at her own weakness. With more anger than skill, she stepped into the onslaught of his foil with a furious lunge. The blades crackled together and he bore his hand upward, pulling her forward until the foils were locked at their base. She hated her own harsh breathing, for he was but inches from her face and could hear her weakening. Damn him, there wasn't even a drop of sweat on his forehead.

Hetty managed to jerk free and leapt back, almost losing her balance. Her free hand clutched wildly at the empty air, in a frantic attempt to keep from falling. Even as she regained her balance, she was aware that the marquess could have been upon her in a second. Yet, he stood silently back, the look on his face curiously dispassionate.

"Damn you," she yelled at him. "Damn you to hell and the devil."

The marquess readied himself for a wild lunge, his eyes, this time, resting coolly upon the boy's right arm. He was fighting bravely and with some skill. But he was tiring visibly. It was time to bring the duel to an honorable end. Odd that he wanted it to be honorable, for Monteith. He didn't understand himself, save that he saw something of what he'd perhaps once been in the boy, a boy who would, nevertheless, give anything to run his foil through his chest. It was a disconcerting thought, but it held him nonetheless.

Hetty wanted to leap upon him, to tear the foil from his hand. It was the severe, rapped out words of Signore Bertioli spoken on a long ago afternoon, that held her back. "Young lord, he who loses his head will most certainly lose his heart. And not, young sir, to a lady." She'd laughed, digested his words and proceeded to feint with such subtle skill that for the only time during his tutelage, she had nearly managed to break through his guard.

She became aware of the calm yet expectant stance of the marquess. He expects me to lunge wildly, she realized with a start. Very well, let him think it to be so.

She clumsily lurched forward, her foil extended its full length, its tip aimed for his heart.

The marquess saw his opportunity, for Monteith had forfeited his guard. He swiftly parried the boy's blade to one side and lunged at his upper arm.

In that instant, Hetty executed the Italian master's most difficult trick: she drew back her blade, jumped quickly to the side, deflecting his blade from her arm, and lunged with all her strength toward his shoulder.

From instinct born of long practice, the marquess whirled about, slid his foil under Monteith's and threw the boy off balance. But he couldn't temper the force of his lunge, and with sickening ease, he felt the tip of his blade slice into Monteith's side.

Hetty jerked her head up, startled that she'd failed. She felt a prick in her side, then a strange cold sensation, as if a slap of frigid air had hit her skin. The marquess stood frozen in front of her, his face pale, set.

She saw that his foil was covered from its tip to almost a quarter of its length in bright red. It is blood, my blood, she thought, but she felt no pain.

She heard the earl of March's voice. "Hold Monteith. Lord Oberlon has drawn blood. It's over."

Over? No, nothing was over. Was the earl blind? Did he and the marquess expect her to crawl away in dishonor because of a slight prick in her side? She cried out suddenly, her voice strong and clear, "Damn you, Jason Cavander. I've just begun with you! *En garde!*" She felt strong, confident, as if her body no longer existed—only her mind and her arm, the foil its extension.

The marquess shot a helpless glance at the earl. He had time for naught else, for Monteith lunged at him with the fury of demons from hell. He leapt back, parrying the thrust. He saw the glazed look of purpose in the lad's eyes and knew that his mind had closed itself to any pain. The lad would bleed to death before he realized how badly he was wounded. The small circle of blood that stained the loose white shirt was spreading rapidly, flattening the material against the wound.

He called out over the hissing of the blades, "Monteith, draw in! Look at your side."

He might as well have spoken to the wind, for though Hetty heard his words, her mind refused to allow her to understand their significance. She heard herself laugh aloud, a strong, triumphant laugh. She pressed him, her blade cutting so swiftly through the air that he backed away and to the side to diminish the force of her thrusts.

The attack was unmeasured, wild. The marquess was very aware that there was no timing or skill in the frantic lunges. The boy's mind keeps him from seeing the truth of the matter, the marquess thought with growing concern. If he didn't quickly bring the duel to a halt, the boy would die. He knew Monteith was beyond understanding, and he swallowed back further words of warning.

For the next several minutes, the marquess gave ground, parrying thrust after wild thrust, his movements wholly defensive. The boy was tiring, his attack so awkward and ill-timed that the marquess could have easily slipped through his guard. Yet, he held back. He was waiting for the instant when he could catch Monteith's foil high near his hand and rip it from his fingers. He watched, parried, his eyes alert, waiting for the perfect moment.

He is weakening and falling back, Hetty's mind told her. Press him, press him harder. That's right, he's afraid now. He's afraid of you, afraid of the death you will bring him. That's right, send him back and back even more. Press him!

The marquess made a mistake. For the instant his eyes returned to the matted, now huge circle of blood that had spread upward toward the boy's chest, he broke his concentration.

Hetty whipped her foil under his, and the suddenness of the impact, at the same instant as his attention wavered, jerked his blade from his fingers and sent it flying to the ground.

What a damned fool you are, he thought dispassionately. He felt the pressure of the boy's blade against his chest.

She'd done it, she'd actually done it. You've won, you've won. She stood poised forward, her weight on her right leg, her foil extended its full length, the tip against her enemy's heart. Why does he not say something? Why does he not plead for his life? The glazed shock that had held her in sway loosed its grip on her vision, and she stared at him. He stood quietly before her and she could see no fear in his dark eyes.

The earl of March forced himself to hold his place, even as he shouted, "For God's sake, Jason, jerk away his foil."

The marquess made no sign that he'd even heard the earl's words. He couldn't be certain why he made no move. There was something in the boy's eyes that held him.

Hetty felt the powerful, single purpose of her mind begin to fall away from her, and in that instant, she saw herself as she used to be. She saw Henrietta Rolland before she'd discovered the marquess's hand in her brother's death. She'd been hollow with grief, hollow with the touch of death. Still, death had not claimed her, and she had savored the full consciousness of life, even in those months when she'd felt most alone. It had seemed so simple to her to plan the marquess's execution, his death a just retribution, a full payment for the grief he'd brought to her. Yet, he stood before her now—proud, arrogant—but alive, just as she was alive. She realized that she'd used the idea of his death to assuage her own grief. But to run her foil through his heart, to rob him of life, to actually bring about another human being's death, was beyond her. Her single-minded hatred, her pact of vengeance crumbled.

She gasped aloud, jerked back the foil from his chest, and clasping it in both hands, plunged it into the frozen ground with all her remaining strength. She jerked her fingers away from it as if it were evil.

She'd thrust it deep enough so that the handle swung back and forth, its gentle hissing sounding softly in the silence.

"Damn you, I can't kill you! Oh God, Damien, forgive me, but I can't do it. I can't do it." Her cry was filled with the deep pain of her spirit and the growing agony in her body. She looked into his face, the face she had hated even in her dreams. His face grew distorted, twisting into a mask of death—Damien's face. "I can't kill you," she said, her voice racked with sobs, wrenching cries tearing from her throat. Her body was taking her over now, closing off any control from her mind. Searing pain tore through her side and she doubled over, clutching her arms about her. She felt hot stickiness on her hands and looked down in dumb surprise at her blood-covered fingers. She looked wildly about her, but saw only blurred images. She heard loud voices, yet they came to her ears as unintelligible sounds. Her knees buckled beneath her and she fell heavily to the frozen earth, her head striking an outjutting rock.

Blackness flooded her.

Chapter Twenty-five

The marquess was at the boy's side in an instant, his hands tearing at the blood-soaked shirt. He had to stop the bleeding. Damn, but he wasn't going to be Monteith's murderer. He acted on instinct, not allowing himself to think about the incredible scene in which he had just played a part. He ripped open the shirt and tugged at the buckskin breeches to bare the wound. It was not bare skin that met his eyes, but a tight-fitting muslin wrap hemmed with blue ribbon. He had torn it apart before the significance of the garment hit him. Though side, ribs, and belly were covered with blood, the inward curving to a slender waist, the soft smoothness of the white skin hit his brain like a stroke of lightning. No, no, there had to be a mistake, he wouldn't believe this, but he had to. He stared at that blue ribbon, at that white soft skin.

Oh God, Lord Harry Monteith was a girl.

"Jason, how badly is he wounded?"

In that instant, the marquess made a decision and acted on it. He jerked the shirt back over the girl's side. "It's bad, Julien. Quickly, give me your handkerchief. Harry, your neck cloth. We must stop the bleeding."

"Mis—Lord Harry. Dear God, Lord Harry." The

marquess glanced up at the valet's frantic face. God, the man had nearly given all away. He looked Pottson straight in the eye and said firmly, "*Lord Harry* will be all right. Don't say anything now. He will survive, I swear it to you."

"Aye, your grace," Pottson said, looking from his mistress's bloody-soaked shirt to the silent warning in the marquess's dark eyes. It seemed the marquess had taken the matter out of his hands. Why? Pottson didn't know, but now there was nothing he could do. He stared down at his mistress. He felt helpless and paralyzed.

The marquess used his body as a shield as he pressed the wadded handkerchief against the wound. "Now your neck cloth, Harry, so I can bind Julien's handkerchief." Gently, he slipped the wide band of material under her back and knotted it over the pad.

He rose, lifting her in his arms. "Julien, I require your carriage. I very nearly killed the boy and now I intend to take care of him." He turned to the valet. "You will accompany me to Thurston Hall."

"Now, see here, your grace." Sir Harry stepped forward, uncertain of what he should do, but knowing that somehow he was the only one left to do anything. He was Lord Harry's second. Lord Harry was surely his responsibility. But the world had taken a faulty turn. Lord Harry had disarmed the marquess. He could have killed him but he'd not done it, and that made no sense. Lord Harry's foil was still gently swaying back and forth in the early morning breeze. And now the marquess was insisting upon taking care of Lord Harry, who hated his guts. None of it made any sense.

"No, Harry," the earl said quietly. He looked searchingly into his friend's eyes, then said evenly, "Lord Oberlon will do what is best, Harry. You may depend upon his word. I would trust him with my life. Surely you can trust your friend's life to him."

As Pottson threw the heavy greatcoat over Hetty, the earl asked, "Thurston Hall, Jason? It will take you an hour and a half to reach. Shouldn't you come back to London instead?"

"I know how long it takes," the marquess said, meeting the earl's eyes. "It doesn't matter. Once the bleeding is stopped, it makes no difference whether Monteith is abed in London or at Thurston Hall. It is better for the lad to be out of London."

"You will keep us informed of his progress, Jason?"

"You both may depend upon it. Now, we must be off. I would cover as many miles as possible before the lad regains consciousness."

"But a doctor," Sir Harry said. "Lord Harry needs a doctor. The best doctors are in London." No one paid Sir Harry any mind as he trailed after the marquess who was carrying his friend as gently as he would a babe in his arms.

Jason Cavander turned as he stepped into the carriage. "Don't worry, Harry. I suffered a like wound several years back and I assure you that I will provide Monteith the best care." He mounted the carriage steps, and said over his shoulder, "Julien, you will see to Monteith's horse, won't you?"

"Don't worry," the earl said. He took Harry's arm and drew him away.

"Now you," Jason Cavander said to Pottson. "What is your name?"

"Pottson, your grace," he said, moving quickly to the carriage door. Lord Oberlon lowered his voice, for he had no wish that even Silken hear his words. "Now, Pottson, what is the young lady's name, if you please?"

Pottson stared vacantly at his unconscious mistress pressed close to the marquess's chest. His promise to her rang clear in his mind, yet, he knew at the same time that all had changed. What the devil was he to do?

"Out with it, Pottson. Don't you see that I must know everything now if we are to pull through this mess without a scandal that would rock all of London? What is the girl's damned name?"

"She's Miss Henrietta Rolland, your grace." Oh gawd, what would happen now? She'd kill him, Pottson knew it. He'd betrayed her, yet what could he do?

Henrietta Rolland, he thought blankly. That lovely young lady at the Ranleaghs' ball who'd fascinated him and who'd liked him very much as well until she'd learned who he was. Sir Archibald's daughter, Jack's sister—she'd left Sir Archibald's house rather than dine with him. And the dowdy female at his aunt Melberry's soiree who'd made his eyes cross just to look at her, yet she'd taunted him and mocked him until . . . until she'd realized that to continue just made him all the more curious. Then she'd become a vulgar, obnoxious twit. And as Lord Harry she'd turned her attention to Melissande, she'd even taunted him that he wasn't enough of a man for his mistress. A girl, no, a young lady of quality had said that to him. He didn't understand any of it. Why the devil did she hate him? Had she assumed the identity of a young gentleman just to kill him? It was fantastic, utterly without sense to him. He pulled himself together. "Ride with Silken. I will see to her. Dammit, man, go now."

He settled her in his arms and yelled out the carriage window, "Spring'em, Silken! If they're blown, we'll change them at Smithfield. Hurry, I want to be at Thurston Hall in an hour."

Silken took his master at his word, and Lord Oberlon clutched her more tightly to his chest to keep her steady as the carriage lurched and swayed over the rutted ground. He gently pulled back the greatcoat that covered her and carefully eased up her shirt. The wadded handkerchief was nearly soaked with blood. He placed his fingers atop the wound and pressed down. He tried to cradle her as best he could with his free hand, and drew the greatcoat over her.

He stared down into her pale, still face. Henrietta was the beauty of the family, Louisa had said. His eyes followed the slender column of her neck to the firm smooth chin, a stubborn chin, he thought, bloody stubborn and determined. Just look at all she'd done. He looked closely at the high cheekbones, the straight, proud nose, the thick, fair lashes lying in wet spikes on her cheeks. How strange that looking down at her now, everything made sense—the myriad parts he had thought about so fancifully now fit perfectly together. She had Jack's blond hair. Curling ringlets were working themselves loose from the black ribbon at her neck, and the thick pomade no longer held the curls back from her forehead. Were she conscious, he knew her eyes would be as light and pure a blue as the summer sky. He also knew she would stare at him with contempt and hatred. She would mock him. She would be more arrogant than he himself had ever been at her age. But she hadn't killed him. She'd pulled up. He could still see the foil as it swung gently back and forth in the early morning breeze.

I think you were born a fool and will most certainly leave this world an equal fool, he told himself, shaking his head at his blindness.

It was often said that the clothes made the man. He was now inclined to believe, rather, that one saw what one expected to see. Lord Monteith dressed as a gentleman, talked like a gentleman and partook in all the gentleman's sports. Everyone had accepted him as such. Now, gazing down at her undeniably female face, he was forced to admit with rueful admiration that she had pulled the wool over everyone's eyes. Even Melissande. He laughed aloud at that. Melissande accepting all the flattery, the riding costume, the mare. It was marvelous, by God, bloody unbelievable and he'd been taken in like all the rest.

Ah, but why had she hated him so much as to force a duel upon him? Why Jack's sister, in particular? It made no sense to him. He could bring Pottson into the carriage with him and demand the reason. Yet, somehow, he wanted to hear from her own lips why she'd planned and executed this outrageous charade. He realized, too, his hand covered with her blood, that his most pressing concern wasn't to discover her motives, but rather to save her life.

The miles pounded by. He began to grow concerned that she didn't regain consciousness. Minutes ago they'd bowled past the signpost for Helderton, a small village not many miles from the halfway point to Smithfield. He gazed down at her again and saw for the first time a dark purplish bruise forming over her temple. She must have struck her head when she fell. He quickly laid his hand over her breast to feel for her heartbeat. It was, he thought, rapid but steady. A blow on the head could keep her from regaining consciousness. He prayed silently that it wasn't serious.

He found himself wondering if he was not a coward. Had he hidden her identity from the others to protect his own reputation? By God, who would want it known that he'd been challenged to a duel by a girl? That she'd managed to have him at her mercy, the tip of her foil against his heart? Was he, in fact, endangering her life to keep himself from being a laughingstock?

He looked up as the carriage drew to a halt in the yard of the Red Rose Inn, in the center of Smithfield.

Silken's small, pointed face soon appeared at the carriage window. "The cattle are winded, your grace."

"Change 'em, quickly, Silken. Five minutes, no more." As soon as Silken had bustled away to search out the ostler, Pottson scratched lightly on the carriage door to gain the marquess's attention.

"Is Miss Hetty all right, your grace? Please, sir, she'll live, won't she?"

"Yes, Pottson. The bleeding has stopped. When she fell, she hit her head on a rock, and it's that keeps her from consciousness. Now, what is it you want to say?"

"Miss Hetty wrote two letters, your grace. One to Sir Archibald and the other to Sir John. If something happened to Miss Hetty, I was to give the letters to her maid. You see, your grace, Miss Hetty always has luncheon with Sir Archibald at precisely twelve o'clock. If she's not there, he'll miss her. There'll be hell to pay."

"Damnation. Well, it must be dealt with. No, be quiet, Pottson, I must think." He stared down at the unconscious girl in his arms. "I've got it. Listen, Pottson. You'll rent a hack from the ostler and return to London immediately. Tell Miss Rolland's maid to inform Sir Archibald that Miss Rolland has been invited by my sister, Lady Alicia Warton, to spend several days with her at Thurston Hall. She will then accompany you to Thurston Hall—by this evening if possible, Pottson. I shall attend to my sister. Do you understand?"

"Yes, your grace. Lady Alicia Warton."

"You may ask my butler, Rabbell, in Berkeley Square, the directions to Thurston Hall. Here," the marquess added, reaching into his waistcoat pocket. "This should be enough money. You must pull it off correctly, Pottson, there is much at stake. You know it as well as I do."

"I know, your grace, I know. It was a mad scheme, but once Miss Hetty had the bit between her teeth, there was no stopping her. I couldn't blame her, your grace. After all, her brother—"

The marquess interrupted him. "No, don't tell me any more. Go now, there's no time to lose. Don't forget, Lady Alicia Warton. I fancy she and Miss Henrietta Rolland are going to become bosom pals."

The marquess thought about Sir Archibald and

his general vague perceptions of his family, and decided that his plan was likely to work. Moreover, Sir Archibald wouldn't question an invitation from Lady Alicia Warton. He must remember to write to his sister this very evening, and warn her not to appear in London.

The marquess lifted her shirt again and saw with dismay that his hand was covered with her blood. The wound was bleeding again. He shouted to Silken to bring him several very clean napkins from the inn.

Gently, he laid her on the opposite seat and unfastened the soaked handkerchief.

He winced at the raw wound, remembering all too clearly the unbearable pain he'd suffered when he'd accidentally been run through the shoulder by a school friend, George Pulmondy. Strange, he thought, that he remembered George's name, for he hadn't heard a thing about him in years.

He didn't let Silken spring the horses until he'd fashioned a new bandage from the clean napkins and settled her again against his chest. She was so bloody slight. How could anyone have ever believed her a young man? And just look at that smooth white jaw. That soft white flesh, the thick lashes, a shade darker than her blond hair. And where were any whiskers? Not in this lifetime, that was for certain.

Fools, they'd all been fools. Sir Harry, Monteith's best friend, had never suspected. Julien St. Clair hadn't suspected. None of them had.

He found himself impatiently gazing out the carriage window for familiar landmarks that would tell him they were drawing close to Thurston Hall. He

had never greatly cared for the rambling mansion
with its forty bedrooms and ghostly draped ballroom, yet when he saw the entrance to the park,
lined with naked-branched lime trees, it was the
most welcome sight he'd ever seen. He breathed an
audible sigh of relief when the carriage drew to a
jolting halt in front of the great pillared front
entrance.

Silken jumped nimbly down from the box and
jerked open the carriage door. "Is he still alive? Aye,
I see that he is. Can I help your grace with the
young gentleman?"

"I can manage," the marquess said as he gently
carried the still unconscious Henrietta Rolland up
the deep-inlaid marble steps. He'd realized for the
past hour that he would be the one to care for her,
no other. He couldn't even let his servants know,
no one must know that the young gentleman was a
young lady. Jesus, he couldn't believe this. What if
she died? No, he wouldn't let anything happen to
her. He pictured again the instant when his foil
sliced into her side. It made him shudder. And she'd
closed her mind to the pain she'd wanted to kill him
so much. Yet she hadn't, when she'd disarmed him,
she hadn't killed him.

Silken reached the great oak front doors a few
steps ahead of the marquess and soundly thwacked
the knocker. Croft, the butler at Thurston Hall
since before the marquess's birth, inched the door
open and looked vaguely out into the gray winter
morning.

The marquess eyed his butler. "Open the door,
damn you, Croft. You're bloody drunk again, you
miserable sot. Just look at you, your eyes are so

bloodshot, you can scarce make out that I'm your master and I'll boot your butt to the next county. Damn you, hurry." Croft, striving desperately for dignity, weaved about noticeably in the doorway.

"Ah, it is your grace. How welcome you are, sir. Ah, here you are, right here on the front steps, waiting for me to open the door for you."

"Foxed again, you blighted specimen. Get out of my sight before I lock you in my wine cellar and throw away the key."

"Your grace, what a fine idea. But what are you doing here? It's early in the morning. You should still be abed in London. Why did no one warn me, that is, give me ample notice that your grace would bless us with your presence? Who is the young gentleman, your grace? He's bleeding. His blood is on your shirt and breeches. It isn't what I'm used to. However, let me take him. It's my duty. I'll make sure he doesn't bleed on you anymore."

The marquess could only growl. "Shake up the servants, Silken. I need hot water, clean strips of linen—very clean, mind you—basilicum powder and laudanum. Cook has a sturdy needle and thread." He whirled about to his glassy-eyed butler. "As for you, Croft, go dip your head in a bucket of cold water. I want you alert in an hour, do you hear me? If you're not alert, you'll be walking to East Anglia. Ah, Silken, don't forget the laudanum." He knew he could count on Cook to have hoarded a supply of laudanum, particularly when there had not been enough to ease his pain when his shoulder had lain raw and open. He took the wide stairs two at a time. The long eastern corridor had never seemed so endless.

He unceremoniously kicked open the door to the huge master bedchamber at the end of the corridor. He was so intent upon his burden that he nearly tripped over a lion-claw leg of a large gold brocade sofa, a remnant of his father's delight in the Egyptian influence that had swept the country some five years earlier.

He cursed fluently, more from habit than from his bruised shin, but didn't break his stride toward the four-postered, canopied bed.

He balanced her on the crook of one arm and swept back the heavy goosedown spread. Gently, he eased her down upon her back and lifted off the greatcoat. To his relief, the napkins weren't soaked through with blood.

He'd just finished baring her side when Silken, accompanied by two stout footmen, entered the room carrying a bucket of hot water and rolls of white linen.

He moved quickly to shield her from the footmen's curious eyes.

"Thank you. That will be all." He waved them all away. If his servants thought it odd that he wouldn't seek their help with the young gentleman, well, so be it. If they thought it even stranger that he wouldn't send for the doctor, well, so be that, too. He was a marquess and they weren't. Whatever he did must be right, must be intelligent. What did they know?

Jason Cavander was thankful that she was still unconscious, for it required more than gentle scrubbing to cleanse away the dried blood from about the wound. Carefully, he pressed his fingers against her side, probing the area. His hand shook. But one more inch inward and his blade would have hit a vital organ.

He threaded the needle with the stout black thread, stared down at her white flesh and drew a deep breath. It required only four stitches. His thrust had been neat and straight.

He sprinkled basilicum powder liberally over her side and bandaged her tightly, layer after layer of the soft linen firm against around her waist and flank. He straightened and gazed down at her. "If I am to have the care of you, Miss Rolland," he said to her, "it's time you were out of your man's clothes and into a man's nightshirt."

He fetched a long white linen nightshirt, exquisitely hemmed by his great-aunt Agnes, and with gentle efficiency stripped off her bloodied shirt. He tugged carefully at the laces on the chemise and snipped the straps with a pair of scissors. Once free of the tight garment, her breasts seemed to swell and round. He found himself wanting to smooth away the sharp lines that the tight laces had cut into her breasts. He frowned at himself. They were just breasts, just like the breasts he'd seen on so many other women in his life.

He pulled off her hessians, stockings, and finally her breeches. Wise of her not to wear tight-knitted pantaloons, he thought fleetingly holding the loose buckskins in his hands. Though her legs were long and slender and her hips rather boyish, anything but the loosest of breeches would surely have given her away. He found himself comparing her body to Melissande's, realized what he was doing, and quickly slipped the nightshirt over her head. He smoothed it to her knees, then pulled the cover over her, bringing it just short of her chin.

After building up the fire, he pulled a large leather chair close to the bedside, sat himself down and prepared to wait. He looked up at the ormolu clock on the night table and saw with a start that it was but eleven o'clock in the morning. It was hard to believe that in just under four hours he had nearly lost his life, discovered that his opponent was a woman, and had decided to take sole charge of her care. He made a steeple with his fingers and tapped the tips thoughtfully together. What the devil was she going to do when she woke up and found the man she hated taking care of her? He couldn't begin to imagine. However, she could have killed him, but she hadn't. Why? It went over and over in his mind, he couldn't seem to stop it. Well, he would know soon enough. When she awakened. *If* she awakened.

He wanted her awake. He wanted to look at her and know it was a woman he was looking at and not a young gentleman.

Chapter Twenty-six

Hetty lay some minutes in half consciousness before she opened her eyes. In those few precious moments before her mind told her that all wasn't well with her body, she looked about her, her thoughts clear and alert. She saw herself, foil in hand, jumping suddenly forward, catching Lord Oberlon's blade at its base. She felt the shattering impact as his foil whirled from his hand to the ground. She clearly saw herself standing in front of him, her arm extended its full length, the tip of her blade against his chest. She saw his face, the clear darkness of his eyes, she felt the fearlessness in him, the odd questioning, though he'd said nothing. He'd waited, not moving. Why? She gasped, remembering how she couldn't bring herself to be his executioner.

"Hello," came a deep familiar voice from just beside her. She turned her head ever so slightly. He was leaning over her, his dark eyes intent on her face. He was whole and she wasn't. Surely there was no justice in that. But why was he here? What the devil was going on?

"You? Can it truly be you? I don't understand."

"How do you feel? Can you see me?"

"Dear God, I must be dead and in hell since you're here. Why are you here? That makes no sense. I wanted to kill you." Without warning, pain that she'd never imagined pierced through her side. She cried out against it, her arms hugging herself, but it didn't help.

"I know your pain is great. I'll try to help you." She heard his words, yet her mind refused to let her understand them. Her eyes were clouding and in but an instant he blurred into the shadows.

"No, dammit, no. I don't want to lose to you, no." She tried desperately to keep control, but it was slipping from her and there was nothing she could do about it. She flung out her hand to ward off the pain that was deep inside her, to ward him away from her. She felt strong fingers close over her hand.

The pain intensified. Her back arched. She twisted sideways, anything to lessen the agony that was making her an animal, without thought, without intelligence, without control. He was lifting her, tilting her head back. His voice was quiet and soothing, the sounds just that, sounds, with no meaning to her. Her mouth was forced open, and she choked on bitter-tasting liquid. She struggled against him. She hated him touching her. Was he forcing poison down her throat? She tried to fight him but the pain was too great and she was too weak. He was holding her very firmly, and she hated it, but she could do nothing about it. She hit at him, but he didn't move, didn't release her or loosen his hold on her. On and on it went. She was crying, knowing that it was so because she tasted her tears in her mouth, salty and hot. The arms went suddenly about her shoulders, pressing her firmly onto her back and holding her there so that she couldn't move against the pain. She tried to draw her knees up to somehow ease the ferocious burning that was ripping through her side. But there was a weight on her legs and there was naught she could do but dwell within herself, within the pain, and know he was there.

Suddenly, the agony grew less intense, like a leashed monster pulling its fangs out of her flesh. She heard an odd sound, pathetic, low ugly sobbing, a sound of utter hopelessness, and she knew it was from her. She was making those animal sounds.

Gradually, his face became clearer above her, his words now distinct. She heard her own name sounding over and over in her ears, low and gentle, but insistent, calling her back into herself. "Henrietta, can you hear me? Come now, speak to me. Is the pain less now? Hetty?"

She managed to focus on that dark face above her. It seemed important that he understand. She said, "I'm not Lord Harry Monteith. Do you understand me? If I die, I want you to know that I'm not Lord Harry. You must tell my father and my brother, else they won't know what happened to me."

"I know who you are," he said, his voice low and deep, his breath warm on her cheek. "You're Henrietta Rolland. Does Jack call you Hetty? Yes, I remember that he does. May I as well? Of course I already have, haven't I? Hold on, I know the pain is unbearable, but the laudanum will soon ease you. Soon now, very soon. Just listen to me, try to focus on my voice, all right?"

"All right," she whispered, her hand now clutching his as if her very life depended on it.

"You are just as I imagined you would be when I met you at the Ranleaghs' ball. Do you remember how I thought I was rescuing you from that drunken

buffoon? You let me know that I wasn't at all necessary, that you would have taken care of him had he
persisted. I thought you full of bluff and bravado. Now
I know that you would have probably slit his throat
had he continued with his foolishness. Do you remember how well we waltzed together? That's right,
squeeze my hand. Do you remember? Just nod,
that's good."

As the laudanum began to dull the pain in her
side, she felt a dull pounding against the side of her
head. She tried to focus on this new pain and
moaned deep in her throat.

"I know you hurt. Soon you'll sleep. We'll sort
everything out when you're better. Yes, you've a
lump and a bruise over your left temple. When you
fell, you hit the only rock within twenty feet. Now,
breathe deeply, that's right. Just listen to me talk
and soon you'll be asleep. That's right." He paused
a moment, studying her face. He saw that her blue
eyes were vague, that the laudanum was taking
effect. About damned time, he thought.

"Now, I will tell you that I visited your lodgings
when I found out you'd been with Melissande. Your
valet, Pottson, nearly dropped dead of apoplexy
when I marched in, murder in my eye. I wanted to
wring Lord Harry's neck for poaching on my mistress preserves. Do you know what happened? I
went into Lord Harry's bedchamber and found a
gown. I thought Lord Harry was a complete young
rakehell. I thought there must be a young girl, quite
naked, hiding in the closet. But it was your gown I
found, Henrietta. When I waved it in his face, Pottson held firm. He has guts, that valet of yours."

She was asleep. He had no idea how much she'd

heard. At least for a while she was free of the god-
awful pain. He gently replaced the covers over her
and straightened. He dipped a strip of linen into
the basin of cool water atop the commode and
lightly bathed her face. The deep purple bruise
above her temple was now ugly and swollen.

She whimpered, jerking upward, then falling back
again. He froze above her. She quieted again and
he drew a breath of relief and he straightened over
her bed. Actually, it was his bed. He hadn't really
thought about it. He'd simply carried her to his bedchamber, a huge dark room with a bed that could
hold a drunken battalion.

He found himself staring down at her, his eyes
searching her pale face. It was such a young face,
and vulnerable, with all the lines and expressions of
Lord Monteith's hatred and anger smoothed away.
Vulnerable bedamned. He saw again the naked
gleam of purpose in her eyes when she'd lunged at
him again and again, until, through his own blun-
dering, the tip of her foil pricked at his chest. He'd
felt her hatred in that moment, a hatred so deep he
couldn't begin to understand it, to fathom what he'd
ever done in his life to deserve such hatred, then
her indecision. He felt the hair prickle on the back
of his neck, uncertain now if he would have been
able to wrench the foil from her hands. He didn't
know. He remembered Julien shouting at him to do
it, but he'd just stood there, held by the naked tor-
ment in Monteith's eyes. Yes, that was it, the boy
had looked tortured in those few moments. No, he
thought, not boy, she was a girl, very much a girl.
What the devil had he done?

She was deeply asleep. He smoothed the covers

over her. He turned away from the bed and strode
to the long windows that overlooked the west lawn.
The morning was gray and eerily silent. Even the
peacocks that habitually strutted through the rose
arbors, squawking loudly as they displayed their colorful plumage, were nowhere to be seen. As he stared
out, her face rose in his mind, drained of color and
laden with fear. They were to duel with foils, not with
pistols as she'd so obviously anticipated. Yet her hatred
of him had been so powerful, her determination so
great, that she'd overcome her fear. Damnation, why?
Jack was his friend. Indeed, Jack had sent him over
to his masked sister at the Ranleaghs' ball. No, he
realized, it had nothing to do with Jack. Jack would
have no idea. Unless she died. He shook his head at
that. No way would he allow that.

He looked back at the bed. What kind of a woman
was she anyway? A girl he would have said, but not
now, not since he'd seen her look blank-eyed at the
foils, overcome her shock and fear, and proceed to
fence with him with all her skill. Hadn't Jack said
she was eighteen? He'd fought a duel with an eighteen-year-old girl. He would wager that no other
gentleman either past or present or future, for that
matter, would have come through what he had.
He'd rarely in his twenty-seven years known a
female who could even bring herself to discuss pistols and foils, much less known one who was so
skilled in this, a masculine domain. She was brave,
indeed, she'd shown herself fearless. It shook him,
this girl who now lay in his bed, this girl who could
die because of his sword thrust through her side.
No, he wouldn't let her die. He wanted to hear her
tell him what he'd done to deserve such hatred from

her, such hatred that she'd become a young gentleman and learned to shoot and to fence, all to send him to the devil, and yet at the last moment, when she'd won, she'd changed her mind. Yes, he wanted her to tell him and then—He didn't know. He strode over to his grandfather's writing desk. He had to write Alicia and ensure that he needn't have any worry from that quarter. Although he was fairly certain that his dashing, very feminine sister was carrying her child-swollen belly in the privacy of Sir Henry's Devonshire estate, he intended to make doubly sure that she remained there. He thought of Henrietta Rolland in feminine ruffles and lace. He'd seen her in a mask and domino, her blue eyes glittering, her lovely mouth laughing. He remembered the feel of her in his arms as he whirled her about in the waltz, her gay laughter, he remembered all of it.

Damnation. She'd tried to kill him. You're a stupid ass, he grunted to himself. He suddenly saw that ghastly, vulgar girl dressed in the pea green gown and ugly spectacles at his aunt Melberry's soiree. Jesus, who had she been? Another role, obviously. She was very talented. And he was, after all, a man with many years' experience and maturity. Surely he would be able to sort all of this out. He wanted to touch her blond hair, blonder than Jack's hair, the curls soft and springy. He was becoming a half-wit. He quickly set himself to the task of writing to Alicia and then to Rabbell to cancel all of his appointments in London for the remainder of the week. Having finished, he rose and rang the bell cord for luncheon and went to his dressing room to change his clothes.

After eating thin-sliced ham, sweet garden peas,

and crunchy warm bread, he returned to his vigil by her bedside. He allowed his mind to wander back to the various encounters he had engaged in with her. Whenever he caught himself either frowning or smiling at one particular memory, he gazed over at her. He was surprised to realize that the afternoon had melted away, and a frown settled upon his brow. She was sleeping overlong and he grew concerned. Perhaps he should fetch a doctor and damn the consequences.

The downstairs clock chimed six deep, resounding strokes. He saw her eyelashes flutter open. There was no awareness in her eyes this time. She stared unseeing at him. A low, aching moan came from deep in her throat. In a jerking motion, she brought her hand up to press against the swollen bruise on her temple, then with another gasp of pain, she dropped her hand and hugged her side.

He laid a damp strip of linen on her forehead, for he could not risk more laudanum so soon. He hoped, without much optimism, that it would relieve the pain in her head. He lowered himself gently down beside her. He pulled her arms away from her side, fearful that her frantic clutching would cause the wound to start bleeding again. She fought against him with surprising strength, but he tightened his grip until she lay still, moaning helplessly.

"Hetty," he said against her ear. "You must try to lie still. I don't want the bleeding to start again. Can you understand me?"

She tried to twist away from him. His arms began to ache with holding her down. Then he simply couldn't stand her pain any longer. He measured a lesser dose of laudanum into a glass of water and forced it down her throat. She choked, doubling forward in a paroxysm of coughing. He pulled her against his chest and held her close, rubbing his hand on her back, until the racking shudders subsided. He began to rock her gently, until finally, he felt the tension in her gradually ease.

The laudanum was beginning to blunt the edges of her pain. She was seized by a sudden sense of urgency. She lurched up, saying, "Millie, where are you? What time is it? Please, we must hurry. Father will wonder where I am. I can't let him suspect. Millie. Oh, hurry." Millie didn't come to her, but there was someone else near to her. A low, soothing voice. "Is that you Signore Bertioli? The *vendetta*, Signore. I mustn't fail. I am nothing if I fail. You must help me, Signore, please, you must teach me. But it's over, isn't it? I was a fool, Signore. I went into battle with naught but a prayer and a foil. No pistols for me, just that damned foil."

A soft shimmering light was shining in her eyes. A dark face was staring at her, dark eyes, deep and fathomless. "My God, it that you, Damien? Please forgive me. I tried so hard and I did win, but I failed because I couldn't do it. I couldn't kill him."

Dry heat consumed her. She was burning, waves of scalding heat swelling deep inside her. There was suffocating material choking her, tightening about her throat, yet she wasn't strong enough to pull it away. She ripped at the material about her neck. Fingers were closing over hers, pulling them away from her throat. There was a sudden lightness of her body, then the touch of warm air caressing her skin. Still it wasn't enough. Her fingers clawed at the mounting waves of drenching heat. The dark eyes were again close to her face. "Please, I'm so hot, so very hot. Please stop the heat."

"Yes, I will." A cool wet cloth smoothed over her face, like a light summer's rain upon a sunbaked earth. Cooling drops of liquid rolled down her face onto her neck, cutting a trail of prickly cold in their wake. The damp coolness floated over her shoulders and breasts, down to her belly, quenching an unbearable heat that burned her legs. She was being slowly lifted, the cooling liquid cleansing away the ghastly burning from her back. The flames of heat in her body surged with new intensity as the cool damp soaked in again and again. Finally the burning was lessening, withdrawing from her. The burning was dying away as would embers doused over and over until they steamed away the last of their existence, hissing and spurting until at last they lay cold and lifeless.

Was that a woman's voice sounding softly near to her? "Louisa, Louisa, is that you? Have you come to curse me? So many lies, Louisa. Too many. I can't bear that Jack must now risk his life because I failed. Please don't hate me, Louisa. I tried and tried, but I just couldn't finish it. It was all lies, I lived nothing but lies."

"Miss Hetty, oh God, Miss Hetty."

"Thank God you've come, Millie. Yes, it's you, I know it's you. You must help me rise now, I can't be late. Father's schedule, I must be downstairs. Help me, Millie, I can't seem to pull myself up. Help me!"

She heard a wrenching sob, then a deep voice sounding next to her face. The cold rim of a glass touched her dry lips and she opened her mouth, greedily gulping down the bitter liquid. Her body felt suddenly light, or was it her mind, floating above her, scornful of the weakness that held her a prisoner? The shuddering sobs were from the helpless weak body, not from her.

"Why is it suddenly so very cold, Millie? Please light the fires, it's so very cold. Millie, where are you? Pottson, please help me. My greatcoat, Pottson, how can I go about in the winter without my greatcoat?"

A chattering, clicking noise sounded in her ears. She could not hold her jaw still. She was weighted down, mounds of greatcoats piled over her, yet she was naked to bitter winter winds. She tried to draw her body up, but the heavy greatcoats held her prisoner. They grew frigid with cold, weighing her down so that she was motionless beneath them.

Suddenly, there was movement next to her and dizzying warmth touched every part of her. She breathed in the warmth, pressing her face against yielding, warm flesh. She clutched at the warmth, burrowing her body so tightly that she felt one with it, fearful at any second that it would fade away from her and she would once again feel the bitter coldness. She felt gentle hands slowly caressing up and down her back, enfolding her, and she nestled close as would a small babe in its mother's arms.

She thought she felt warm breath on her hair. She thought she felt the warmth of breath against her ear. Her teeth stopped their chattering, her shuddering eased. Deep shadows closed over her mind and gently, she fell into a silent, warm sleep.

Vaguely, she became aware that her face and body were being gently touched with a damp cloth. She tried to turn away from it, unwilling to relinquish the peacefulness of sleep. There was a feather-light probing at her side, and she cried out at the unwanted touch. Then it was gone. With a soft sigh, she drifted back into a deep sleep.

Hetty awoke suddenly and blinked away the last scattered remnants of the laudanum. She felt only a moment of confusion at the unfamiliar room, for memory stirred, and even before her eyes fell upon the marquess seated in a large chair near to the bed, a newspaper in his hands, her mind flashed over the duel and his presence with her before she'd fallen unconscious. As though he felt her eyes upon him, he looked up and she saw a smile of relief.

He spoke as he rose to come to her. "Now I trust you're really back to me again. How do you feel, Hetty?"

Feel? How should she feel? Should she be feeling less pain in her side or should she feel relief or anger that she hadn't killed him? She felt light-headed and uncertain at the moment how to answer him. She said only, "I'm with you. Where am I?"

"You're at my home just south of London—Thurston Hall. After I discovered Lord Harry Monteith wasn't what he claimed to be, I thought it wise to bring you here."

She wasn't listening to him. She was staring at the lengthening shadows of the afternoon sun on the far wall. "Oh no. I must go now. Father will worry, he'll find out, and all will be lost." She tried to rise. A stab of throbbing pain shot through her side and she fell back panting against the pillow. She felt his hands upon her shoulders, holding her down.

"Hush now, Hetty. You're causing yourself needless pain. If you will but listen to me, you will realize that the world is not quite as you left it."

"What do you mean? Oh God, how long have I been here?"

"It's been three days since our duel." She stared at him, unwilling to believe him. "Don't you remember anything?"

"I remember stabbing my foil into the ground. It was hard to do because the ground was frozen. I remember so much pain I wanted to die. Three days? My father, dear God, my father. What will he have done? Oh God, what's he thinking?" His hands left her shoulders. She stared up at him. Carefully, slowly, as if she were afraid of further betrayal by her body, she let her fingers gently trail down to her side. She felt the bulky strips of linen binding about her waist, and remembered with sickening clarity the dizzying pain and the huge pool of blood like splayed red fingers pressing her shirt against her body. She looked at her hand. She realized she wasn't wearing her own nightgown, for the material didn't fasten at her wrist with tiny pearl buttons, but rather flopped over the ends of her fingertips.

"My father," she said again.

"I'll tell you everything."

She turned her head slightly, carefully avoiding any sudden movement, and regarded the marquess's face above her. She remembered for a brief instant the raging fever, then he'd wiped her down over and over with the damp cool cloth, soothing away the fever. She trembled at the memory of the bitter frigid cold that had frozen her from within. Then the soothing, giving warmth . . . it had been him. He'd held her against him, pressed her against the length of his body. Stroked his hands over her back.

"Is this your nightshirt?"

"Actually you should thank my great-aunt Agnes, for it is her tenacious needlework that's kept you clothed. Yes, it's my nightshirt."

"Where is the doctor? Millie? I know I heard her voice. Has she taken care of me?"

"Hush now and ease yourself. You've asked me a great many things. Would you like a drink of water?"

She drank avidly, choking. He lifted her gently, patting her back. It seemed a normal thing for him to do.

"I told you you've been with me here for three days. It's been three days since you've eaten. Are you hungry?"

She realized suddenly that she could devour anything that called itself food. "Oh yes, please. Anything at all will do, just bring it now."

He grinned down at her. "I'm glad you're hungry. I've had all sorts of broths made for you daily in hopes you'd come about."

He tugged the bell cord. At the soft knock on his bedchamber door, he walked quickly to the door. As he'd done since he'd brought her here, he stood in the doorway to shield her from the servants. She looked so much like a young girl that he couldn't imagine anyone else seeing her any differently.

She felt light-headed. She supposed it was because she was so very hungry. Yes, that was it. As soon as she ate, she would deal with this man. He was still the same. He was still evil and ruthless and didn't care about anyone except himself. Even though she hadn't killed him, he'd still killed Damien and she would make him pay for it. Just not yet. But as soon as she was better, then she'd think of something and he would pay for what he'd done, he'd pay dearly.

Had he really taken care of her since he'd wounded her? She couldn't bear that thought.

Chapter Twenty-seven

Croft stood owl-eyed and quite sober, amazingly alert to receive his master's orders. The marquess grinned, hoping this transformation would last, though he doubted it would. Croft would be back to the wine cellar the moment the marquess left Thurston Hall. He rapped out his orders and shut the door.

He turned and walked back to Hetty. He thought she looked rather flushed, and in that instant dreaded the onset of another fever. As he reached out his hand to touch her forehead, she jerked away, her back stiff against the headboard of his bed.

"Good God, what is this?" He'd forgotten for the moment that although he knew her body almost as thoroughly as was possible, she, on the other hand, was unaccustomed to either him or to any intimacy from him. Also, she hated his guts. Well, for the moment, it was too bad.

"Look, Hetty, I merely want to see if you've another fever. Don't be afraid of me. I have no intention of assaulting you or trying to hurt you."

She just stared up at him and tried to inch away toward the center of the large bed, but another sharp pain in her side held her rigid. She closed her eyes tightly. "None of this makes any sense at all. I don't have a fever, damn you, but I suppose since you're the stronger then you'll have your way."

He did, lightly laying his palm on her forehead. Thankfully, her skin was cool to the touch. "You're fine, thank God. Now, I imagine you're ready to eat your water glass. It shouldn't be much longer now, Hetty."

"My name is Miss Rolland."

He looked faintly amused. "Het—Miss Rolland, I believe that I know you well enough to dispense with such formality."

"You don't begin to know me, your grace. But I know you, I know all about you."

"Do you also know that I've taken care of you? There's been no doctor. I see you don't like that at all. Well, just remember, Miss Rolland, I fought a duel with Lord Harry. Lord Harry you must remain if we are to pull through this mess without a scandal that I personally wouldn't want to have to live through. I've really done quite well by you, you know. You'll live. You'll have a scar on your side, but you're alive and soon you'll even be eating."

He wished he'd kept his mouth shut. Her eyes darkened and narrowed. He wondered if she had a pistol she'd shoot him. She'd had so much to adjust to that her hatred of him had been momentarily forgotten. He wondered with amused irony whether feeding her was wise. The moment she gained back some strength, she would be at his throat.

"Ah, food." He walked away from her before she could speak.

Hetty eyed the steaming bowl of soup and fresh warm bread. She tried to struggle to a sitting position, only to fall back, biting her lower lip, as the wound in her side sent a ripping pain through her.

"Listen to me, Hetty, you must keep still. I don't want those stitches to tear. I don't want you to start bleeding again. Just hold still. No matter what's between us, for now just let me feed you. All right?" He frowned at her, saw how very near to tears of pain she was. "Please, allow me to help you."

She was simply too weak to resist. She was also dizzy with hunger. As much as she hated it, she knew she'd have to lie here in his bed like a weak fool and let him feed her. She lay limp as he slipped one arm behind her shoulders and the other under her legs. He carefully eased her to more of a sitting position and plumped the feather pillows behind her head.

"There, you're ready to dine."

He pulled out the wooden legs of the bed tray and set it across her lap.

"I hope it isn't corn soup," she said, eyeing the steaming bowl warily.

"Corn soup? Why the devil not?"

"Father's a Tory."

"Good God, do I ever know that. Your father and my uncle between them would run England if allowed. It's a frightening idea. You aren't speaking of the Corn Laws, are you? No, don't answer. Let's feed you now." He sat on the bed beside her. He picked up the spoon and stirred the hot soup.

To have him feeding her was simply too much. Besides now she was sitting up, not lying on her back like a lump. "I don't need your help now. I'll feed myself."

"As you will," he said, and handed her the spoon.

She couldn't make her fingers do any more than curl weakly about the handle. She slid her thumb closer to the bowl of the spoon and dipped it into the soup. Her hand was trembling and before the spoon reached her open mouth, her thumb lost its leverage and she grimaced as the hot soup splashed onto her nightshirt, rather his nightshirt sewn for him by his aunt Agnes.

"Damn but you're stubborn," he said and pulled her fingers from the spoon. "Now, lie back, open your mouth, and stop trying to prove how invincible you are."

She did, and opened her mouth.

The bowl was empty and the fresh bread rested comfortably in her stomach and still she felt her mouth watering. She wanted more. She wanted the entire pot of soup. She wanted another loaf of bread, buttered liberally. He stood and removed the tray. As if he read her longing, he said, "No, any more and you'll get ill. Trust me in this. You can have some more in a couple of hours."

She turned her face away from him and he saw her fingers bunching at the cover.

"Are you in pain?"

She shook her head, then suddenly turned to face him and whispered, "I know Millie is here. I heard her. I wish to have her, please."

He said cynically, "Really, Hetty, it is I who have looked after you for the past three days. You have no need of Millie. Come, what is it you want?"

"Damn you, get me my maid."

Understanding dawned. "Very well, but listen to me, Hetty. Millie will have only fifteen minutes with you. I can't allow any gossip to start among the servants. As you know, that would be fatal. You're Lord Harry, don't forget that."

He said over his shoulder as he strode to the door, "I'll be back in fifteen minutes. Then, Hetty, we must talk, if you feel up to it."

It seemed an age before Millie's large, spare figure appeared in the doorway, and Hetty wondered if the marquess had been giving her all sorts of orders. Probably so.

"Oh, Miss Hetty, oh my poor little lamb."

A poor lamb she was destined to be at least for the next fifteen minutes, for Millie clucked over her like a mother hen finally returned to her lost chick.

Hetty's more basic needs having been attended to, she nervously eyed the clock. "Quickly, Millie, tell me everything you know before the marquess returns."

"Well, his grace isn't a dreadful man as I'd sworn he would be. It's a tangled state of affairs he's saved you from, and I'd say he's taken better care of you better than any doctor. Not, of course, that I approve of an unmarried man being so intimately familiar with a young girl, but I agree with him that it had to be this way. Yes, you must remain Lord Harry, else I shudder to think what might happen."

"Did his grace tell you it would be all right if you brushed my hair?"

"Now, Miss Hetty, no need to get snippety." She grinned down at her mistress. "I daresay I'll have to since his grace hasn't seen fit to render you this service."

Millie was gentle, Hetty gave her that, still the pain grew with each gentle stroke of the brush. She sought to distract herself. "What have you been doing the past three days? How did the marquess justify your presence here?"

"Naught of anything, Miss Hetty. His grace said I needed a holiday after all the wild doings you put me through. Of course, Sir Archibald believes I'm attending you here during your visit with the marquess's sister. As for what he told his servants, they simply think I'm a visitor from his sister, here to see if she would like anything changed when next she visits. I don't think they believe it, but they've kept quiet. I like most of them. That Croft, now, he's a handful. Careful as a vicar he is while the marquess is here not to fall into drunken stupors. He's always peering around corners, afraid his grace will catch him with a bottle in his hand."

Hetty pulled away from the hairbrush. "Millie, listen to me. It seems you've begun to think his grace is a virtuous, kind man. You know what he did. He's cruel and ruthless. If his behavior now belies that, well, it's because he doesn't want a scandal, he told me so himself. His nobility is only word deep. He's a sham, Millie, he's—"

"Is arrogant or evil next on your list of compliments, Miss Rolland?"

She looked up quickly to see him standing in the doorway. "Very probably," she said, her voice as cold as the ice storm of the previous week. "I also should say devil. Oh damn you, you've made my side hurt." She wanted to cry, but she wouldn't let herself, not in front of him.

The marquess said calmly to Millie, "The fifteen minutes are gone. You can see your mistress again— perhaps later this evening when it is likely that she will prefer your services again to mine. I'm sorry, but we mustn't risk giving you more time with her."

"I quite understand, your grace," Millie said. "It will be as you wish."

Hetty watched Millie curtsy to such an obsequious depth that she would have liked to kick her.

"And now, Hetty," the marquess said after Millie had closed herself out of the bedchamber, "we have, I believe, much to talk about. I find Miss Rolland as viciously insulting as the indomitable Lord Harry. Would you now care to inform me exactly why I am a vile, cruel, and arrogant—"

"Don't forget devil."

"Yes, naturally I'm a devil, and evil to boot. Do you hurt or do you want to talk to me now?"

He pulled a winged-back chair close to her bed and sat down. He leaned back, crossing his arms over his chest.

"It doesn't stop hurting but that doesn't matter."

"Very well. What do you have to say to me?"

She stared at him. For so very long she'd planned on telling him why she'd killed him. He was to have been mortally wounded, lying at her feet. But not this, not her lying here, hurting, with him saving her life, taking care of her. God, she wished she had a gun so she could shoot him, but she didn't, even a cane so she could strike him over the head.

At her continued silence, he said, "You know, Hetty, while you were in a high fever, you were delirious. You spoke of many things. You thought, for instance, that I was your brother, Damien, and screamed at me that you couldn't do it—that you couldn't kill me."

"So you admit your guilt?"

"Guilt? What wretched guilt? I just wanted to know what Damien has to do with any of this." He tapped his fingers together. "You seem to think that I was or am involved in some way with Damien.

Come, Hetty, you've never been at a loss for words in any guise I've known you."

"You killed my brother. Damn you to hell, you killed Damien!"

He stopped tapping his fingers and stared at her. "What did you say? You think I killed Damien? What arrant nonsense is this? Your brother was killed at Waterloo, in a very ill-advised cavalry charge, at least that's what Jack told me."

"Yes, he was killed at Waterloo. And you're right, of course, about that charge. At the last moment before the battle, he was assigned to lead a cavalry charge that meant certain death. You killed him, your grace. You sent him to lead that suicide charge."

She fell back, gasping as a sudden jab of pain ripped through her side. As the waves of pain wouldn't subside, she hugged her arms about her waist and gritted her teeth. To her shame, she felt tears swimming in her eyes and tightly closed her eyelids. She couldn't be weak now, not now.

When she felt his hand upon her forehead, she didn't have the strength to draw away.

"Drink this," he said. She didn't want to, but she opened her mouth. He held her head in the crook of his arm and held the glass to her mouth until she'd drunk all of it. It was barley water. She hated barley water.

It was several minutes before the laudanum began to take effect and dull the pain. She concentrated all her energies on not moaning aloud. She was only vaguely aware that he was clasping her limp fingers in his hand. At a particularly sharp wave of pain, she realized that she was clutching his hand, in some way seeking comfort from him. She heard him say something to her about sleep, and when the laudanum dulled her mind and her body, she willingly obliged.

When she again awoke, it was night. She had no idea how late it was. She turned her head carefully and saw the marquess standing in front of the fireplace, staring down into the crackling embers, a thoughtful expression on his face.

She queried her body, received no painful reply, at least for the moment, and slowly began to pull herself back up in a sitting position.

Her movement caught his eye, and he smiled as he strode over to her.

She held herself in stiff silence as he put his arms about her and eased her up. He straightened over her. "If you promise not to yell at me, I'll feed you."

"You changed my nightshirt."

"Well, yes. The soup you spilled was very sticky."

She felt beyond embarrassment. She felt strangely out of time, as if this man wasn't the same man she'd hated and sought to kill for the past nearly five months. Everything had gone awry and she felt herself floundering. She didn't know what to do, so she said, "I'm very hungry."

It was near to midnight before Hetty had finished another ration of soup, more bread, and Millie had left after her fifteen-minute allotment.

The marquess closed the door, locked it, and walked to the bedside. He eyed her intently. "The fact of the matter, Hetty, is that you didn't kill me when you had the opportunity. You either doubted my imagined guilt over your brother's death or you hadn't the stomach for murder. Which is it?"

She cocked her head to the side, staring at him, perhaps even through him, trying to understand why she'd done as she had. She saw so clearly the tip of her foil against his heart. One thrust, that's all it would have taken, just one thrust, yet she hadn't done it. She said aloud, "I've never doubted your guilt for a single instant. But when you just stood there and stared at me, no fear on your face, just waiting, looking at me, I knew I couldn't do it. When Damien died, part of me died with him, but yet I still lived, still knew I lived and was grateful for it. You lived as well. I couldn't be your killer. I couldn't be like you."

"You were close to your brother?"

"He was part of me."

"I gather you must have some sort of proof, some sort of evidence, that makes you believe me guilty of your brother's death. It must really be something for you to arrange your elaborate charade as Lord Harry. Now, tell me."

"Very well, we shall see how well you can lie, Lord Oberlon. I trust you do still remember your wife—Elizabeth Springville."

His eyes darkened at his dead wife's name. "What has any of this to do with Elizabeth?"

"You've a short memory, your grace, so I will refresh it. Not such a long time ago, you, Sir William Filey, and my brother, Damien, were all enamored with a beautiful young lady named Elizabeth Springville. Evidently your respective assaults to win her hand led you to lay a wager at White's—a large wager, I understand—to see which of you would succeed in winning her. Is this true?"

"Yes, it's true," he said, grim lines etching about his mouth.

"Although I'm disappointed that Damien would do such a thing, and indeed, I can't excuse him for that, what followed bears witness to your true nature. You're correct in one thing, your grace, I do have proof of your treachery. Pottson was Damien's batman. It was he who found a letter from Elizabeth to my brother. The letter damns you. She damns you. You will have to tell me the details of your plot to rid yourself of Damien. I will tell you what I know. Elizabeth chose Damien. Then you, your grace, getting wind of your defeat, used your influence with the ministry—through your uncle Lord Melberry no doubt—and we both know he has more than enough influence, and you had Damien quickly removed from England to be sent on a series of dangerous missions that, you hoped, would lead to his death. It is my belief, your grace, that Elizabeth gave herself to Damien as a proof of her love. When she discovered she was pregnant with Damien's child, she had no choice but to wed her lover's murderer.

"Perhaps the reason she died in childbed, your grace, was that she loathed you so greatly, particularly after hearing of Damien's death, that she simply had no further wish to live. There is much on your conscience, if you have one, for even Damien's child didn't survive."

Chapter Twenty-eight

The marquess stared at her long and hard. Then he jumped to his feet and strode to the fireplace where he stared down at the warmly glowing embers. Then, without speaking, he strode back to her, stood over her and said, his voice remarkably level, ah, but she could feel his rage, a deep rage, but he was controlling it, "I damned well don't believe this. You're telling me you engaged in your suicidal charade all on the basis of a letter written from Elizabeth to your brother? You planned to track me down, insult me until my eyes crossed with anger. And I challenged you to a duel, and then kill me all because of a bloody letter from Elizabeth to your brother? Jesus, this is madness."

"Yes, it was enough, more than enough."

"By God, you're a fool, a damned irresponsible, blind as hell female fool—and God knows a female fool is the very worst kind. No, I take that back. There can be no greater a fool than a man brought low by a woman. Now you will listen to me. When you've recovered, I shall want to see this infamous letter of yours. In the meanwhile, allow me to disabuse you of your romantic, ridiculously idealized reading of the entire sordid affair. Despite what you believe of me, I'm a man of some scruples. Were I not, I wouldn't have kept quiet about the true facts, and none of this need ever have happened.

"On several points, you are quite correct. The three of us, Filey, your brother, and I, all wanted Elizabeth Springville. Obviously, you have heard that she was an exquisite girl, sought after and feted from the instant of her coming out. Foolishly, too, one evening when all of us were deep in our cups, Filey suggested the wager—to add spice to the chase, he said."

He stopped and she knew he was debating with himself what to tell her. He gave her a look of utter loathing, then began to pace back and forth beside the bed. "Ah, to hell with it," he said more to himself than to her. "Let's get it all out in the open. Listen, Hetty. Although the next day both Damien and I regretted our action, it couldn't be undone. Elizabeth was courted like a princess. Like a woman with all the wiles of Cleopatra, she gave each of us encouragement in turn, yet never declared her preference. Although you may not choose to believe me, after several weeks of this sport, my supposed affection for the young lady began to wane. I began to believe her vain, cold, and quite calculating in her actions."

Again, he seemed to struggle with himself for a moment, then shrugged. "No, I must tell you all of it. Neither of us will ever be free of this unless I tell you everything. So be it.

"I'll never forget coming to White's one afternoon to be told that Damien had left suddenly for the continent. I thought at the time that he, like I, had grown tired of Elizabeth's capriciousness. Filey seemed vastly amused by what he termed *Captain*

Rolland's defection and taunted me to declare him the winner of the bet. Although, as I said, I was no longer much interested in the lady, I didn't believe that he had succeeded in winning her favor. That, along with his taunting, made me tell him to go to the devil. Not long thereafter, I began to revise my opinion, for Elizabeth appeared to be in his company more than in any other's.

"You can imagine my shock several weeks later when Elizabeth, hooded and masked, arrived at my town house near to midnight one evening. I won't sully your ears with the particulars of that memorable night—although why should I spare you? You took my damned mistress all about London. There can't be anything you don't know now. Very well, I'll say it outright, after all, you've been a gentleman for five months. You've seen more of this sordid world than any other young lady. Elizabeth didn't leave until near to dawn the following morning. I bedded her several times. I'm not going to try to justify my actions of that night. I have repeatedly cursed myself for my galling stupidity. Suffice it to say that Elizabeth, before her most innocent and artful seduction of an experienced man, ensured that I had consumed half a bottle of brandy.

"Three weeks later, I was tearfully informed by a hysterical Elizabeth that she was pregnant. Fool that I was, I accepted her word without hesitation and offered her marriage. We were married by special license three days later, then removed immediately to one of my estates near to Billingsgate."

Hetty could contain herself no longer. "By God, you still want me to listen to this outlandish tale you're spinning? It makes me want to puke. You have the gall to accuse me of romanticizing the entire affair, yet you've told me the most outrageous lies. Damn you, you must have been the one to send Damien from England. There is no one else. You've made this whole thing up, perhaps for my benefit so I won't try to kill you again, or else you're simply trying to lessen your guilt over murdering Damien."

She expected explosive anger from him, she expected more of his banked controlled rage. But she got neither. He said very quietly, "I will tell you, Hetty, I would have offered your brother half my estates had he but returned to take Elizabeth off my hands."

"God, that's a bloody lie! She was pregnant with Damien's child. They loved each other, he would gladly have wed her. He never wanted to return to the continent. He didn't want to die."

"You've looked too long into only one side of the mirror. Elizabeth wasn't pregnant with your brother's child. It was Filey's seed that grew in her womb."

"No, damn you no, that's bloody absurd—your final lie. I won't listen to any more of this."

"I have absolutely no reason to lie to you, Hetty," he said, his voice weary, now nearly emotionless.

"No, Elizabeth couldn't have—the letter, I read her letter to Damien. She loved him, not that foul lecher Sir William Filey."

"It's entirely possible that if your brother had remained in England, it would have been he who would have led the pregnant Elizabeth to the altar. But no, Hetty, she didn't love your brother. As best as I could tell, she loved no one but herself. Wait, please don't interrupt me. I have no desire to speak of this private human tragedy, much less remember it, but I see that you will never believe me otherwise."

He was silent a moment, remembering the ugly scenes, the growing hatred. For an instant, he was sorely tempted to tell Hetty to believe what she liked and to go to the devil. Yet, there was so much pain and confusion in her blue eyes—Damien's eyes, Jack's eyes—and only he held the key to the maze of distorted truths.

"Elizabeth's father, Colonel Nathan Springville, was a stern taskmaster, a ruthless martinet whose word was undisputed law in his family. I tell you this to help you understand why perhaps she acted as she did. She hated her father and wished only for escape, but her escape had to be through lawful marriage, else he would have consigned her to perdition. I can't prove it, else I would have killed Filey with my bare hands, but it is my belief that he seduced her, then instead of offering her marriage, asked her to be his mistress. Damien was gone. She had no one to turn to save myself. Filey doubtless thought it fine sport. Perhaps you are right; perhaps she and Damien were lovers and she would have preferred marriage to him rather than to me. Perhaps she felt some affection for your brother and her letter was a plea for his forgiveness. I can only speculate, as can you."

"Yes, your grace, I can also speculate. You paint the picture of a vain, unscrupulous woman, a woman who cared for no one save herself. But there is the letter, your grace, a letter that damns you. But more, there is Pottson. He told me of Damien's unhappiness, not, of course, that Damien ever confided the cause to his batman, but Damien was affected, your grace, and deeply saddened."

The fire was dying in the grate and the night shadows deepened between them. The marquess turned away, not answering her, and with mechanical movements lighted several candles and placed them near to the bed. He turned then, still silent, and added new logs to the fire. He kicked up the embers with the heel of his boot and watched the flames dance into life, then fall back upon themselves.

He walked back toward Hetty, and she saw naked pain in his eyes. She drew back from that knowledge of him. She drew back from the humanness in him, the honesty of that pain. She didn't want to see pain, only guilt. But an instant later, his face was expressionless. But she wasn't wrong, she'd seen that pain. She felt a small seed of doubt begin to grow within her. She hated it, wanted to squash it, but she couldn't. When he spoke again, his voice was curiously flat, as if he were reciting an impersonal story.

"As I told you, after I married Elizabeth, we immediately left for Billingsgate. By the time we reached Blanchley Manor, we were scarce speaking to each other, nor did I ever again touch her. After but a month of marriage, her belly was round with child. I pressed her to tell me the truth of the matter, but she only laughed at me and hurled half-veiled taunts until I could bear the sight of her no longer. I had no desire to return to London and instead visited some cousins in Scotland until I knew her time was near.

"Upon my return to Blanchley Manor, her hatred

of me was as heavy as her huge belly. The night the child was born, she had consumed a great deal of wine at dinner. I remember to this day thinking that her angel's face had become cold and hard, as if mirroring her true nature. How she laughed at me that evening, for she knew that I wouldn't divorce her, that I would accept her child as my own." He could still picture her face, hear her low laughing voice. "Ah, so you do not care for your fine, beautiful wife, your grace?" He remembered how she had bared her swollen breasts, leaning over the table. "See all the milk I have! What a fine bouncing child I shall present to you, your grace." He drew a breath and got a grip on himself.

He continued with an effort, and she saw it. "There is more ugliness, of course, but suffice it to say that my fury grew to such heights that finally I grasped her shoulders and shook her. She tore away, all the while laughing at me. In her drunken state, she tripped and fell heavily over a chair. The fall brought on her labor, and it was I who delivered my wife of another man's child. It was a little girl and she lived but a few minutes. Her mother lay in a half-drunken stupor, uncaring."

He paused a moment, then added in a voice devoid of emotion, "Elizabeth didn't die in childbed as I have allowed everyone to believe." He pictured again in his mind for perhaps the hundredth time what must have happened from his frightened groom's account. Elizabeth had ordered his curricle without his knowledge, his half-wild bay stallion harnessed between the shafts. She'd whipped the animal about his head until in a spate of fury the stallion had kicked out the flooring of the curricle and sent Elizabeth hurtling down a steep incline. He said to Hetty, "She died in a curricle accident about two weeks after the birth of her child. That is all, Hetty, there is no more that I can tell you. It is, of course, up to you if you wish to believe me."

He turned and walked away from her. As he had spoken, she had felt almost as if she had been there, standing near to him and Elizabeth as they wreaked their anger on each other. She had seen the bitter pain lighting his eyes, had sensed his unwillingness even now to unbury his painful ghosts. But the letter, she always came back to the letter. The letter and Damien's unhappiness, as described by Pottson.

She lay staring into the dark shadows about the room, trying to make sense of things. She realized something she didn't want to realize, but she had to. Deep within her she knew that he had spoken the truth. She simply had no doubts even though she wanted them, wanted to curse him for his lies, but they weren't lies and she knew it. She simply *knew* it. She also realized that she wanted to believe him.

She thought of her life as Lord Harry, of the decision to make herself into a gentleman. Lord Harry had given her life meaning and focus. The sharp pain in her side was preferable to the wrenching pain that now filled her. Had Lord Harry's existence been for naught? She felt hollow as she forced herself to ask, "You said that Elizabeth would never tell you who fathered the child. Yet you believe that it was Filey."

He turned to face her and she saw surprise in his dark eyes, surprise that she was no longer challenging him. "Yes, that's true. I told you that if I had been certain, I would have killed him. The babe carried his general features, very fair with a thatch of reddish hair. There was no resemblance whatsoever in the babe's features to Damien or to me. There is nothing more I can tell you, Hetty."

She lay back against the pillow and closed her eyes. "No, there's nothing more. I believe you've told me everything." Suddenly she felt such relief well up inside her that she wanted to shout with it. She was awash with it until it hit her hard what she'd done. She'd set out to kill a man, a man who was innocent. She struggled up on her elbows. "God, I've been like Don Quixote, fencing with windmills, searching for vengeance, when I had naught to do but speak to you, to show you Elizabeth's letter, to ask for the truth. You were my *vendetta*. I used you to help pull me from my grief. I made you my nemesis. I made you evil, all on the basis of a single letter. May God forgive me, what if I had killed you?"

She was crying, for the first time in so very long, she was crying. She felt stripped bare. She felt guilt and relief and such despair for what could have happened that she couldn't bear it. She stared at him wildly.

"Hetty, no, you must not—"

"Oh no, there's no forgiveness for me. I believed you guilty over nothing more than that bloody letter. I shall never forgive myself for my blindness, for my stupidity."

She turned her face away from him, muffling her damnable tears into the pillow.

He strode to her and gathered her in his arms, rocking her gently against his chest. She offered him no resistance, but he sensed her struggling with herself against the tears. He stroked the soft curls atop her head and waited quietly for her to regain control. He found himself smiling as her sobs dissolved into hiccups. He shifted her in his arms so that he could see her face.

"Come now, Hetty," he said as she tried to burrow her face into the open neck of his white shirt, "Lord Harry would stare me straight in the eye and call me a damnable fool to have fallen into such a horrible situation. Surely Lord Harry wouldn't weep all over my neck." She continued to sob against his neck. "Lord Harry is also an honorable young gentleman. His courage and strength of principle are admirable, and since you, my dear Hetty, are Lord Harry, I would that you would stop this display of guilt. Surely Lord Harry would very quickly find another bone to pick with me. No, still not ready to come back to me? All right, Lord Harry thought I was vicious, that I was a predator. Perhaps I'm not those things, but I am an excellent gambler. I could take you at whist and at piquet and at faro and win your entire dowry. I could leave you humiliated, lying in the dust, no more money to your name. You wouldn't have a chance against me. What do you say?"

Hetty raised her face, aware of his eyes, dark and tender upon her face. Why tenderness from the man she'd meant to kill? It warmed her. It made her feel strangely urgent. She sniffed loudly, then said right in his face, "You've seen me naked."

Now this was unexpected. Interesting, fascinating even, but unexpected. But he was a cautious man, upon occasion. "Well, yes, I suppose that's true enough, but I didn't really think of you as a woman."

"You're lying," she said, still staring at him straightly. "I was at Lady Buxtell's establishment with Harry and Scuddy. There wasn't a single man who wasn't extremely interested in every inch of every female who was there."

"You were in Lady Buxtell's?" There was awe, but no particular surprise in his voice. "You actually went to a whorehouse?"

"How could I avoid it for five months? I tried, but Harry wouldn't let me weasel out of it. I did something good, though. I saved a young girl who'd been befouled by Sir William. She's now Little Jack's nurse."

"You go to a brothel and you manage to bring out a whore to stay with your nephew?"

She told him about Mavreen, about the death of her Uncle Bob. "What really made me angry was Sir William Filey. He'd treated her horribly."

"Sir William isn't a nice man," he said, and dropped a kiss into her hair. He was so startled that he just looked at her. Hetty cocked her head slightly to one side, then smiled at him. "I also learned that men tend to think about sexual matters all the time. It was disconcerting until I got used to it and learned how to say my own titillating things. Everyone believed that I was keeping Mavreen and I let them believe it. It kept me out of Madame Buxtell's house."

He just shook his head at her. "It's unbelievable" was all he said.

There was silence between them then, a silence filled with questions and curiosity.

Then she raised her face. He kissed her very lightly on her closed mouth. "I remember wanting to do that at the Ranleagh ball," he said. "I wanted to touch you, too. I loved your laughter, it flowed over me and made me feel the warmth of you. You charmed me, Hetty, charmed me to my toes. I thought you fascinating. I couldn't figure out why you'd disliked me, why you'd leave your father's house just to avoid me."

"You charmed me as well," she said. "I don't know anything about men and women, your grace—"

"My name is Jason. Do you think perhaps you could say that to me?"

"Jason, as in the Greek Jason who was ever so heroic and noble and adventurous?"

"The same one," he said, and kissed her again. "Now, about you knowing about men and women, I would say that you have a perspective on my species that no other woman could have. I would like to hear all of your exploits. I like to be terrified and astounded."

"You really didn't think of me as me when you took care of me?"

The night had ended very much differently than he'd expected, he thought, and lightly kissed her yet again. She tasted warm and sweet and he wanted her very much. Not that it mattered. "You're beautiful. I'm not blind. But believe me, I'm in charge of you—your health—as your doctor if you will, not as your husband. One doesn't shirk one's duty, Hetty. Surely you would have cared for me had there been no other choice. Would you have looked at me naked and felt a woman's lust for me?"

"I don't know," she said slowly, frowning deeply in thought. "I realize that the gentlemen, as I told you, all think about sex nearly every hour of the day and night. I think it's strange. I don't know much of anything about a woman's lust. Is there really such a thing?"

"Next time we duel, I shall contrive to be the one who is wounded. I will see if you end up kissing me and holding me as I am you. We will see if you feel such a thing then. Lust is a very nice thing, Hetty."

"I think I'd rather learn about lust in a happier circumstance than with you wounded." Suddenly, she shuddered, ducking her head again against his neck. "You know, I really enjoyed my fencing lessons with Signore Bertioli. Yet when it came to the sticking point—"

He tightened his hold on her shoulders and finished her unspoken thought. "There's always a sticking point. There's no sport, no dashing romance in slicing up a man, or a woman, as the case may be."

"You wouldn't want to kill Sir William Filey?"

There was a sudden, dangerous gleam in his dark eyes. "That's different. He's different. Yes, I have wanted to for a very long time, but my hands are tied. After Elizabeth's death, I returned briefly to London and confronted him. Sir William is many things, but he isn't stupid. He knows me to be his better with foils and pistols. Thus, he denied any involvement with Elizabeth and sullenly swallows my insults as he did that night at White's when I tried to intervene and protect you."

"I would like to kill him, too," she said. "I think I could kill him after what I saw he did to Mavreen."

She moved slightly against his chest to relieve the sudden sharp pulling in her side. He became very much aware of her soft breasts pressing against him. He became very much aware of how hard he'd become in just the past few moments. He didn't want to embarrass her. He didn't want her to feel she couldn't trust him. Damnation.

He rose quickly to stand over her. She was young and beautiful and so damned female that it made him harder than a stone. He saw her laugh, felt the energy and pleasure in her when he'd whirled her about in the waltz. She was also Lord Harry. He knew her better than he'd ever known another human being. All her different parts were his now. It felt very good and very right. There could be no other woman like her. The black despair that had held him for so long was gone. "You must rest now, Hetty. We've had an evening I doubt I will ever forget. I pray you won't either and try to stick a knife in my ribs on the morrow."

"No, I shan't do that," she said and let him pull the covers over her. "Jason."

"Yes?"

"Do you think you can forgive me for all I've done to you?"

"Perhaps," he said quietly, taking her hand in his. "In twenty years or so."

She smiled at him. Twenty years, she thought. That sounded nice. Odd that it should, but it did. For the first time since Damien's death, she felt something besides guilt, despair, and blind determination. She felt a bit of peace. She knew it wouldn't last, that she couldn't let it last, for the person who was responsible for Damien's death was still out there, still unknown. But for now, she hugged the peace to her and when she slept, she was smiling.

Chapter Twenty-nine

She awoke up to complete silence. Sunlight filled the large bedchamber. That wonderful feeling of peace was still with her. There was still a smile on her face. She remembered him clearly, holding her, kissing her. She felt clean and whole, despite the constant pulling in her side, but that didn't matter, she could bear that. She was alive.

And so was he. She stared over at him, watching him write, his dark head bent, his right hand moving swiftly over a piece of foolscap. He was wearing a white shirt, open at the neck, the sleeves loose to the tight cuffs, and black knit pants that made him look quite nice indeed. As for his black hessians, she had to admit that Lord Harry had never looked quite so excellent in his.

But what was most important was that he'd told her the truth. He was innocent. There was honor in him, deep honor, and honesty. Again, she felt the surge of guilt, then forced herself away from it. It was over now. He'd understood. He'd forgiven her, at least he said he would in the next twenty years.

That still sounded very nice to her this morning.

"Who are you writing to?" She struggled up on her elbows, trying to reach for the carafe of water.

He paused, his pen poised in midair, and quickly rose. "No, hold still. Let me give you water."

He held the glass as she drank. "I'm writing a letter to Sir Archibald."

"Oh my, you're what?"

"I'm writing to your esteemed sire. Hetty, Lady Alicia Warton is an excellent hostess, though she sincerely apologizes for not informing Sir Archibald sooner of the delightful visit she is having with his daughter. She is, at the moment, endeavoring to create and recount the various activities you've enjoyed since your arrival at Thurston Hall. I fear you've been fairly debauched. Perhaps you've even flirted overly with too many gentlemen. It also appears that you are very fond of your host, Lord Oberlon. Perhaps he even is attracted to you. It remains to be seen."

She just stared up at him with those clear blue eyes of hers. "I think I'd like to be debauched."

He looked stunned, then forced a light smile. "What, no duel for me today? No knife in my black heart?"

She just shook her head at him and drank some more water.

"Call me Jason. I like to hear you say my name."

Instead she choked on the water. He thwacked her back, then sat down on the bed beside her and pulled her against him to gently rub his palm over her back. She'd stopped choking long before he stopped rubbing.

"Jason," she said against his shoulder. "Is Lady Alicia your only sister?"

He didn't let her go, just began to rock her slowly back and forth. "Yes, and fortunately for us, she is

pregnant and thus unlikely to venture this time of
year into London. Now, as much as I would like to
hold you until you'll undoubtedly want Millie again,
let me order your breakfast and finish this letter.
Pottson must leave shortly to deliver it."

"Have I really flirted outrageously with my host?"

"You've been fair to tripping on your tongue you
want him so much."

"That sounds quite odd to me. What about the
host? You think he's equally interested?"

"It's certainly possible, given that he's washed you
and fed you and already kissed you, but not enough
to ease him."

She liked the sound of that as well. "Is there
nothing you've forgotten?"

"There's a lot I don't want myself to think about
right now," he said, rising. "Yes, I'm thinking venal
thoughts of you, Hetty, very vivid debauched
thoughts, but let me answer you as a gentleman and
your doctor. I hope I haven't forgotten anything. I've
also just finished writing my daily note to the earl
of March on Lord Harry's progress. He, I assume,
will keep his brother-in-law informed."

Hetty lay back quietly and thoughtfully chewed
on her lower lip. "When is Henrietta Rolland
going home?"

"In about three days, I expect. Lady Alicia has
begged your father, very prettily, I might add, to
allow you to extend your visit to a full week. Even
then, Hetty, you'll be damnably weak and there'll
still be pain."

"I don't like it at all."

"I don't blame you. Now you asked me about Miss
Henrietta Rolland. Which one? The one I wanted

to kiss and tease all night at the Ranleaghs' ball or the one at my aunt Melberry's soiree who called me a spanking fine fellow and was so vulgar I wanted to smack her?"

She laughed, regretted it, and settled for a smile. "I fooled you, I surely did, but not at first. You're very perceptive and I knew I had to stop taunting you."

"Yes, you were wise to stop it. Perhaps I would have recognized you eventually. But not immediately. There were so many of your parts strewn around London. You're an arrogant woman, Henrietta, do you know that?"

"Yes, but Lord Harry gave it to me. He couldn't afford not to swagger and boast and be ruthless. He taught me a lot. So did Miss Caroline Langley. She's infatuated with you. I had to listen to her chatter on and on about how wonderful you are. I had to bite my tongue since I was firmly convinced that you were a villain."

He could only shake his head at her as he moved quickly at the knock on the door. He took the breakfast tray from the servant and quickly closed the door again. "I know the servants are mad to know what this is all about. Pottson tells me that they hound him and Millie both, but they've kept mum. Now, porridge for you and some toast with lots of butter and Cook's special honey."

She ate a goodly amount. It settled well on her stomach, which relieved both of them. She said, "Do you believe that Sir William Filey could have had the influence to have Damien sent out of the country?"

"I've wondered about that. I wouldn't have

thought so, but then again, I don't know all the influence he wields with the war ministry. We still have a mystery on our hands. Does Lord Harry feel he still has more work to do?"

She frowned into her coffee cup. He misinterpreted her gesture. "Thank God you're ready to send that imperious young gentleman back to the wilds of northern England or was it Scotland? It was a foolish and dangerous game you played, Hetty. Just thinking about all you did—at least all you did that I know about—makes my belly cramp. Now, at least, you may again don your skirts and leave me to do the hunting."

It was the stupidest thing he could have said.

She eyed him with dangerous calm. "Ah, let me understand you, your grace. You mean that it is time for the *real* gentleman to search out the truth? The lady will return to her proper place, simpering and serving tea?"

He was annoyed and yet, at the same time, rather pleased to see the vinegar back in her. It must mean she was feeling much better. How to get himself out of this hole? His offer wasn't meant to offend. He was being just as he should be. He said easily, "Naturally you will return where you belong. I said nothing of simpering and serving tea. However, I can't now see you donning your breeches again and prancing off to White's or to Lady Buxtell's, for God's sake."

"*Prance*? Why, I believe you should go directly to the devil."

"We aren't even lovers yet and already we're arguing. What did you say? You want me to do what?"

"Go to the devil," she said again, stressing each word. She saw a muscle twitch in his jaw. "If I wish to remain Lord Harry and button up my breeches, I won't ask your permission or anyone else's. You have absolutely no authority over me, and I shall do exactly as I please." She frowned at her clasped hands. "Well, perhaps that was a bit too strong. As you said, we're not lovers yet and here we are arguing. I don't want to argue with you, but I won't let you just step in and take over everything. Damien was my brother. I owe it to him to find out the truth and that is what I must try to do."

"Damnation," he said, and skimmed his fingers through his hair, making it stand on end, "I don't want to understand you, but you always seem to force me to. In this instance though I must stand firm. I won't allow you to ever return as Lord Harry to society. That I can stop, and I will if you try it. We will simply have to come up with another idea, but no more Lord Harry. It's away from London with that young gentleman."

"I'll think about it, that's all I can promise. Could you come here and kiss me, Jason? Perhaps it will clear my head."

He didn't hesitate. He looked at her pale face, framed by blond curls that tumbled over her ears. She looked young and innocent and very clever. She also looked very interested in him. He pulled her to him and kissed her. "Open your mouth," he said, his breath warm against her flesh. She did and was thoroughly distracted.

"Oh, that's very nice. Can I have some more?"

"If you promise you won't do anything in the future without discussing it with me first."

She thought about it long and hard, and he thought, he should have kissed her more thoroughly, made her more urgent, for he'd not awakened enough passion in her and now that very smart brain of hers was working at full speed.

He tried arrogance, knowing that would bring her back to him quickly enough, and with a good deal of annoyance, he imagined. "I've saved you, Henrietta, saved both of us from a scandal that would have been at the top of the gossips' list for a good six months were it to become known that you, a gently bred lady, had charaded as a young man and challenged me to a duel. Will you admit that I have done well so far?"

"I'm alive and that's good. Other than that, I have only your word for the rest of it. For example, maybe this sister of yours doesn't even exist."

He laughed, tousled her hair, hugged her until she squeaked, and said, "You will obey me. I intend to marry you. I suppose I must now that I've seen you naked, looked at every delightful inch of you, spent days alone in your company and you wearing only my nightshirt. I'm a gentleman and see no other honorable path for me to tread. I'm still too young and now I'm caught again."

He got all he'd hoped for. She shoved against his chest, then shoved her fist in his belly. It wasn't hard enough and she tried again, but he was laughing now because she couldn't gain enough leverage.

"Maybe I won't marry you. I don't even know you. You've been a bad man to me for a very long time. Perhaps that was just a stray part of you at the Ranleaghs' ball. Perhaps that was the only night in your life that you were charming. You do look nice and you kiss well enough, but even then, I've never been kissed before so perhaps you're a troll with no talent or skill at all or—"

He kissed her just to shut her up.

"Oh, another thing, your grace," she said when he allowed her to pull back for a moment. "You play that arrogant role of yours and I'll cosh you. You know that I could simply announce to the world that the wonderful Marquess of Oberlon, that famous Corinthian and black-hearted knave who's wicked and amusing and fascinating, fought a duel with a girl. I shudder to think what would happen to your reputation. Would anyone speak to you again?"

"You're very good," he said, his fingers lightly stroking over her white throat. "If I squeeze just a bit, will you whimper for me? Will you call me cruel and—"

"I'd die before I'd whimper for anyone," she said. She lightly touched her fingertips to his mouth, to his jaw, to his nose. "Yes, you're a spanking handsome fellow."

"And you, Henrietta, you have a tenacious will." He could probably threaten her all he wanted, but it wouldn't matter. She'd just look at him and probably laugh and poke fun at him. No, she wouldn't be bowed by any threats from him. He realized that the last thing he wanted was to make threats or demands or give her orders. He probably would want to in the future and he could just begin to envision what would happen between them when he did. It seemed quite a nice future to him. Four days ago, he couldn't have begun to imagine such a thing. Life was, he thought while kissing her ear, very strange and unexpected. He decided that the marriage he'd jested about with her would come to pass. He wanted her.

He looked at her and everything he was thinking was in his expression. She ran her tongue over her bottom lip. He stared at her tongue and that bottom lip of hers. He wanted her right now. He wanted to love her and caress her and not stop.

"Damnation, this has got to cease. I know things, Hetty, things that you know about as a gentleman but have no notion about as a young lady. They're fun things, but I can't share them with you yet, else I'd have to challenge myself to a duel." He gently eased her back onto the pillow. "I'll fetch Millie for you. Rest now. I'll be back soon enough. I can't seem to keep away from you. All very odd, but there it is."

"I know," she said. "I know."

Chapter Thirty

Hetty gritted her teeth and held herself as still as she could. He was gentle, he was matter-of-fact, as he carefully snipped away the dressing from her side. The wound had closed nicely and the flesh surrounding it was a healthy pink. The black thread looked obscene but that couldn't be helped. She'd grown thinner, he thought, as he gently bathed her side with warm soapy water. With great deference to her modesty and to his own control, he'd slipped the nightshirt only midway up her chest and the sheet down to the middle of her belly. She trembled as the soft washcloth touched her skin.

His hand paused momentarily in the hollow of her belly. He spoke his thought aloud. "You're beautiful, even a doctor would have to recognize that, but your father would think that Lady Alicia has been starving you. You must force yourself to eat more, Hetty. We've but a day to fatten you up. By God, your flesh is white and soft, and—I'm sorry. This is not well done of me. I'm your doctor again, bloodless, with no thought beyond that the wound is closing well. Millie will remove the stitches after you're home again."

She was silent as a stone. He felt a tightening of her muscles beneath his hand, and gingerly moved to another spot. In but a few more minutes, he'd dried her with a soft linen towel and was reaching for the basilicum powder.

"This is very embarrassing," she said after he'd covered her again. He looked up, expecting to see her face flushed, and was taken off guard to see her staring at him, wide-eyed, with a kind of stunned expression on her face. She'd felt something for him, despite the pain she must still feel in her side. She liked him touching her? Oh God, he liked it as well.

He tried to make himself feel like a bishop at a baptism as he slipped the linen beneath her waist to bind the wound loosely again. It was damned unnerving and he felt sweat break out on his forehead. He felt a clumsy oaf, thinking that he must be hurting her.

"Do you really want to marry me?" she asked, staring at him straightly.

"Yes," he said, standing over her now. "I must as I told you. I've taken more advantage of your innocence than a man is allowed to take. Yes, I must hie myself to the altar with you, noble fellow that I am."

"You haven't asked me if I'm even interested in becoming better acquainted with you," she said. She watched his face closely as he pulled the nightshirt back down and rose from her bedside.

"I already know you're interested. You smile at me, you ask me to kiss you, and I fancy you like it. Now, you'll be a bit sore for another week, but Millie will be able to see to you quite sufficiently after you're home. Would you like to become better acquainted with me? Learn if I can mind my tongue and be gallant and flatter your very pretty eyebrows?"

"Are they really?"

"What's really?"

"Do you really like my eyebrows?"

He rolled his eyes, strode back and forth three times beside her bed, gave her a crooked grin and took himself off.

She told herself as sleep tugged at her again, as it always seemed to do, this weariness that was so deep she didn't even know where it came from, this weakness she hated, that he knew at least that she wasn't like many females. She wasn't helpless or fragile or soft, as men seemed to like women to be. She'd never be remotely helpless, regardless of what he would admire.

Enough of that. She had to think. Just because he'd turned her life upside down in four days, there was still Damien and still the man out there who'd been responsible for his death. Someone had forced Damien to leave England; and that same person, still maddeningly unknown, had sent him to his death at Waterloo. Lord Harry still had much to do.

The following morning, dressed as Lord Harry and leaning heavily upon Lord Oberlon's arm, Lord Harry bade a silent farewell to Thurston Hall, a mansion she was quite certain she could come to admire, if the opportunity were offered to her, which it had been, but had he been truly serious?

As she expected, Sir Archibald's carriage was standing in front of the gothic-pillared entrance, with both Millie and Pottson standing by the open door. She pulled her greatcoat more closely about her shoulders to ward off the frigid winter wind. Of course, she had to leave Thurston Hall as Lord Harry—for the servants' sake—the marquess had said, and naturally she'd agree with him. She didn't relish the prospect of changing back into women's clothes, even with Millie's assistance, in a cramped carriage.

She looked at his set profile. He was in close conversation with Pottson. She felt a knot of loneliness. She didn't want to leave Thurston Hall. She didn't want to leave him. She wasn't going home. She was leaving it. She realized the marquess was speaking to her and turned up her pale face to meet his.

"I'm sorry, but I can't accompany you. Millie and Pottson have my instructions. You'll be well taken care of. I shall call upon you in a couple of days to see how you're doing."

"I've been well taken care of all my life," she said. "When will I see you?"

"In three days. I doubt I could last longer away from you. You madden me and I want to kiss you, very badly. Oh lord, I hope that Jack the footman didn't hear that, else I would quickly gain a reputation as a pederast. Go, Lord Harry. Take care and rest. I'll see you soon." He wanted to touch her face, but he knew he couldn't. They had to maintain the charade.

He closed the door to the carriage. He turned and walked back up the steps. "Silken," he shouted, "have the carriage ready in half an hour. We're going back to London."

Tired and somewhat depressed, Hetty arrived dressed modestly in a woman's gown at the stroke of noon. Thinking that her father would demand all sorts of details of her visit to Thurston Hall, she had carefully invented several parties and outings. She was rather unnerved when her sire, after greeting her with a negligent kiss on the cheek, asked only, "I understand the marquess was in residence during your visit and that you got along very well with him."

"He put in an occasional appearance, Father." She picked up a roll, but still, from the corner of her eye, she saw his speculative look. She smiled to herself. If her father only knew.

After luncheon, Hetty excused herself and trailed wearily up to her bedchamber. She lay very carefully down on her back and stared up at the ceiling. She thought of Jason Cavander's manly command that she was never again to appear as Lord Harry. Still, no matter how much she just wanted to stare at him and kiss him, she couldn't let him dictate to her. She knew what she had to do. She had to find out if Sir William Filey had indeed been responsible for Damien's death. Nor could she turn her back upon poor Isabella's plight. The thought of Sir William even being near Isabella made her ill. My motives are of the highest order, she told herself, and if the marquess goes into a snit, then so be it. Damn, why couldn't gentlemen, the marquess in particular, not realize that they weren't the sole guardians of honor and pride? Actually, truth be told, she hoped he didn't really feel that way.

"You intend to do *what*?" Millie stared stupefied at her mistress the next afternoon when Hetty evenly informed her of her intention to invite Sir

Harry and Mr. Scuddimore to dinner at Lord Harry's lodgings.

"You heard me, Millie. If you don't choose to accompany me to Thompson Street, I shall just have to go alone. But go I will. Lord Harry isn't done yet. The marquess is innocent, but that leaves the man responsible still out there. I must get him."

"But the marquess—"

"To the devil with the marquess. I'm your mistress, and he has no say whatsoever in whatever I choose to do. Now, will you help me or no, Millie?"

Short of tying her mistress to a chair, Millie found that she had no alternative but to escort her to Lord Harry's lodgings. When she tried to argue with her young mistress, she received only cold, uncommunicative stares.

Pottson served only to make Hetty want to strangle the man she was going to marry. "But no, Miss Hetty, the marquess told me that he would see to things now, that you were a young lady, after all, and you were still weak from the wound, and you would need to rest and remember how to wear your skirts again, and, well, he gave me strict orders to pack away Lord Harry's belongings. He said that *he* was going to find out who was responsible for sending Master Damien away."

Her hands were on her hips even though it made her side hurt more than necessary. "Oh, he did, did he? Well, he certainly has his nerve, doesn't he?" Then she just grinned at Pottson. "All right, both of you. Lord Harry is still very much in existence, and it is I who will decide just when he will disappear from London. If you don't obey me, I swear that I will go directly to White's and yell the truth of this entire matter to the world. Just keep on with me and I'll do it. Do either of you wish to take that chance?"

Millie glanced at Pottson. They knew they'd lost, but just for the moment. Hetty guessed that, at the first opportunity, Pottson would take himself to Jason's town house and fill his ears with Miss Hetty's obstinacy.

Although Hetty suspected that Pottson, after delivering her invitation to Sir Harry and Mr. Scuddimore, had paid a visit to the marquess, she didn't question him, just stared at him coldly, making him feel the perfect traitor, she hoped.

As she vigorously pomaded down her blond curls and drew them severely back at the nape of her neck, she found herself wondering just how Sir Harry and Scuddy were going to react upon seeing her. They would have many questions, of that she was certain. I shall just have to take them as they come, she decided, as she pulled on her breeches. She directed a grunt of disgust at the thin body looking back at her from the mirror. If her breeches had been loose fitting before, now they positively hung. She heard a loud knocking on the outer door, and with a final glance at herself, she turned and strode from the room, hopeful that during her illness she hadn't lost her masculine swagger.

"Good God," Sir Harry said, clasping her hand and pumping it. "You've become a damned scarecrow. You still feeling pulled, old fellow?"

"Ho, Harry, it is only that I thought of you and became too ill to eat." How strange it was that she had slipped back so easily into Lord Harry's role.

"Well, Scuddy here ain't the worse for wear. Ate like a man mountain, he did, in sympathy for you, at least that's what he kept telling me."

"I thank you, Scuddy. It's good to be alive. It's also good to see both of you again."

"Well, we're surprised to see you, Lord Harry," Scuddy said.

"Surprised? Why? Did you believe I'd curl up my toes and pass to the hereafter?"

Sir Harry said, "What Scuddy means to say is that the Marquess of Oberlon informed Julien—my brother-in-law, the Earl of March, you know—that when you recovered from your wound you would be returning home. We're dashed glad, though, that you returned to say goodbye before going back to that barbaric place."

Damn him, she thought. It was nicely done. She said in a cool voice, "I'm not quite ready yet to say my farewells. It appears the marquess was a bit premature in announcing my leave-taking." She turned before either Sir Harry or Mr. Scuddimore could offer any further comment and led the way to the table.

They were midway through the first course of a raised pheasant pie when Sir Harry asked her the inevitable question.

"I say, Lord Harry, will you tell us now just why the devil you forced the marquess to fight a duel?"

Hetty paused a moment and lifted her wineglass to her lips before saying with just the right dash of hauteur in her voice, "I certainly have no intention of telling you the cause of our disagreement. It wouldn't be honorable to do so. Suffice it to say that the marquess and I have amicably resolved our differences. I now call him friend."

"Well, I'm glad you decided against killing his grace. It would have been a messy business," Sir Harry said. "I would have had to second you out of the country."

"That was clever, Harry," she said. She'd started to say that it had been the other way around that it had been the marquess who'd done her in, but she didn't say that. What Sir Harry said was the truth. She could have killed him, perhaps, if she'd still had the strength. She'd felt invincible at the time, but now, she didn't know what would have happened. "He took me to Thurston Hall and cared for me. I owe him a debt of gratitude."

Scuddy said simply, "You deloped, Lord Harry. I was very proud of you."

"Deloped? Come, Scuddy, one delopes with a pistol. Our duel was with foils."

"No, Scuddy's hit the nail on the head. Same thing, at least in principle," Sir Harry said. "Damned brave thing to do. Like I've told Scuddy here countless times, you had the tip of your foil at Lord Oberlon's chest—could have sliced him up right then—but chose to let him live. Yes, you deloped."

"You can't disagree, Lord Harry," Mr. Scuddimore said. "The marquess himself could talk about nothing but your honor and bravery."

"The marquess?" Hetty asked, at sea.

"Button your trap, Scuddy—after all, they were *my* letters. Well, at least, they were my brother-in-law's letters and I was the one who read them. You see, Lord Harry, while you were on the mend at Thurston Hall, the marquess kept Julien informed of your progress and also how he had developed the greatest respect for you, despite your wild ways and your tender years."

She wished he hadn't done it with such leveling sincerity, yet it warmed her to her toes. But enough of the marquess. She quickly turned to Sir Harry, "Enough of my affairs. Tell us, Harry, may Scuddy and I yet toast your impending wedding with the lovely Isabella?"

A deep frown settled on Sir Harry's smooth brow.

"Proper mad, he is," Scuddy said.

Sir Harry did look harassed. "Damned if I know what the chit's about. Seems she ain't so adverse to Sir William Filey's suit anymore."

"Sir William Filey is a disgusting old man. Explain yourself."

"It's just as I said. That old lecher is making himself very agreeable to Isabella. Showers her with flowers and silly notes praising the ribbons in her damned hair, even takes her riding in the park. He had the damned gall to approach me at White's, smirking all the while, to lay a wager on which of us would win the chit."

Hetty felt herself go cold. Did Sir William want to repeat with Isabella what he had done to Elizabeth? "Come, Harry, this is nonsense. Surely Isabella doesn't welcome his attentions. If anything, it's her damned mother forcing her to be pleasant to the satyr."

"What's a satyr?" Scuddy said.

"A very unlovable creature," Hetty said.

Harry stared down into his glass of sherry.

"Damn you, Harry, answer me. Have you proposed to Isabella, told her of your feelings? Has she turned you down?"

Harry's hand tightened around the crystal, and the stem broke. He looked up and said, anger filling him, "Oh very well, you interfering bastard. If you must know, she hasn't given me the chance. And I've told her time and again not to be taken in by that old roué's flattery. I've told her he just wants to seduce her, that he liked young girls, and he can't be trusted."

She stared at him thoughtfully. "So what you're telling me is that when you're with Isabella, you spend all your time raking her down and telling her how stupid she is. It's you who are the stupid one, Harry. How can you be such an idiot?"

There was a sudden gleam of understanding in Mr. Scuddimore's eyes. "By jove, Lord Harry's right. A girl can't like to be preached to all the time. Bet when you leave, Sir William comes by and tells her that she's the light of his life. Deuced stupid, Harry, deuced stupid."

Hetty knew Sir Harry was on the point of knocking over their dinner and smacking Scuddy in his rounded jaw. He'd already broken his sherry glass. She said quickly, "Harry, heed me. There is much that I know about Sir William, things that you or Scuddy would scarce believe true. Suffice it to say that Sir William need not necessarily have marriage to Isabella in mind. He likes young virgins, Harry. He likes to take their virginity and then leave them, perhaps even leave them pregnant. I know of one proven example."

"Just how the devil do you know that?"

"It's just as I said. The man is vile and he will do anything to achieve his ends. He is a man of much experience and Isabella knows nothing about the sordid world in which he lives. She is innocent and pure. If you don't take action, she will be ruined.

Even if it is marriage Sir William must offer, he will very quickly turn her life into a living hell. All he wants from her is her innocence, Harry. He doesn't want her, not like you do."

"Oh damnation. What if she won't have me?"

Hetty regarded him steadily for a long moment. "If you care for her, Harry, then you must haul her off to Gretna Green. It would be an act of true chivalry."

Sir Harry nervously gulped down a full glass of sherry. "I must think. Bedamned, I must think." He rose unsteadily from the table, jerking at his cravat as if it were suddenly choking him.

Sir Harry suddenly crashed his fist upon the table, having reached the most portentous decision of his life. "By God, I'll do it. Yes, I'll marry her. I'll haul her over my shoulder and carry her to Gretna Green if I have to. And you're right, damn you, Lord Harry, I want her virginity and her purity, it's true, but I do want all of her and I want all of her forever. I'll do it. Listen, Lord Harry, if Isabella refuses me, will you help me? I will kidnap her if I must, but will you help me?"

Lord Harry looked at him and smiled. "Of course I'll help you. First, Harry, you must press your suit to Isabella. Be all that is romantic, mind you. If she refuses, well, of course then we'll do what we must."

"I have more horses," Mr. Scuddimore said. "Horses are always helpful, you know."

"Indeed they are, Scuddy. We will need horses, won't we, Harry?"

"Eh? Oh yes, certainly."

Hetty said to Sir Harry, "Send me a note here as to the outcome of your proposal to Isabella. If she refuses you, I'll come by to see you at your lodgings and we'll make plans."

"I'll be there as well," Scuddy said.

When at last she had seen them out, she leaned heavily against the closed door. She admitted to herself that she was weary, the wound in her side was aching dully. Her thoughts went inevitably to the marquess. She found herself wondering if it were truly possible for a gentleman to love a lady who was also a gentleman.

She gazed down a moment at her breeched, booted person. Lord Harry Monteith had granted her the greatest freedom, had allowed her adventures that no lady would ever experience. Yet, she thought, she felt now that Lord Harry was trapping her, holding her prisoner in a role that she no longer desired. She wanted out.

She walked wearily into Lord Harry's bedchamber, wondering just precisely how one went about eloping to Gretna Green.

Chapter Thirty-one

"Good morning, Grimpston. His grace is in the drawing room?"

"Yes, Miss Hetty. I offered him tea but he said he preferred to wait for you."

"If you please, fetch tea now, Grimpston." She went immediately to the gilt-edged mirror and looked at herself. Her blond curls were sparkling clean and brushed neatly into place. No pomade for Henrietta Rolland. She supposed she looked well enough. The blue muslin gown, though a trifle short, at least didn't remotely resemble buckskin breeches. That in itself was an improvement over the last time he'd seen her.

She opened the door to the drawing room quietly and saw the marquess before he was aware of her. Bedamned but he was handsome, she thought, with the flavor of Lord Harry. She didn't realize it, but the marquess had dressed himself with rather more care than usual this morning, the powder blue coat of broadcloth having just yesterday arrived from Weston's, and his hessians polished to such a bright shine that he could see his reflection. He stood by the tall bow windows, his back to her, gazing out onto the square.

"Good morning, your grace."

He turned quickly and for a long moment said nothing, but merely stared at her.

She stared back at him. "Good God," he said slowly, whistling under his breath. "Louisa was really quite right."

"Right about what?"

His dark eyes twinkled in amusement. "What is this? You sound as though it must be an insult. You'll get no answer from me. You must ask Louisa. I do wonder, though, where your spectacles are. And do not let us forget that hideous pea green gown and cap. A *lasting* effect. If I close my eyes and think bilious thoughts, I swear I can still see it."

He advanced upon her and lazily lifted her hand and kissed her fingers. "How are you feeling?"

"A little sore, that's all. Your cravat is really quite well done."

"It's my own design. Lord Harry may disabuse himself of the notion of copying it."

"I daresay Lord Harry does just fine for himself. Actually, it's the Mathematical he aspires to. It's not as easily achieved as it looks. My lord March does it nicely." It didn't occur to her to remove her fingers from his hand. His fingers were strong and warm and she wished they were on her arm, perhaps on her face, her throat. She sighed. It might even be nice to be back in his bed again.

Things seemed so very different now that she was a female and in a gown and in her father's drawing room.

She retrieved her hand when Grimpston, bearing tea and morning cakes, loudly cleared his throat upon entering the drawing room.

"Ah, sustenance. Please set the tray upon the table. I shall serve his grace."

Grimpston did as he was bid and during his placement, he managed to study the marquess quite thoroughly. Before he left, he nodded to Hetty.

"It appears your butler finds me acceptable husband material," the marquess said blandly.

"You're male, of the nobility, not doddering toward the grave, you have all your teeth, so yes, he approves of you."

He grinned at her. "I don't carry extra flesh either, though a butler would scarce consider that, I doubt. Grimpston has been with your family forever, am I right?"

"I sometimes think he's been with the family since the seventeenth century. He seems to know everything about every ancestor. Cream, your grace?"

"Yes. Thank you for pouring it, Hetty. Is that a simper I hear? No, certainly not. Incidentally, do call me Jason. I don't like this withdrawal of yours. It makes me feel insecure. It makes me feel like you no longer regard me as your white knight. It makes me think you don't want me to kiss you again."

"I feel the same way, sitting here just like a proper young lady." She laughed. "My life has been so very odd for the past five months. Tell me, Jason, are we really betrothed?"

"Yes, but I will speak to Sir Archibald. We don't want to shock him, Hetty."

"I agree," she said. "I should like to kiss you though whether you're a Jason or a your grace. Perhaps at Thurston Hall it was just my weakness that made me want to kiss you so very much and all of the time. Do you think that's possible?"

"No, it's not. I will kiss you, but not just yet. Tell

me, dear one, how did you enjoy your evening with Sir Harry and Mr. Scuddimore?"

"They were much pleased to see me. Oh, the devil. How did you know I'd seen them? I would have told you without you having me followed by one of your minions."

"I quite understand, but a little prodding never hurts. Pottson was understandably concerned and practically begged me to 'break you to the bit,' I believe was his colorful way of putting it."

"I can't believe he'd betray me to you," she said and slammed her teacup into its saucer. "I *knew* that he would take it upon himself to interfere. He always gives me those wounded looks of his, no matter what I wanted to do as Lord Harry. I even saw him praying once. Breaking me to the bit? How very gothic that sounds and well, maybe lots of fun, but just with you."

"Does it really? Be careful what you say, Hetty, else I just might leap on you right now, right here in your father's drawing room. Now, forgive me but I did ask him to keep an eye on you. I found a gray hair in my head yesterday morning. Since I want to be with you for the next fifty years or so, I had to do something. Also, you must know that Pottson rather has to obey me since he'll be in my employ for many years to come."

That sounded very nice to her and she gave him a smile that hit him down to his toes. God, she had a wonderful smile, a very female smile. He couldn't imagine her as Lord Harry, he truly couldn't. She was beautiful, her breasts full and soft. Lord, he wanted to kiss her and hold her, perhaps even cup her buttocks in his hands and raise her against him.

He nearly groaned at the thought. He saw her naked so clearly, so beautifully naked and white and soft and his dark hand in the hollow of her belly and the contrast between them, ah, it was too much. He would surely expire on the spot if he didn't elevate his thoughts immediately. He pictured her breasts and choked on his tea.

"Shall I hit you on the back? You're all right? Of course you are and now you're giving me one of your wicked looks that I like very much. But enough. I find it odd, your grace, that you were so very adamant in sending Lord Harry back home on the one hand and praising him to London society on the other. I find your actions difficult to fathom."

What had she said? His thoughts were so powerfully real that he was utterly blank for a moment. Finally, he managed to say, "Do you really?"

She looked at her feet. What was the matter? He frowned at her, wondering what was going on in that beautiful head of hers when she blurted out, "I'm not at all like Melissande. I'm sorry, but I'm not and I'll never be. I'm just me and I'm quite plain, but I am nice and I do have a sense of humor and I promise to make you laugh and—"

"It's true," he said calmly. "You're not at all like Melissande. She's really quite voluptuous, her breasts are more than a man could ask for. She also knows every trick to please a man, to make him lie panting at her feet. I might also add that she rapidly becomes a dead bore. Her brain isn't of the highest order, but then again, most men wouldn't want that in a mistress. Listen, Hetty, she is what she is. And what she is is a mistress. She's good at it. I'm damned thankful you're not like her. You're you and you're beautiful and you're everything a man could want in a mate. But, of course, you, I am persuaded, are already much aware of that fact. Surely you know I'd slay every dragon in England for you."

She sighed. "Would you really, Jason?"

"Every bloody one," he said. "Well, I might leave one for posterity, but that's all, just one."

"Melissande is rather silly, I expect, but so very beautiful."

"I would like to know what the devil you said to her to make her pine so for Lord Harry."

"Men don't understand women. That is, women like Melissande need to be nourished on the most outlandish flattery. It makes them quite malleable, you know. At least that was my experience with her."

"Can you be more specific, sweetheart?"

Ah, she liked the sound of that. "I likened her first of all to Aphrodite, being fairly certain that she would have heard of that lovely goddess. When images of Aphrodite began to pale, I cast her first as the romantic Helen, the most beautiful woman in the world, then threw in a dash of Daphne with handsome Apollo in hot pursuit. I must admit though that I did buy her a riding habit. That, I think, was the clincher, which doesn't say all that much for my flattery."

He threw back his head and laughed deeply. "You should have kept the habit for Miss Henrietta Rolland. It would have suited her fair coloring most admirably."

"Oh no, I couldn't. It was far too short for me. Melissande lacks inches, you know."

"Only in height, my dear Hetty, not, I assure you, anywhere else."

"You're dreadful and I will get you for that."

"I can't wait," he said, and it was difficult for him to remain seated in his chair. He wanted to scoop her up in his arms and kiss her until they were both silly with it. He drew a deep breath. "Tell me about Sir Harry and his problems."

Oh well, Hetty thought, this is at least safe ground. She hesitated only a moment before recounting to him Sir Harry Brandon's difficulties. He listened to her without interruption, his dark eyes never leaving her face. "So, you see, depending on Isabella's answer to Harry, Lord Harry may very well find himself in the thick of another outlandish situation. Do you believe, your grace, that Sir William would dare to offer Isabella a *carte blanche*?"

"Jason," he said absently, his thoughts elsewhere.

"I think of you as both. When you raise that right eyebrow of yours to quash me, then you're a definite 'your grace.' When you smile at me and there's lust in your eyes, then you're Jason. I like both. Perhaps there's even lust when you raise that right eyebrow as well."

"You've just leveled me. Please stop it. Now, listen. You've done right in telling me. Would Lord Harry be much insulted if I took some direct action at this point? I think Gretna Green a most extreme measure. Surely it isn't necessary. It could severely hurt Isabella's reputation."

"What would you do that I can't do?"

"Don't be stupid, Hetty. First of all, I have no intention of allowing you to race off to Scotland with that ridiculous couple. I told you that Sir William holds me in healthy fear. In no less respect would he hold the earl of March, when and if Julien decided to involve himself in the matter. Will you allow me to see to the affair in my own way, without Lord Harry's colorful interference?"

"I think Lord Harry would much enjoy putting Sir William's nose out of joint. To have to forego such excitement is asking a lot of him, Jason. Perhaps it's simply too much. Perhaps you'd best convince me."

"Hetty," he said, his dark eyes becoming even darker. She liked those dark eyes of his, so deep and menacing. She said aloud, "Gothic, that's what you are, quite gothic. Not that it's bad of course. I shall have to watch you when it comes to our daughters. Oh, all right, I suppose it's only fair that you be given *your* chance. Lord Harry, shall, of course, closely watch your progress and decide in due course whether or not he'll be needed."

"Thank you for your vote of confidence. I shall return later this afternoon. You will have your note from Harry by then?"

"Yes, as I said, he means to try his luck this morning. If Isabella turns him down, I will begin to think she has butterflies in her head, if, that is, Harry doesn't botch it, which is a strong possibility."

"She's lovely, she appears sweet-natured and the two of them should suit just fine. And look at us, just the opposite from those two. Just look at what I'm voluntarily seeking to have for the rest of my blighted days. Well, there is no accounting for taste and I suppose it will always be true." He grinned. "Did I tell you that you're a complete sweetheart? Of course I did. Now, to other matters before I haul you up to your bedchamber and do wonderful things to your body. Lord, now I'm making myself sweat.

Stop looking at me like that, Hetty." He drew a deep breath. "I would see your brother's letter now, if you would fetch it to me."

Hetty nodded and whisked herself out of the drawing room, though in truth she truly liked the sound of unspeakable things he would do to her. She was back in a trice, clutching the folded square of paper tightly in her hand.

"Hmmm," was all that he said after his third reading of Elizabeth's letter to Damien.

"What do you think, Jason?"

He said slowly, "It would seem to me that regardless of Elizabeth's true feelings in the matter, Damien was sufficiently involved with her to make his keeping of her letter understandable. The manner in which she tied my name to her predicament is rather ambiguous, yet, Hetty, I now understand how you drew such a conclusion."

"You're just trying to make me feel better. No, it was inexcusable. I won't ever forgive myself for serving you such a false turn, I'll—"

He dropped the letter onto the side table, rose and was at her side in a moment. He lifted her from the chair and pulled her closely to him. He felt the pounding of her heart against his chest. He felt the softness of her, the warmth, the utter surrender of her, her yielding to him, and he knew deep down that she was the only woman for him, and he was so damned bloody lucky to have found her, or, actually, she had found him, but it didn't matter, they were together now and they would be forever. God, he wanted her.

"I love you," he said against her mouth. "I love you and I'm the luckiest man alive to have Henrietta

Rolland. You did nothing wrong. You acted, Hetty. Most women wouldn't have acted. Most men wouldn't have either. You did what you believed was right, with no thought to your own safety. I love you. Forget the rest of it. Together we'll figure this all out. All right? Do I feel to you like I'm holding you any grudge?"

She looked up at him thoughtfully. "You're hard against me. I know that's because you're a man. It feels very nice, Jason. When can we marry?"

He groaned, there was nothing else for him to do. "Jesus, as soon as I can manage it. But first we must discover the truth of things and you know it."

"Yes, I know. Don't you want to shout at me just a bit more, like you did at Thurston Hall? It would make me feel less low, less like a blind worm."

"Go ahead and feel guilty, if you wish. Doubtless it will make you all that more admiring of me." He kissed her hard and deep, then gently set her back into her chair. "I can't think with you so very close to me. And both of us must think. Now, your other evidence is conversations Pottson related to you, conversations with Damien?"

She was breathing hard. There he was just standing there, looking as if nothing at all had occurred between them and she was having trouble breathing. It was odd and it was exciting. "Yes," she said. "And, of course, the fact that Damien was, at the last moment, ordered to lead that cavalry charge. Pottson said Damien knew it was on purpose, that he knew he was going to his death. He didn't want to, but it was his duty, he accepted it."

Jason shook his head. "I simply can't imagine that Sir William has the kind of connections in the ministry to direct Damien's orders like that."

"Then who, for God's sake, sent Damien out of the country with such speed? Who could have directed his activities with such a close hand? Who could have sent him on all those dangerous missions, then sent him to certain death at Waterloo?"

"That's precisely what I intend to find out, Hetty. Now, sweetheart, I must leave. To erase all doubt in our minds respecting Sir William's involvement with Damien, I shall search out his lordship this afternoon. I wish to converse with him, in private, about his entanglement with Harry's Isabella."

"You swear you'll keep me informed?" she said, rising. "About everything?"

"I swear. No, don't get close to me," he said. "I can't take it. Yes, I'll be back this afternoon and tell you what I've learned."

He said softly, squeezing her fingers, "Believe me, Hetty, I wish to finish this damned business as quickly as possible. Then, we will speak of the future, our future."

"And you'll kiss me as much as I wish?"

"At least. Trust me."

She watched him stride to the door, his legs long and strong and he was so certain of himself and of his abilities and she supposed that she had to be as well. "Jason," she called after him, "do take care, else Lord Harry must needs come rescue you."

He cocked a black brow and was gone.

Chapter Thirty-two

Toward the middle of the afternoon, the Marquess of Oberlon walked into the gaming room at White's. He hoped that Sir William Filey would be here, he usually was. He had scarce time to begin his search when his attention was caught by a loud commotion and the rising of angry voices. Intrigued, he walked unobtrusively toward a far corner of the salon, where a small knot of gentlemen formed a wide circle.

He drew up short at the sound of Sir William Filey's voice. "Go lick your wounds in private, Brandon. If you're not enough of a man to hold the lady's affections, then go back to the infantry where you belong. Country girls, I understand, like young rustics like you trying to raise their skirts. Don't come whining to me about it being all my fault."

Damnation and hellfire, the marquess cursed silently. He could readily have strangled Harry Brandon for interfering in his plans. He moved quickly forward, edging his way through the circle of gentlemen.

Sir Harry Brandon stood facing Sir William, his hands balled into fists and his face red with rage.

"You old lecher," he shouted, "Isabella is not for the likes of you. She's young and innocent. You've pulled the wool over her eyes with your damned flattery. You've bribed that wretched mother of hers, haven't you? I demand satisfaction, do you hear?"

It struck the marquess that Harry was copying Lord Harry's behavior. He wanted to be a hero. He was going to force a duel. He stepped quickly forward and grabbed Sir Harry's arm. Before Sir William could answer Harry's challenge, he said smoothly, "Hold, Harry. Though I would never disagree your reasons, I must confess that my grievance with Sir William predates your own. I'm sorry, old boy, but surely you must yield to my prior claims."

"Prior claims? What the devil, your grace?"

Sir William sneered, no other way to put it, but the marquess saw from the corner of his eye that he had backed away a step.

"Yes, Harry, prior claims. As a gentleman, I of course can't disclose to you just what is involved. Further, I believe your argument with Sir William is a trifle premature. Allow me, I beg, to hold a brief discussion with Sir William. It is my belief that he will wish wholeheartedly to offer you an apology for his actions in this affair."

"Apology," Sir William shouted, his face red with rage. "If this young puppy can't keep the silly wench in line—"

"Do shut up, Filey," the marquess said quietly. "Well, Harry, will you give way to my request?"

Sir Harry stood uncertainly, wondering what the devil he should do. Isabella's cold refusal of his proposal had left him in such a fury that he wanted nothing more than to blow Sir William's brains out. That he had not followed Lord Harry's advice and had, indeed, bawled Isabella out for her common slut's behavior, had made him all the angrier. She'd just stood there, staring at him, her only words being, 'I'm not a slut and well you know it. Get out, Sir Harry. I never want to see you again.' And that had been that. Well, he would show her that he was more the man than was Sir William. He would make her regret her words.

"Harry?"

Sir Harry pulled himself away from his thoughts to meet the marquess's eyes. "Very well," he said finally, "but he will be mine when your grace is done with him."

"You shall have him or an apology, Harry. Does that suit you?"

"Yes." Sir Harry bowed curtly to the marquess and strode away, leaving a group of very interested gentlemen in his wake. The marquess gazed about him, his brows raised. "If you would now excuse us, Sir William and I have a small problem to solve." He smiled sweetly at Sir William and said gently, "Come, Filey."

Sir William deplored this sudden turn of events, yet realized that if he were to refuse the marquess, he would be the butt of humiliating jokes for a very long time. He nodded coldly and followed the marquess from the room.

"I believe we can be assured of privacy here," the marquess said, drawing to a halt in a darkened corner of the vast reading room.

"You've no quarrel with me. I can't help it if Brandon forces a fight."

The marquess said, "My quarrel with you is of long standing, Filey."

"I had nothing to do with Elizabeth and you can't prove otherwise, damn you."

"No, as you say, I can't prove otherwise. Yet when I see you playing the same game once again, I cannot help but grow perturbed. With Elizabeth though, you enjoyed much more sport. After all, both I and Damien Rolland were involved. And that, Filey, has led me to wonder exactly how you managed to have Rolland removed from England with such exquisite timing."

"Rolland? Your grace pulls the girth in the wrong direction. How could I have known what Rolland was about?"

"You must admit it was a curious coincidence. Elizabeth veered away from both of us, toward Damien. Then suddenly he is gone and the field is once again yours."

"And yours as well, your grace."

"Yes, but you see I had nothing to do with Damien's leaving England. Whereas you, Filey, are really quite a bastard and would stop at nothing to gain what you wanted. Now I ask you again, what do you know of Damien Rolland?"

Sir William was uncertain. He would have liked very much to tell the marquess to go to the devil, but he knew that such a gesture would very probably cost him his life. He tried for an indifferent shrug. "Maybe Rolland realized that Elizabeth would make a very poor wife for an aspiring politician. Damn, I tell you, I know nothing about it. It's the truth. I wondered when Damien left England, but I had nothing to do with it."

He saw that the marquess was staring at him, an arrested expression in his eyes. Filey couldn't figure out for the life of him just why the marquess should be so interested in Damien Rolland. Ancient history, he was, and Rolland, by all accounts, was killed last June at Waterloo. Who cared?

"Did you say Damien was an aspiring politician?"

Sir William was held a moment by surprise, before he said impatiently, "Something like that. Mentioned it when he was deep in his cups one evening. I gathered he didn't want it bruited about. Yes, he was going to be a politician. I remember I laughed."

The marquess looked decidedly thoughtful for several moments. "Very well, Filey, I will believe you—but only in that matter. Now you will listen to me carefully. As I said, I grow perturbed that you play a new game with Isabella Bentworth and Harry Brandon."

"It's not a game, damn you. I intend to marry the chit. She pleases me. Yes, I'm going to marry her."

"So she carries a more appetizing dowry than did poor Elizabeth, does she? Her innocence draws you more than Elizabeth's? No, don't bother to deny it, Filey. I grow quite bored with you. I will tell you this only once. You will never again speak to Isabella and you will apologize to Harry Brandon before the day is over. If you fail to comply with either of my requests, I'll make you this promise: your dissolute son, whom I understand is following quite closely in your footsteps, will find himself the head of the family before the end of the week. Do I make myself clear?"

Hatred and fear blended into an indistinct blur in Sir William's mind. He seemed suddenly not to have enough breath to fill his throat. There was a curious knot forming in the pit of his stomach.

"Do I make myself clear, Filey?"

He raised his eyes. His long-nurtured sense of

self-preservation rose to the fore. He nodded slowly, hating himself for nodding, hating the marquess for making him feel such bone-deep fear.

"Excellent. I fancied that we could arrive at an amicable solution." The marquess turned, then said over his shoulder, "Incidentally, I'm quite certain the earl of March will be at White's this evening. He will, of course, be very interested in your behavior." Without waiting for Sir William to reply, he strode away, leaving his defeated adversary to roundly curse a hapless footman.

The marquess arrived at Sir Archibald's town house within the hour, his mind greatly relieved on one score and utterly scrambled on the other. He didn't disbelieve Sir William in his recounting of Damien's political ambitions. Sir William had, he was certain, thought it most unimportant, and thus blurted it out without a moment's hesitation. Indeed, the marquess wondered, as he pounded the knocker, *was* it important? Surely Sir Archibald must have known if Damien had wished to follow in his footsteps. He had to have known. God, Sir Archibald breathed politics. It was his bread and his wine. It was everything to him. As painful as the subject must be to Sir Archibald, he had to ask.

"Your grace."

"Good afternoon, Grimpston. I trust our Miss Henrietta is home?"

"I shall ascertain, your grace," Grimpston said, giving him a fat smile.

"Oh my God, Jason, thank goodness you're here."

The marquess looked up to see a distraught Hetty speeding down the staircase toward him. "Quickly, oh my goodness, we must do something now. I've just gotten a message from Harry. The silly nodcock, he means to take matters into his own hands. The bloody fool, he promised he'd let me see to things. Oh, I'll kill him for this."

The marquess clasped her hands. "Why don't we discuss this in the drawing room, Hetty? Grimpston, some brandy, if you please. Your mistress's nerves seem to be teetering on the edge. The first time I've seen her in such a state. It's disconcerting. It's very female. I will tolerate it, but I don't like it."

"Yes, your grace. Certainly, your grace."

She managed to get ahold on herself. "I'm sorry for sounding like a ninny. I'll thank you not to mock me. This is important. Please come to the drawing room and I'll tell you everything."

No sooner had Hetty snapped the drawing-room door closed, than she whirled about. "Jason, you'll not believe this but the most terrible thing has happened. Harry wrote me—that is, he wrote Lord Harry—a letter. Yes, a letter. I didn't even know that Harry could pen more than one sentence without dire concentration. But a whole letter. He wrote that he intended to resolve the matter just as Lord Harry had done. Jason, I know what he intends. It's a duel, of course. My God, Filey might kill him. We must do something."

"I have."

"Oh my God, it's all my fault. If I—that is, if Lord Harry hadn't insisted upon such bravado, such arrogant behavior, I'm persuaded that such a thing would never have occurred to Harry. That is, it might have occurred to him, but he would have sought counsel from the earl of March. Only Lord

Harry can talk him out of this. I must go, don't you see, I must."

"No, you must not."

"It's easy for you to be so bloody calm, for Harry isn't a special friend. Don't you understand, Jason, only Lord Harry can put a stop to this?"

"I suspect that there are others just as persuasive as Lord Harry."

She stamped her foot and heard the rip of muslin. "Damnation, just look at what you've made me do. I have only three gowns and now I've ruined another one. No, that's idiotic. Who cares? I have no more time to indulge in useless arguments with you. I don't care what you may think of me, but Lord Harry must come out again. I'm sorry, Jason, but it is something I can't ignore. It's my duty and Harry is my friend."

"But I'm not arguing with you, Hetty. Now will you be seated and calm yourself?"

"I'm quite calm, I will have you know. You will not be condescending or treat me like a half-wit. Now, your grace, if you will excuse me."

"I won't excuse you. Now sit."

"Ha! Go to the devil."

The marquess sighed. "You've already consigned me to that rather warm clime, and, despite your repetition, I have no intention of complying. Now, before I have to tie you down, come here and listen to me."

"Oh very well, but only for five minutes. Surely five minutes is more than enough time for whatever you have to say, which can't be all that much of interest. Very well, talk." She sat down on the very edge of her chair, her toe tapping, her fingers tented together.

"Didn't you promise to give me a chance in this affair?"

"Yes, but—"

"You doubt my abilities so much, Hetty?"

"No, it isn't that. It's that everything has changed, gone awry. Now it's not a question of fleeing to Gretna Green, it's a question of saving Harry's damned life."

"No, it's not a question of Gretna Green. Indeed, it is no longer a question of anything, even Harry's damned life."

"No longer—what the devil do you mean?"

The marquess grinned down at her. "My dear, if you would but adopt the habit of listening to me, you would save yourself a lot of wasted energy. As it happens, I was present at White's when Harry was in the midst of flinging his gauntlet in Filey's face, so to speak. I, of course, put a stop to it. As a matter of fact, Filey will be apologizing to Harry this evening at White's. Further, he will never again speak to Isabella, so you can put your mind to rest. And Lord Harry Monteith. The good Lord grant him peace forever, in the North somewhere."

"You put a stop to it? Truly?"

"Wouldn't you have expected me to?"

"Yes, of a certainty, but—"

"It's not kind of you to doubt my word, Henrietta. Now, please sit back, I don't want you to fall off your chair."

"You mean it's all settled?"

"Please don't sound so disappointed, sweetheart. Lord Harry can't be expected to right every wrong. We other poor mortals do occasionally succeed, you know."

"Of course I'm not disappointed. Well, not precisely. You did all that? Filey will apologize to Harry? Goodness, that's very impressive." She bounded out of her chair, ignoring the slight pulling in her side, clasped her arms around his back and stood on her tiptoes, her lips pursed.

"Open your mouth, love," he said, his breath warm on her lips. Even as she parted her lips, she felt the warmth of his breath inside her mouth, the touch of his tongue. "Oh," she said, and just stood there, holding him tightly to her, feeling all of him, letting him kiss her and kiss her yet again until her eyes were closed, her mouth soft and wet from him, and he was hard against her belly.

"Hetty, I must stop," he said, and his voice sounded wonderfully tormented. He didn't want to stop, she realized, and she didn't want him to. It was new, all these feelings that were raging through her, making her urgent and warm and wanting to grin like a fool, making her want to moan with the pleasure of his mouth, the pleasure of him holding her, the pleasure of having him just be him.

"Please, don't," she said. "This is so very nice, Jason. Can't we have a bit more?"

He wanted to curse. She didn't realize, she had no idea what she was asking of him, but he—"All right," he said, and his hands were all over her, caressing her breasts through the muslin of her bodice, wild on her bottom, pushing her hard against him, pressing her, feeling her and knowing she was enjoying all of it and wanting more. He looked at the sofa. He looked at the Aubusson carpet in front of the fireplace. Even the winged chair was good sized. Oh hell, she was a virgin. He had no intention

of teaching her about lovemaking on a damned carpet. Then he smiled. Why not? Very gently, he eased
her onto his lap and sat in the winged chair that
faced the fireplace. He kissed her, never stopping,
and his hand eased up beneath her gown. He felt
her stockings, felt the garters at midthigh. He felt
her breath hitch when his hand touched her bare
thigh. "Ah, Hetty, you're so warm. Do you want me
to stop, sweetheart?"

She looked up at him. "What are you going to do?"

He eased his fingers higher, so close, so very close
to her warm female flesh. He paused. "I want to
make love to you but you're a virgin. When we make
love it will be on our wedding night and in a very
large soft bed. But for now, I just want to give you
pleasure. Will you let me? Will you trust me?"

"What are you going to do?"

His fingers lifted then came down gently over her.
He cupped her, his fingers dipping inward.

"Oh," she said, staring up at him. "No one has ever
touched me there before. Are you certain it's done?"

"All the time," he said as he leaned down and
kissed the tip of her nose. "You'll like it very much.
Will you trust me to give you pleasure, to let you
know that I want you very much and that what you
feel is important to me?"

She felt those fingers of his, one of them easing
slowly inside her and she couldn't believe it, yet, as
Lord Harry she did know just about everything, but
still, she didn't know about this. Then another finger was touching her, lightly stroking, lightly, then
more forcefully and she blinked even as she moaned
deep in her throat and her hips pressed up against
those fingers of his.

"Jason, I don't know about this. I don't really feel all that normal."

"Hush," he said and leaned down to kiss her. His tongue touched hers even as his finger was moving more deeply inside of her. His thumb was now caressing her and she couldn't believe what it made her feel, what it made her want to do, and that was to cry out and move and jerk about and go into an absolute frenzy.

She did several minutes later. She cried out into his mouth even as the incredible climax sent her spinning into an oblivion that held him and her together and it was something she couldn't have imagined. It was something she wanted forever.

"I love you," he said into her mouth as the rhythm of his fingers gently slowed, as he stroked to calm her rather than excite her. "Yes, that's it. I'll make you feel those wonderful things every day of your life. All right?"

"Yes," she said, feeling vague and a bit dizzy and perfectly wonderful. "But I know that your sex must come inside me for you to have pleasure. Do you like that as much as I just did?"

He grinned down at her. "You can't begin to realize what it will be like between us. Not just me being inside you, but there's so much more. We will marry in two weeks. No, in a week, all right? I can't wait longer, Hetty. Actually I don't think you can either. If I'm to protect my reputation, no more than a week. All right?"

"Oh yes," she said and sighed. "I thought that the entire sex business was really rather foolish. Men drooling over females and females just letting them do it since they were paid to let them. But that was wonderful. Why would you want to pay me? I'll pay you."

"Ah, your unusual education rears its head again. We're special, Hetty. Very special. Will you trust me on that?"

"I suppose I must since you saved Sir Harry and rubbed Filey's nose in it."

He smoothed down her skirts. "How do you feel?"

"I feel full of energy," she said, sitting up on his lap. "My side doesn't even hurt now. Is that odd? I want to dance. I even want to tease you about something. I want to laugh and kiss your ear. This is all very new to me, Jason."

"To me as well, Henrietta. Now, sweetheart, we must get back to business. It kills me, but we must. No, don't touch me. Oh damn." He picked her up and set her on her feet. Then he led her to a chair, sat her down, and took three steps away from her. Still he could feel her soft flesh on his fingers, breathe in the sweet scent of her. Oh God, he couldn't wait any longer than a week. He drew a deep breath. He had to gain control of himself.

He said finally, "I have something of a more serious nature to tell you. While I was chatting with Filey, I accused him of knowing what happened to Damien. He swore that he knew nothing, indeed, he was quite bewildered, and I believe him. But there was something he said, Hetty, something that meant nothing to him, so he blurted it out in an attempt to appease me. He said that Damien had talked about 'political ambitions' one evening when he was foxed. Filey evidently taunted him about Elizabeth making a very poor wife for a politician."

Hetty frowned, then shook her head. "Jack said

something about Damien's feelings on the growing poverty in the industrial cities. He said Damien likened the people's lives to bondage and slavery, and that it could but grow worse. But Jack said nothing about Damien wishing to take an active role in political life. I'm afraid that I really don't see the importance of Filey's statement, Jason."

"Hetty, don't you see? Only someone highly connected in the ministry could have had Damien sent so quickly and permanently from England. Only someone very powerful in the government could have put him at the lead of that cavalry charge."

Hetty nodded slowly, her mind working furiously. "Yes, perhaps someone who didn't agree with his politics. Perhaps even a group of men who feared he might succeed and displace them."

She pulled up short, rubbing her palm against her forehead. "Ah, that's ridiculous. I just pulled that out of a hat, like a rabbit. It's all speculation. I can't credit such a motive."

"There are some men, powerful men, whose very lives are consumed by their political beliefs. Don't forget our English history, Hetty, it's filled with powerful men struggling to govern the country as they wished. It's a bloody history."

Hetty rose, her hands pressed against her temples. "Even so, Jason, it is 1816, and the vicious struggles for power are over. There's no more Cromwell, no more bonnie Prince Charles. And even if it could be true today, who could have done such a thing? Who could have even known what Damien believed and feared him for it?"

"I did."

Chapter Thirty-three

Both Hetty and the marquess whirled about, open-mouthed, to see Sir Archibald standing quietly in the doorway. Jason's first thought was that he'd been a fool not to have checked that the door was locked before he'd loved Hetty. Well, that wasn't important now. Sir Archibald said again, "I did." He smiled at both of them impartially.

"Father," Hetty said, running to his side. "What are you talking about? No, you didn't hear what Jason said. We were speaking of Damien and who would have had the power, the motive, to have him removed from England. Certainly not you. Damien was your son."

Sir Archibald gazed fondly down at his daughter and fought down the stab of pain he felt whenever he thought of his second son. "You must forgive me," he said, his eyes searching out the marquess, "for overhearing your discussion, but I was coming to greet you, my boy. I understand you were at Thurston Hall with my darling Hetty here. Did you much enjoy yourselves?"

"Yes, sir, we did. But what do you mean that you did it?"

Sir Archibald sighed deeply and laid his hand upon Hetty's shoulder. "I didn't realize, my child, that you had even discovered that there was more to Damien's leaving England than a simple reassignment. I had hoped to spare you further pain. Now I see that you and the marquess have become embroiled in the affair. You must understand, my child, there was no other choice. You see, Damien had become a traitor to his country."

Hetty stared in shocked silence at her father.

The marquess said, "Surely, sir, that can't be so. What do you mean, Damien a traitor? That makes no sense, he died for England at Waterloo."

Sir Archibald sighed again and shook his silver head. "Alas, it's all too true. I never told either you, Hetty, or Jack, for I didn't want you to think less of your brother. I didn't want you to hate him. I wanted to protect both you and Jack from what he'd done. But now that you and Jason here seem to understand more than I'd ever believed possible, then I must tell you the truth. I'm sorry for the pain it will cause you, Henrietta, for the hatred you will doubtless feel for your brother."

Hetty gazed at her father, a gentle man, yet a man impassioned by political fervor, a man whose life was dedicated to directing English affairs as he envisioned them.

She placed her hand on his sleeve. "Please, Father, you say that Damien was a traitor. I must know what you mean by that. I can't believe it."

Sir Archibald looked at Lord Oberlon. "I must tell Henrietta the ugly truth. And since she has obviously confided in you, my boy, then you will hear it, too. I beg both of you to leave Damien's shame in this room, to allow it to go no further. I have intended you all along as the husband for Henrietta, and since soon you will be one of the family, it is your right to hear of our disgrace. If you wish to cry off, then surely even Henrietta will understand. It's a sad tale, Damien's story is, but I fancy that he gained redemption at the end, as I meant him to."

"I don't understand this," Hetty said flatly. "Stop speaking in circles, Father. What do you mean that Damien was a traitor? A traitor to whom? Father, please, you must tell me if you had anything to do with Damien's death. How could you ever believe Damien a traitor?"

"Very well, my child," Sir Archibald said finally. "You must be brave, for you will be as shocked as I was when you learn of your brother's actions. I trust when I'm done, you will understand why I had to take such drastic steps. It was for the honor of our family. For the honor of England."

The marquess moved next to Hetty and took her hand in his. He squeezed it. Neither of them said a word. Sir Archibald moved wearily to the large winged chair near to the fireplace, one so shortly before that had given rise to Hetty's first sexual pleasure, and sat himself down. He stared a moment into the glowing flames before continuing in a surprisingly strong and forceful voice. "You hadn't yet come to London, Henrietta. For some reason that I did not at first comprehend, Damien asked for and received an extended leave from his military duties. I believed at first that he had finally decided to find himself a wife and settle down. I was disabused of that notion when your brother informed me that he intended to run as the Whig candidate from a borough in Somerset, under the patronage of that infamous, thieving Lord Grayson. I was, of course, appalled that my own son would desire to join in the political fray against me, and I reprimanded him sharply. He told me that Tories—Whigs—they were all one and the same to him, and that he sought only justice for Englishmen. His notion of securing justice, Henrietta, was to join forces with the baser element of the Whig contingent to incite the rabble in Manchester and Leeds to riot. You won't wish to credit this, my child, but he then called me a mindless old fool. Accused me, he did, of trying to hold England back from her rightful destiny—and that was the destruction of the aristocracy. Only their destruction would elevate the common man to political equality with his betters. His subsequent words were even more fanatical and traitorous, and I refuse to sully your ears with his raving insults, his vile accusations. He accused me of fanaticism. Me! I couldn't believe that I'd spawned such a vile creature. I finally became convinced that my blood—my son—was one of that lot bent upon destroying the very fabric of England. I couldn't allow it.

"So you see, my child, I had no honorable choice left to me but to use my influence with Lord Melberry in the ministry to have your brother removed immediately from England. I wanted only distance between him and that damnable fool Lord Grayson."

Hetty said in a peculiarly quiet voice, "You're telling me, Father, that because Damien held radical political views, you had him ordered from England? You arranged that he be engaged in dangerous missions in Spain and Portugal? You arranged that his orders be changed so at the last moment he led a suicidal cavalry charge at Waterloo?"

"Yes, but not Waterloo until I learned that Lord Grayson was in contact with your brother even then.

They were planning together what they would accomplish when your brother returned to England. They were going to join the Luddites, Henrietta. The Luddites! They planned to have men infiltrate the factories and destroy them from within. They would have men march on the House of Lords itself and demand reform. It was then that we all knew we had to act, to remove the stain on my family, to remove the stain on all of England."

"You killed your son because he didn't want to be what you were? You killed him because he disagreed with you politically?"

Sir Archibald gazed at his daughter with some surprise. "You make it sound as if I dismissed your brother out of some fanciful whimsy. You question my actions in this affair?"

The marquess said quietly, "What then was your role, sir, in Damien's activities?"

Sir Archibald's voice suddenly became stern, a strange glint of inflexibility in his blue eyes. "As I've told you, Damien was a traitor to every honorable belief that I had instilled in him from his youth. He had shown himself a radical bent upon the destruction of all that any decent Englishman holds dear. You can quite imagine that Lord Melberry and indeed many of the gentlemen in the ministry were appalled when I told them of my own son's subversive activities. It was my request that Damien be forced to serve his country, to shed his blood, if need be, so that he would in some measure lift the dishonor from our house. I gave no direct order for him to lead that cavalry charge. I later learned that an overzealous general under whose command Damien had been placed dispatched him to the battleground. You must know that I grieved at your brother's death. But he died as a hero of his country. The world will never know that without my actions, your brother would have heaped shame and dishonor upon all those who cared for him, upon all those who loved him, who trusted him."

By God, the marquess thought, gazing at Sir Archibald, he is quite mad in his saneness. He suspected that his uncle, Lord Melberry, was as deeply involved in arranging Damien's missions as was Sir Archibald. He gazed past Sir Archibald to Hetty. Her face was pale and drawn with shock, her eyes unseeing. He shook himself into action.

"Sir," he said to his future father-in-law, "you will understand, of course, that your words have caused Henrietta great surprise and distress. Needless to say, that since I am to become her husband, you can rely implicitly upon my discretion in this matter. If you wouldn't mind, I think it best that you leave her with me alone for a time, so that she may recover from her shock."

"I suppose since I chose you for her that it wouldn't be improper. See to her, my boy, don't let her despise her poor brother. Don't let her hold his memory in abhorrence." Satisfied, Sir Archibald rose with surprising grace for a man of his years, smiled down at his daughter in his gentle way, then turned and stretched out his hand to the marquess. "I accept you into my family, my boy. I told Henrietta all along that you would make her the perfect husband. Such a dear child she is—always obeys her father's wishes, always wants to please her family." He patted Hetty's stiff shoulder and let himself out of the drawing room.

The marquess gazed at Hetty, wondering just

what the devil he could say to her. He strode over to her and sat down beside her, clasping her limp hands in his. "Hetty, my love, I wish to be here for you forever. And I will be. We will talk about this. It's incredible. I suspect that my uncle Melberry is in just as deep as is your father. That he believes he saved your family from dishonor leaves my brain waving in the wind, but, Hetty, he believes himself to have behaved appropriately, to have behaved in the only way open to him."

She looked at him, straight in the face. "I would rather you leave, Jason. This is a home of tragedy, of murder, and it's the murder of a son by his father. It's not a nice family, Jason. No, I want you to leave. I can't marry you. I carry my father's blood. Jesus, there's nothing I can salvage from this. My father's blind honor, it doesn't surprise me all that much, but to kill his own son. His own son! You don't want a wife who's so tainted."

His black brows met over his eyes and his hands tightened over her fingers.

"Poor Jason," she said in a soft, singsong voice. "I've done naught but unearth old wounds and create new ones for you. How strange it is that you, whom I believed to be a vicious, cruel devil, are the innocent one. You who are the kind one, the man who wants to see justice done. But that's not possible. Damien is long dead, rotted on that damnable battlefield, and my father killed him, no matter how you slice the bread, that's what happened. You want to leave, Jason. You can't want me for your wife now."

She felt strong arms enclose her, and for an instant held herself stiff and unyielding. The tears that were not far from the surface welled up and she collapsed against him. He held her until the hoarse sobs became rasping hiccups.

He pulled a handkerchief from his waistcoat pocket and pressed it into her hand. She clutched at him, burrowing against his shoulder. Finally she raised a tear-streaked face, her voice forlorn between the hiccups. "Whatever shall I do? I can't remain in the same house with my father. Of a certainty, Lord Harry cannot challenge Sir Archibald to a duel."

The marquess took the handkerchief from her unresisting fingers and efficiently wiped her face. "Of course, my love, I realize that you can't wish to remain in this house. I want you to come with me, Hetty, for we can be wed as soon as I can procure a special license. It will take me just a day."

To his utter bewilderment, she pulled away from him. "Listen to me, damn you. I told you that you won't be held to your offer of marriage. I will have none of your pity, do you hear? I would now, your grace, that you leave and contrive to forget all that has passed here today. God knows I can't do anything about it. God, how I wish it had been Filey."

The marquess rose and clasped her arms, forcing her to face him. "That's really quite enough, Hetty. You must have lost what few wits remain to you if you ever think I would take a wife out of pity. Hetty, can you not understand that I care very much for you? That I love you? That I held you on my lap and stroked you with my fingers until you gained your pleasure and cried out in my mouth?"

"No, don't talk like that. How many women have you held like that, caressed like that? It can't mean all that much to you. You have told me yourself that you felt no love for Elizabeth, yet, you offered *her* marriage. Wasn't that from pity? From some sort of misplaced gentleman's honor?"

"Damn you, it's not the same thing and you know it." He wanted to shake her. "Hetty," he said, gentling his voice, "you must know how I feel about you. Stop being at cross-purposes with me, it serves no cause. We are what we are and Sir Archibald won't change, ever. We must accept him. We must accept the situation. We will mourn Damien, the damnable waste of it, the tragedy of it, but we will do it together."

She regarded him coldly, in dead silence.

He continued softly, "You can't make me believe you don't care for me, Hetty. I have gotten to know you quite well, you know. You cried out in my mouth. I gave you pleasure you've never had before, I've made you feel things you want forever. Admit it."

He would have preferred to haul her over his shoulder and get her away from this house, from her father, this very moment. But he knew Hetty. She would very likely tell him to go to the devil if he became the least bit autocratic, even if it was for her own good. Yet he hated to leave her to deal alone with her grief and sense of betrayal. She had turned away from him, presenting a board-stiff back. He had no idea what she was thinking. It scared the hell out of him.

"Hetty," he said. She didn't turn, so he continued addressing her back. "I don't want you to believe that I shall continue pressing you. I've told you how I feel, and I would that you think about my words. I also know that you love me, that you love me deeply. However, I know that you're not thinking clearly right now. Neither am I. We both need some time, you especially. I will leave you now and if you wouldn't mind, I would like to come for dinner this evening. Perhaps then we can more rationally discuss what we are to do."

"Very well," she said, and he had the impression that she wasn't actually agreeing with him, merely acquiescing at the moment so that she could be alone.

Rabbell entered the library, his face set in deep worry lines. "Your grace."

The marquess pulled his attention from a sheaf of papers that, in all truth, he'd been reading and rereading and he still had no idea what the content was. "Yes, Rabbell?"

"It seems, your grace, that an odd person has arrived—knocked at the front door, he did— urgently demanding to see your grace. He informed me, your grace, that it was a matter of the gravest importance, concerning a Miss Rolland."

"What?" The marquess bounded to his feet. "Don't just stand there, show the damned fellow in."

But a moment later, the marquess was facing a pale, out-of-breath Pottson.

"Oh my gawd, she up and skuttled the pike, your grace."

"She's what?"

"Loped off, gone without a word, your grace, fleeced the rod. Millie's fit to be green with worry, begged me she did, to come to you, seeing as how you'd know what to do."

The marquess felt suddenly quite cold. Damn, but he was a fool for ever leaving her alone. "Why does Millie believe that Miss Rolland has run away, Pottson? It has been but three hours since I left her." Even as he spoke, the marquess found himself gazing toward the windows. It was already dusk. Night was soon coming.

"She told me, your grace, that Miss Hetty was acting oddlike, not saying a word, merely staring off when there was nothing to look at. Millie leaves her for only five minutes and when she comes back, Miss Hetty's gone. Nobody even saw her leave, your grace, even the scullery maid, Agnes, who knows everything everyone does."

"I see," the marquess said. "Even Agnes didn't see her. You've done right to come to me, Pottson." As concisely and quickly as possible, the marquess told Pottson what had happened during the afternoon.

"Gawd," Pottson said, then whistled softly. "Master Damien's own father. Jesus, it's well nigh unbelievable. It makes a man glad he didn't even know which man were his father when something like this happens."

"I know I can rely on your discretion in this matter. Even her brother, Sir John, will never know what happened. Now, we must try to determine where she would have gone."

"Miss Hetty adored her brother, worshipped since she was a child, if your grace knows what I mean," Pottson said after but an instant, his words making perfect sense to him. The marquess, however, didn't understand.

"Sussex, your grace. It's Sir Archibald's country home, Belshire Manor, I believe is the name, near to Atelsfield. It's where Master Damien is buried."

"Thank you, Pottson. We needn't worry about Sir Archibald, I don't think. If he misses her at all, he will merely believe that she accompanied me to Thurston Hall. Yes, I'll pen him a note from my sister. It will serve."

He clasped Pottson's hand and shook it. "Don't worry. I'm leaving now. I'll fetch her home."

Chapter Thirty-four

The marquess sat on the edge of a ditch and raised his voice to the heavens, his curses fluent and loud, despite the fact that he was quite alone. A curricle wheel was still spinning just beside his elbow, and his horses were stamping and whinnying. He pulled himself to his feet and soothed his horses as best he could, all the while searching out the scurrilous, half-hidden rock that had so arranged itself just beyond the turnpike entrance past Hatfield that it had ripped a curricle wheel cleanly from its axle and sent both the curricle and the marquess off into the ditch. He wondered without humor if the elements were conspiring to script a farcical play with him as the bumbling, ill-fated hero.

It didn't help matters when the bay hack he was forced to hire in Hatfield proceeded to throw a shoe not many miles beyond where his broken curricle still lay at odd angles in the ditch. Leading his horse some five miles to the village of Davondale did nothing to improve his temper, and it was only after three mugs of strong local ale that he was finally able to review the day's events with a modicum of good humor. The marquess was slightly foxed when he finally made his way up the old winding staircase of the Gray Goose Inn to fall in between the none-too-clean sheets of a rather rickety, too-short bed. He found that he could not long nurture his sense of ill-use, for images of Hetty, perhaps courting the same types of minor disasters that had befallen him, made his stomach knot with cramps. The shrill, off-key cuckoo chirped one o'clock in the morning before he was finally able to squelch his more dire imaginings and make peace with the lumpy bed.

The following morning, after an indigestible breakfast of watery porridge and rock-hard toast, he strode out of the inn and gazed grimly at both the slope-shouldered mare and the gray sky. He had no doubt that before the day was out, he would be drenched to the skin. Damn, he thought, if he caught a chill from this escapade, he would force Henrietta to wait upon him hand and foot for at least five years. He smiled at the thought of what he would have her do. He smiled more widely at the thought of what he was going to do with her. When he caught up with her. When he made her come to peace with herself and with him.

It wasn't until midafternoon of the following day that the marquess drew up his sweating horse in front of a set of rusty iron gates just off the main road from Briardon and read the deeply etched sign, BELSHIRE MANOR. He was so certain that Hetty had reached her birthplace before him, for whatever else she was, she was endowed with an overabundance of ingenuity, that he began to picture their meeting. He couldn't believe that she would really be surprised to see him. What would she say? He couldn't wait to see. However, he knew that deep down there was such pain in her that he wouldn't be able to trim her sails for leaving him. Ah, her pain. He didn't know how he would deal with it, but he knew that he would have to. He still couldn't believe that a father had sought his own son's death. All because of politics, all because Sir Archibald had convinced himself that Damien was a traitor not only to the family but to England. It boggled the mind. He couldn't begin to imagine how Hetty was dealing with it.

He led his horse through the creaking iron gates and found himself facing a three-story pink brick house, dating, from the looks of it, from the Stuarts. It was set amid a small park. The grounds showed only superficial signs of care. There was a general air of a long absentee master about the manor, and, he thought, of a less than sterling staff in attendance. He drew up his horse in front of deep-set flagstone steps and looked about for a stable boy. No such luxury, he thought, and tethered the mare to a bedraggled yew bush.

It was some minutes before his loud knock was answered by a gaunt-featured, bent old man wearing a shiny black suit with oddly pinned-down lapels that reminded him forcibly of the garb his agent, Spiverson, habitually wore. Prim lips were drawn tightly into a line of suspicion as the old man looked him up and down. As if I were some sort of peddler, the marquess thought, not realizing that in his dusty, travel-stained clothes, he could hardly fit anyone's idea of a peer of the realm.

"I've come to see your mistress," he said without preamble. "Tell Miss Henrietta that the Marquess of Oberlon requests her presence immediately."

Even though Dawley had rusticated for over twenty years, he still knew well the voice of Quality, and the line of suspicion became one of perturbation. Miss Henrietta? He didn't believe that he could have overlooked her presence in the manor. But he doubted an instant, for his grace sounded so very positive.

He cleared his throat. "Forgive me, your grace, but Miss Hetty hasn't been in residence for close to seven months now. I believe she's in London, your grace, with Sir Archibald."

The marquess frowned. The butler was telling the truth, he didn't doubt that, but it simply didn't seem possible that he could have arrived here before Hetty. He grew suddenly cold. He, himself, had suffered several mishaps. "It's likely she will arrive shortly from London. I trust it will not disaccommodate you if I remain for the night, for it's urgent that I see her."

Dawley thought that the marquess's presence would very much set Mrs. Dawley on her ear, but of course he didn't offer this observation to his grace. He bowed low, silently praying that Mrs. Dawley had something beside the pig's cheek to serve the marquess for dinner.

The pig's cheek didn't end up on the marquess's table, but rather several slices of overly salted ham, unearthed from the larder by a frantic Mrs. Dawley. At least the port was passable, he thought idly, as he stretched his feet toward the warm fire set in the parlor. He drummed his fingers together with rhythmic precision, trying to trace what would logically have been Hetty's movements from the moment she fled from London, but found himself almost immediately stymied, for he couldn't really be certain if she'd traveled by horse, on a coach, as a female or as Lord Harry. He felt extraordinarily helpless, a circumstance he truly detested. His life had been too much out of control of late.

He rose and absently kicked a crackling log with the toe of one dusty, mud-caked boot. Where the hell was she anyway? He had even delayed his journey until the morning, thus giving her many hours to reach her destination before him. At the moment, he seemed to have very little choice but to remain at Belshire Manor until noon on the morrow. If Hetty hadn't arrived by then, well, either she had been delayed, or had never intended to come here in the first place. He thought of Jack and Louisa and their home in Herefordshire. Perhaps the very fact that they were in Paris would induce Hetty there, for she could be alone.

He didn't find Hetty at Sir John's home in Herefordshire, and it was an extraordinarily weary and worried man who reined in yet another hired hack at the front steps of Thurston Hall, six days after his frenetic and fruitless search had begun. There had been no main road or village that he had passed without inquiry, and, now, he admitted, he simply had no more ideas. He hadn't the energy to continue back to his town house in London. Deep within him, he knew in any case that there would be no news of Hetty awaiting him were he to return.

He mounted the steps, and without bothering to sound the knocker, pushed open the great front doors. As the afternoon was gray and overcast, the entrance hall seemed chill and dim, both the weather and his home reflecting, he thought, his own depression.

It was with sudden tight-lipped anger that he greeted the obviously tipsy Croft, who was weaving his way toward him, consternation paling his flushed face at the unexpected sight of his master.

"Oh dear. Oh my goodness. Oh Lordie, it is your grace, is it not?"

"You miserable sot! Damn you, Croft, get belowstairs immediately. I don't want to see that bulbous nose of yours again until you've sobered up from drinking my port."

"Er, it was the sherry, your grace. We're low on the port. Your late father was never very fond of port."

"Damn you, I should sack you right now, it's no more than you deserve."

"But your grace—" Croft tried to lower his voice to a more dignified pitch, but the marquess interrupted him brusquely.

"Out of my bloody sight, Croft. I've no patience left for you. God, you reek." He turned on his heel and headed for the quiet of the library. "Send a footman with brandy and don't you taste it."

He didn't see Croft wave his hand frantically at his back. He flung open the library door, kicked it closed with the heel of his boot and strode directly to the fireplace. It didn't occur to him to wonder why such a brightly blazing fire was burning in the grate, and he splayed his hands toward the warmth.

"It's about time you have returned home, Jason. After five days, I must tell you that the servants had seriously begun to doubt my word. Croft even started tippling again, so that proves that he believed me an imposter."

He spun about so quickly that he had to grab the

edge of the mantelpiece to retain his balance. For a long moment, he stared at Hetty, not one word taking form in his mind.

She stood quietly, her hands resting on the back of a chair. She was dressed in a modish yellow jonquil gown, her blond curls tied with a yellow velvet ribbon. She looked very beautiful and very serious and very pale.

"You, Hetty, you're here? I don't believe this. You've been here at Thurston Hall all this time?"

"Yes," she said, walking slowly toward him. "I've put you to a good deal of trouble. If you wish to yell at me, I will grant you the opportunity without interruption. Do forgive me, Jason, please."

"Yes, I damned well want to yell at you and shake you and kiss you until you're senseless. Bloody hell, I've been frantic with worry. Everything went wrong. I went to Belshire Manor, then on to Jack's house in Herefordshire. I prayed, by God, I've turned into a Methodist this past week."

Then he opened his arms to her. She covered the distance between them on a dead run. He pulled her roughly to his chest, burying his face in her hair. He tightened his hold about her back, as if afraid she'd disappear.

"I'm truly sorry, Jason," she whispered, raising her head from his shoulder to gaze into his dark eyes. "Pottson told me where you'd gone. Lord Harry thought for a while to set out after you, but I decided it ridiculous for both of us to be riding the roads of England. Please forgive me for being so foolish. It's just that I didn't know what to do. There was just too much and I couldn't seem to sort through it all. All I could think about was Thurston Hall and you."

He thought fleetingly to inquire just how the devil she'd spoken to Pottson, but he wanted to kiss her— her mouth, her stubborn jaw, the tip of her nose. He wanted to inhale her scent, to kiss her soft hair, to mold his hands around her breasts. God, if something had happened to her—

"Do you forgive me, Jason?"

She didn't let him answer, but stood on her tiptoes. As his mouth closed over hers, feather light, she felt his hands stroking up and down her back, cupping her to bring her hard against him. She loved the feel of him, the differentness of him. She loved him. It was some moments before he drew back and looked down at her. There was a dark, dreamy quality in her eyes he'd never before seen. Tenderly, he kissed the tip of her nose, her chin, the soft curls at her temples. The weariness and concern that he had worn like a heavy mantle slipped from him, and he gave a shout of pure joy.

She giggled. "Does that mean you forgive me?"

"It means that I'm so grateful I'll be pure of heart for the rest of my years on this earth."

"Will you promise me something, your grace?"

"I shout with joy that you're all right, and you have the gall to call me 'your grace'?"

"It's about marrying me. Promise me that if you have any doubts, if it bothers you what my father did, that you won't go through with it. I don't ever want you to think I trapped you into marriage like Elizabeth."

"Shut up."

He kissed her, this time, his hand stroking from her breasts down to her belly until he was resting his hand against her, feeling the heat of her through her gown. He hoped she felt the heat of his hand.

"If you ever again compare yourself to Elizabeth, I'll thrash you. I mean it, Hetty. You aren't Elizabeth. What your father did, both of us will have to come to understanding about it, and we will. I am sorry for it, for the pain it's giving you. But we shall marry just as soon as I can procure a special license."

"All right," she said, gave him a fat smile, then fell to kissing him again. He was nibbling on her ear when she said, "Oh goodness, you're exhausted, you must be ready to eat a horse and have a hot bath. Shall I ring for Croft?"

"No. The sot is in the cellar drinking my sherry. I should have booted him out years ago, but dammit, he's been here since I was born."

She kissed him again, then said, "When dear Croft wasn't foxed, he treated me in the most suspicious manner. I swear he thinks me one of your mistresses."

"He's in for a surprise, isn't he? Yes, I can't wait to see him sneaking the champagne from our wedding breakfast. Now, before I take myself off for a bath, when did you see Pottson? He came to me, you know, panting that you'd skuttled the pike. He was the one who sent me to Belshire Manor."

"I did pack a portmanteau and buy a stage ticket to Sussex. But early the next morning I realized there was nothing there for me at Belshire Manor. I couldn't bring myself to return to Father's house, so I paid a final visit to Lord Harry's lodgings and sent Pottson with a note to my father explaining that I'd accepted an invitation from Lady Alicia to again visit Thurston Hall. Pottson thought it a rather clever idea, though he felt terribly guilty that he'd sent you to the far reaches of England."

"You have a lot to make up to me for, Hetty."

"That sounds a bit alarming but ever so much fun."

"Ah, yes," he said, as he kissed her again and forced himself away from her.

"Is Lord Harry finally content to return to the wilds that disgorged him?"

He saw the wistfulness in her eyes, heard the reluctance in her voice when she said, "I guess there's no choice. He has to disappear. I'll miss him, Jason. He was so free. He could do anything he wished. He shot at Manton's. He held the faro bank at White's, where he was a member. He drank as much as he wanted. He went to a brothel. Henrietta Rolland could never do any of that."

"Henrietta Cavander."

"Even a female Cavander wouldn't be welcome at White's or at Manton's, or at Gentleman Jackson's or at Lady Buxtell's—"

"Please stop, you're making my hair curl even as it turns gray. Will you make these sacrifices for me, Hetty?"

"It will be difficult, Jason."

"I'm giving up Melissande."

"Thank you," she said in the sweetest voice he'd ever heard from her, then she sent her fist into his belly.

He grunted, then grinned down at her. "Poor Melissande, she's losing both Lord Oberlon and Lord Harry."

"Lord Harry didn't really care for her all that much, truly."

"Naturally not. Lord Harry wasn't able to partake of her most, ah, awesome offerings."

He closed her mouth with a light kiss, then drew back and said, "I don't want you to ever feel anything but free, Hetty. There's no reason why we couldn't set up our own version of Manton's, here at Thurston Hall. You've been bragging much about your prowess with pistols, my girl, but you have yet to test your skill against a master's. Now, let me leave you for a bit to scrub off the dirt of our English roads. Then there are things we must discuss. All right? You swear to me you won't leave again?"

"I swear." She stroked her fingertips over his beloved face. "I've known you as my love for such a short time, but I have no doubts at all. I want you with me, Jason, forever. I think I will bring you a good-sized dowry. You will have to visit my father for those matters, and for that I'm sorry. I must have him at our wedding, for it is proper and Jack and Louisa would wonder were he not to be here."

"Can you forgive him, Hetty?"

"Oh no, I'll never forgive him for what he did, yet there's nothing I can do to change him now or in the future or alter the past. He is as he is, Jason. All of it makes sense to him and to Lord Mulberry and to others. But there's Jack and I don't want him to know."

"No, I don't either, nor does your father, but for far different reasons."

There was a light scratching on the library door. "Damn," the marquess said. Reluctantly he drew away from Hetty.

"Your grace. Miss Rolland." Croft stood in the doorway, his bulbous nose like a red beacon in the candlelight, a tray holding a bottle of champagne and glasses held firmly in his hands.

"He's dipped into the champagne even before our wedding breakfast," the marquess said, then just shook his head.

Hetty held his arm as laughter tumbled out. "How very thoughtful of you, Croft. Do you not think, your grace, that it would be most proper for us to have a toast—among the *three* of us? After all, you told me that Croft has been here since before you were born."

Croft beamed at Hetty, choosing to ignore the dark frown on the marquess's face.

"It's a wonderful event," he said, and quickly poured the champagne into the beautiful crystal glasses.

"To the marquess and marchioness of Oberlon," Croft said grandly, and without further ado, emptied the glass in one long drink.

"My immense thanks for your thoughtfulness, Croft," the marquess said. He clicked his glass to Hetty's, then sipped at his own champagne. "Tell you what, Croft, why don't you take the rest of the bottle and get out. If we require your presence, we'll take the initiative and ring for you. We'll even take the initiative and hunt you out in the pantry where you'll doubtless be snoring away."

Croft bowed low, hastily picked up the tray, and weaved his way happily out of the library.

"He's an original," Hetty said. "Truly, he is an original."

"There's another original."

"And who is that?"

He clicked his glass to hers.

"To Lord Harry, that daring young gentleman who gave me the love of my life."

By the year 2000, 2 out of 3 Americans could be illiterate.

It's true.

Today, 75 million adults...about one American in three, can't read adequately. And by the year 2000, U.S. News & World Report envisions an America with a literacy rate of only 30%.

Before that America comes to be, you can stop it...by joining the fight against illiteracy today.

Call the Coalition for Literacy at toll-free **1-800-228-8813** and volunteer.

Volunteer Against Illiteracy. The only degree you need is a degree of caring.